SLAUGHTER:
Book 2

BY: JAMES BELTZ
www.JamesBeltz.com

Table of Contents

Chapter 1: Clouds of White

Everything he had recently become, the damaged parts of his soul that had been painstakingly reassembled, the joy he had only recently rediscovered, was slipping away right before his very eyes. And, there didn't seem to be anything he could do about it.

Far below him, down in the frosty Kentucky valley, DJ could see a lone figure moving around in the bed of a pickup truck. As he squinted into the distance, he could see the man just now casually positioning himself over the cab of the truck with what could only be a rifle. A rifle that would soon be aiming right at the two most important people in the world to him.

They were in danger. They were going to die. He was powerless to stop it.

Maybe...

There was a chance. The smallest of chances. An almost impossible chance. But, it was still a chance.

DJ held in his hands one of the most accurate rifles on the planet. A special bench-rest target-shooter with the unique ability to fine tune the harmonics of the weapon to whatever round you loaded into it. Every round, when fired, created vibrations traveling up and down the barrel. The resulting harmonics affected accuracy. This one allowed you to fine tune those harmonics with a torque wrench, and shrink your shot groups by an amazing amount.

It was mated to a pretty accurate round as well. The 6.5mm Creedmore was a fairly flat shooting round capable of taking out a groundhog at over 800 yards when paired with the right rifle.

His was.

But DJ went a step further by developing a reloading technique to make it even more accurate. He discovered a secret process for making the burn rate of the gunpowder brilliantly consistent. And in the world of precision rifle shooting, consistency translated to accuracy.

There was just one problem. Actually, there were several. The first one concerned his new wildcat technique for reloading this particular round. While he had tested and perfected this technique using a special version of a .357 bolt action, bench-rest pistol, he was standing up here on this hilltop to test this new technique in the rifle he now held in his hands. And while this rifle was zeroed, it was not zeroed for this new experimental round. He was certain it would be within six inches at one hundred yards, but his target, the stranger now taking aim at the only two people he loved in this world, was somewhere north of five hundred yards away. This meant he could be off by as much as a few feet or more.

Secondly, without knowing the exact distance, he would have to guess on how high above his target he would need to shoot. Normally, in ideal conditions, he would laser range the target for exact distance, look for a cross wind that could cause the round to drift left or right, do some math to calculate bullet drop and windage adjustments, then dial in those changes to his scope.

But he did not have his range finder. Nor did he have time for math and adjustments. He didn't even know what the math for this new round was yet. And besides, the man below him would have fired long before then.

DJ would have to do something called "holding over". Just use his best guess and aim somewhere above where he needed the round to go. It's what a hunter from the south would call "using Kentucky Windage".

Thirdly, DJ was standing high above his enemy on a hill. But, he had no idea how much above his target he was. If he had to guess, maybe four hundred feet? More? It meant shooting down at an extreme angle. And it would throw any math he could guess at for bullet drop right into the trashcan.

It was an impossible shot.

No, DJ thought, only nearly impossible. There was a chance. A chance he would take. A chance he *had* to take. Abbi and her mother were unknowingly depending on him to make the best guess he could.

Reality told him the odds of making this shot were like a blind man swinging at a fastball and hitting a homerun. But, recent history told him anything was possible if he simply believed.

He was running out of time.

He threw his pack to the cold rocky ground and dove in behind it, placing the competition rifle across the top like it was a sandbag. With his right hand, he dug out the small box of experimental ammunition from his coat pocket. He cycled the bolt back, slipped a round into the chamber, and pushed the bolt forward to lock it in place. Next, he focused on his scope. It was a high dollar 6-32 power adjustable rig, but he needed to find his target first. A hard task, zoomed all the way in. So, he dialed it back down to 6 in order for him to locate the truck. He found it quickly, then he reached around with his left hand, and began to zoom in until it was maxed.

There he was, barely visible through a narrow slit in the trees, a murderous dirt-bag with what appeared to be a rather old rifle. Zoomed in as he was, DJ could see the other's breath in the still morning air. The assassin was just now sliding the rifle into position across the top of the cab, and preparing to take aim.

Who was this guy? After realizing the man was in possession of a rifle and climbing into the back of the truck to get a better view, the first thought that came to him was that Big Chuck must have friends. They tracked them down and were about to exact revenge on him for what he did to their empire. But now that DJ could see him clearly, he didn't have the look of a professional killer. A professional killer would possess better equipment.

He would reason through all of the questions later. First, the man needed to die.

His scope jumped all over the place, magnifying every slight, barely imperceptible movement of his body. Every breath made the view look as if he were looking through the porthole of a ship. Every heartbeat was an earthquake of motion in the reticle. He took a long, slow, measured breath to calm his heart and still his body.

Far down in the valley, he imagined the killer was doing the same.

His heart would not respond to the commands of his brain, and to his deliberate breathing. It was still trying to deliver oxygen to all his bits and pieces from the long climb up the hill. Plus, adrenaline, driven by cold fear, fueled his pounding heart. It boomed in his ears. It throbbed in his fingertips.

STOP, he silently screamed at himself.

He breathed again and paused at the end. Still, his racing heart stubbornly refused to listen. The magnified view in the scope leaped with every drumbeat deep in his chest.

With his own body refusing to obey his commands, his monumental task became an impossible fantasy. There was just no way he could hit the man. This was futile.

Wait! He didn't have to hit him, he realized. He just needed to make him duck for cover. Just scare him. Just send a round somewhere close and make him run. It could be enough to save the two people he loved. To save Abbi. It had to be enough.

Refocusing himself, he prepared to send a hasty round down-range and get as close to his target as he could.

He never got the chance.

The sound of a distant shot cracked and echoed through the valley. Finally, all too late, his heart seized in his chest. His eyes went wide with shock. The will to breathe vanished, and the will to live was being pulled along behind.

"No…" The word escaped his lips with the sound of a small, frightened child.

He closed his left eye and refocused on the killer. Maybe there was still time to save one of them. But which one had been killed? Which one was left?

Not Abbi. Please not Abbi, he silently pleaded.

Behind the scope, DJ drew aim on the mysterious killer once more. He could see him there, leaning over the cab behind his own scope. But something was off. Something about the way the man lay hunched there didn't seem right.

As he watched, with his trigger finger slowly applying pressure, the man down below him slid backwards away from the rifle. Slowly at first, then faster as he went.

DJ held off pulling the trigger any further as the man slid completely off of the cab and collapsed into the bed of the truck, disappearing from view.

The shot DJ heard, he realized, was not from the killer below, but from someone else. Someone had just saved the people he loved by taking out the assassin. Some hidden angel had done his job for him.

But who?

Despite the killer in the truck no longer being a threat, DJ was still concerned for the two women. Something wasn't right.

"OK, Mom. What's the plan here?" Abbi stood there in the greenhouse with her hands on her hips looking around. The greenhouse stood on the north side of the older farmhouse, and was her mother's sole focus in life right now. Her mom loved digging in the dirt and prodding things to grow. Every spring would find her on a small plot of tilled up earth, roaming up and down neat little rows, and hovering over tiny buds and shoots. In the summer, she could be seen picking, spraying, and canning. The fall found her clearing, and planning for the next season.

But this was new to her. Owning a greenhouse was a whole new opportunity for her mother.

While the January air brought a staunch chill to the world outside, inside the glassed-in box was quite comfortable. Thanks to small electric heaters warding off the chill at night, and the walls of glass windows for the day, her mother could grow all winter long. Abbi already unzipped her lightweight jacket in response to the temperature change.

They were standing here because her mom, Mary Jackson, had come up with an idea to improve growing inside the small building. Abbi waited patiently for her mother to explain the plan.

"You see," Mary began, "the problem is not temperature. We have enough heat to allow for growing. At a slower pace, of course. The real problem is a lack of light. In the winter, the sun has a lower arc through the sky anyways. Then, you add in these high hills and it takes till past nine in the morning for the sun to peek over the top and shine in through these windows. And it's gone way too early in the evening as well. Plants like tomatoes," she said touching the leaves of one of them close by, "need as much direct light as you can give them. So, I was thinking we could add in some growing lights. Maybe four long ones hanging from the ceiling. You think we could hang them ourselves? Just you and I? We'll leave DJ to his guns and tinkering. I just thought it could be our thing."

Abbi smiled and walked over to hug her mother. "I think that would be great, Mom."

"Good. I was thinking we could hang them here, here, there and there," she said, pointing at spots along the peaked roof. "Maybe we could go into town this morning to see if we can find what we need local. Maybe have a bite to eat? Talk a bit?"

Abbi cut a sideways look at her mother and was instantly suspicious. She knew the other was up to something over the suggestion they could talk. After all, they lived here together in this old farmhouse and talked all the time. Why did they need to go have a bite to eat all alone just to have another conversation? Something was up and Abbi planned on getting to the bottom of it right now.

"Mom… We talk every day. What's going on?"

"Nothing's wrong. There are just a couple of things we need to discuss before you go off to school in the spring."

"Like what?"

"It can keep for now," Mary said with a wave of her hand. "Do you think the breaker for out here can handle the electricity of a few big growing lights?"

"I don't know. We can ask DJ. Now quit changing the subject. Spill it." Abbi had her hands back on her hips and gave her mother a stern stare. Her mom may have her reasons for wanting to delay, but now that Abbi was on to her, it would bug her to no end. She needed to know what her mom wanted to talk about.

Her mother matched Abbi's firm gaze with one of her own. "I said, it will keep."

Abbi poked her chin out with stubborn resolve and glared back, but her mother would not yield. They stood this way for what seemed like a long few seconds. Neither was willing to concede defeat.

A gunshot shattered the chilled Kentucky morning. Abbi knew right away it wasn't DJ. At least not DJ practicing. He never practiced close to the house, and this shot was close.

The look the two women shared, changed to one of concerned curiosity. Both made for the door to the greenhouse with Abbi leading the way. She took only a few steps outside before stopping to look around.

She didn't see any sign of DJ, and heard nothing more out of the ordinary. She did, however, spot a truck parked further down the road. She could just make out the top of it above the tall dead grass next to their fence line.

Strange. There were no neighboring houses anywhere close, and across the street from them was only acres and acres of dense trees. Did someone break down? It was not there last night. Was someone there needing help right now?

She took a few steps towards the truck, and cleared the front of the greenhouse with her mother in tow, when she heard distant shouting to her right. Abbi stopped and scanned the trees back behind the house, working her eyes up the hill to where DJ had his gun range.

She spotted him then. DJ was in a full run down from the top, arms waving frantically above his head, flashing in and out between the bare trees. Something was wrong. Very wrong.

All the events of the past summer rushed into her in a stampede of sudden fear. Big Chuck may be dead, his children may be buried with him, but the man could have friends. He could have accomplices who could still track them down and murder them all.

She wheeled around, grabbed her mom's hand, and tore for the house with a shout. "RUN!" Abbi was much faster than her aging mother, and she practically dragged her along behind. As soon as she could, Abbi cut back to the left towards the back of the house, putting the greenhouse between her and the truck back down the road, yanking her mother along with her. But, not before feeling a hot stinging sensation along the back of her neck, and hearing the crack of another gunshot split the morning from somewhere behind her.

She had been shot. For the second time in her life, she had been shot. Thankfully this one seemed to be only a graze, a narrow miss attributed to her sudden change in direction.

Another sharp crack, and the sound of breaking glass to her left. Whoever was trying to kill her was now shooting completely through the greenhouse. They could obviously see the both of them from the other side. From the truck? She had to get low. Now!

She skidded to a halt, grabbed her mom in an embrace, and pulled her to the ground on top of her. The lower part of the greenhouse was wrapped in stone, and should offer them protection.

On top of her, there was fear in her mother's eyes. "It's OK, Mom," Abbi said, nose to nose. "DJ is coming. I saw him through the trees. He'll save us. It'll be alright. Promise."

Her mother shook her head slow, closed her eyes, turned her head to one side, and coughed. Blood sprayed out of her mouth and red spittle covered her lips.

With a spine jarring jerk, Abbi's world crashed to a halt.

DJ abandoned his rifle. Without it being zeroed, it was nothing but a hindrance. But buried in his pack like a long-lost friend, was his silenced Sig Sauer P320, confiscated from his confrontation with Big Chuck last summer. He had it in his right hand now, weaving his way down through the trees with break-neck speed.

Below him, he had seen Abbi wrap up Mary in her arms and drag her down behind the greenhouse for safety. They were OK for now. His priority was the shooter. With three shots now fired from the unknown person, DJ had a pretty good idea on the area where the hidden shooter was targeting them from.

At first, even though the assassin in the truck had been taken out by whoever was firing, he had wanted to make sure the two women were safe. He left the rifle on the ground and slung his pack over his shoulder. He charged down the hill, waving and shouting at Abbi to get her attention when he spotted them emerge from the greenhouse.

Then the second shot, obviously aimed at the two below him, told him everyone was a target. Not just the guy in the truck. No one was safe.

The third shot sent Abbi diving for the ground with her mother. DJ slid to a halt in the leaves and dug out his pistol. Dropping the pack where he was, he barreled down the hill towards where he guessed the shots were coming from.

Nothing was making sense right now. Why take out someone who was about to kill both women, and then try to kill the women too? Why save them only to target them yourself? The questions burned their way through him, but he would have to shove them aside for now.

Right now, he was using the downward slope of the hill to cover the distance between himself and the shooter as fast as possible. He leaped over fallen logs and darted left and right to throw off the shooter's aim. Gravity was his friend now, pulling him down the hill at a rapid pace. In a hundred feet, he would reach the edge of the field and have no more tree cover to make it harder for the sniper to hit him.

His plan was to cut right, move along the trees to the north, and head for the woods that sat parallel to the shooter. If he made it that far, then it would get tricky. He would have to make his way through those woods towards a concealed enemy, cross the road with no cover, all the while trying to find a sniper that was likely already aiming at him.

As if on cue, bark flew next to his head as he broke left around a giant elm. The sound of the rifle firing it following along behind a split second later.

Another round split the air near his ear as he cut back right at the edge of the field and started his flanking maneuver. DJ put his head down and sprinted for all he was worth.

A final round splintered the top of a fence post on his left, separating the trees from the field, and then he was into the safety of the forest and brush on the far end.

He was even with the shooter now. He slid to a stop and listened. Here is where it got hard.

———————

"Listen to me, baby," Mary Jackson whispered to her daughter. Abbi had rolled her carefully to the ground next to her, and was trying to examine her for the wound Mary could now feel burning high up under her left side. She knew the bullet had taken her as her left arm was extended outward, being drug along by her frantic daughter. She also knew it had passed all the way through her upper chest, and exited somewhere out of her right side. The exit wound didn't hurt for some strange reason. But she knew it was there.

"Don't talk, Mom!" Her daughter was frantic. "Stay still. I have to go get the Jeep. I'll be back. I'll get you to the hospital."

Mary latched onto her daughter's arm in a death grip. "No. I don't have that long."

"Mom, stop! You're going to be fine."

"No, listen," she said softly. "I can feel it. There's too much damage. Not enough time. You need to hear what I am about to say. You need to listen."

"We don't have time for that. I need to get you out of here. Now let me go."

"I was dying anyway."

Her daughter froze, the pain painted across her face suddenly mixed with confusion. "What are you talking about?"

"The doctor I went to see last month. I didn't want to say anything until I knew for sure. I'm sick. Sicker than I thought."

"You didn't look sick," Abbi stated, sitting and pulling Mary's head into her lap.

"Was feeling weak. And getting weaker. Went to see the doctor. Ran some tests. He called me yesterday. Gave me six months tops. Said when it happened, it would come on quick. I wouldn't have been able to hide it much longer."

"Mom..." Abbi was crying now.

She gripped her daughter's arm tight. "You hush now, Sweetie. You have to listen. Cry later. I have to tell you something."

Abbi tried her best to stop her sobbing and listen to her mother. "Yes, ma'am."

"DJ is a strong man. As strong as I have seen. But there is a weakness in him as well. That weakness is you."

"Me?" Abbi wiped her eyes.

"You, baby. You. If he thinks you'll get hurt, it'll cloud his judgement. He'll sacrifice everything for you. When that starts to happen, you need to snap him out of it. He's a good man. Too good and too capable to keep him wrapped around your finger and all to yourself. He's a natural fixer. When he sees a problem, he fixes it. Makes it better. When he sees a wrong, he corrects it. But if it pulls him too far away from you, he'll back off from doing what is right. If he thinks you may get hurt, he'll sacrifice others just to keep you safe. You can't let him."

"Mom, I don't understand." She looked down at her with confusion.

"Somebody just shot me. We thought we were safe. But here I am bleeding all over the place. There is more to do. More for *him* to do. You have to make sure he does it, or this will never be over." She could feel a tickle in her throat. It had been creeping up in her the whole time she was talking. It was growing too hard to keep from coughing, and she knew what would happen when she did.

She could hold it back no longer. She coughed, hard, and blood flew out in a small explosion of red. Her daughter wiped the blood away from the edges of her mouth. Abbi was crying freely now.

There was more Mary wanted to tell her. More she needed to say. She wanted to tell her she loved her. Wanted to thank her for the way they had been hanging out since the summer. She wanted to tell her she appreciated Abbi making her feel like her best friend.

She made the effort to tell her daughter, but the words were not forming. She was feeling lightheaded. Like she could float. Like she didn't weigh a thing. Her vision was blurring. Everything was softening into a white haze. Like a glowing fog was settling over the valley. A warm, glowing fog.

Her daughter was gone then. Everything was gone then. And she floated. Just floated along on clouds of white. She could hear something then. Something far away, but getting louder. Was that music? It was, she realized. It was beautiful. The most beautiful music she ever heard. And the sweetest singing to go along with it.

Chapter 2: The Professional

He survived this long by following a core set of rules. Rules, he knew, defined the difference between the predator and the prey. He most assuredly viewed himself as the predator. As such, he never broke one of his own rules.

Until now. And he was paying the price.

Rule Number One: Observe first. Kill later. Take the time to learn all you can about your prey, and develop a detailed and specific plan.

He had just broken "Rule Number One". His greed and pride had uncharacteristically gotten in the way. And it was nipping at him like a bothersome dog.

His mind turned back the clock to what had brought him to this point.

David Slaughter had skills, he determined. The man had single-handedly taken out the notorious mobster known as Big Chuck. Plus, he had killed many people along the way just to do it. Instead of sticking his chest out and bragging about his great deed, he let an opportunistic FBI agent take all the credit. The evidence and the eyewitnesses he interviewed told the real story, however.

Then, the man vanished into the night with two women he obviously cared about. No one ever really disappears, though. There was always a clue. A thread always dangled out there waiting to be pulled.

In this case, he knew to disappear properly, you would need a great background. A convincing background that would pass all scrutiny, could only be generated by a small group of people. Many of those were connected to the government in such a way, that they had access to the resources required to get it done. Those people usually worked in the FBI, the US Marshalls, or the CIA. There were still flaws in fake backgrounds generated by those individuals, as their resources tended to be compartmentalized.

The best new identifications and backgrounds came from a small group of skilled hackers out there on the Dark Web. And those people had a tendency to brag about their accomplishments with one another.

It took him a while, but eventually he tracked down the hacker involved with Mr. Slaughter's transition to his current identity, Mr. Kirsch. The hacker, going by the moniker Beaver Nuggets, gave up the secret willingly under threat of torture.

Then Beaver Nuggets, whose real name was Brad Puffer and who lived in his parent's basement located in the Bronx, died from asphyxiation in a horrific house fire. His parents died too.

Tragic, really.

That is what led him here to the redneck hills of Kentucky.

When he did his first drive-by, Slaughter was easy to spot, walking to the house from his shop. Surprisingly, the man did not have the look of a killer. He appeared just like some nameless, unsuspecting sheep he would pass in a supermarket somewhere. He had encountered enough killers in his time to be able to tell the difference between the wolves and the sheep from a mile away. But this man was different. In fact, he wondered if he even had the right person the first time he laid eyes on him.

His second encounter with Slaughter was at a gas station. The man was filling up a Jeep, while he filled up an SUV at the next pump. He was certain of the ID, then. But he was still baffled by the absence of the killer presence he knew to live inside the man.

Different for sure.

Once he established a firm ID, the next step was to observe and make mental notes about his habits and routines. For that, he needed a good observation point. There was only one real course of action considering the terrain surrounding the house.

Slaughter lived in a white two-story farmhouse out in the country. It was bordered on the north and south by fields of tall dead grass. There were five or six acres on either side, and no way to get close enough to observe without being spotted.

Behind the house were woods and forest that covered a high hill. His second drive-by told him that Slaughter traversed that hillside often. He spotted the man coming down from the top, following a well-worn path through the trees. Observing from back there was out of the question.

Across the street stood a densely wooded piece of property of many acres. It was wrapped in barbed wire fencing with several "Posted" signs being displayed. If he could get up in one of those trees, maybe just before where the field started on the other side of the road, and right at the corner of the Slaughter property, he would have a great vantage point.

The best way to defeat those posted signs and avoid an accidental run-in with the law, was to get permission of the owner.

So, he did.

Turned out, the property owners lived on the opposite side of the same piece of land. He approached them under the guise of a wealthy business man looking for a place to hunt. He drove up in an expensive British SUV, wearing a nice suit. After waving a lot of cash around, the old couple were all too willing to allow him to set up a tree stand anywhere he wanted, and to hunt as much as he desired.

The next day, he showed up at the old couple's house with a tree stand, and the promised first installment of cash. It was about a mile hike through the woods to the opposite side, and across from the Slaughter house. He located a suitable tree and dropped the portable stand into the leaves next to it. Setting it up then may have revealed himself to the targets across the street. He would need to do it under cover of darkness.

After explaining his intention to show up well before dawn the next day to the owners, he drove two towns over to a privately run, cash only motel. He parked the SUV with fake plates in the owner's garage, paying him extra for the privilege. The owner did not question why a rich dude in an expensive ride would want to hang out in his roach infested motel. He just took the wad of cash and smiled through missing teeth.

He pulled into the driveway of the property owner's house at just before three in the morning, switching off his lights as he turned in. The house was quiet, with only a single bulb glowing under the back porch. He was quiet as well, as he parked and eased the door closed when he exited.

He traversed the blackened woods using night vision, carrying his expensive sniper rifle in a black bag, and shouldering a pack with a ghillie suit stuffed inside. He had the tree stand set up, was dressed in his ghillie suite, and was observing the Slaughter house well before five with a pair of low light binoculars.

He spotted his prey slip out the back door and head up the hill with a rifle and a medium-sized backpack around seven. The valley was rapidly turning grey as the sun was rising somewhere on the other side of that hill. But it would not peek over the top for quite some time.

Fifteen minutes later, the problem occurred.

The problem manifested itself in the form of an unknown assassin showing up in a beat-up old pickup truck. The stranger cut the engine, and coasted past him for about fifty yards, parking on the side just as the two women emerged from the back of the house. They didn't notice the man below. The morning air was brisk, and they seemed more focused about getting to their destination, a glassed-in greenhouse that stood on the north side of the house.

The man below opened his door quietly, and made his way to the back. He lowered the tailgate softly, and reached for a weathered old rifle case.

Right then, his blood began to boil as the man below pulled out the rifle, then climbed into the bed of the truck. It was clear he was going to shoot the two women.

He could not allow that to happen. They were *his* targets. His alone. Who did this man think he was?

The women were in the greenhouse, and the stranger below was taking aim at them over the cab of the truck. If he let the man kill them, Slaughter was sure to head this direction because of the gunfire. He would be alerted and on edge. Slaughter was a highly skilled and trained killer. If the man below could not kill him after taking out the two women, Slaughter would be actively looking for threats, and far harder to deal with. In fact, he may never get another shot at Slaughter ever again.

He could not let that happen either.

Fine, he decided. *They would all die. Right now.*

And, for the first time, blinded by frustration, pride, and greed, he violated his first rule.

He shot the would-be assassin below him and turned his attention to the two women. They emerged from the greenhouse and looked his direction.

He decided to take the cute one first. He hated cute. Cute was always worthy of death. He drew aim on her as she walked towards him, searching for the source of the shot. He mentally calculated what he needed to adjust to the scope for hold-over to take her through the bridge of her nose, and placed his finger on the trigger. Then, distant shouting to his left interrupted him.

Keeping the rifle trained on the two women, he looked left and up the hill. There he was. The Big Chuck Slayer. The man who took down the Colorado mafia. Slaughter was running like a madman down the hill, and waving his arms to warn the ladies at the greenhouse.

Perfect, he thought. *Slaughter can watch his loved ones die.* He smiled at the thought.

He looked back through the scope, only to see the cute one latch on to her mother's arm and bolt for the house. Still an easy shot, to be sure.

She turned hard left and darted back behind the greenhouse just as he squeezed off his shot. He obviously missed her because she never even slowed. His decision to break Rule Number One was already taking its toll. He never missed.

His rifle was a semi-automatic, and he had attached a bag to the ejection port to catch the spent ammunition. Two empty casings were now captured by the bag to limit the forensic evidence at the scene.

Rule Number Two: Leave no evidence behind unless it resulted in profit.

He could see them through both glass walls of the greenhouse. They were in full stride and there was a chance at maybe one more shot. The older one was slowing the younger one down. Take the old bag out, and it may present another opportunity to shoot the cute one.

He aimed carefully. All of his experience came in to play as he adjusted for a person on the run, outside of the zeroed distance of his rifle, and through two walls of dirty glass.

The rifle jumped at the moment he willed it to, and he knew he mortally wounded Grandma.

He smiled.

The cute one hit the brakes, then wheeled about, wrapped her mother up in her arms, and yanked her down behind the safety of the lower part of the greenhouse. Had the bottom twenty percent been constructed of wood, he could have still sent several more rounds through and taken them both out. But it was stone.

It would have never been a factor had he not violated Rule Number One. On realizing that, a flash of hot anger coursed through the back of his neck. Through his birthmark.

He was born with a red patch of skin along the back of his neck. A three-inch oval of pink skin his mother called an Indian Burn. He was sure it was not really politically correct to call it that, but it was all he had known it by. When he was angry, or embarrassed, it glowed a deep red like a stop sign.

He could feel it glowing with a soft warmth right now.

He turned his attention to Slaughter then, and tried to take him as he ran down the hill. The man bounded and hurtled down the steep slope like a jackrabbit. Through the scope, he could see Slaughter now had a pistol in his hand.

Great. According to his investigating and interrogation of one of Big Chuck's incarcerated minions at the Colorado State Prison, Slaughter was very good with that pistol. In fact, the man at the prison suggested Slaughter was almost too good with that gun. He claimed the man had shot a comrade through the throat from a hundred feet away. Unlikely, to be sure.

The prisoner then, having revealed all of his secrets to him while he was disguised as a guard, was later discovered dead in his cell. He apparently decided to end it all by hanging himself with a bedsheet.

So sad.

Now here was Slaughter, leaping down the hill with his main weapon of choice, heading right for him as if he considered himself to be impervious to bullets.

He aimed carefully and released a round, but the man juked at just the right time. He tried again just as his target reached the edge of the trees. Again, the man changed directions at just the right moment. A third time he aimed and released as Slaughter was charging along the edge of the field, obviously attempting to flank him. The round clipped the top of a fence post and altered the bullet's flight path.

Slaughter was parallel with him then, hidden in the dense trees on the other side of the road.

And now, here he was, back to the present, sitting up here in this tree stand and contemplating just how many issues had piled up since he decided to break his own rules. Those rules had kept him alive. They had kept him out of the hands of the law. They had helped to create his almost legendary reputation for getting the job done. Every time. Without fail. Without exception.

Until now.

What to do…

If he stayed where he was, the odds were firmly stacked in his favor. It would be next to impossible for Slaughter to get close enough for a pistol shot, no matter how good he was. He was hidden in a sniper's ghillie suit, high up in a tree stand. He had elevation and concealment. There was simply no way he could be approached without him seeing Slaughter first.

What about from behind?

In response to that revelation, he jerked his head around and looked behind him. He had positioned himself alongside the road and facing the house. But if Slaughter kept swinging wide before making his way to the road, he might be able to cross behind him without being seen. And even if he saw Slaughter cross, the angle was too difficult for him to get much of a shot. He would have to shoot behind himself, around the trunk of the tree.

He considered the body count of Slaughter going against Big Chuck. Back then, the odds were solidly stacked against the man as well.

That did it.

As fast as he could, he descended the tree. Time to leave. He had already broken Rule Number One, and was witness to the domino-like collapse it was having. Violating Rule Number Three could only make matters worse.

He was not afraid. Of course not. That would be silly. A man of his skill and experience did not suffer from fear, even when going up against someone with the mythic reputation of David John Slaughter. It was just… Prudence.

Yes, prudence. *Follow your rules*, he told himself.

Rule Number Three: Never force the plan. If the plan is not working, fall back and follow Rule Number One.

Of course, he was not following a plan here. He already trampled all over that rule. But the idea was still the same. It was time to leave.

He quickly made to stow the rifle in its bag, and adrenaline suddenly coursed through his spine.

The bag mounted to the side of the ejection port meant to capture any spent brass, was missing a round. He did the math in his head to make sure. The mysterious stranger, the missed shot on the girl, her mother, and three missed shots on Slaughter. Six shots fired all together. But there were only five empty casings in the mesh bag attached to the rifle. One must have slipped through the narrow gap along the side. It happened rarely, but it happened. Maybe it flew free when fired. Or, it could have fallen out in his haste to get down the tree.

He needed that casing. He was always careful to load ammunition using surgical gloves for just this type of failure. But in this case, the last pair of gloves he had were worn when cleaning the weapon ahead of time. He failed to pack enough. He thought he had more, but there was just the one set. They became slick from gun lubricant, and the rounds kept slipping as he tried to push them into the box magazine. So, he removed the gloves. After all, he had the bag to fall back on.

He had a well-established plan for loading and handling his weapons. He had made an exception and violated that plan, thinking the bag would do its job. It always did its job.

Rule Number Three: Never force the plan.

He should have stopped right then, driven to the nearest pharmacy, and picked up another box of gloves. He had now violated his own rules twice in less than twenty-four hours.

He had been angry at Slaughter since first learning about him. It bubbled underneath the surface from the first moment he became aware of the man. For months now, it festered like an open wound that would not heal. He thought he had it under control.

He was wrong.

Anger and arrogance had allowed for two colossal mistakes back to back. He could not remember the last time he made a mistake. Mistakes landed one in prison. Mistakes cost you your life. That is precisely why he created the rules in the first place. To avoid mistakes. But here he was, acting like a rookie guided by raw emotion rather than following rigid planning and discipline.

He kicked around in the heavy leaves looking for the shiny piece of brass. He willed it to appear, as he searched for that small yellow glint among the leaves in the rising grey light of morning.

Nothing.

He fell to his knees and moved the leaves around with his gloved hands.

Nothing.

He was running out of time. There was no choice but to chance fate. As a last act, he tried to smooth out the leaves as best he could. It was an effort to camouflage to any that came after him that he had been searching for something. That would assuredly prompt others to search as well. It was hasty, but it was all he could do at the moment.

He scrambled to his feet, finished stowing the rifle, and fitted his pack into place behind him. Next, he drew his own pistol from beneath the folds of his ghillie suite, and set off at a jog towards the old man's house. There was one thing left to do when he got there, and then he would vanish for a time until he could reacquire his target.

Besides, he was pretty sure he knew where Slaughter would run to next. The hacker formerly known as Beaver Nuggets had given up more than one secret before he died.

At a full jog, it did not take him long to cover the distance from the far west side of the wooded property. As he got closer to the house on the far side, he tucked his pistol back out of view.

A good choice, too. Emerging from the trees close to the house, he spotted the old man standing out on the porch drinking a steaming cup of coffee. He waved at him and slowed down to a casual walk.

"Mornin," the old man called out. "I'm assumin all that shootin I heard was from you? Did you get one?"

He smiled at the old man as he approached. "I did. Yes, sir. But I shot at three, and only managed to hit one of them. I guess this is harder than it looks."

"Well at least you got one. Give me a minute and we can take my side-by-side to fetch it. What did you get? Buck or doe?" He placed the cup down on a section of railing and set about zipping his coat.

"Doe. Thanks for the help. I'll pay you extra for the service," he promised the old man. "Where is the wife this morning?"

The old man finished zipping the coat and pointed back over his shoulder. "In there putting up the breakfast dishes. Might have a little left, if you're hungry. She makes a mean breakfast casserole."

He casually produced the pistol from the folds of his ghillie, and shot the old man right between the eyes. The Glock G17 was suppressed, but not silent. It produced a subdued clapping sound like a car door being slammed. He was already stepping over the body and reaching for the kitchen door, before the old man finished falling.

The dead man's wife was right on the other side, drying her hands on a dishtowel as he opened the back door. There was a look of disbelief on her face as he leveled the pistol right at her. He dropped her where she stood.

He moved to the counter top and quickly field stripped the pistol. He dropped the barrel in the sink with gloved hands, then disassembled the slide and removed the firing pin. Next, he reached back underneath his clothing and pulled a second, brand new barrel and firing pin from a small pouch attached to his belt. It was a pouch commonly used for small flashlights, but he used it for far more sinister purposes. He reassembled the handgun with practiced precision, reattached the silencer, and made for the door.

Cool thing about preferring Glocks to other handguns, because of their popularity, one could readily find parts and accessories at any sporting goods store or online retailer. Swapping out both parts for new ones and leaving them at the scene of the crime meant that if he were apprehended by law enforcement with the weapon, it could not be traced back to any of his murders.

It was not a violation of Rule Number Two, as there was nothing about the barrel that could be traced back to him. The original factory barrel possessed a serial number that matched to the weapon. But after-market barrels, like the one he discarded, possessed no serial number or identifying markings.

There was nothing unique about a firing-pin that would allow it to be traced back to him, as well.

He could reuse the same weapon over and over again, killing countless people. As long as he kept swapping out those two pieces for new ones, it could never lead back to him.

At the SUV, he tossed the Ghillie suit, his rifle bag, and the pack into the back seat. At this point, because he never made it to the planning stage for the assassination of Slaughter and his female companions, there was no plan for disposal of the rifle. He would keep it with him and figure that out later. First, he needed to hit the road and place as much distance as possible between himself and the two crime scenes he just created.

He pulled casually out of the drive. Forty-five minutes later and he was in the slow lane on the highway headed east. The northeast, to be specific. It was only a matter of time before Slaughter did the same. He would be there waiting for him when he arrived. When his prey finally showed, he would be back to following the rules.

Sure, he had a momentary, and very rare, lapse of judgement. As much as he would hate to admit it, he was still only human. But that was behind him now. He would learn this lesson well. He would be back to following the rules when next he encountered Mr. Slaughter.

After all, he was a professional.

Chapter 3: Outnumbered

DJ swung wide around where he imagined the shooter was hiding. He approached from behind the assassin rather than a side angle. His opponent possessed a high-powered rifle and could shoot from long distances. He only had a handgun, and was better up close. He could also assume his enemy required elevation to engage the whole area around DJ's house. That likely meant his adversary was up in a tree.

So, DJ swung wide, approached from the rear, and kept his eyes scanning the trees as well as the underbrush.

After a few minutes of moving just a bit at a time, he finally found the shooter's nest. The guy was long gone. DJ was not much of a tracker, but he was pretty sure whoever it was, headed east from here. While he would have liked to go after whoever tried to kill them all, he decided he needed to gather up Abbi and her mother, throw some things in the Jeep, and rabbit out of this valley before the cops were called. After all, there was a dead guy in the back of a pickup truck on the side of the road next to his house. And because this road got very little traffic, DJ was going to have to be the one to make the call.

Not only that, but whoever just tried to murder everyone he cared about was definitely not done. They would be back. Staying here was no longer an option.

First, he wanted to check out the dead man in the truck. It might offer him a clue on who just tried to kill them, and why there seemed to be two assassins competing for the kill.

The only thing he could think of that could explain everything, was that a hit had been taken out on them, and the payout was being offered to whoever could get it done first. Two killers must have shown up at the same time, and one took the other out to keep the payout for himself.

Or herself. Let's not be sexist here. He guessed there could be women assassins too.

Something that really bothered him, though, was Beaver had sworn up and down that their new identity was rock solid. It would be very hard for someone to be able to find out where they were. They had complete backstories and a full history of their pasts. For the love of Pete, they even had fake shot records from when they were fake kids.

So, what the heck happened? How were two killers able to find them? He would wring Beaver's neck for this.

The good thing was, over the last six months since they had gone into hiding, DJ worked with Beaver to come up with multiple backup plans just in case. It was only logical that Big Chuck might have friends. Not only that, but the Feds were never going to stop looking for them either. Even though Beaver insisted that it was overkill, he was only too happy to take his money.

So, he set up two other complete identities for them all, as iron clad as the first. Or so he had hoped. However now he wasn't so sure, after seeing what happened this morning. Additionally, this past summer when he had been attacking Big Chuck's riverside complex, he had done battle with a guy that had three other complete identities stuffed in his backpack. He was the only person that knew about those. It's not like he was hiding them from Abbi and her mother, it just never came up.

They were in the backpack he was wearing now.

The only problem was, he did not have additional ones for both Abbi and her mother. Just the three for himself. He was not sure if he wanted to fall back to one of the other two that Beaver had made for them all, or start new using the ones he picked up off the dead guy back at Big Chuck's place.

He could decide that later. First, investigate the dead assassin in the truck, then scoop up the girls and get out of here.

Arriving at the truck, and peeking over the side, revealed the other guy face up and staring into the sky. There was a bullet hole, probably the exit wound, right in the center of his chest. Blood was pooling outward still, and covered most of the empty bed.

On the roof of the cab was the empty soft case for the rifle. The would-be killer was using it to cushion his weapon. It was frayed and worn.

The rifle itself was an old one. And pretty beat up. It certainly did not look like a professional killer's choice of weapon. His suspicions were at least confirmed on that one.

So, who the heck was this guy? Him being a second contract killer didn't seem to add up.

Something looked familiar about him. Like they had met? Or maybe he had seen the man somewhere?

And then realization slammed into him like a freight train full of guilt. He had seen this man on the third floor of the same building that Big

Chuck was in months ago. On his way up looking for the Mob Boss, DJ ran into this guy. He had been unarmed. He had sworn he was a victim of Big Chuck's brutality. DJ was not sure if he believed him, but he had taken a chance on letting him go because he wasn't armed.

He remembered thinking to himself back then, if it ever came to light the guy was truly a victim, he would not have been able to live with himself knowing he killed an innocent man. So, he let him go instead of putting a bullet through his head.

Now here he was. Only by a shear stroke of luck in showing up at the same time as another assassin, and trying to take the other's kill, did he not manage to take out Abbi and her mother.

The guilt he felt about accidentally placing them in harm's way was overwhelming. *He* did this. His gut told him back then that there were no innocent people roaming around the complex of a mafia leader. He didn't listen. And it had almost cost the lives of Abbi and her mother.

If they had died…

DJ left the guy where he lay and investigated no further. Time to move on. He needed to get them all out of here.

He took off at a trot, making his way down the road along his fence. When he got close, he tossed his pack over the top, and ducked through the barbed wire. He snatched the pack from the ground and proceeded around the corner of the greenhouse, expecting to see Abbi and her mother waiting for him, hiding in the shelter of the short stone wall. What he found instead drove him to his knees in the dirt, his world shattered.

Abbi looked up at him from a sitting position, her mother's head cradled in her lap. There was blood everywhere. His trained Corpsman eye instantly took in everything. She never stood a chance. The wound tract the bullet left caused way too much damage. Had it happened in the emergency room of the best hospital, there would have been nothing they could have done. It had destroyed all the vital organs in her chest cavity.

Abbi's eyes were devoid of emotion. She had been crying, he could tell, but no longer. She was now empty inside. She was shutting down. He recognized the look. He had been there once himself.

The unknown shooter in the woods may have pulled the trigger, but it was his own decision to take out Big Chuck that caused this. He might as well have been the one with the rifle in the trees. *He* killed Abbi's mother. *He* did it. *He* was responsible. Guilt poured over him and soaked him to his core.

He should pay the price for his sins.

He looked down for a moment at the silenced Sig Sauer in his hand, and considered placing it to his head. Not now, of course. Not in front of Abbi.

Abbi was suddenly full of heated emotion. Somehow reading his mind in that one simple action. "NO," she shouted. "You are the strongest man I know. And you will NOT take the cowards way out of this! I need you now more than ever. So, you man up right now or, so help me, I will punch you in the throat!"

DJ could only stare at her. "I…."

"I don't know how you could possibly think this was your fault. You did the right thing taking Big Chuck out. Whether you were able to rescue your family or not. He was a vicious killer that hurt an untold amount of people. He needed to go. Someone had to do it. You did. You are not responsible for whoever did this." She sat there yelling at him, bubbling with fury. He had never seen her like this. "Just tell me you killed the guy that did this," she demanded.

DJ shook his head. "He got away."

She paused and seemed to soak that in. "Fine," she said. "You'll get another chance. And when you do, you'll make him pay for this!" She looked down at her mother's head still cradled in her lap.

"Abbi…" He needed to tell her. He had no choice. She needed to know. "This *was* my fault."

"DJ, I love you so much it's hard to breathe when I think about you sometimes, but if you think I wasn't serious about punching you in the throat, you're about two seconds from finding out the cold, hard truth!"

"Abbi, just listen. Please." He told her then of the man in the truck. How he had run across him on the third floor of Big Chuck's warehouse. How he let him go. How making that choice put them all in danger. How it was only by sheer coincidence that another assassin showed up at the same time to throw off the plans of the first, or they could all be dead.

As he spoke, he expected understanding to flood her eyes, followed by the hatred for him that he deserved. But she only shook her head at the end and said something he was not prepared for.

"She was dying anyways," she said bluntly.

For a second he only stared at her with a blank expression. Then, "What?"

"She just told me. She said she only had a few months anyway. Remember when she went into town for a check-up?"

He nodded his head.

"She lied to us. Didn't want to scare us. She didn't tell me what it was. Just said she didn't have long." Her voice developed a far-away sound as she talked. Then she appeared to snap herself out of it.

"Abbi…" Again, words were lost on him.

"Don't you see," she said. "None of that changed anything. She was dying anyway. In fact, in some ways, it may have been better this way because she went so fast. As far as I'm concerned, she gave her life for mine. If anything would have happened differently… If the guy in the truck would have showed up a day earlier, or a day later, this could have been even worse. We could all be dead. But we're not. And now, the man that did this, he's in real trouble." She smiled at DJ at the end, but the sparks in her eyes said that it was not really a smile of happiness. It held a darker purpose.

"How is he the one in trouble?" DJ asked her, confused.

"You think that was the first time the man in the trees has ever killed someone? Of course not. Who knows how many people he is responsible for putting in a grave. But, you see? Now it's over. His reign of murdering is over. He won't kill another innocent soul."

"I… I don't understand," DJ said. Was she losing it? Was this somehow all part of the tragedy ripping her mind to pieces?

Abbi gently laid her mother's head on the ground, then stood up, walked over, grabbed his hands, and pulled him up to her. DJ looked down at her, and she reached up softly and stroked his cheek with one hand. The tenderness she had expressed to him so many times was now back. Like nothing happened. Like her mother was not lying there murdered at their feet. Like the same guy was not going to come back to try it again.

"Because, sweetheart," She smiled. "We're going to kill him, of course." Her grin deepened as she considered that. "He doesn't have a chance. He's outnumbered. There's only *one* of him. But there are *three* of us."

"I'm sorry?" DJ was stunned looking at her and listening to her talk. It dawned on him that he may not really know who she was at all. She seemed so calm about tracking down a trained and seasoned contract killer they knew nothing about. And what did she mean by saying the three of them? Was she expecting the ghost of her mother to help them in some way? Had she really lost her mind?

But her next sentence put it all into perspective.

"We'll call him when we find a place to stop tonight. Now help me get her in the house. I am not leaving her out here like this."

DJ knew right then who the third person was, and he was remembering the last time the two men talked. Brett had threatened him with handcuffs and barred windows. Now Abbi was expecting him to call the FBI agent, and all three of them teaming up again like it was old times. Abbi must have really lost her mind.

Chapter 4: Brain Itch

Brett was very good at being able to put the pieces together. He had a natural gift, his mentor and former boss, Tim Neville used to say. That gift had served him well over the years. Not only did it put quite a few bad guys away, something Brett was proud of, but once upon a time, it saved his former boss's life.

It was part of the reason the powers-that-be went ahead and put him in charge of the Denver Field Office. Despite being pretty sure he may have bent the law, if not outright broken it, when he took down Big Chuck and twenty percent of the corrupted Denver Field Office.

Special Agent in Charge Brett Allen Foster, or commonly called "SAC", flashed a grin inwardly at himself over the title. It had a nice ring to it. Of course, he had a lot of help gaining that title.

DJ Slaughter made most of it happen, but Brett received most of the credit. They both helped each other out on that little adventure, however. DJ would be dead were it not for Brett, and Brett would have cashed it in a few times were it not for DJ. Not to mention Brett's wife and DJ's in-laws were saved because of their working together.

In another life, they would have made a great team.

He wasn't the only one who benefited from the take-down of Big Chuck and the dismantling of the Denver Field Office. His old boss, Tim Neville, got the largest recognition one could probably ever receive in the FBI. A new United States president had been elected a few months prior, and he had finally pulled the trigger on firing the current director of the FBI. This new president was an outsider to the political game. He was a successful business man who managed to turn normal presidential elections on their ear. In a decided upset, the man somehow won.

He set his sights on replacing the director of the FBI early on, but held off for whatever reason. Then, the discovery of a host of on-the-take agents running a corrupt field office exploded into the news, and the new president used this new opportunity to demand the director's resignation.

This left a hole needing to be filled at the top. The president proclaimed it was foolish to ever put a politician in charge of a law enforcement agency. According to him, only a person spending a lifetime of catching bad guys should ever be qualified for the job. Tim Neville, having sent Brett to Colorado, got a lot of credit for Big Chuck and the uncovering of corruption in the field office. As such, this new president nominated him to fill the position of director. The confirmation hearings went well, and right now, soon to be Director Neville was awaiting a final vote by the full Senate this weekend. It was expected to be a near unanimous approval. After all, Tim knew half of those guys quite well.

Brett snorted at the thought. It was likely his old boss knew where most of the bodies were buried for most of those Senators. Weren't most of them corrupt anyways? His old boss was about to become his new boss all over again.

Brett turned his attention away from his musings, and directed it back to the pile of papers on his desk. He tried to will his natural ability at seeing through the fog, to manifest itself and to connect the dots. Brett did not always fully understand how the dots were related. But eventually, over time, he usually could connect them together.

When he spotted one of those obscure, seemingly unrelated details, it was like a nagging itch developed in the back of his brain. The longer it went without him being able to filter through to the truth, the more bothersome that itch became.

Right now, that itch was driving him nuts.

Brett looked at the three dots on his desk and worked through the facts one more time.

The first dot was the death of a prisoner in the Colorado State Penitentiary. Johnson Mulvaney was found in his cell having hung himself with a bedsheet. Mr. Mulvaney was a mid-level lieutenant in the Big Chuck army. He was also the right-hand man to Remmick Sheckerley. Remmick issued orders on behalf of Big Chuck. Mr. Mulvaney assisted Remmick to distribute those orders, and ensure they were followed.

There was a rumor that Remmick and Johnson were involved in a much deeper relationship. When Brett followed up on that, he discovered the rumors were true. They were secret lovers.

Lovers meant there was pillow talk shared between the two. His rank, and his involvement with Remmick, made him a focus point. He became a central part of the ongoing investigation into everything connected to Big Chuck. With both Big Chuck and Remmick dead, Johnson Mulvaney was the only one who knew where all the bodies were buried. He also knew all of the people and entities that had working relationships with Big Chuck, and the details of those dealings.

Johnson worked out a deal for freedom in exchange for information and the willingness to testify. Until then, he was being held in solitary confinement away from the rest of the population of prisoners.

With freedom and a new identity only a few months away, he had a lot to live for. No way he killed himself. Mulvaney was murdered. Brett was sure of it.

The only people with access to the man were federal prosecutors, the FBI investigation teams, and the staff at the prison. This had to be an inside job.

Brett was leaning towards the thought of more corrupt FBI agents that still hadn't been discovered yet. After all, two of them tried to kill him over the summer.

Regardless, it was the first dot that caused his brain to itch.

The next dot, he stumbled across by coincidence. He was reviewing a file he was asked to hand off to any available agent under his command. Just a run of the mill interagency request.

Turns out that a triple homicide went down in The Bronx. The responsible party tried to cover it up with a house fire, but the fire marshal's investigation team was really good at their jobs. Once they knew the fire to be arson, they started looking into the victims a little closer. The FBI was called in for an assist with their lab. The FBI owned the best equipment on the planet for forensic investigation, and it was all sitting right in the heart of New York City. Just a hop, skip, and jump away.

Those guys discovered a trace amount of a rarely known, seldom used chemical compound called trimethylphexate. TMP, as it is known by, is used in plastics manufacturing for medical devices that would find uses inside the human body. A layman's description of it would be that it ate oxygen.

Using it in medical plastics meant any microscopic air bubble that might form in the construction of the pieces would be destroyed. Otherwise those bubbles might carry harmful bacteria into the body. It was mainly used in synthetic heart valves.

If enough TMP were injected directly into an artery, it could result in chemically induced asphyxiation. It would consume the oxygen right out of the bloodstream. It could even devour it straight from the lungs before the lungs could even do anything with it.

In addition, TMP was not something that would show on any typical toxicology report. But in this case, the FBI ran an extended panel as the first yielded no results. Plus, since they knew arson was involved, the agent in charge ordered one just to be on the safe side.

TMP had been found in all three victims. Since TMP is controlled and difficult to come by, the New York office launched a full investigation. That investigation turned up some proprietary software on a giant computer discovered in the basement of the burned out house. The software discovered could only mean that one, or all of the victims, was into the manufacturing of elaborate, fake identities.

Most of the identity history was destroyed by the fire. But they did discover one strange thread of evidence. They passed it on to the Denver Field Office with the request for someone to check it out.

It was that strange piece of evidence that made the back of Brett's brain itch.

A company in the Cayman Islands, thought now to be a shell company, purchased two grave plots at a small cemetery in Gerrard, Colorado. One to put a body into at the time of purchase. One for the spouse to follow later when their time came. Those graves were exactly three miles from South Fork, where the Jacksons and DJ used to live.

Fake identity manufacturing. Murder. Shell companies in the Caymans. A burial plot near the Jackson home, where Henry Jackson had been murdered. Coincidence? Brett didn't think so. But he did not know how it was connected or why it made the hair on the back of his neck stand on end.

Besides, he knew where Henry was buried, and it was nowhere near that location. The agency had the place under surveillance for months now on the off chance that Abbi and Mary might make a visit to the gravesite, and pay their respects.

The third dot was from evidence discovered months ago by an enterprising young man he hired in his forensics department. It came from a tiny smear of blood no larger than a nickel, located on the third floor of Big Chuck's office warehouse, about six feet from the stairwell.

In the crushing amount of forensic evidence discovered at the large riverside compound, it was amazing it wasn't overlooked. Even then, because of its insignificance, it was almost stuffed away into an evidence box, and lost forever to the mountain of data known as Big Chuck.

In an effort to finally close that crime scene, the new hire decided to cross compare all blood evidence found at the scene with each other, and with every known associate and family member known to Big Chuck.

That small tiny bit of blood was discovered to belong to a family member of the Mafia leader. A son. A son that was not in the system. A son no one knew anything about. A son that was still missing, but had obviously been there on that fateful night.

Someway, somehow, they were connected. He knew it for certain. He just didn't know how.

As the head honcho of the entire Denver office, it wasn't like Brett didn't have huge piles of other things to attend to. In fact, he knew he should shove all of this onto another agent and let them figure it out. He was the boss, after all. He had foot soldiers to carry out his orders and do what agents were trained to do.

The problem was, it wasn't so long ago he was one of those foot soldiers himself. Doing the legwork to catch the bad guy was still too fresh in his system.

Even though he lived for this kind of thing, he should stop consuming himself with this and hand it off right now.

But he couldn't.

Itch, itch, itch.

Right in the back of his brain.

There was a knock at his open door, and Brett looked up to see a familiar face. Agent Bradford Cashin, or Cash as everyone called him, had a very concerned look on his face. Despite his young age, Cash was as steady as they came. He was never very animated about anything. To those who didn't get to know him, he came off as cold and calculating.

Calculating, always. Cold, never. Cash believed emotion was something best kept outside of his job. Besides, there was a role model he was trying to live up to.

No one knew, except for Brett, that Cash had a secret identity. His mother and father divorced when he was still in diapers. She remarried rather quickly. So quickly, the real father, a personal friend of Brett's, was always suspicious she had been cheating on him the whole time.

The stepfather adopted him, which legally changed his last name. The truth was, his original last name was Neville. He was Tim Neville's son. The same Tim Neville who was Brett's best friend and former boss over at the Dallas Field Office.

Cash refused to let anyone know who his father really was, so anything he accomplished through the FBI would be done all on his own. He wanted to live up to his father's sterling reputation, but he preferred to chart his own course.

Brett recruited Cash to follow him from Dallas, as he knew beyond a shadow of a doubt he could trust him with anything. He was one of the agents who drove to Oklahoma City this past summer and picked up DJ's in-laws. Cash, because of his unique relationship with Brett and his own father, knew everything that happened that night. The whole story. Not just the bits and pieces spun and twisted for everyone else.

Brett felt he needed someone he could trust and count on when he took over the Denver office. He would always be suspicious they never chased all of the rats out of the building. Cash was there to not only support him in his new role, but to secretly spy on his coworkers.

Additionally, as part of his goal to become his own man with his own reputation, when he transferred out of the Dallas office, Cash refused to tell his father where he was headed. He also made the man promise to not look into him or track where he was going. He was afraid his dad might not be able to resist temptation and would stick his nose into Cash's career.

Tim Neville, for his part, did his best to honor his secret son's request. He signed a set of blank transfer documents and gave them to Cash to fill in as he desired. Brett's old boss had no idea Cash was working for him. And Brett promised to do everything in his power to keep it that way.

Now, here was the young man with his steely blue eyes and his barely five-foot seven frame, looking like he had been poked with something electrified.

"Boss," the agent said with an even more serious expression than usual. "We have a problem."

There was an edge to his tone Brett did not usually hear. Had he not been so aggravated by the itch in his brain, he would have responded differently to the young man. Instead, "How long have you been an agent? Dealing with problems is what we do here." Brett shot him a look of annoyance.

He felt a brief moment of guilt over barking at maybe the only person in this entire building he could truly trust. After all, it wasn't his fault Brett's brain was itchy. But then the youngster's next statement had him hitting speed dial on his desk phone to call his wife.

"Authorities outside a small town in Southern Kentucky just discovered the body of Mary Jackson." He never got a chance to provide more information because Brett silenced him by holding one finger to his lips. The finger on his other hand was already punching the speed dial button even before he got to the end of the sentence.

The phone rang twice before Lisa picked up. Lisa never even got a chance to say hello, as Brett was already talking. "Something big just came up. I need you to pack a bag. I have some men coming to get you and bring you here. You'll be staying in the office for a couple of days. That thing that happened this summer may not be over. Hurry quick, please. They'll be there in ten minutes. And I won't be in the office when you get here, because I have to go chase this down. I love you but that's all the information I have at the moment."

"Um… OK," Lisa replied. She had been the wife of an FBI agent long enough to know that when things of a more serious nature happened, everything started moving at the speed of light. As a spouse of an agent, you either got on board and let the process play out, thankful you could see your other half when you could, or you bailed out of the relationship. It's why few agents were married more than about ten years. It was a lot to ask of the other person.

Within the compound of buildings Brett now called his second home were a set of apartments. Five of them. They were used for everything from visiting brass and dignitaries, to keeping a witness secure and safe. In this case, it would become Lisa's new home until he could sort this all out.

"I love you, sweetheart," he told her. "It's going to be fine. I'm sorry."

"Number one, I love you more. Number two, I know it will be fine. Number three, you owe me a date. And I'm saying you need to go all out, Mr. Agent Man. I want to be swept off my feet."

"Absolutely."

"You better come through on that. I mean it. Knock me right out of my socks. Now, tell me how our friend is doing. Is he alright?" Lisa was referring to DJ, of course, but she was smart enough to never use his name across a phone line.

"I can't answer that question, yet. My gut says he's fine, for the moment. But it won't stay that way for long if I can't get a handle on this. I love you, but I have to go."

"Go save the world," she said simply, then she hung up the phone.

"It's what I do," Brett replied to no one.

He punched another button on his desk phone. This one was connected to his secretary in the next room. Just like Lisa, as soon as he heard her pick up, he did not even allow her to speak before he started issuing orders. "Find my A-SAC and tell her she is in charge for the foreseeable future. Forward only the most important issues directly to me, and redirect everything else to her." A-SAC stood for Assistant Special Agent in Charge.

He continued. "Call ahead and get me a jet. I need to be in the air in twenty minutes. Tell them to file a flight plan for the closest runway to…" Brett trailed off and shot a questioning look at Cash.

"Ritner," he replied.

"Ritner, Kentucky. Make sure you get me some well rested pilots. I don't know where I'm going after that."

"Sir?" the female voice on the other end questioned him.

"What is it?"

"Sir, Agent Cashin gave me that message when he came in the door. He said the request came directly from you. They have probably already pulled it out of the hanger by now."

Brett looked at Cash annoyingly. "He did, did he?" Brett never took his eyes off of the youngster, "Did he also ask to have some local agents meet us at the airport with transportation? Enough for me and a tactical team?"

"Um… yes, sir, he did. I have a call in now, but the SAC on that end is going to want to know why."

"You tell him I will call him once I'm in the air. I need you to also send a recovery team to my house and secure my wife. There may be an imminent attempt on her life. Probably not, but I want to be sure. Put her up here until further notice. Keep her under watch, and don't let her leave for any reason."

"Yes sir," his secretary said with a suddenly worried tone to her voice.

Brett disconnected and stood up. "I take it you already dropped my name and have a tactical team in route to the airport?"

Cash simply nodded his head.

Brett shook his head and shot a perturbed look at the young man. "Well, get your Go Bag, kid. You're coming with me."

Cash had been standing in the doorway the entire time. In response, he reached out of view into the hallway to his left, and slid a rolling luggage bag into view.

Brett's eyebrows knitted together at the sight of the agent already anticipating his moves. "You need to stop reading my mind. That can get annoying really quick," Brett deadpanned at the young agent.

In a monotone voice, and displaying not one ounce of humor, Cash replied. "I can't help it, sir. You're too predictable."

Brett slipped his laptop into a messenger bag, then walked to the far corner and grabbed his Go Bag as well. In this business, you always had a packed bag with extra clothes ready to go at a moment's notice.

"Lead the way," Brett commanded. "Fill me in once we're in the car."

Brett now knew precisely why he was having issues connecting those dots. One of them didn't belong. Only two of them did. And those two were connected to a third he didn't even see.

Until now.

DJ and Abbi were in very serious trouble. But at least that annoying brain itch was gone.

Chapter 5: Let's Go Swimming

It was just now 11 a.m. Colorado time, and Brett was pulling to a stop in front of a police barricade in rural Kentucky. It was located outside of what could only be the most recent home of DJ Slaughter. When you have your own personal jet to order around, you could get to anywhere pretty quickly.

Too bad the reason he was here sucked to no end.

Once in the air, Brett reached across to the local Field Office in Louisville and explained why he was personally headed to their neck of the woods. As a result, they were gracious enough to have a few vehicles and drivers standing by for an assist.

Brett already learned that quite a few SACs were a tiny bit miffed over his promotion in Colorado. In order to get that job title, you would normally have needed to run a major division out of D.C. He was in charge of one in Dallas, but that was not quite the same thing. While Brett's career was stellar up to that point, and he was surely on a steady rise up the food chain, no one skipped ahead of the line that fast. Ever.

While many in the lower ranks were probably impressed with him for bringing down the Colorado Mafia, and gutting an entire field office of two-faced agents on the take, the upper management teams were largely unhappy with his rapid rise.

So, when attempting to share resources between other field offices, Brett was often met with pushback and resistance. But in this case, the other person was only too willing to help him out. And that was not something he was used to.

He was met with three full size SUVs at the airport, and three drivers to go along with them. All three agents were so polite it made him uncomfortable. It was just... Odd.

Brett used two of the vehicles to distribute his six-man Tactical Team, and the last for himself and Cash. Thirty minutes after parking the plane, they were arriving at the farm outside of Ritner.

He instructed the Tac Team to dismount but stay by the vehicles, while he and Cash had a look around and talked to the local FBI agents on scene.

According to what Cash told him on the plane, the state police was running the show at first, until a fingerprint scan of one of the dead bodies confirmed her to be Mary Jackson. Since she was a known fugitive thought to be consorting with a wanted murderer and possible hitman, the FBI jumped into gear quickly when she popped up in the system.

Brett was assured the local agents would offer no issues with letting him poke around and ask questions. After all, this was the case that got him promoted, and DJ in the wind was the one thing missing on finally closing out every aspect of the case.

Of course, no one really knew that Brett let the man walk to begin with. And he never even admitted it to his former boss Tim Neville, or his incognito son tagging along on this trip. Although he was pretty sure they both knew.

An agent was waiting for him with a big smile and a handshake. "Hi, sir. Welcome to Kentucky. I understand you're anxious to finally close this out, and hope our two DBs here can help you out in that regard."

DB stood for dead body. "That's the idea," Brett responded. He was instantly suspicious that something wasn't quite right. Between the SAC that ran Kentucky, the agents that picked them up at the airport, and the one he was talking to now, he was feeling a toothache coming on. There was just a little too much sugar flowing around. The question was, what were they all up to?

"Well, sir, it looks like you may have wasted a trip all the way out here. It's pretty cut and dry about what went down. We could have shipped all of the paperwork to you by the end of the day."

So that was it. Let him waste a bunch of resources, and spend a ton of money out of his budget flying a private jet around, only to come up empty handed and look like a noob that was clearly out of his element. Then, of course, secretly inform the upper management how inexperienced he was and how he should clearly be demoted.

Obviously, these idiots didn't know him very well. His instincts nearly always yielded results. And this time, as soon as he heard the first words come out of Agent Cash's mouth, his instincts screamed at him to get to wherever the crime scene was as fast as possible.

"Waste of time, huh?" Brett's voice had a hard edge to it, and the other's friendly, but fake demeanor, evaporated.

"I just meant that-" the agent began hastily.

Brett cut him off. "Why don't you show me what all your incredible investigating has revealed so far?"

The other agent had a surprised look on his face. It was apparent he thought their polite smoke screen was working. But Brett was on to them now, and he was torqued. He issued a sharp one-word order. "Move!"

There was a slight hesitation, and then the agent wheeled about. He may be on orders to try and make Brett look stupid, but Brett still had more pull than this little jerk dared to go against. Calling out over his shoulder, he asked Brett and Cash to follow him. Which they did.

The idiot, whose name he did not know, led them both to a waiting single cab pickup on one side of the road. It was an old clunker. The agent explained this was where the whole thing started. The dead body in the back was the assassin of Mary Jackson. Although they did not have ballistics back yet to confirm it, it was pretty obvious. He had tried to kill both women, but only managed to bag the one. He knew this, he said, because the clear footprints in the dirt over by the greenhouse showed they were both together. He pointed off into the distance to show Brett where the greenhouse was. They were both fleeing for their lives, but Mary bought it, he told Brett.

Brett was fuming inside, and his fists were clenched tight enough his fingernails were biting into his palms. He forced himself to relax. He could bark at the moron all he wanted, but he could not lose control. At least not around witnesses. If he did, he would be providing ammunition to his political enemies.

Political enemies? What the heck was he turning into? He never had political enemies prior to accepting this stupid promotion. He had colleagues, friends, coworkers, but *political enemies*?

"How about we treat the deceased with a little respect, Agent. We don't refer to her death as 'getting bagged'."

"Yes, sir. Sorry, sir." The agent looked sheepishly at Brett and then continued. He explained how another party, probably Slaughter, had managed to kill the assassin in the back of the truck, but not in time to save the mother. Then Slaughter and the daughter hastily packed a bag, placed the mother in the living room, called the cops, and then left as fast as they could.

It was a pretty clear case, he insisted.

Brett looked at the dead body in the back. "Have you identified the body yet?"

"No, sir. Fingerprints have not showed up in the system, and we have not gotten results back on DNA. But it's still early for that."

"Is it, agent?" Brett's voice was like a hurled dagger. "Because I already know who he is. I just flew halfway across the country, spending all my time just getting here and doing no investigation on my own. Now, how come I know the ID before you do?"

"Um…" The agent, whose name he still did not know, began to stammer.

"Great response. Um. Perfect." Brett turned to Cash. "Call home and get the DNA results that identified a third familial match to Big Chuck. The unknown son that wasn't in the system. Have that forwarded to their lab for comparison."

Brett then turned back to Agent Idiot. "So, I have never seen this guy before," he said pointing to the DB in the bed of the truck. "But what do you want to bet that the DNA report my office is forwarding to your office, matches this guy that I have never seen?"

The other agent merely blinked and stared.

"No reply. Of course not. Then answer me this, hot shot, has anybody stood in the back of this truck yet?"

"Well, no, sir. The entire bed is covered in blood."

Brett walked around to the passenger side door, reached into his pocket and retrieved a pair of purple rubber gloves. After snapping them into place, he then opened the door. He placed one foot into the cab, and reaching in to grab the edge of the door, hauled himself up to examine the top of the roof. Seeing what he was looking for, he dropped back down and closed the creaky door with a slam.

He walked back to the tailgate and began to visualize the flight path of the bullet that killed the man in the back. He turned around and faced behind the cab, and into the trees on the opposite side of the road back behind the police barricade. After a second of scanning the trees, he turned back to Agent Idiot.

"So, Agent… Where was Slaughter at when he shot this man?" Brett threw the question at the man, knowing he had no clue.

"Well we aren't certain yet, but somewhere back down the road. We have already used metal detectors to search along the road looking for brass. We haven't recovered anything, so the working theory is he used a bolt action rifle and just never cycled the bolt to expend the casing."

Brett appeared to consider that for a moment, and simply nodded his head slowly up and down. "I suppose that a rookie, you know - someone in training - might come to that conclusion. But I was under the impression that your SAC had put a seasoned agent in charge of the scene. I guess I was wrong. I guess your SAC likes to put noobs in charge and let them stretch their legs a bit. I would suggest informing your boss you just aren't ready for this type of thing. Not yet, anyways. You still need to grow up a bit."

The look on Agent Idiot's face rotated from extreme anger to extreme humiliation, over and over again, like he couldn't make up his mind what emotion seemed to fit the moment. Brett let him sit and stew in those emotions for a minute. It was comical watching the man wanting to scream obscenities at him but knowing what would happen to his career trajectory if he did.

Finally, Brett spoke up. "Let me show you how this is done. Follow me, Agent. Make sure you stay back about ten feet. I wouldn't want you to accidentally step in a crime scene."

Brett crossed back through the barricade and headed to the Tac Team at the rear. Agent Idiot followed along at the ordered ten-foot distance. Cash followed back behind even further. Presumably to enjoy the schooling he was going to give Agent Idiot. Brett asked a Tac Team member for his binoculars, and the young man dutifully gave them up without question. He then asked that man to follow him as well.

He led them all back down the road for about forty more yards, then turned left, crossing to the opposite side and carefully picked his way through a barbed wire fence. Brett didn't even wait to see if the rest were following. He knew they would be. From there, he weaved his way through the light underbrush until he found the tree he previously spotted. The chain ladder to a hunter's tree-stand stretched upward along the trunk for about thirty feet, ending in a small shooter's platform.

He turned and called out to Agent Idiot. "This is where your killer shot from. Not the road." The man was staring at the tree stand in embarrassment.

Brett turned back and began to ascend the tree. He imagined he must be a sight to see in his two-piece suite, climbing a tree stand, but sometimes you needed to do things yourself. Once in position on top, and looking through the binoculars, he scanned the truck first. Then he looked towards the greenhouse. Finally, he turned further left, scanning the far side of Slaughter's field until he saw something of interest. He thought he knew what it was, but could not tell for sure. Lastly, he worked his way up the hill behind the house and field.

Brett pointed to the hill. "What's up there, Agent?"

Agent Idiot turned back to verify where Brett was pointing before responding. "A hilltop shooting range. We have already looked it over once, and didn't really find much. Looks like the guy liked to practice up there, is all."

Brett climbed back down carefully and handed the binoculars to the man. "Put your gloves back on and get up there."

"Sir?"

"Climb, agent. Are you scared of heights?"

"I… No, sir." Agent Idiot put his evidence gloves on and scurried up the ladder, obviously confused on why he needed to be up in the stand.

"Now," Brett called up to him, "use those binoculars and check out the truck on the road. Is there a clear shot to that point?"

"Yes, sir," the Agent replied still looking through the binoculars.

"And would you also have a clear shot all the way to the greenhouse?"

"Yes, sir." The agent's voice had turned a bit more dejected as he realized Brett was right.

"Make note of the trajectory from up there. You will need to look for rounds fired along that flight path. Now turn and look across the field at the base of the hill." The Agent did as he was instructed. "Take a look at the tops of those fence posts over near the tree-line. You will see one that has fresh wood exposed at the top. Like maybe someone shot it from all the way over here. You will need someone to verify that, of course. But do you want to bet I'm wrong?"

The Agent looked down at him from the tree stand. "No. No, sir, I don't." His countenance had completely reversed itself from cocky and smug to one that reminded Brett of a puppy caught taking a wee on the carpet.

"First smart thing you've said since I pulled in. Your shooter was not Slaughter. Your shooter was an assassin that was sitting up there observing and calculating out a plan for assassinating all three. Then that truck pulled up and everything changed. You will discover once DNA comes back, that man in the truck was the illegitimate son of Charles Kaiser. The very same King Pin that I took down, and the reason I am a few pay grades over your head.

"The assassin in the tree stand, where you're standing now, was not happy that the one in the truck was about to take his kills. So, he shot him instead. I know that for sure, because I bothered to take a look at the top of the cab. If you will look through your binoculars again, you will notice a deep gouge in the roof. One with no rust on it, indicating it's fresh. The bullet passed through the man in the truck, and then ricocheted off the roof. It's what told me that the angle you were theorizing about was all wrong. It told me the angle would have made more sense from up where you are now."

Brett could see the now thoroughly humiliated agent was indeed looking at the top of the truck with his binoculars. But, he wasn't done with the man yet.

"Now," Brett continued. "if I am right about that fence post, and I know that I am, the shooter in the trees turned his attention to Slaughter. He was firing at him as he ran down the hill. Follow the angle that you are on now, instead of that winding trail I can see headed up the hill behind the house, and you might be able to gather more evidence as you follow that pathway up.

"Our assassin in the tree missed his intended target in the process. We know that because the tipster that called all of this in was male. Slaughter himself. The assassin would never have bothered. So, we know he missed. And instead of sticking around and trying to finish the job, the assassin decided to high-tail it out of here. Maybe he thought it was too risky knowing Slaughter's reputation. His intention is to probably try again at a later date.

"Now when you come down out of that tree, you need to have those guys with the metal detectors sweep around the base for spent brass. The shooter probably took it all with him, but you never know. Maybe we'll get lucky.

"Class isn't over yet. Now climb down out of that tree. We have one more piece of evidence to follow up on, that you neglected to see because you didn't actually investigate. You just showed up and presumed to know everything."

The man climbed down, but all the wind had been taken out of his sails. His psyche was beat up and bruised like it got tossed into a cage with a ninja.

Good. The jerk needed a good bruising.

"Now standing right here, knowing that the real shooter was above your head, what is our next course of action?"

"Look for brass," the Agent said meekly.

"Yeah, but how about something we haven't already discussed." Brett, satisfied that the young man had been humiliated enough, had taken the hard edge out of his voice. Now it was time to start building the young man back up again. After all, he was still a fellow agent. As long as he accepted defeat, then Brett was willing to start restoring some of his confidence again.

The man appeared to be trying to collect his thoughts and getting himself back on track. He likely had not received an embarrassing dress down like this since his academy days. Brett walked up and put one hand on his shoulder.

"Look around. Tell me what you see," he instructed in a much warmer tone of voice.

The agent did as instructed, eyes combing the woods all around him. Then, "He went this way." The Agent was pointing to a barely noticed path of disturbed leaves leading deeper into the forest.

"Correct. You." Brett pointed to the single Tac Team member with him. "Can you see that trail well enough?"

The man silently nodded. He automatically raised his Sig Sauer MCX rifle and led them all into the shadows.

A short while later, they found themselves at another crime scene. It was apparent what happened here. It was also apparent that he was correct on who the real shooter was. That was confirmed in his own mind, at least. Only a professional would leave the barrel and firing pin sitting in the kitchen sink.

He debated on voicing who he thought the shooter to be.

Politics said that if he was correct, he would have no real way to back that up other than his gut. He certainly could not explain how he knew for sure who they were after.

Practicality said that if he spilled the beans on his suspicions, however, it would get resources moving that might be able to help DJ and Abbi.

If he ended up being wrong, it was really going to hurt his career. And with so many people out to see him taken down a notch, it wouldn't be pretty.

He decided to risk it. "Agent, what did you say your name was?" The man looked at him nervously. He hesitated for a moment before replying.

"Hall, sir." Agent Hall swallowed.

"Agent Hall, are we on the same page now? Do you trust that I have a knack for this sort of thing?"

"Yes, sir. Sorry, sir. I was out of line."

"OK, we'll see if you're lying or not. I am going to tell you something. I know who the real shooter is. And if you help me bag him, it will do a lot for your career. A lot more than finally taking down Slaughter. Few agents get a chance to take down someone with as much of a legendary reputation in the criminal world as the assassin I am about to name.

"But, here is the deal. I have nothing to really back up my claims. If you run back to your boss with this, they will use it to say I'm in over my head.

"You can make a career changing decision right now. But I can promise you this, if you run back to your SAC with this, and I turn out to be right like I've been all along, I'll make it my mission in life to make sure your career is over.

"So, you ready for who I think the shooter is?"

The agent merely nodded in reply. Brett could not tell what he was thinking. Brett knew where the man's loyalty would normally sit. He should be loyal to the one he called Boss. But he felt like he had no choice. He needed help on this one. A lot of it. And he had few places to pull that help from.

"Agent Hall," he said, taking a deep breath. "We are looking for none other than the famed hitman known as El Gran Blanco. The Great White himself."

Agent Cash let out a long whistle, then spoke up for the first time since landing in Kentucky. "Time to go swimming with the sharks."

"I'm sorry," Brett said, looking stunned at Agent Cash. "Did our resident Vulcan just attempt a joke? Because that was just horrible."

Chapter 6: Frozen Treats

It didn't take DJ long to get them both loaded up and gone. He had long since prepared them for a hasty exit just in case. They stuffed a bag full of clothes, Abbi's laptop, DJ's pack he carried with him everywhere, and a few guns into the back of the four door Jeep parked behind the house.

The large box-truck full of weapons he drove away from Big Chuck's compound had been dealt with long ago. The guns, ammo, and other weapons stored in the back had been distributed in various places over the last few months. Most of them in storage facilities registered under the fake names he acquired at Big Chuck's facility. He stashed some in this state, and some in others. Some were even hidden at the farmhouse they just left. As long as Super Sleuth Brett Foster didn't show up to look for them, he felt reasonably sure his stash wouldn't be found this time.

And when the state seized the property and eventually auctioned it off... Well, he had a plan for that as well. The same one he had for dealing with his old ranch back in Colorado. He had a hard time giving up that piece of property, so he and Beaver had come up with an ingenious plan for re-acquiring it. It involved stealing a large sum of Big Chuck's electronic funds, allowing the property to be sold at auction, and then offering a substantial increase to the person that won the bid.

With Big Chuck's leftover funds, Abbi and Beaver found as many innocent people the criminal had hurt as possible, and secretly started dividing up his funds as anonymous donations into their bank accounts.

But the guns and other stuff in the back of that truck, DJ kept.

When he finished distributing Big Chuck's stolen weapons, he drove the truck into a very questionable neighborhood in a nearby state. After removing any DNA and fingerprint evidence, he left it running with the keys in the ignition. He was pretty sure it was stripped into parts and sold by whatever gang ran that part of town. They probably had it down to the frame within hours.

Leaving the farmhouse behind, DJ made a snap decision to switch to one of the other sets of fake identities Beaver had already set them up with. He was pretty sure the man that was killed in the back of the truck simply followed them all the way from Colorado when they ran that night. It was too big of a coincidence. The assassin in the tree-stand probably tracked DJ and the girls down by tracking down the man in the truck first. After all, the only other person who knew their new identities was Beaver.

What was not clear, was why the dead guy waited until this morning to try and kill them. Did it take him this long to work up the nerve? No matter, DJ thought. With that man now dead, and by switching to alternate ID's that had barely been used, it would be hard for the unknown assassin to try and track them down.

After hitting the road, Abbi used her phone and jumped on the dark web to try and reach Beaver. It had now been a few hours and the hacker had not responded. DJ would have thought since he was such a good paying customer, the hacker would have responded by now. That concerned him. They needed his help in the worst way.

The second thing she did was to make a phone call back to Colorado. There was a friend of the Jackson family in the mortuary business. The man dated Mary way back in high school and always thought highly of her. When the events of the summer went down, they arranged for a secret swap with Henry Jackson's body.

DJ used a shell company to buy two grave plots in another cemetery not too far away from where Henry was supposed to be buried. Then, Mary's friend took possession of the body. But instead of having it buried in the location as planned, he switched the paperwork around, and an empty casket went in the ground instead. Henry was now buried in one of the two alternate grave sites.

Abbi called him and arranged for her mother's body to be picked up, and have the same swap performed. The man was deeply saddened at the news and promised to take care of everything. DJ promised her they would make a trip out to visit their gravesides in the spring.

After that, they both sat in silence while DJ drove. He was headed east, to Boston. DJ had secretly, under the second set of identities he was using now, purchased a home last month just over the river from MIT. His plan was to surprise the girls with that information pretty soon. He had just been working out the best way. As they snaked their way east, he told her of the home and the planned surprise.

There was still time to enroll for the spring semester under the new identity for Abbi, and there was no reason to change those plans. Her mother would have insisted, DJ told her. Abbi just shook her head in affirmation and went back to watching the scenery sweep past the windows.

They had been driving non-stop since they got on the road. Nearly four hours straight put a lot of distance behind them, and they were now well into West Virginia. He needed a break. They both did. And the Jeep was coasting on fumes. He was sure Abbi would not feel like eating, considering the recent events, but he would force her to anyway. She needed her strength.

Up ahead, right alongside the two-lane blacktop they were traveling, he saw a small diner and gas station. It sat on the other side of a bridge, and was moderately busy. He would fill up, and they could go in and sit down for a meal. And, he really needed to go to the bathroom.

He crossed over the bridge, and instantly knew he wanted to take a closer look at the place. The gap under the bridge was narrow, but deep, housing a fast-moving mountain river. The diner had a parking lot stretching right up next to a straight drop down into the churning white water, probably about forty feet over the surface. Further behind the diner, a waterfall cascaded through thick evergreen trees and helped to feed the swollen rushing river. It then passed under the road, winding its way out of view on the other side.

It was beautiful.

The sign out front of the diner read, "Fast Falls Feedin' Hall," and the building was built to look like a log cabin. This was a perfect spot to fuel up, eat up, and rest up.

As he swung into the parking lot, he glanced at Abbi. He was really worried about her. The tone of her voice never really displayed the grief he knew was there. She talked little on the trip so far, other than making that phone call to arrange the transport and swap of her mother's body. When she did engage in idle conversation, however, he could tell she was doing her best to ignore the emotions.

She was angry. She was hiding it, but he could tell. She was doing her best to control it. To direct it. She was committed to teaming up with Brett somehow, and hunting the assassin down. DJ wasn't so sure of that himself. He had a feeling if he called Brett, they would both would end up wearing matching steel bracelets.

He could sense the pain in her voice as well. It was far away, buried behind a thick layer of resolve to move forward. But, he could hear it back there. He traveled this road before and recognized that familiar tone.

Looking at her was like looking at a smoldering volcano. There was a hint of steam, and an occasional tremble. She possessed just enough of a hint for one to know there was pressure and turmoil, boiling and burning, just beneath the surface. That pressure was going to blow at some point. It would be fearfully violent. And just like what happens when a real volcano erupts, it would not only destroy the mountain known as Abbi, but it would fling debris far and wide, damaging and wounding anything close to her.

Their relationship could become a casualty of that eruption. That understanding sent a thin sliver of fear right through him. It was selfish to be thinking of himself right now and what he stood to lose in all of this. But he couldn't help himself. Nothing was more important to him in this world than Abbi Jackson.

If he didn't find a way to pull her out of what was going on in her mind, he may never have the opportunity to change her last name. For real. Not through building a fake ID on the Dark Web, but by slipping a thin gold band on the ring finger of her left hand.

DJ pulled in to the first available pump and set about topping off. Abbi made a bee-line into the building to find a bathroom. The shooting pain in his side informed him he would need to do the same, and soon. He had spent far too long in the bouncing Jeep with no break.

He stretched as he filled up and accidentally caught the eye of the guy next to him pumping gas into his ride. DJ smiled casually at him, then offered up some small talk. "You know if this diner is any good?"

"Sorry, friend. I have no idea," the man politely replied. "Passing through myself." The gentleman seemed well educated by his dress and DJ thought he could pick up a northeastern accent.

"Well, anything with the words 'Feedin Hall' has to be tried." DJ pointed at the sign as he spoke.

"We *are* in the hills of West Virginia," the man nodded in agreement. "I am sure that whatever they serve will taste like chicken."

DJ laughed and said, "You know, I *thought* I heard a banjo a few minutes ago."

The stranger smiled. "Just make sure you refuse any canoe trips down that stream if you're asked."

"I'll do that." DJ nodded in agreement. "Though that stream seems more like a small river."

"Must have gotten a lot of rain."

They stood in awkward silence a minute more until the man's pump shut off. DJ wished him a good day, and the other returned the pleasantry. But instead of pulling off down the road, the man just moved to park in front of the building, and then disappeared inside. Must be hungry as well, DJ thought. Or maybe his bladder is about to explode like mine.

The pump clicked off for DJ as well, and he didn't even try to squeeze any more into the tank. His eyes were floating. He quickly hung up the nozzle, scrambled into the Jeep, and hurried to park near the front doors.

Once inside, he focused his attention on anything that might indicate a bathroom location. Spotting a sign, he tore to the back of the store with single-minded purpose.

The building was divided into two halves. The one on the right, the same side as the waterfall, was devoted to giftshop items and convenience store goods. The left side consisted of the diner. The entrance to the women's and men's restroom were side by side. Abbi was coming out as he was headed in. He paused a moment to speak to her, asking her to get a table and order him a burger and a shake. He would meet her in a minute. She softly nodded with a far-away look in her eyes.

She was having a rough time. Abbi kept cycling back and forth between that heated anger and a deep sadness. She was trying desperately to deal with it, but she was struggling. And for the life of him, he had no idea how to help her.

Despite having dealt with similar circumstances in his own past, he felt powerless to assist her. He had no idea what to say in order to help her cope. Words emptied out of his head every time he looked at her. He felt so stupid and weak. If only it were something he could shoot, something he could place in front of a set of gun sights, maybe then he could help her out. When it came to affairs of the heart and the mind, he was a blind man groping desperately along an unfamiliar path, with no cane to help him find his way.

One thing was for certain, his heart clenched in his chest every time he looked at her. He loved her so much. He just wanted to sweep her into his arms and hold her. Just hold her until it all faded away in the background.

She was past him then, headed to the diner to find a table and place their order. His eyes followed her a moment more, then he was racing through the door, searching for the first available place to pee he could find.

He almost couldn't unzip fast enough, and then… blessed relief. He closed his eyes and tilted his head back, relaxing into the moment. Man, he really could not have waited a single second more. Any longer, and he would have been changing his clothes.

"Long trip?" The voice was familiar, but it startled DJ nonetheless. In his desperate search for the closest place to relieve himself, he failed to notice the stranger from the gas pumps standing in the next stall. He was partially hidden from view, and DJ had been so very focused on his pressing need.

"Yeah," DJ replied.

"Where you headed?"

DJ regretted ever saying anything to the man. He was just trying to be cordial to the stranger, and now here he was, trying to engage DJ in conversation while both of them, quite literally, had their hands full. There was nothing worse than someone trying to get chatty in a bathroom stall. To DJ, it was just… well… *weird*. It kind of creeped him out. No need to be rude, however. He at least should answer the question. "Boston," DJ replied.

The man turned his head to face him fully over the partial wall. "No kidding? I am too. Are you headed home?"

"No. My girlfriend is thinking about going to MIT. We are going for a campus visit." DJ wished the guy would finish and just go away. The man talking to him was affecting his… concentration.

"Ah, well I am going there to check out a hospital. Boston General. I'm a thoracic surgeon. I've been offered a job there. Thought I would check out the hospital and the city before making my decision. I've never been to Boston. Have you?"

SHUT UP MORON, I'M TRYING TO PEE, he screamed at the stranger in his head! Out loud, however, he replied with a polite voice and answered the man's question. "This will be my first trip, too."

At last, the man turned back to his business. But just when DJ thought that might be the end of the conversation, the idiot started talking again. "Thought I would drive instead of flying down," the man said. "I hate flying, really. I have to fly all the time for my job. Work frequently takes me out of the country, but I would drive across the Atlantic if they would build a bridge."

"Really?" DJ asked "You have to fly overseas a lot for medical conferences?"

"Oh, no. Surgery," the man said with a light-hearted lilt to his voice. "You would be surprised how many people need me to go to another country and stick a knife in their chest." The man then turned his head towards DJ again and gave a big smile.

DJ nodded his reply. He had nothing to say to that. And it was now official, DJ was creeped out. In his haste to get into the building and relieve himself, DJ's daypack with his silenced Sig stored inside was left in between the seats of the Jeep. He was starting to regret his oversight. He wasn't seriously thinking of shooting the guy, of course. He was merely joking with himself. But the stranger certainly was starting to make him feel on edge. "You actually fly to other countries to perform surgery?" DJ asked him.

"Let's just say, I have a highly refined skillset," the creepy stranger answered. His perfect little pearly-white teeth practically split his head in two.

DJ thankfully finished with his business and zipped himself up. He eagerly turned away from the stranger and headed to the sink. To his dismay, the stranger did the same.

That's just fantastic, DJ thought.

As they stood side by side again, this time over a pair of sinks, the man continued. "Yep, I've been in this business a long while. You might say that I've developed a bit of a name for myself. I get paid top dollar to go all over the place," the man said matter-of-factly.

"Wow," DJ replied, glancing at the man's reflection in the mirror across from him, and trying to sound sincere. "A man of reputation."

The gentleman turned to face him completely. "Oh, you have no idea. But if you did, you would have never pretended to be me when you went against Charles Kaiser."

It was then DJ saw the Glock the man was casually pointing at his belt buckle. There was a long, meaty suppressor attached. It had apparently been hiding in the folds of the man's expensive polar fleece.

A millisecond after he realized the danger he now found himself in, he suddenly knew who was standing before him, and why everything had happened since this morning.

The man in the bathroom with him was the assassin El Gran Blanco. The same man he had portrayed this past summer when trying to bluff Big Chuck into making an exchange of hostages. The ruse had been done to convince Big Chuck DJ was a ruthless man and not one to be messed with. It had been Brett's idea, and it worked.

But right now, he wanted to kick Brett between his legs. With both feet. Twice.

"This is what's going to happen," the man said, the tone of his voice changing to a bizarre, sinister-like calmness. "You're going to turn around and walk back out the front door. At a normal pace. Do what I tell you, and your girlfriend lives. She doesn't matter to me. Give me any reason, and I will make sure to kill her slow."

Along with the tone of the man's voice shifting, the man's accent had changed as well. DJ could no longer pick up the trace of a northeastern flair. Now it was… Well, it did not seem to have an accent at all. Having served in the Navy with people from all over, he learned that everyone had an accent. People from Southern California had a different sound than someone from Washington State. Mississippi sounded different than Tennessee. Every region sounded different, if you listened for it.

But now that he let the disguise drop, this man had no accent at all. He was probably just used to adopting a regional accent to suit whatever masquerade he was using at the time in order to conceal his identity.

There were two things going through DJ's head at the same time. The first was a question.

What was the best manner in which to kill this man? He left his firearm in the car. So that wasn't a consideration. There was a spring assisted folding knife with a two-and-a-half-inch blade clipped to his pocket. That seemed like the best choice, but he would need a distraction long enough to pull it free, flip it open, and stab him somewhere fun.

DJ smiled inwardly at himself as he envisioned all the wonderful places he could put that blade.

That settled it. He would just have to find a suitable distraction. Not a problem. Something would present itself.

The next thing bouncing around between his ears was the safety of Abbi. Firstly, he needed to keep Mr. Great White away from her. If she in any way sensed that something was wrong, or that DJ was in trouble, she would come after the guy with hands and feet flying. That could get her killed.

The Great White. What a stupid name, DJ thought.

The easiest thing to do in order to try and keep Abbi out of this was to exit the building like Shark Bait ordered him. That would carry them both further away from her. So, he did as Shark Bait instructed and casually left the bathroom. As nonchalantly as possible, he moved back through the building to the exit. Shark Bait followed behind, concealing his gun underneath his heavy fleece.

"Head left through the door. Make your way to the waterfall," Shark Bait ordered in hushed tones.

Perfect, DJ thought to himself.

Over next to the drop off of the black mountain river, there was a short retaining wall to keep cars from driving in. The air was misty from cascading water, and since it was winter, no one wanted near the thing for fear of getting wet. That meant the side of the building was devoid of witnesses. Shark Bait likely intended to shoot him, let him fall over the wall, and watch him just disappear downstream.

Being out of the view of witnesses was ideal for DJ as well. This way, when he stabbed the man and tossed him over the wall instead, no one would see him take the life of the murderous dirt-bag. He could go back inside and have a nice leisurely meal with the love of his life. He could focus his full attention on how to fix her and make her better. No more distractions.

DJ turned sideways, and shouldered his way through the door with his right side. As he did, with that side shielded from view, he slipped the pocket knife free and palmed it in his hand.

This was going to be so much fun.

He walked along the front of the building, passing a couple with their teenaged son headed to the front door. He glanced over his shoulder at Shark Bait, watching him tense up as they moved past. Probably sensing that DJ might use them as a distraction.

This man thinks I'm just like him, DJ thought. *He thinks because I took out so many of those guys, that I sit in the same category of cruelty as all of those I killed. He thinks I'm a common criminal. Only a low life would use an innocent bystander as a shield or a distraction.*

The assassin's misguided belief that DJ was just another criminal thug would be all the distraction he needed. After all, wasn't most criminal activity birthed into existence by greed and the love of money?

Well, Big Chuck's stolen horde should be a great lure, then.

As DJ turned the corner of the building and started moving along the side, he spoke over his left shoulder. This allowed him to keep his right hand with the folded knife hidden from view. "Just out of curiosity, exactly why did you feel you needed to track me down? Please don't tell me it was just because I impersonated you."

"Shut up and keep moving."

"Because I would think you would be flattered."

"I said close your mouth. Now move over to the stream."

DJ obeyed and started angling across the parking lot. This part was empty, as the closer you got to the edge, the more mist there was swirling around in the chilly mountain air.

"Or is it because of the money?" DJ asked. "Because if your plan is to torture how to get to it out of my girlfriend, I can promise you're wasting your time. She has no clue where I stashed it."

DJ was not sure, but he thought he heard a slight hesitation in the killer's foot falls. He was only twenty feet from the edge now. He had to do something soon. "It's true, I have all of the account numbers written down. Who could memorize that many? After all, it's over two hundred million dollars. But no one knows the banks I stashed it in. I have all of that stored right here," DJ said pointing to his temple with his left hand.

Shark Bait had stopped talking, and they finally reached the end of the parking lot. DJ had his back to the short wall. If the man shot him now, he would fall backwards over the wall, and Abbi might not ever know what happened to him. But Shark Bait was hesitating. DJ could see him trying to decide what to do. That was a lot of money. He was processing whether he should just shoot DJ in the head as planned, or see if he could get to the cash. That would make anybody a nice retirement package. Too bad he had already given it away to many of Big Chuck's victims.

Now was the time. He needed to make his move.

DJ kept his wallet in his left back pocket. He started doing that ever since he started carrying a side arm in a concealed manner. This would ensure that when he pulled his wallet out at a store, he wouldn't accidentally expose his weapon concealed underneath his shirt.

The plan here was simple. He would remove his wallet and dangle it over the chasm with his left hand. He would tell the man that the account numbers were inside. Kill him, and there would be no way to retrieve the money. He would talk and stall until he saw his opening. Then he would toss the wallet into Shark Bait's face, step in close past the gun, and stab him in the Adam's Apple.

"I don't think you understand," Shark Bait said. His voice took on a sharpness that had not been there before. "I don't know if you're serious or not about the money, but I don't care. You pretended to be me. You didn't have much of a reputation on your own, so you stepped in and stole mine. I've worked hard to develop the reputation I have. And you think you can simply step in and use my name with impunity? Who do you think you are?" His eyebrows had fused together as he talked, and spittle flew out of his mouth at the end.

It looked like DJ was not going to get the opening he was planning for. This man was ragingly fired up. Money was not going to be an adequate distraction. Prior to this summer, DJ would have started to panic by now. With seemingly no way out, he would have figured this was the end. But times had changed. DJ learned that there was always a way out. It was like he had a higher purpose to take down bad guys, and as long as he didn't get a big head about it, things always seemed to work out. A way forward would always present itself.

And then he saw it. The distraction he was searching for. True, it was not exactly what he was hoping it would be, but it would do. It would do nicely. And maybe using this distraction would provide a way to help him with his other problem.

DJ smiled directly at Shark Bait. Then a snicker slipped past his lips. Next, a rumbling chuckle. Finally, a full-on, belly clutching laugh burst from him, causing him to bend over a bit at the waist. It was real. It was genuine.

The look on Shark Bait's face was priceless. The idiot had no idea what was about to happen, and that caused DJ to laugh all the more.

His real name was Thomas Huntley, but he had not gone by that name since he was in his teens. Nowadays, he went by fake names that changed from week to week.

When he was seventeen years old, he decided to murder his parents. They had it coming, of course. They were very abusive.

His pill-popping mother berated him over the pettiest of issues. Nothing was ever good enough for her. Every word that came out of her mouth was designed to tear him down instead of lift him up. To embarrass or belittle.

His father loved to slap him around to prove what a man he was. Especially when he was drinking. If Thomas wasn't fast enough with something he was told to do, he paid the price in bruises. If the chore he was given was not perfect in its completion, Thomas would accidentally fall down the stairs, or suffer a skateboarding mishap. At least that is what the ER nurses were led to believe. "Tommy is such a klutz, sometimes," his father told them.

One day, he decided enough was enough. He would take them both out. But he would do it with skillful planning. He wouldn't just go on a killing spree like those idiot people you hear about on TV. He would murder them both, get away with it, and then start a new life. One where he would never be abused again.

He had made friends with a Mexican kid named Paco. Paco was an illegal. His whole family was in the country illegally. And, Paco's father made a living helping other "border jumpers" slip through the cracks. The man did that buying social security cards with valid numbers through a connection he made in the Social Security Administration. He would sell

Social Security cards and fake birth certificates to anybody who could cough up a thousand dollars.

The first thing Thomas needed to do to murder his parents was to get Paco to secure him new sets of those papers. Ones saying Thomas was twenty-one years old, and not seventeen.

He used his new paperwork to get a driver's license. With those three forms of identity, he became someone else.

The next thing he did was volunteer to give blood. He did it at two locations in town, two weeks apart. He found the personnel in these blood banks were not very tight on security. After all, who would steal the blood they just donated on the way out of the door?

The last thing he needed to do was wait for the right time. This meant waiting for the next thunderstorm to come through. And in the summer, it was a frequent occurrence where he lived.

Their house had a large drainage canal that ran behind it. Living in Southwest Louisiana meant those canals always had water in them. When there were no heavy rains, those canals moved at a leisurely pace. When there were heavy rains, they turned into engorged, fast moving rivers. It seemed to be commonplace that when a heavy rainstorm came through children would occasionally get swept away if they played too close.

When the next storm showed up, he was ready.

As the wind and rain began pounding on the windows of his home, he put his plan into motion. His dad always drank bourbon and Coke every night watching TV. This night, Thomas offered to make it for him. Instead of using traditional Jack Daniels, he used a bottle of Bacardi 151. The rum was decidedly more potent than his father's regular whiskey. He also crushed up a couple of his mother's sleeping pills into the mix.

Dad was alerted to the flavor difference instantly, but attributed the difference to too much rum. He actually acted proud of his son for trying to pour his father a drink worthy of his station.

The man was passed out in his chair an hour later.

He did the same thing to his mom. He crushed up a handful of sleeping pills and slipped them into the warm milk she had every night before she went to bed. That, along with the two pills she routinely devoured anyways, had her sleeping soundly quickly.

The next step was to wait for it to stop raining. He didn't want the rain to wash away the evidence he would plant in the backyard. When it stopped, and he was sure the storm had moved on, he first checked the drainage ditch behind the house to make sure it was flowing good.

Then he grabbed an old pillow, his two bags of blood, and went to the kitchen. He shoved in both bags, slipped on plastic gloves, grabbed a large kitchen knife, and plunged the knife through the pillow casing. Blood soaked the casing and spilled out onto the floor.

Next, he dropped the knife onto the floor, and dragged the blood-soaked pillow through the kitchen as if it were a dead body. He went out the back door, across the porch, and through the yard to the edge of the drainage canal. He let it slide down the steep slope into the water, and watched it get swept away from view. He removed the gloves and tossed them into the canal as well.

He returned to the house and went to his parents' bedroom. In his father's nightstand was a .45 caliber 1911 pistol with "We the People" inscribed across the side, and stars etched into the grips. He placed the barrel into a pillow, and then the pillow against his mother's head. The .45 bellowed like a beast, and despite the pillow to muffle the sound, made his ears ring. It was loud enough the neighbors might have been wakened. Apparently muffling a gunshot with a pillow was a Hollywood joke.

His father might have been wakened… He needed to hurry!

He tore into the living room only to see his father still unmoving in his recliner, sleeping like a baby. Carefully, he eased his father's hand around the grip of the pistol, and slowly lifted his beefy hand to his head. The same hand that used to enjoy pounding on him from time to time.

The gun roared to life again, and this time Thomas could enjoy the carnage that ensued. The slug tore through his father's brain like it was a giant soft marshmallow. It exited on the opposite side with a bloody explosion splattering the far wall. Thomas actually laughed out loud at the wonderful glory of it all.

The bedroom was dark and murky where he had slain his dear mother. But this? This was fantastic! An incredible rush of adrenaline coursed through him and he felt like his brain was lit up like a Christmas tree. It was almost magical.

He wanted to sit, pour himself one of his father's Jack and Coke's, and enjoy the moment. But he needed to get out of here as fast as possible.

He had already prepared for his exit. There was a duffle bag packed, wrapped in a plastic bag, and stored in some bushes at the edge of a park a few blocks away. He only needed to grab some money. His father had a lunch box under his bed with a few thousand dollars. He took the box, along with a snub nosed .22 revolver and a box of shells, and never looked back.

He paid attention to the news long enough to know that his ruse worked for the murder, however. Back then, they did not have the level of forensic evidence collection they did today. The cops all thought his father had stabbed his son and threw his body in the canal, murdered his wife in bed, and then killed himself. The man had a reputation with the law. In their minds, it was what it looked like. The father killed his family and offed himself.

He lived on the streets for a while after that, trying to make his money stretch as far as he could, and roaming from town to town. Eventually, however, the money ran out.

He found himself in a bar in a seedy Chicago neighborhood, sitting on a stool next to a man drowning his sorrows in a drink with an umbrella. Thomas asked the man if he had any odd jobs he could do for cash. Jokingly, the man said he would pay him five hundred dollars if he could make his wife disappear.

Thomas smiled and told him he could make that happen. Over the next hour, what started off as a joke turned into an actual plan. Thomas told him he needed all the money up front, and a week to observe and plan.

A week later she was gone, and Thomas walked into a new profession.

There were a few mistakes along the way, and some close calls that nearly got him caught. Twice they almost killed him. But, he learned from those mistakes, and eventually came up with a core set of rules to keep him out of trouble.

Those rules, eight of them, not only ensured his success, but allowed him to develop a complete system for acquiring contracts and exchanging money without ever meeting his customer face to face.

Eventually, he got the one high profile job he needed to launch his career and start commanding the big bucks. That one job helped to cement his reputation. He got so much work after that, he decided to grow his one-man operation into a multi-employee business. He transitioned from a one-man show to a ten-member organization of assassins. He recruited and trained them himself.

None of the ten knew who the others were. Each operated independently as a sort of free-lance contractor. Thomas negotiated all contracts, and farmed them out to the one he felt could fulfil it per the contract agreements. If it was an elaborate job, he usually handled it himself.

He even had three retainer contracts with various organizations. They paid him a flat rate annual fee, and he made their problems go away. If the requirements were explicit, or the time frame conditional, there were always additional surcharge options.

Life was profitable. Therefore, life was good.

Then, David Slaughter came along and tinkled in his Kool-Aid. The man pretended to be him when he went up against Charles Kaiser. Charles then called in a hit on El Gran Blanco. Called it in to ten different contractors, no less. Two of them belonged to his own network and worked for him.

Both of the ungrateful traitors took it. Didn't they know where their bread was buttered?

He was attacked three different times before he figured out what was going on. Only his skill and his aim allowed him to avoid death. He had to kill the two that worked for him, of course. Their act of defection was completely unforgivable. The third, he tortured until he learned of the contract placed on him. Then it was painstaking investigative work to determine who the other seven were that agreed to take the contract.

He killed them all. With the help of his network, of course. He was only human, after all. Despite the legend associated with his name.

But Slaughter, he saved for himself. It was personal. He had an emotional connection to this kill. He wanted to see the man's brain explode. He wanted to press a dagger through Slaughter's ribs and pierce his heart.

Those emotions allowed him to make mistakes the first time he tried to kill Slaughter. Thomas violated his coveted rules' structure because he allowed his emotions to get the better of him. The man was left still breathing, and Thomas had to run lest he be forced into a much closer combat situation.

On the trip away from the farm, headed to Boston for another chance, he kept analyzing himself. The truth was, he was scared that Slaughter was his better in every sense of the word. Thomas had met no one that was better than him. Equal, sure. Better, never. His speed in hand to hand combat was lethal. His marksmanship in close quarters combat, or extreme distance, was as good as it got. He was deadly with blades, guns, and his own two hands. For years he had been sure that no matter the circumstances, there were few that were his equal.

But Slaughter made him nervous. What the man had been able to do to Big Chuck and his men, and in the span of time he did it, was something Thomas had never run across before. He was crazy good. And that scared him.

It was an unfamiliar emotion. Fear.

Fear transitioned into even more anger and hatred. Hatred for Slaughter. Hatred for himself for fearing him. And that hatred of himself only turned around and fueled his emotional blindness to Slaughter.

The man had to die. And soon. His existence was jeopardizing a career that was nearly two decades in the making. Not that he had to worry about Slaughter taking his business. He was taking his mind. The fact he knew the man was walking around somewhere, was like a needle in the back of his eye. It gave him a migraine and distracted him from his true love. His passion. Murder for hire.

The ability to get paid, and paid well, for the thing he loved most, and for the thing he did best, was hanging in the balance as long as the man existed.

But follow the rules, you moron! He yelled that command at himself, over and over again as he drove east from Kentucky. *Follow your stupid rules!*

He'd paused twice so far on his trip away from Kentucky. Once to answer the call of nature and top off with gas. Once to dispose of the rifle by hurling it off a bridge into a deep river.

His plan was to get to Boston ahead of Slaughter, and to stake out the house the man had purchased there. It was added information gleaned from torturing the now dead hacker known as Beaver. He would go back into his practiced routine of observation and planning. He would bide his time until he could kill the nuisance that needled his mind and induced uncontrolled emotions.

But then it happened. The guy actually pulled up at a gas pump across from him with his cute little girlfriend. He was right there, less than six feet from him, stretching like he had not a care in the world.

Are you kidding me, he asked himself?

Then the man caught his eye, and Thomas switched into chameleon mode, becoming just another person in the crowd. He could have controlled himself, still, waiting for Slaughter to fill up and leave. But the man had to be polite and say something to Thomas. As soon as he did, that needle behind his eye began poking away, again. The pain in his brain started anew.

Seriously, he questioned Fate? *Are you really going to tempt me like this?*

He was saved by the pump shutting off and giving him an excuse to pull away. He shrugged off temptation and made for the bathroom. He would relieve himself and get back on the road as fast as possible. He would do his best to get back out ahead of Slaughter and put himself on track to complete this mission like the well-disciplined assassin he was. Fluid, smooth, precise.

But fate intervened again. And then the man was standing alongside him, at the very next urinal, head back and eyes closed, oblivious to the simmering hatred of Thomas standing next to him.

The needle. Oh, how it poked at him. It was making his eye twitch.

And then stupidity happened. Thomas opened his mouth and started talking to him. He couldn't stop himself. The rules, like a living thing, yelled at him to stay true to the guidelines he knew always worked. But he ignored them. It was like he was stuck in an out-of-body experience. Like he was on the outside of his corporeal form, listening to himself babble on about being a surgeon. He was a runaway train, pressing ahead despite all the warnings going off. His foot was off the brake, hands up to enjoy the ride like the train was nothing more than a children's roller coaster in an amusement park.

He pressed ahead with reckless abandon. That needle behind his eyes shoving him forward as if he were at gunpoint. He stumbled forward with his stupid tale of surgery like he had no choice in the matter.

He was blinded. He was foolish. But reason, no matter how it screamed at him to divert from his course, would not be listened to. The Rules were made to be broken. The Rules were but mere guidelines, anyway.

In his out-of-body experience, he watched himself helplessly as he drew his gun and forced the man back through the store.

He was committed now. There was no bailing out of this ill-conceived plan. He had no recourse but to see it through. He would lead the man to the edge of the parking lot, to the edge of the falls. He would pass a bullet between his eyes and shove him into the rushing mountain stream. Then, he would pray no one saw him. He would pray he left no evidence behind.

If he was lucky in this foolhardy endeavor, he would leave this place. The girl was meaningless. He would just kill Slaughter and then move on with his life.

But as he marched Slaughter across the parking lot, he heard the man speak of money and account numbers. When he heard the amount, he momentarily searched to see if there was a way he could torture the truth out of him. But there wasn't a way. Another time and another place, and perhaps he could have worked it into the plan. But he was here now, seconds away from ending that poking needle in the back of his eye.

Seconds away from splendid relief. So he ignored the avarice temptations briefly coursing through him.

But first… First he would tell Slaughter why. He would tell him his money meant nothing. He would tell him how pretending to be the greatest assassin ever was an unforgivable sin.

So, he did.

He expected to see a flash of fear and a sudden understanding that the end was finally here flicker through Slaughter's eyes. Instead, what was he now doing?

He was laughing at him. He was standing here an instant away from the end of his life, and Slaughter was laughing at him. It was not the defiant laugh of a doomed and dying man. It was honest humor. Like a funny joke had just been told to him by his best friend.

Thomas stood there looking at him with confusion, his finger resting on the trigger ready to end the man for good. Thomas stood now at the precipice of satisfaction, ready to finally rid himself of that needle. That annoying needle.

Worse now than the needle, was the laughter. How someone so close to death could find genuine humor in such a bleak situation? He had to know.

"Before I end you," Thomas asked the man. "What exactly about this situation do you find so funny?"

Slaughter tried to contain himself before answering. "I was trying to decide the best way to distract you," he said through snickers. "Before I grabbed that gun of yours and tossed you over this wall."

Thomas sneered at him. "Your little temptation with the money isn't going to work. You don't seem to get it. The only thing I want is for you to die. Right here. Right now." Thomas was seething on the inside. Who did this guy think he was? This insulant little bug of a man! He would step on the bug. Crush him under his foot!

"But then," Slaughter continued. "I never thought the distraction would come in the form of a chocolate milkshake."

Stinging shock rolled through Thomas's body, starting from the right side of his head. Something smashed him hard, causing him to flinch and close his eyes involuntarily.

His brain processed everything in a micro-second. The stinging sensation in his ear, his head, and his neck, was likely caused by the girl. She had hit him with something. Something cold. A whiff of chocolate invaded his nostrils as he sucked in. A milkshake? That's what Slaughter had said.

She snuck up behind and got as close as she could without tipping him off. He was focused on Slaughter laughing. The man successfully distracted him long enough for her to get into hurling range with her frozen chocolate treat. Then, she beamed him in his ear as hard as she could.

He pulled the trigger a millisecond after he recoiled from the milkshake, but he already knew it was too late. Slaughter had moved. The bullet passed harmlessly to one side of his target.

He felt a talon-like hand clamp onto his gun wrist. He tried to correct and bend it toward Slaughter to get off another shot. He pulled the trigger a second time, but even though soft ice cream clogged his vision, he knew he wasn't even close.

As he struggled to get his eyes opened and focused on his target, he felt his wrist being bent over and knew what was going to happen next. That was OK, Thomas thought, he was well trained in the art of hand to hand combat. He quickly stepped in to keep Slaughter from gaining leverage. And blindly threw an opened palm strike at Slaughter through the fog of chocolate ice-cream.

But Slaughter stepped in too, around his move, and they were chest to chest.

Then the most horrific pain he ever felt struck him in his left butt cheek. It was brutally intense. It stole the air from his lungs, buckled his knees, and ripped every thought of self-defense from his brain. Every muscle in his body sagged in instant weakness, and for a moment, he was no longer in control of his entire body.

Slaughter had stabbed him. He had plunged a knife from out of nowhere, deep into the meatiest part of his backside. Right through the left back pocket of his jeans.

He was being pushed then. Propelled along by the strength of the man, and his own weakness, as his body and mind failed him under the intensity of the pain.

He felt the low wall hit him in the shins. The same wall he meant to shove Slaughter over. And then he was falling through the air as he finally managed to see through chunks of sloppy milkshake. As he watched the cold mountain river rushing up to meet him, he was dimly aware that his pistol was no longer in his hand. What was most prevalent in his mind as the frigid waters swallowed him whole, was that he had been soundly defeated by only a girl with a chocolate milkshake.

Chapter 7: Covenants & Vows

DJ loved that girl. He loved her with all of his heart and soul. She was amazing on so many levels and in so many ways. But right now, where she seemed to stand out the most, was her throwing accuracy. When it came to tossing milkshakes, the woman was positively lethal.

He would have really liked to sit back and enjoy the moment when the white cup of chocolate delight smashed into Shark Bait's right ear. He would have loved to savor the instant it broke apart and covered the man's head and face in milky ice cream. But, he needed to take advantage of the distraction Abbi provided him.

He stepped hard right and narrowly avoided being gut shot, then gripped Shark Bait's wrist that held the gun. Blinded, his adversary stepped in to keep DJ from gaining leverage and being able to snap his wrist over.

DJ answered by stepping in as well, so close he could smell the chocolate shake, and now he had the knife open and ready. Shark Bait made a futile attempt at another shot, but DJ was well inside, and safe. With gleeful satisfaction, he plunged the blade into the man's left buttock, all the way to the hilt. The killer sucked wind, and DJ felt the man's whole body sort of sag against him.

DJ stepped aside then, and using the still imbedded knife, pushed Shark Bait hard at the retaining wall. The man flew over with no fight whatsoever. His gun slipped from weakened fingers and clattered to the pavement. DJ watched the man plunge into the river and vanish from view. He emerged a moment later further to his right, being swept along in the current. Then, he was under the bridge and being carried along to the other side.

Abbi skidded to a halt next to him, searching for the killer as well.

"Is he dead?" she asked.

"Not hardly," DJ answered.

"You're getting better at that wrist move. Training pays off, doesn't it?" Oddly, considering the situation, Abbi was grinning at him ear to ear.

DJ had been training with Abbi in some basic self-defense moves. She was a good teacher, and he certainly did not mind getting all tangled up with her in practice. But while he enjoyed thinking about those moments spent with her, he had other things to do. And he was running out of time.

"The GPS in the Jeep said that black top curves around and crosses back over the stream about a quarter of a mile down the road." DJ pointed in the direction he was referring. "I need you to get the Jeep and meet me there. I am going after him on foot. I have his gun, so he is probably unarmed." He paused to think a moment before continuing. "He might have a backup, though. I know I would. Anyways, if he makes his way out of the river, I need to be there to end this."

DJ was running then, not waiting to see if Abbi was following his instructions, the killer's confiscated weapon tucked inside his jacket. He sprinted hard across the parking lot to the edge of the road. He paused to let a couple of cars go past, and then charged for the other side. Once there, he scrambled down over the steep rocky slope to the river's edge, eyes probing up ahead, looking for any sign of his enemy.

Down here by the river, everything was wet and slippery. He needed to be cautious or he could snap an ankle. He moved quickly though, hopping from rock to rock. Pausing every few steps to search for movement. He scanned for Shark Bait, wounded and wet, to be seen crawling from the water.

From boulder to boulder he moved, searching and probing ahead, looking for his adversary. A few minutes passed by with him seeing nothing, and he wondered if the man already floated too far downstream to catch up with.

On this side of the road, and at the edge of town, there were no buildings or signs of human life. Just dense evergreen trees and wet boulders on both sides of the gorge, broken up occasionally by a fallen tree. There were plenty of places for a wounded man to hide behind and conceal himself from view. If he was armed with a backup pistol, like DJ had to assume, then DJ would make an excellent target out in the open like he was.

The hair on the back of his neck bristled at that sudden revelation, and DJ abruptly turned and bolted for the safety of the trees to his right. He barely heard the sound of an unsilenced weapon over the roar of the rushing water, but he certainly felt the wind of the bullet's passing across his cheek.

DJ flinched and picked up speed, zig zagging as he went. Another round whipped past him, and this one took flesh with it, grazing his left ear.

Finally, he dove right behind a large boulder, landing on his side in the hard rocks at its base. An angry whine of a ricochet told him he had suffered yet another close call.

This guy could shoot.

Of course he can, you idiot, he berated himself. *He's an assassin.*

He was trapped where he was, only twenty feet from the concealing shadows of the trees. But something told him if he bolted that way now, his enemy would cap him before he made it three feet. Plus, he had no idea where the man was. He could be on this side of the river, or the other. He could be close, or far away. Right now, he could be carefully aiming with a weapon braced on a rock, or he could be maneuvering for a better angle.

DJ needed to figure out where the man was before he could decide on a course of action.

Laying his weapon aside, he took off his coat. Then, pressing up close to the large boulder, he raised himself into a crouching position, facing the boulder and the river on the other side. Finally, he took his jacket, and tossed it to the right. At the same time, he popped up for just a moment.

The assassin was not fooled. DJ had been hoping the man would take a quick shot at the jacket, and he would be able to spot the shooter's location. The man did take a shot, and DJ did spot where he was shooting from, but the shot was taken at him. The round smacked the top of the boulder right in front of him, and sent pieces of rock shotgunning into his face. A larger round, and he would likely have died from the ricochet. As it was, he was only cut up pretty good from rock fragments. He had debris in his eyes, and he could feel blood trickling down from various places. The round itself must have been deflected enough to miss him.

The man was a better shot than he thought. That was some serious distance to cover. He was on the other side of the river hiding behind a log. And the gun he was shooting appeared to be a smaller gun with a shorter barrel than the one DJ confiscated. It was an extreme distance for a pistol shot. Maybe forty yards separated his own hiding place from the assassin on the other side of the river.

He was going to have to stop taking chances, or he wasn't going to make it out of this river bed. He wiped his face with his hand and it came away bloody, but not as bad as he feared.

Time to make this guy flinch as well. He readied himself. In his hand was a Glock G17, and he knew the man had fired twice back in the parking lot. This meant there was at least fifteen rounds left. Possibly sixteen if the man always loaded it with a round in the chamber along with a full mag. So, let's say fifteen to be safe. It was a weapon with which he was quite familiar, and it had a long-proven history of accuracy even at extreme distances.

He popped back up again and aimed at the man's last known location. Only he wasn't there.

Crap.

He turned and bolted for the trees behind him, and there were no shots this time as he ran. As he crossed into the shadows, he quickly turned left and continued parallel along the river. He was headed down stream, and to where he hoped Abbi would be waiting.

He ran only about thirty feet, and stopped. He peered through the evergreen boughs, back across the river to the other side. Where was he? Did he climb out of here and double back to the diner? Was he hidden in the shadows on the opposite side waiting for DJ to show himself?

He noticed then the tree cover on the other bank. He could tell each row of trees seemed to be taller than the row in front. This could only mean that the ravine walls on the opposite side must climb upwards at a very steep angle. His target was hurt. Hurt badly. His leg would be stiff and difficult to move. There was no way he could climb out. Not here. The man's only choices would be to double back the way they came, stay put, or press forward.

He searched the opposite side, eyes trying to see past the thick green wall of fir trees, seeking his target. He wasn't sure, but he thought he saw a shift in the shadows directly across from him.

He aimed and fired a round at the shadow. The shadow moved. He fired again. Thirteen rounds left.

Shark Bait fired back, and a small branch flew free from the tree against which he was leaning. Before he could even scramble for more cover, a second shot followed and an angry whine behind him told him the bullet ricocheted into the unknown. DJ turned himself sideways behind the tree trunk and prayed for the best. A third round smacked the trunk solidly somewhere on the other side of his shoulder. It was a sickening, heart-stopping sound, because DJ knew that is what it would sound like if it had hit him.

A fourth and fifth round passed close. One whizzed past right in front of his eyes, and he swore he caught a glimpse of it as it raced along. A sixth tore another limb from the tree. Bark and chunks of wood sprayed him in the face, momentarily blinding him with debris, and causing him to flinch and blink. A seventh passed behind his head.

This was cover fire, DJ realized. A non-stop, sustained barrage of gunfire designed to keep your opponent's head down. The sole purpose for expending that much ammunition, was so you or your friends could move to a new location.

DJ risked a glance around the tree trunk. Sure enough, Shark Bait was moving. He hobbled and shambled over the rocky surface of the river bank, advancing towards DJ and the river's edge. His left hand clutched his wounded butt cheek. His right, putting round after round at DJ.

This gave him a new appreciation for Shark Bait's deadly efficiency. Firing one handed, on the move, at such an extreme distance, and to place his rounds so close to his target meant this killer was well practiced.

Another round passed dangerously close to his head, and DJ involuntarily jerked his back around the tree.

He forced himself to peek around the edge of the tree again, and Shark Bait was now knee-deep in the water. As he watched, the man dove headlong into the rushing river and vanished.

DJ suddenly realized what the man's plan was. He was wounded in such a way as it made it excruciatingly painful to walk, and impossible to run. Shark Bait was trapped in this gorge, surrounded by rough terrain, and having very limited ammo. He knew DJ only needed but a moment to take careful aim, and it was over for him. There would be no coming out of this the victor. His only way out was to let the river carry him from here, knowing that DJ could not keep up on foot.

DJ tore out of the tree line, hopping on and over big rocks. He moved at an angle, trying to envision where the man would resurface downstream. He spotted him, further away than he imagined. Then he was gone again, and DJ did not even have time to take aim.

The river took a turn around a bend to his right. A large mound of rock from a collapsed cliff face blocked his view around the corner, sitting right at the bend as the river made its turn. If he could make it to the top of that pile, he might be able to get one more good shot at the guy before he pulled too far ahead. DJ changed his angle, trying to get into position before it was too late.

He reached the base and scrambled up as fast as he could. As he reached the top, he could see the bridge up ahead where the road crossed back over. And there was Abbi, seventy-five yards away, parked on the bridge, and standing on the other side of a short cement railing looking for them both.

Gasping for breath and winded from all the energy spent over the last few minutes, he stood there, weapon at the ready, looking for Shark

Bait. Finally, he spotted him, bobbing along like a fishing cork, being swept away from him. He had time for one more shot. He willed his breathing to slow, raised the Glock, and took careful aim.

The gun bucked in his hand, and he saw the round smack the water next to his target. Shark Bait raised his own weapon out of the water as he approached the bridge. He wasn't aiming at DJ, however. He was aiming at Abbi.

DJ heard the crack, then saw Abbi fall backwards out of view behind the wall.

Weakness hit his knees and his vision swam, tunneling into blackness. Endangered of passing out from shock, he simply squatted down on the boulder lest he fall off. From far away in the distance, he thought he heard a scream. A desperate cry of pain and horror. It wasn't Abbi, he realized. It was him, his vocal cords burning from the strain told him the truth.

Shark Bait passed under the bridge and disappeared, then. But he didn't care. His only thoughts were of Abbi. He needed to snap himself out of his shock and get to the bridge. Just because she was shot, didn't mean she was dead. He was a former Navy Corpsman, for crying out loud. Saving people was what he did.

He dropped the pistol, leaped from the rock, and raced along at break-neck speed for the only thing that really mattered to him. As he ran, faster than he should over the treacherous surface, he made himself a promise.

No. Not a promise. It held more weight than a promise. It was a covenant agreement with himself. He would kill Shark Bait no matter what it took.

Thomas drifted along in the rushing water, tossed about like a piece of floating debris, grimacing at both the pain in his backside, and the frigid cold that wrapped him completely. His extremities were growing numb. Plunging in was his only choice, though. He was outgunned and in severe pain.

He now only had one round left in his Glock G26. The standard magazines for a short barreled G26 allowed for only ten rounds. But any double stacked 9mm magazines for a Glock would fit inside. So, he opted for a fifteen-round mag from a G19. The short barrel allowed him to tuck it behind his belt buckle but still be able to sit down without jamming himself in the testicles. Plus, the longer magazine gave him more to grab onto, as well as more ammunition.

As the rapids carried him along, he would duck underneath for about twenty seconds, before popping back up for air in order to throw off Slaughter. He was convinced that in a few more minutes, he would be out of range with the man no longer able to keep up on foot. The rocky terrain was just too rough.

He had no plan at the moment, other than to get away. Another repeated reminder that failure to follow his rules meant the loss of control and danger to his very existence. It meant you might find yourself stabbed in your left butt cheek, floating along in freezing water, with nothing more than the wet clothes on your back and one measly bullet in your gun.

He never felt more pathetic in his life. How could someone of such a legendary status in the world of assassins find himself in such a condition? He was an embarrassment to his name and his profession.

He was ashamed.

Wounded and ashamed.

Freezing, wounded, and ashamed. Those were three crappy words that should never find themselves grouped together into the same pile of skin.

Yet here he was.

Thomas came up for another breath of air and saw his first break since he screwed up at the urinal and pretended he was a surgeon. Up ahead, standing on a bridge, leaning across the barrier and looking for him, was that stupid girl who used a milkshake as a lethal weapon.

If he couldn't harm the man pursuing him physically, he could destroy him psychologically.

He drew aim, ignoring the bullet that slapped the water next to him. It was a tough shot to try and take, tossed about in the rapids like he was, but tough shots were part of the mythos of his reputation. He aimed dead center of her chest, pulled the trigger with confidence, and watch her fall back out of view.

Deal with that, Slaughter. I hope that stabs you through the heart just like you stabbed me where I sit down.

He made a promise to himself, then. He made a commitment. No matter what, no matter how long it took, he would kill Slaughter. It was an unbreakable vow he made to himself. Slaughter needed to die. Preferably slowly. But he no longer cared if it was by his own hands.

Just die, Slaughter. Just die.

Chapter 8: A New Target

About the time he couldn't take the freezing water anymore, Thomas spotted a house on a tree-covered piece of property, pressing right up to the water's edge. It was a small single-story building with a roof-wrapped porch running the entire back length of the house. Whoever owned it had a fire going in a fireplace. He could see smoking rising from the chimney, filtering its way through the pines. The cabin-like house sat at the apex of a lazy turn in the river as it flowed around a point to the left.

It was a perfect place to get out of this water, get warm, and re-evaluate his circumstances. Maybe he could come up with a plan to fix what had quickly turned into a steaming pile of excrement.

He let the water carry him around until he was close to the cabin, and then he gratefully hauled himself out. The cold air on his wet body was even worse than the river. It motivated him to move as quickly as he could to the back door.

Thomas shambled up the steps, and then beat on the back door with a balled-up fist. The act sent tingling pain through his blue hand and he knew he was on the verge of severe hypothermia. His teeth were chattering and he couldn't feel his face.

He beat on it again. There had to be someone home. No one would leave a fire in the fireplace and just drive off somewhere.

Suddenly a deep, long, throaty growl could be heard close behind him, and he froze. On a normal day, Thomas would not have been concerned about an angry dog. He could draw from concealment and shoot with deadly skill. Even unarmed as he was, he knew how to slap a dog around and send him yelping in short order. But his leg was stiff from being stabbed, and his muscles were seized up and lethargic from the cold.

He turned as slow as he could to face the threat behind him. The growl came from a black mixed breed mutt. It was a fairly large animal. Maybe eighty pounds or so. It was staring at him intently with his head down and teeth bared, just a few feet off the porch.

Today was turning into the worst day ever.

Thankfully, the door jerked open behind him and a sharp command from a weathered old voice told the dog to be still. Thomas turned at a creeping pace to address the voice, and saw it was attached to an old man, probably in his late sixties to early seventies.

He was wearing a black baseball cap that read, "US ARMY RETIRED" in gold thread. White hair poked out from around the edges of his cap. He stood about 5' 9", and despite his age, looked to be in good shape. Like a man that was used to a lifetime of working out, and did not choose to give up the routine in retirement. He was wearing a pair of gray sweatpants, a simple black undershirt, and he was standing in socks. But the part that Thomas cared about the most was the Mossberg 590 Shockwave the crusty old veteran was pointing right at his navel.

The Shockwave was a modern-day version of a sawed-off shotgun. Only it was built that way on purpose, instead of being illegally modified from a regular shotgun. It was a 12 gauge with a fourteen-inch barrel, and a handle that looked almost like it had the shoulder stock cut away. Except it was actually molded polymer. It held a maximum of six rounds, and at this distance, they would do incredible damage. With the right ammunition, it would practically rip him in two.

Thomas did not take his eyes off of the end of the barrel, and only uttered one word to the grizzly old man. "Help," he said meekly.

"What in tarnations happened to you?" the man asked with a graveled voice. Despite it being a question, it was phrased like an accusation.

"Fell in," Thomas said weakly. Weaker than he was feeling, of course. But it wasn't hard to fake considering how he felt. "Went out on a bridge a mile up the road to take a picture with my cell phone. Got too close. Fell over the rail. Saved the phone, but it's probably useless for calling for help." Thomas slid his useless, water-logged phone out of his front pocket to show the man.

Surprisingly, the man did not move the barrel. He kept it firmly where it was, pointed right at his stomach. The look on his face told Thomas the old guy was still deciding if he believed his story or not.

Thomas looked into his eyes, and through chattering teeth said, "Shoot me if you want, but can you at least do it over by your fireplace?"

The old man paused for a moment more, then lowered the muzzle. He still held it in both hands, however, and could quickly bring it to bear if needed. His eyes were stern and held mistrust, but the stranger nodded for him to come in and stepped out of the way. Thomas staggered through the door. Partially from acting the part, and partially from truth. His right leg was overly stiff. Every step was met with waves of pain driving through his buttock. Both feet were tingly, sending a million poking needle into his soles with each new step.

Thomas made his way to the fireplace across the wooden floor. The old man kicked the door closed, refusing to take a hand off of his weapon. He watched Thomas with the eyes of a predator. Getting this man to drop his guard was going to be difficult.

"What's wrong with your leg?" the old man growled.

"Struck a rock when I fell in. I'm not sure if it fractured anything, but it at least has a deep bruise." The dark, wet blue jeans camouflaged any sign of blood that might still remain. He was pretty sure the extreme cold helped the wound to stop bleeding for the most part.

Thomas reached the fireplace and stood as close as he dared with his back to the old man, sucking up as much heat as he could, and rubbing his hands together near the flames.

The room was a large one that included the living room, kitchen, and dining area. It was divided by a long leather couch that faced the fireplace, with support columns on either end stretching to exposed rafters and an open ceiling. The front door sat opposite of the one in the back that Thomas came through. And in between the dining area and kitchen, there was an open doorway that led back to the rest of the house. Even though all of these details were located behind him, Thomas took it all in when he first stepped through the door.

He already determined the man lived alone from the multitude of clues surrounding the place. There was a pair of socks located on the end of the couch. Something a wife would never allow, even though the picture of his lost bride was still on the mantel near his head. An ashtray with the stub of a cigar laying in it sat on an end table next to a large comfortable chair by the back window. A wife would probably not allow smoking in the house. The table in the eating area held a few dishes from an earlier meal, and nothing to decorate the surface. No flowers in the middle. No placemats. In fact, there were no feminine touches anywhere in the place, other than pictures on the wall. The man likely lost his wife a long time ago. The photographs and pictures would be the last thing to remain in place after the death of a spouse.

"I have cash in my wallet," Thomas said. "If you will let me warm up a bit, and then give me a lift to my car, I would gladly pay you for the trouble." He turned around to start warming his backside, and face the homeowner.

The man still stood where he was over near the back door, both hands on the Shockwave. His eyes told Thomas he didn't trust him. Not for one minute. Not as far as he could throw him.

"I'm dripping all over your floor, sir. I feel terrible about that. Do you have any old towels? Maybe a couple that I can stand on. Maybe one to dry off with? I promise you I can pay you." He pulled his wallet out of his right back pocket, opened it, and leafed through wet bills. Out of the corner of his eye, he could tell the old man did not care one thing about how much cash he was willing to give up.

Thomas needed this guy to relax. If he didn't, there was no way Thomas could go forward with the plan he was hastily putting together on the fly. He brought out two $100 bills and held it out to the man.

"Don't need your money," the man growled. "I'll get you some towels. Stay where you are. You hear me?"

"Yes, sir! I promise there is nothing more important to me right now than the warmth of your fire."

The old man snorted. Finally, he pulled one hand away from the Shockwave to let it hang down by his side, finger still alongside the trigger, and vanished through to doorway to the back of the house. Thomas didn't move, but stayed planted right where he was. In fact, he turned back around to face the fire, in order to help sell the illusion Thomas had no intention of causing any harm. He was just a wet, injured stranger in need of some help.

"Here," the old man barked a few seconds later. Thomas turned back around to see the man drop a stack of towels down on the couch. He stepped back away in order to keep Thomas at a safe distance.

Thomas glared at the man for a second, then shambled over to the stack. He angrily snatched one from the top and began to towel dry his hair with his right hand. The wallet was still in his left.

"You know," Thomas began. "I get I may have inconvenienced you. And I am pretty sorry about that. It's why I offered to compensate you for all of the trouble I've caused you. But, I'm having a pretty bad day as well. I fell twenty feet into a freezing river. My leg is beat up pretty good and I probably should get myself to a hospital. I was dangerously close to hypothermia when I dragged myself up on your back porch." Thomas casually moved around the couch and took a slow conversational step into the old man's direction, taking the towel and looping it over one time while talking.

"I thought," Thomas continued, pointing at the old man with his wallet, "that this state was known for its hospitality. But instead, when a stranger finds himself in need, in real my-life-is-in-danger kind of need, I find myself threatened by a dog and a cranky old man with a sawed-off shotgun. Now I told you I would compensate you for your troubles, and I meant it."

Rule number 7: Everything is a weapon. Everything.

With a flick of his wrist, Thomas tossed the wallet into the man's face. The old man flinched and turned his head away involuntarily. Thomas followed by swinging the looped-over towel like a club, aiming for the side of the old man's head. He intended to stun him, then step in and remove him of the shotgun.

But the old man moved and responded in a manner that said he had been in a few scuffles. He curled his left arm up, bending it at the elbow and effectively blocked the towel. He then started to swing the Mossberg up with his left. That is where the old man's age kicked in and was his undoing. Or it should have been. Had he been a younger man, he might have had the forearm strength to bring the shotgun up, and shoot it like a pistol with speed and efficiency. As it was, Thomas grabbed the end of the barrel with his left hand and pointed it away.

The shotgun went off harmlessly with a window rattling clap of thunder, but then it was the old man's turn. His left fist shot out and connected to Thomas's chin with a hard left cross. Again, his age impeded his effectiveness. Were he younger, it might have been lights out for Thomas. As it was, Thomas was knocked backwards and sent staggering across the side of the living room. He reached out and steadied himself on the end table next to the large chair along the back wall.

The old man grabbed the shotgun and pumped a new round into the chamber. That's when the ashtray with the cigar was sent spinning through the air like a throwing star by Thomas.

Rule number 7 had saved him a few times. But it required for him to always be alert to everything around him, and constantly thinking how it could be used. From the first moment he stepped into the house, he was already processing the environment looking for things to be considered as weapons.

The pictures on the mantel, the tablet computer on the coffee table, the remote control sitting on the couch cushion. All of them could be used for weapons in the spur of the moment. And right now, they were. Thomas used the glass ashtray first, slinging it like a ninja at the old man. It caught him right in the Adam's apple. The old man recoiled backward from the blow.

As he staggered, the man jerked the trigger again and the Shockwave issued another clap of thunder. The pellets flew harmlessly to Thomas's left, scattering the old man's pictures of his wife from the mantel above the fireplace.

Thomas took a large step forward, ignoring the shooting pain from his buttock. There was a crossword puzzle book on the arm of the couch with a pencil sticking out from the folds. He grabbed both, tossed the book at the man for a distraction with his left hand, took another large step towards the old guy, and then jammed the pencil into the grizzled old veteran's throat.

The Shockwave dropped to the floor, both of the man's hands grabbed for his own throat, and he fell backwards at the base of the dining room table. He gasped for breath, and his mouth worked trying to find air. His eyes jerked back and forth like he could not believe what was happening, looking into the rafters above.

Thomas gingerly took a knee, groaning from the pain of his stab wound. Scooping up the Mossberg, he pumped a new shell into the chamber. Then, pressing the barrel to the floor, he used it like a cane to push himself back upright. Once on his feet again, he casually put a three-inch magnum into the man's shocked face. The crotchety old veteran arched his back off the ground, as practically every muscle in his body convulsed one good, hard time. Then, he relaxed and quit moving forever.

He cycled the shotgun again, shuffled to the back door and pulled it open. The black mongrel was still there, but had moved to the porch. The Shockwave went off a fourth time and pulverized the dog's head like it had been through a meat grinder. The mangy mutt didn't even have a chance. Thomas moved over, bent down gingerly, grabbed one black leg, and brought the stupid thing inside.

Thomas quickly developed himself a list of things he needed to do and began to work through them in order.

First, he cleared the house to make sure there were no other people or pets lurking around that could cause him issues. At the same time, he locked every door and window, pulled the shades and blinds, and located every possible escape route out of here should the need arise.

In doing so, he located the man's keys in a bowl next to the front door. A shiny red pickup sat in the drive. Its lights flashed when Thomas hit a button on the key fob in his hand, confirming the truck belonged to the corpse behind him.

He then found a couple boxes of shells for the shotgun, reloaded it, and discovered a handful of other weapons that could be handy.

There was a loaded Taurus .357 with a four-and-a-half-inch barrel and a box of ammo. In the bedroom closet was an old Remington .243 with a scope, but only a handful of rounds for it. The old man probably used it for hunting back in the day.

Then he hit nirvana and discovered a bright spot in an otherwise crappy day. In a decorative wooden box at the top of the closet was a Ruger 22/45 variant that made him smile. A 22/45 was a .22 caliber pistol best used against rabbits and other small game, or for plinking at the range. It had grips, however, like a 1911 style pistol with the weight and feel to match. This model came equipped with a red dot sight mounted to the top, two extra magazines, and best of all, it had a silencer screwed into the end.

Thomas could see no practical reason why the man would own such a weapon, and then go through the extra trouble of purchasing the tax stamp for legally owning a suppressor. Other than the old guy just wanted it because he thought it was cool.

What made Thomas so happy about the discovery was, even though it was a small caliber weapon that would be hard pressed to take down a full-sized man, it was near silent in its operation with subsonic ammunition. Which he found a few hundred rounds of. And even though you would seldom use it for self-defense, the truth was, just one of those little bullets between the eyes would drop the biggest, baddest bruiser right into the dirt.

This was an assassin's weapon.

The next thing he did was find first aid supplies to patch himself up with. Including some old antibiotics in the medicine cabinet, and some Percocet for pain. He took a triple dose of that.

Next, he confiscated some clothing from the bedroom. Just some old jeans and a sweatshirt. The man's shoes were too small, so he grabbed socks instead. He set his own shoes to dry next to the fireplace.

He stripped completely in the living room, sucking up as much warmth from the hearth as possible, and began to doctor himself. He cleaned the wound carefully, and did his best to seal it closed with Steri-Strips he found in a hall closet. What he needed were stitches, but there was no way to do it himself at the angle it was, and going to the doctor was out of the question. Finally, he covered the gash with Super Glue.

Normally, when he was headed to a job, he would reach out through the Dark Web and find an under-the-table contracted physician. Someone that would patch you up for cash, off the books. There were always a few of those types in the area he would be working. He would book services in advance just in case, and pay them a retainer fee even if they were never used.

He only had to use one once before. A piece of shrapnel from a ricochet lodged in his back while fleeing a location. It was a chance scenario off of a missed shot by a member of a security detachment.

In this case, though, he wasn't on a job, but he was pretty sure there would be no one nearby out here in the hills of redneck country. Steri-Strips and Super-Glue would have to do. The sad thing was, because he wasn't going to receive the surgery he knew he needed to properly fix him up, there was a good chance he would never walk the same again. The muscle would probably never mend like it should on its own without the skills of a physician.

He shook his head in anger and disgust. *Freaking Slaughter…*

Once he patched himself up and dressed in his borrowed clothes, he grabbed the tablet off of the coffee table. It was locked and password protected, but it was the kind that unlocked with a fingerprint. So, it was an easy fix using the stiffening corpse of the old man.

He needed to make several video chats, and the first one was going to be uncomfortable. He would toss the tablet into the river out back when he was done.

He jumped onto the web browser and made his way to a complicated URL he had memorized. The page looked like an advertisement for a porn site. In fact, click on any of the links, and they would indeed take you to legitimate sites for porn. But press just outside of one picture in the lower left-hand corner in a very specific spot, and it would take you to a location with a video feed of a scantily clad young woman.

She could see you through your device's camera, and you could see her. If someone were to accidentally click on the hidden link, she would go through all of the motions of trying to get you to cough up a credit card, but then you would lose connection a few seconds in.

If, however, you covered the devices camera with a piece of tape, a Band-Aid, your thumb, etc, as well as provide her a code word, she would then ask you for your destination. She functioned as a sort of switchboard operator like the telephone companies used to work a long time ago. You would give her the party you were trying to reach, a criminal underworld operator that subscribed to the service, and she would patch you through.

In reality, your connection was routed through several different locations around the world. One of those was in the Ukraine. When it hit there, the signal was scrambled with unbreakable IP masking software, and if anyone was trying to trace the signal, it would effectively hit a brick wall.

From there, it finally connected to your party. If no one on the other end answered, she would take a message and hand it off. The ingenious system was a mix of high-tech wizardry and good old fashioned low-tech subterfuge.

Thomas used a small bandage to cover up the camera and clicked the tiny hidden link. After a second, a window popped up, and there was the actress, a topless brunette in red panties. He gave her the code word, the person he wanted connected to, and his alias. A second or two more, and a familiar face on the other end popped up.

"El Gran Blanco! My boss has been anxious about an update," the man said with a thick Russian accent. He was dressed in an expensive black suit and a bright blue tie. His black hair was slicked straight back and he wore sunglasses tinted a slight blue.

"There have been delays," Thomas responded.

"Mr. Romanoff pays you handsomely so there are never delays." The surrogate on the other end tilted his head over and leaned a bit into the camera for effect. It was designed, of course, to intimidate. But Thomas did not intimidate.

"Unforeseen circumstances," Thomas simply replied.

"Seen, unseen, these things do not matter to Mr. Romanoff. Only results." The man's face split in two by a smile that was less than sincere. Perfect teeth reflected the light from the computer screen the man was staring into.

"When have I ever failed to produce?" Thomas asked the man.

"Oh never, to be sure. But you are paid well. Well enough that any failure on your part would be unforgivable. I simply remind you of this. And it is hard to see how a man can live up to his contracted agreement that is due in less than 72 hours, when his last reported location was in the state of Kentucky." The smiling face leaned back again. He knew the revelation would have an effect on the unseen assassin.

And it did.

How in the world did Sergei Romanoff know where he was? How was it possible he had been followed and tracked? It was an unnerving discovery.

"You're tracking me?" Thomas asked with incredulity.

The man looked off the screen for a moment at something else, then turned his attention to Thomas once more. "Oh, do not look at it as tracking. Look at it as monitoring an investment. An investment I now see is in West Virginia. You know, you must really get over your fear of flying. It is such a hindrance in your line of work."

If Sergei was able to have him followed or tracked, then more than likely he knew exactly what he looked like. So, there was no more need to cover the camera. He reached over and ripped the bandage off, allowing the man on the other end to see him. He expected the act to have a sobering effect on the personal assistant to Mr. Romanoff. After all, those who knew the face of El Gran Blanco ceased to exist shortly thereafter. But the man's reaction was quite the opposite of what Thomas was hoping for.

"Why hello, Thomas. So good to have a face to face conversation at last." The man's smile broadened even more, as he waved to him through the camera.

"You dare to have me followed? You dare to try and track me?" Thomas's voice cut through all semblance of professionalism and nicety. He was angry at the violation. He was fuming at the insolence of the man. Who did he think he was, talking to Thomas this way? He was a common underling. Just a lapdog with a higher opinion of himself than he deserved.

And then it hit him. The go-between on the other side of the screen called him by name. No one called him by name. No one even knew his real name. He had stopped using it the second after slaying his parents and walking away from his home in Louisiana so many years ago. How was this even possible?

As the cold realization slammed into him, words caught in his throat. His ability to speak vanished into thin air.

The man on the other end tapped the camera with one finger. The mic on the man's computer picked up the sound and carried it all the way from Russia to Thomas's ears. *Tap, tap, tap.* "Hello?" the man on the computer asked. "I am sorry, it looked like the screen froze for a second. Or was this fear gripping your heart, Thomas? I did not mean to frighten you so. Don't worry, Thomas. I won't tell anyone your name. It's our little secret."

That one act spoke volumes to Thomas. Sergei Romanoff knew everything about him. And in that knowledge, there was power. Power held over him to control him and bend him to Sergei's will. With an inaudible click, Thomas felt the leash of control snap around his neck. He had just become another one of Sergei's lap dogs. Someone to be ordered around and commanded.

Well, they may know who Thomas was, and they may have figured out a way to track him, but it did not mean they understood the man.

"I just need a few more days," Thomas began.

"No," the man's reply answered. "You have the time that was agreed on. After that, if the job is not complete, Mr. Romanoff will consider our contract with you to be..." He leaned in to drive this last point home. "...terminated."

And, just like that, the video feed went dead.

Thomas sat there for a second, unmoving, unthinking. Well, this could only mean one thing. As soon as Slaughter was dead, Thomas had himself a new target. Sergei was now number two on his list of annoying people to remove from the earth.

Chapter 9: Heaven

Abbi stood in the parking lot of the diner quietly fuming. But not over the assassin making another attempt on them. She was cranky over the good-looking man she was in love with currently sprinting across the parking lot after the killer. Abbi felt like she should have aimed that chocolate shake at DJ instead of the murderer.

He just didn't get it. She was not some fragile, dainty, overly feminine lady with high heels and a Gucci bag. She was a chick. And there was a difference.

Ladies fretted over their nails and dresses. Chicks mowed the yard. Ladies would spend an hour in the makeup store. Chicks put their hair in a ponytail and got in a sparring match before breakfast. Ladies fixed their face in the mirror while driving down the road. Chicks passed them on the shoulder and yelled at them as they raced on by.

If other women were different that was fine by her. It just wasn't who she was. She was a chick, and she would have thought DJ understood that by now.

This assassin murdered her mother, so Abbi now had a job to do. Two actually. First, she needed to make sure DJ stayed focused and did not worry over her, or he would become next to useless in trying to catch the man. Secondly, she had to make sure the killer paid a price for what he had done. And not jail time and a lengthy trial by the justice system, either. He needed to die.

She watched as DJ ran off after the murderer, trusting she would be a good little woman and drive the car around like he instructed. She bit her lip and resisted the urge to chase after him, knock him to the pavement, and lock him up in an arm bar until he cried like a girl.

No, she thought to herself. She would work with him for now until she could beat some understanding into him later. She loved the man, even if he was a doorknob sometimes. But he was crazy if he thought she was just going to drive around and meet him like she was a driver for a ride sharing app.

Not hardly. She would get ahead of the floating killer and ambush him. She would put a bullet in his face.

Abbi took off for the jeep, pulling her keys out of the small purse she slung crossways over her chest. She fired it up, and tore out of the parking lot heading down the road like DJ instructed, but as soon as she was out of eye-shot of the diner, the last building on the edge of town, she peeled off on the side.

She opened the door and raced around to the passenger rear. She needed to equip herself for the job. DJ had been teaching her to shoot a bit with both a pistol and a rifle. She was nowhere near his level, but she was competent enough to load and ready one of them without shooting herself in the foot.

Opening the back door revealed several choices for her. DJ had brought a few of them along, choosing to conceal the rest back at the house for retrieval later. He had a plan for that, but she was uncertain of exactly what that entailed. Right now, she had four rifles, two shotguns, and three pistols to make her selection from.

At first, she eyed the AR-15 he custom built himself. It was a pretty dark green and black, with a shiny red trigger and attachments hanging off of it. There was a foregrip-thing up front that made holding it easier, and this cool holographic sight like she used on her favorite first-person shooter video game. She liked shooting it, but she could never conceal the thing from view if she needed to.

She picked a pistol instead. Abbi was partial to the Smith and Wesson M&P. She just liked the feel of it in her hand more, and this was the medium-sized version. It was made for people with smaller hands like herself, or for those needing something smaller to conceal.

DJ liked to store his weapons with a full magazine loaded, but no bullet in the barrel. Round in the chamber, she corrected herself. The pistol he usually carried in his backpack or on his person, always had a round in the chamber ready to go. When he stored one away, however, he liked it to be in a safer condition.

She grabbed the Smith, pulled the slide back with purpose, and released it. The Smith drove a round into the chamber with a satisfying, butch-sounding *chink*. She then tucked it in her waistband up under her shirt.

What else could she use?

DJ was really into this gun stuff. He owned not only weapons galore, but all of the cool stuff to go along with them. He had a myriad of holsters and storage devices, bullets, clothing, bags; you name it. There was a small sporting goods store in the back of the Jeep. Something she was thankful for now.

She moved things around looking for anything that might help her in her fight, anything that might give her an edge. Settling on something that looked promising, she made herself ready, then jumped back into the driver's seat. Dropping the Jeep in drive, she left the shoulder with wheels spinning.

The murderer was not going to get away from her, she vowed, as she kept her foot planted into the accelerator. But reason kicked in a second later and she dropped back down to the speed limit. Last thing she needed was to draw the attention of a cop should one happen past.

The GPS was already mapping her location on the large screen in the dashboard. She could see the road did swing around in a casual arc until it crossed back over the river, just like she was told. Her plan was to set up there as DJ instructed, but wait for the murderer to come floating past and then fill him full of holes. That's if DJ had not caught up to him yet.

As she continued the slow left-hand turn, she eventually met up with a bridge crossing over the river. This was it. She slid to a stop on the bridge, waited for a car to pass going the opposite direction, then jumped out and bolted to the other side of the bridge to lean over the rail.

The river made a sharp turn to the left around a point of stacked up boulders and loose rock. A collapse of the steep embankment above had created a wall of rock she couldn't see past. She was sure any minute her quarry would round that bend. Either on foot, fleeing DJ, or still floating along in the water with her boyfriend in hot pursuit somewhere along the bank.

Her boyfriend. What a weird thought. It didn't really sound right. It sounded weird. He was not her boyfriend, she mused. He was something more special than that. He wasn't her fiancé because he had not bothered to ask her to marry him yet. So technically, that wasn't quite right either. So, what the heck was he? Her live-in lover that she didn't have a sexual relationship with?

And what was up with that? She certainly wanted it. She had pushed him that direction on more than one occasion, but he said he wanted to do this the *right* way. That it would honor her father if they waited. There was something noble in that. Something sweet and special. But she was definitely ready to jump him.

A flash of fire rose up inside her as she pictured them both, bodies intertwined with each other on a giant white bed, giving themselves over to frenzied passion.

She heard a car coming from her right and it snapped her out of her heated thoughts. For the briefest moment she felt embarrassed, but shoved that notion aside. Without looking at the car, she motioned it past with her right hand, eyes still scanning the river area below. But it didn't make its way past. It stopped.

She turned her head and gave the driver a look of annoyance. But she took it back as fast as she could. For a second, a wave of panic coursed through her. A police cruiser had pulled up. He hadn't turned his lights on, but just pulled to a stop in the middle of the bridge.

She shoved the panic aside and focused. She was a girl. She was a cute girl. Cuteness had a way of disarming men. Plus, she was standing on a bridge looking for something. He probably stopped to help a damsel in distress. He would help her find whatever was lost. That was it, of course. She could talk her way out of this. She would turn her cuteness up to the max and charm the socks off of him.

The police officer dropped the cruiser in park and stepped out of the car.

It was a woman.

Abbi's heart sank.

"Lose something?" the officer asked good naturedly.

Abbi was standing sideways to the officer, and was pretty sure even if she faced her full on, she would never be able to tell she had the pistol tucked under her shirt. "My fiancé and I lost our dog back down the road at the diner. He's following the river bank and I jumped ahead to see if we could catch it between the two of us."

"Well, I'll see if I can give you a hand," the lady said still approaching. "But I will need you to pull off the bridge and park the car on the shoulder. We can't be blocking the bridge like this."

"Oh… Right. Of course. I am so sorry!" Abbi turned to the officer intending to shake her hand in mock gratitude. Then she would twist her arm around behind her back, and put her into a sleeper hold. But as soon as Abbi turned toward the officer, the woman dropped her gaze downward, away from Abbi's eyes and towards her middle. A look of surprise washed over her face and suddenly went for her gun.

Abbi had no time to think. She only acted out of instinct. She stepped in fast and threw a left jab, and then followed it up with an even harder right, throwing her whole weight behind the punch. The poor woman never even cleared her holster. She dropped down onto the pavement of the bridge like a felled tree. Completely knocked out.

DJ would not be happy.

She bent down and removed the officer's weapon, placing it behind her own back, and went to work securing the woman. Abbi removed the handcuffs, and locked the policewoman's hands behind her back.

Now she was not sure what to do next. Another car could come along any minute. If it did, she was in real trouble. She and DJ both. Her Jeep was on one side of the bridge, and the police car on the other. She was blocking both lanes of traffic with a cop car, a Jeep with a bunch of guns, and a handcuffed and incapacitated officer lying face down on the asphalt.

There would be no talking her way out of this.

She stood up and tried to decide what to do. She could try to drag the woman to her car and then move the thing, but she didn't think she had the strength or the time.

She could just jump in the Jeep and try to get away before anyone ventured along, but then DJ would be left on his own until she could catch up with him.

That wasn't acceptable in the least.

The hum of tires on asphalt behind her told Abbi her fears were realized. She turned back the direction of the diner to see a black sedan slowing because of the blocked bridge. Again, Abbi acted out of instinct and began to wave her arms over her head like she was in trouble.

The man came to a stop behind her Jeep and opened the door. He stepped out and Abbi approached him with as much manufactured fear and concern on her face as she could muster.

"Help," she commanded. "I don't know what's wrong with her. I think she may have had a heart attack."

The stranger took a couple of hasty steps towards the downed officer, passing Abbi and speaking as he went. "Are you undercover or something?"

What kind of question was that, she wondered. She looked down at herself and suddenly knew what tipped the police officer off. Well, she would take care of that in a second. First, she needed to knock this guy out as well, before he saw the handcuffs.

So, she did.

As the man made his way past her, she struck him with pin-point precision behind his left ear with a hard right. The man's knees buckled and he plowed face-forward into the asphalt covered bridge.

She winced. That was going to leave a mark. Man, DJ was going to be seriously mad at her. First a cop, now an innocent bystander.

DJ... He and the murderer should be getting close! She ran to the side of the bridge, looking for her boyfriend and the man he was chasing.

She spotted the killer instantly, floating in the rapids. She saw DJ a second later, standing far back on the bank at the peak of a large rock, at the point where the river swung back out of view.

He was aiming.

Get him, she thought to herself. Even *she* knew this would be an impossible shot from DJ's distance, but she silently urged him on. DJ was a great shot. The man could do anything with a gun. He was like a storybook hero.

He missed.

She looked down at the bobbing assassin, suddenly furious the man was about to float away to safety. In a second or two more, he would pass beneath the bridge and just disappear downstream. And there was little she could do about it. There was no way she could get down to the bank on the other side of the bridge to get close enough to take a shot. Especially at a moving target. As fast he was moving in the water, by the time she made it down, he would likely be long gone anyways. And there was certainly no way DJ could catch up to the man.

He was going to get away. And that meant he was going to sneak up on them again sometime in the future, and make another attempt at them from the shadows. He would have a severe advantage over them.

Then, the man lifted his arm out of the water. He was pointing at her. *Oh crap! He has a gun*, she realized.

A hard, piercing force drove itself right into the center of her chest. In all the sparring and training Abbi had taken part in, she had been hurt a few times. Some of it doled out severe and excruciating pain. But this? This was on a whole new level of hurt.

It drove her backwards from the edge of the bridge. She stumbled and staggered. Her legs were suddenly unsure of what their purpose was, and she went down flat on her back. Then, in an instant, everything tunneled away into a spiraling darkness.

DJ's heart thundered in his chest. Not from exertion as much as from the overwhelming fear for Abbi's safety. Watching her fall away from the bridge railing was like a fist to the stomach. If she were gone, he was not sure he could take another blow like that. Living through the death of his wife and two children was nearly impossible. It almost ended his life. If the same scenario happened again, he was pretty sure it would push him over the brink. That kind of pain was just too much to be endured twice.

He clawed and scrambled his way up the steep embankment of the bridge. His desperation to get to the top grew with each foot he climbed. She would be bleeding-out up there. Her precious life's blood would be pumping out onto the pavement with each beat of her slowing heart.

His brain was already preparing himself for various medical things he could encounter, and what he could do to overcome them.

A sucking chest wound: Roll her to the side and plug the hole on her exhale with his plastic driver's license, and then secure it in place with his belt. His belt should be just long enough to fit around her chest.

Perforated artery: Use his pocket knife to make an incision so he could find the artery and then pinch it closed with his fingers.

Punctured heart: He would have no choice but to make a long incision just below her sternum, then reach in with his arm all the way to his elbow to try and plug the hole with a finger. God help him if he had to do that.

Simple flesh wound: Kiss her long and deep on the mouth and vow to never leave her side ever again.

When he made the top of the embankment, he was momentarily stunned into inaction by what he found. Instead of one body lying on the ground, there were three.

And one was a cop.

He quickly diagnosed what must have gone down on the bridge before Abbi was shot. The ex-corpsman in him kicked into gear, and then he was racing at full speed to where she lay.

He was there in a moment. He practically leaped to the ground on his knees beside her. First his eyes went to her face for signs of consciousness, but there was none. Next, he worked down her body looking for the bullet hole that laid her out like this. Frantically, he tried to determine where the entrance wound was.

He froze in disbelieving shock. His breath caught in his throat, and his eyes didn't quite accept what he was looking at. He blinked and looked again. The scene was the same. The truth sent his emotions cartwheeling. He closed his eyes, pointed his face to the heavens, and laughed long and hard with relief and joy.

Abbi, in an effort to gear up and help DJ go after the assassin, went into the back of the Jeep and put on the black bullet proof vest he had saved from his encounter with Big Chuck's gang over the summer. She was knocked unconscious from smacking her head on the asphalt, but he could clearly see the 9mm slug embedded into the middle of the vest.

She was going to be fine. Bruised, maybe. A mild concussion, possibly. But safe and sound. He was going to beat her, of course. He had to beat her for creating all of the carnage on the bridge like she did, but after that, he would kiss her until his lips fell off.

"Hey, you!" snapped a female voice from a few feet away. It was the police officer. He could see now that she had her hands cuffed behind her back. "Get away from her now! She's dangerous!"

"Oh, you don't know the half of it," DJ replied. "You should see what she's done to my heart." He looked at the officer and smiled. "Sorry," he shrugged his shoulders with his apology. "But I'm with her." He got up and ran to the other guy plastered face first in the pavement to check him over. He was starting to stir as well. When he got to the man, he saw his wounds were superficial with a scraped-up face and a smashed bottom lip.

DJ helped the man to his feet, telling him he was going to be alright, then he promptly pinned his arm up behind his back and told him to move over next to the officer and have a seat. The police officer already managed to wiggle herself into a sitting position, and simply glared at DJ.

"Believe me or not," he told them both. "But we're the good guys. Move a muscle, however, and it's lights out again for the both of you. Try me and see." He pointed one finger at them both.

"DJ?" Abbi spoke softly behind him. He spun on his heels in response and took a few fast steps to her side. She had already rolled onto her knees and placed one hand to the back of her head, while the other rubbed the center of her chest where she was shot.

"You're going to be fine," he reassured her. "The vest stopped the round. You hit your head, though, and you might have a concussion. We need to get out of here. I'm going to pick you up, OK?"

Initially, Abbi started to protest, but then she allowed DJ to sweep her into his arms and hurry to the Jeep. He rushed her around to the passenger side, then set her down next to the door. He opened it for her as another car rounded the corner coming from the direction of town. Seeing the bottleneck up ahead, the car slowed.

DJ raced to the other side, clambered into the seat, and rolled the window down as he pulled even with the two sitting down in front of the police car.

"Call the FBI," he ordered the officer. "Colorado Field Office. Ask for Special Agent in Charge Brett Foster. Tell him you have a message from DJ Slaughter. Got it? DJ Slaughter. Tell Agent Foster that I'm going to take the one responsible for all of this to school. Those words specifically." Behind him the car had stopped and someone was already out and approaching them. DJ gunned it and continued to accelerate until he rounded another corner, and the bridge vanished in the rearview mirror.

They were about two miles from the main highway, and DJ held his breath the whole way to the entrance ramp. But once there, he began to relax a bit. He set the cruise control for four miles per hour over the speed limit and then kept checking his mirror. After just a few minutes on the road, they passed a highway patrol vehicle, but it stayed put as DJ drove past as nonchalantly as possible.

He was worried about the license plate, and he really needed to change it, but getting as far away as possible was the main priority right now. Besides, there were millions of black four-door Jeep Wranglers on the road. He would blend right in unless he gave a policeman a reason to look closer.

They rode in silence this whole time. But now with a few miles behind them, and the appearance of not being pursued for the moment reassuring him that all was well, he felt it was time to talk. He needed to confront her about attacking the cop and the stranger.

"Listen," DJ began.

"No, *you* listen!" she corrected him with a stern voice.

He glanced at her, surprised at her reaction. What on earth did she have to be mad at? He pressed on anyway with his own agenda. "What were you thinking back there? You almost got us both caught, and yourself killed."

"DJ, look at me," she barked. "What do you see?"

DJ stumbled over his words a second before responding with a complete sentence. "I'm not sure I understand."

"That's obvious." The two-word sentence was coated in sarcasm.

"What do you mean?"

"I mean, when you look at me, what do you see in me as a person?"

"I... I see you as a sweet, kind, loving woman. You care about people. You're fun loving, and good natured. You're also one of the smartest people I have ever known. And you're... You're beautiful." She was, indeed, beautiful. Just looking at her right now, even though she was mad over something he did not understand yet, made his heart pound in his ears.

"That's wonderful. But, there's more to me than that. And with all of the time we have spent together in the last six months, you would think you would have caught on by now.

"I am also a fighter. I don't run from one, and I look forward to getting in one. I like to scrap. I find enjoyment in it. Like it's a sport I love to play. It's not that I'm an evil person, but I enjoy figuring out how to beat someone else. It's like a competition for me.

"I'm not a pretty little flower in a dainty vase you have to be cautious around, fearing you'll break me. I'm not someone that needs to be protected. I can take care of myself. I was doing it before you were around, and if this guy kills you, I'll be doing it long after you're gone."

Her words snapped and bit at him the whole time she was talking, but that last remark cut him deep. "Are… Are you saying you want me to just back away?" He was scared of her next few words. The small diamond ring in the little red drawstring bag, buried deep in his right front pocket, seemed to burn against his thigh. Would it remain forever buried in a dark place, he wondered? Would he ever have the chance to take a knee? Had this whole ordeal taken away their chance of a life together?

She looked at him for a long few seconds before responding. Like she was carefully considering her next words. Like she was reaching some decision.

Finally, she spoke. "DJ, you're an old-fashioned kind of guy. I love that about you. There are few men like you anymore. And I don't want you to change one bit. But you have to understand that I am not quite as old fashioned as you are. I'm not telling you to back off. I'm telling you to include me."

DJ said nothing. He was partially relieved she did not tell him to get lost, and partially confused. What did she mean by including her?

She spoke again. "This man killed my Mom. He tried to kill me, and he tried to kill you. Twice. And he's going to try again. What I'm telling you is, we cannot run from this fight. We have to meet it head on. And you better find a way to include me in it, or I'm going to go after him all on my own. No matter the cost. I'm either going to kill him myself, or we're going to do it together. But if you decide to do it with me, you're going to have to back off in trying to be my knight in shining armor. Protect me like I would protect you. But don't put me in a box and think you are going to shield me from all of this. Because I won't let you."

DJ said nothing immediately. He just turned his attention back to the road and tried to process all of this. Could he do what she was asking of him? Could he look at her as a partner in this fight? Was it possible for him to look at her as a comrade in arms, and suppress her true worth to him?

If this were a combat situation with a platoon of Marines, he would lay his life down for any one of them, but never at the cost of sacrificing the mission. The mission would always come first. In war, you used your buddies as a weapon. You used them each as a strategic tool for defeating the enemy. You trusted them to do their job while you went and did yours. And if they fell along the way, you pressed on to complete the mission.

Could he do that with her?

Abbi had become another part of him. The better part, he reasoned. She was precious and valuable. Something to be treasured and protected. Could he just simply turn that off enough for them to work together as a team to defeat an enemy? Could he ignore his feelings for the sake of the mission?

He already decided that running was out of the question. He would not try to hide from this enemy. In fact, he was already working out a plan to attack him head on, like Abbi claimed was necessary, but only after he safely tucked Abbi away in a nice hidden spot somewhere. And now she was telling him if he tried that, she would leave him to strike out on her own.

Well he certainly could not allow that to happen.

There was really only one logical course of action. While he was uncertain if he could treat Abbi as a warrior comrade, at least not fully, and at least not all at once, there was no way he could risk her taking off on her own.

Besides, if allowing her to fight alongside him was the only way to keep her in his life, then the solution was clear. He would back down and capitulate. At least he could keep an eye on her this way.

He just wasn't sure how much he could truly give in to her desires. He was who he was, and he could not be expected to change overnight. And it was best to be honest with her about that.

"OK," he started. "You're right. I am a bit old fashioned in a lot of ways. The truth is, I could probably use a hand going up against this guy. But you need to understand something. There is no way I can be expected to totally abandon my principles. In my opinion, you are to be placed on a pedestal and cared for. And I won't change that. But I will allow you a broader roll in taking this guy out. However, if it comes down to something being overly dangerous, something that will risk your life unnecessarily, I won't let you do it. I just won't. You're too important to me.

"Additionally, being involved in the death of someone, justified or not, changes you. And not in a good way. It takes away a part of your innocence. And that is something I love about you. So, when it comes time to pull the trigger, I don't know if I can allow you to do that. I think that needs to sit with me and be my burden to bear. I can't make that part of the plan.

"But… I will include you. I will use you. I promise to let you make a difference."

Abbi took a long thoughtful moment before replying. "Fine. That's a compromise I can live with. But you need to promise me something."

"What's that?"

"If I *do* get the drop on him, if I have the chance to take him out, even though you want to save me from that burden, you let me do it. You let *me* make that decision."

DJ paused, then nodded. "I love you. I love you so much."

Abbi smiled, then. Her eyes lit up with that old familiar twinkle. It was a sparkle that held just a hint of youthful mischievousness. "I love you more," she said. "Now, how are we going to turn this thing around and bury this dirt-bag?"

"Well… I have a rough idea in place. But truthfully, we could use some help. Shark Bait will come at us again, and we won't really be in control of how he'll do that. But, we can bait him into a trap. We just need more help in order to spring it."

She gave him a confused look. "First of all, Shark Bait?"

"That's the guy's name. I'll explain in a minute who he is and why he's after us."

"OK… Secondly, you finally admit that we need Brett's help?"

"He could sure come in handy," DJ admitted. "Problem is, how do we have a conversation with Brett without tipping off the entire FBI? That's why I told the cop to give him the message about going to school. Brett knew you were thinking about going to MIT. He'll know where we're headed, and he'll know I want him to show up there because I need his help. But now I'm not sure how to talk to him after that."

"And this is why you need to start including me on everything so we can work together," Abbi shot back. "I can make that happen. First, we need to get as far away from here as possible. Then I need a stable internet connection. Something better than a cell signal. A hotel would be perfect. So, get us safe and get us a hotel. And something nice. We have money. Spend some of it. I want a nice bathroom with one of those big garden tubs."

DJ smiled. "Yes ma'am. Anything else I can do for the little lady?"

Abbi tilted her head to one side and acted like she was thinking about it. Then a thought seemed to pop into her mind. "Yes! Pull over on the shoulder."

"What?"

"Right now! Hurry!"

Against his better judgement, he did exactly as he was told. He knew he should keep putting highway behind him, but she had him wrapped around her little finger. He knew it, and she knew it. Despite the danger of a cop happening by to see a description matching Jeep Wrangler parked on the shoulder of a major highway, he gave in to her request.

As soon as they were stopped, he checked the rear-view mirror for a cop car. "Now what's going on?" he asked her.

"I need one more thing from you," she replied. "Kiss me."

He did. And it was heaven.

Chapter 10: La Minita

The odds Shark Bait could have tracked them from the diner to the small town of State College, Pennsylvania were slim. He was hurt pretty bad and would have to take care of his wound. Secondly, he lost his SUV and would have to come up with other means of transportation. By now, just because Abbi beat a police officer into unconsciousness, the cops would be all over the diner collecting evidence. They would have already started tracing the history of every car in the parking lot.

If they managed to find any fingerprints from DJ or Abbi, and you could bet they would, the FBI would be involved shortly thereafter. Not to mention the message DJ left with the police officer in the middle of the bridge. If she followed through on that, Brett would have dispatched a team to collect evidence and ask questions. Or he would have contacted local agents to do the job.

No matter, Shark Bait returning to the scene to pick up his SUV was out of the question. And, he would have to tend to the stab wound in his left butt cheek. DJ couldn't help but snicker at the thought. It would slow the assassin down considerably. Which, in turn, would give Abbi and DJ some time to work and figure some things.

Secondly, while DJ might have divulged their destination as being Boston, Shark Bait would only have one clue to follow up on in a city of that size. DJ told him they were going on a school visit to MIT. Shark Bait would have no choice but to stake out the campus and wait for either one of them to show their faces.

And that is how DJ would lure him in and spring their trap. He was unsure of exactly how they were going to do it, but he would work out those details with Brett once he managed to talk to him face to face.

Speaking of Brett, talking to the agent face to face was going to be a logistical challenge. DJ couldn't just tell him to meet them at the house he secretly purchased near the campus. After all, Brett was still an FBI agent. DJ couldn't be sure to where Brett's loyalties really leaned most. So, DJ opted to meet Brett on neutral ground with a well-planned escape route in case the man decided to arrest them.

In order to plan this move out, DJ needed to be in Boston first. He needed to walk around and lay out his well-conceived plan of escape. It needed to be someplace nowhere near their home. DJ was reasonably sure the new ID's they were using were still safe, with the FBI and Shark Bait clueless. But he didn't want to be living nearby just in case. It needed to be further away from where he was going to call home for the time being.

As far as the Jeep still registered under their old names was concerned, DJ purchased a brand new one under their new names from a dealership here in State College before checking into a hotel. After leaving the lot, they transferred all of their belongings, and then DJ had Abbi follow him. He drove the old one, and Abbi the new. A brief internet search told him the worst location in town. He pulled up in a convenience store parking lot with no security cameras, left the engine running, and then jumped in their new ride with Abbi.

She made fun of him to no end about purchasing yet another Jeep. This one a clay gray four door Wrangler with a dealership added lift-kit, modified hood, snorkel and a mean looking bumper with a winch. He informed her she could make all the jokes she wanted, but as far as he was concerned he would never own anything else.

From there, they drove to the hotel. He made sure it was the nicest one in town to ensure Abbi got her garden tub. He gave a slight hesitation at the counter when the lady on the other side asked about the room arrangements. There was no way he would let her out of his sight and risk ordering two rooms. Partly because he was afraid she would run off on a solo mission on her own, and partly because he wanted to keep her safe.

As he was deciding, Abbi spoke up. "One King, please." He looked at her, but she ignored him. He wasn't sure what she was up to, but if she thought he was going to break his commitment to her father's memory by taking her to bed before marriage, she was dead wrong. He would sleep on the couch. And if the room didn't have one, he would curl up on the floor like a faithful dog.

The room was a big one. A suite with a bedroom, a living room area, and a kitchenette. Abbi went straight to the bathroom and confirmed it had the tub she requested. He handled their bags while she snooped. From the depths of the bathroom he heard her speak loudly that before she did anything else, she was going to get her bubble bath on.

After the day she had, she could spend a week in the tub if it helped her feel better, he thought to himself.

He walked to the bathroom and stood in the doorway. Abbi was sitting on the edge of the big tub, reading the labels on the complimentary soaps. There was nothing particularly attractive about the pose or the act, but right then, despite his earlier commitment, he wanted to sweep her into his arms and carry her to the bed in the other room.

He shook his head, silently correcting himself. He had to think about Henry. And, her recently deceased mother, he added.

She looked up at him. "What's wrong?"

"Nothing. It's just that… I could really use a cup of coffee." He wanted to confront her on the room choice and set expectations with her, and himself for that matter, but he just couldn't do it. He could stare down a killer with a gun pointed at his head, but he couldn't have a frank conversation about sex with the girl he loved. He really didn't have a firm handle on the whole fear priority thing.

"Well, make a cup. I saw a coffee pot in the kitchen. I'm sure they have some packets."

"No, not that cheap house junk. Not now. I need *real* coffee. Take your bath. Take your time. I'm going down to the bar to get them to brew some of *my* stuff. Then, I'm going to find me a corner and watch anything sports related, and drink about three cups. When I'm done I'll bring up room service and we can call Brett."

Abbi shook her head at him in mock exasperation and flashed him a playful grin. "I don't care what you say, coffee is coffee. And until you make it foamy, sweeten it with vanilla, and top it with whipped cream and a pinch of cinnamon, it's all nasty."

DJ sighed. "I'm not having another pointless conversation with you about the finer points of real coffee, or why real men either drive a Jeep or, if they don't, secretly have a profound respect for them, or why I'll never own a cat. I won't be baited into another silly argument about things I find masculine. Not now. I'll see you later."

She stuck her tongue out at him and proceeded to run the bath water.

DJ turned on his heels, grabbed a bag of his special coffee beans from the top of his pack sitting on the dresser, and made his way out of the room. Before he could close the door behind him, Abbi tried to bait him into a fake fight one more time.

"By the way," she called out from the bathroom over the sound of running water. "Camouflage is *not* a color."

"Yes it is," he yelled behind him, and slammed the room door loud enough so she could hear it. "I don't care if I did run away from her in the process. I think I won that one," he said aloud to no one.

He made his way down to the bar area and checked his watch. It was a little after eight, and there were a handful of patrons hanging out. Not a one of them was alone. All were paired off into small groups. Just people passing through, killing time over a few drinks before turning in.

The room was shaped like a rectangle with a double-wide doorway near one end of the stained bar. Two of the adjoining walls were lined with windows looking out across landscaping and eventually the parking lot. The bar ran the length of an entire inside wall on one of the longer sides, facing one of the walls of windows.

DJ stood at the distant end of the all-wooden bar waiting patiently for four older women to give their order to the lone bartender working the room. Their drinks were colored a turquoise blue, and apparently complicated to make. By the time the bartender made them happy, several minutes passed. DJ tried to remain patient, but was getting cranky the longer the delay stretched. He was ready for his day to end.

When the bartender finally approached, he could sense DJ was mad for having to wait so long. "Sir, I am so sorry. There should be two of us here, but there's just me. It's not an excuse, but it's the truth. How about if I make this drink complimentary? What can I get you?"

"I know it's not your fault. Don't worry about it. But I have a serious request and it's going to sound odd."

"Well if I don't know what it is, I am sure I can find out how to make it. The internet is a wonderful thing." The bartender obviously thought DJ was about to order an obscure cocktail.

"Can you make a French press coffee?"

The man blinked before responding. "Oh, yeah sure. No problem."

"Good," DJ said. "Now make it with these beans. And use distilled water, please." He placed the bag of coffee on the bar. Surprise flowed over the young man's face as he looked down at the silver colored package.

"You travel with your own beans? Now that's what I call a serious coffee drinker."

"You have no idea," DJ replied. "Make me a French press with those beans and I vow to give you the best tip out of everyone here."

"Coming right up." The young man left quickly with the bag and immediately started the process of grinding the beans and preparing the press.

DJ climbed up on the last stool and turned his attention to the TV mounted high on the wall behind the bar. Some news channel was on, but he spotted the remote control sitting across from him on the back counter. Without asking, DJ stepped around the bar, grabbed the remote, and channel surfed until he found ESPN. He placed the remote back where he got it and glanced at the bartender. The young man was doing his best to pretend he didn't notice. After all, DJ promised a big tip.

A few minutes later, with DJ's brain officially in the off position from the hectic and worrisome day he had, the French press showed up in the hands of a smiling barkeep. He dropped it off with an empty cup and saucer placed on a white cloth napkin, along with cream and sugar. He then offered to pour the first cup. DJ thanked him but declined the offer, sliding the cream and sugar away. Good coffee was meant to be enjoyed black.

A few seconds later and he was in coffee heaven. There was nothing like the cup he held in his hands. It was about as perfect a cup of coffee as you could get. He sipped it slow and let the flavors coat his tongue. Before going for a second sip, he waited to taste the afternotes in the finish.

No matter how often he drank it, he always came away with the same impression. This was a great cup of coffee.

The bar steadily filled up over time, and a second person finally arrived to help the overworked bartender. At the end of the bar where DJ sat in quiet solitude, now only two empty stools separated him from two business men talking about politics. But that was fine, as he was about to leave.

"You mind if I sit here?" The question came from a medium height young man in a black coat and tie. Another business man passing through and looking for a moment to unwind. He wore a short cropped, neat haircut and a clean-shaven face. His eyes were a piercing blue like DJ had rarely seen. Even though his face didn't smile, his eyes did in a sort of polite manner.

"Help yourself," DJ responded. "I'm about to leave anyway." He waved at the first bartender to get his attention, and the man hurried over. DJ dropped two $100 bills on the bar as he thanked the young man.

The barkeep was stunned by the amount. "Wow... You didn't lie about it being the best tip I would get! I don't know what to say. Thank you! Hey, how about I keep that coffee and arrange for another French press brought up to your room in the morning? No charge, of course. I think you paid enough."

DJ considered the offer and then agreed, asking for a 7 a.m. drop off and to please include the rest of the beans. The man promised he would, shook his hand and turned to leave. Before DJ could follow suit, the stranger next to him interrupted.

"Excuse me," he said. "But did you just tip that guy $200 for making you coffee?"

"It's not just any coffee."

"If you don't mind me asking, what's so special about it?"

DJ smiled. "It's the perfect bean, perfectly roasted at the perfect time."

The blue-eyed stranger cocked his head to one side. "OK, now you have to explain. I am understandably curious."

"In order to get the perfect bean," DJ began, "you need to first grow it in ideal conditions. In this case, the fertile soils of Costa Rica. And you need to do it at an elevation of between four and six thousand feet above sea level."

"The elevation matters that much?"

DJ nodded. "For two reasons. It promotes the best growth of the plant and therefore the bean it produces, plus at that elevation, pests are limited. It allows you to grow it without chemical pesticides."

"OK, I can see how that would help, but there has to be more to it than that."

"Correct," DJ replied with confidence. "Then you have to not only pick the beans at the perfect time, but you have to turn around and sort them to take out only the best of the best. In this case, out of every million pounds of beans, only twenty to thirty percent actually make the cut for this particular blend. They have to be perfect or they get kicked aside to make less perfect blends. But when you go through all of that trouble, you get a perfectly smooth coffee with no bitterness, and a very pleasant finish that will last for minutes after drinking it."

"You know," the blue-eyed stranger said, and smiled "I don't think I've met anyone more serious about a cup of coffee."

"You should order some just once."

The man nodded and reached into his jacket pocket for his phone. "What's the name of it? I'll look it up."

"Hacienda La Minita Tarrazu. I actually buy mine custom roasted from a company out of Tyler, Texas. Just look for Distant Lands Coffee on the internet. But I would wait until you heal up before you drink any."

The stranger gave him a blank stare. "I'm sorry?"

DJ punched him in the face with a left cross as hard as he could, and the stranger flew off the stool backwards onto the hard-tiled floor.

Ever since the summer when DJ had to fight through hordes of Big Chuck minions, he had been suspicious of strangers. He was pretty sure the only reason Shark Bait was able to sneak through his defenses back at the diner was because he had to pee so bad, his thinking clouded by the color of yellow and the intense pain in his kidneys.

But now, with a fresh jolt of La Minita caffeine flowing through his synapsis, he was hyper-alert to everything around him.

When the stranger first asked to sit down, DJ was mistrustful and did a quick scan of the room. Another stranger sitting silently at a small round table behind him and wearing a leather jacket seemed to be paying attention to their conversation. Though, he was doing his best to try and act like he wasn't. Two more were over in the far corner looking sideways at him while pretending to be looking at a menu. A final one had taken a seat at the far end of the bar, and pulled a baseball cap down low over his eyes. But the real kicker for the four positioned in a semi-circle around the room behind him, was even though they all were wearing different tops, all were wearing matching black cargo pants.

Finally, when Mr. Blue Eyes pulled out his phone, DJ caught a glimpse of the butt of a Glock tucked away in a cross-draw configuration on the man's right-hand side. This meant Blue Eyes was a lefty.

The presence of so many men with guns could only mean that Shark Bait somehow tracked them down once again. Since he was wounded, he must have decided to employ others to help get the job done. They were probably all waiting for DJ to exit the bar so they could deal with him away from witnesses.

Well, if they were going to jump him, he was going to make sure it was a fair fight. He would beat them to the punch and even the odds.

As Blue Eyes was still on the way to the ground, DJ followed after him and snatched his Glock out of the holster with his right hand. Next, he focused on the one sitting behind him. This man had a small scar across his left cheek, and DJ already assigned a nickname for him.

Scarface was in the process of standing and going for his gun. DJ kicked out and shoved with all his might using the ball of his foot. He sent the table hard into the man's groin area. Scarface stumbled backwards, torn between trying to catch himself on the table and chairs behind him, or continuing the effort to draw and aim at DJ.

The plan was straight forward from here. He would plug Scarface through the nose. Next, he would pivot to the left and take out the two in the far corner. They were on their way to a standing position as well, but were slower trying to draw their weapons. Real slow, in fact. They were hesitating on purpose for some reason. Maybe they were shocked the other two hadn't been able to contain him using subterfuge and surprise.

Whatever their reason, it would be their undoing. DJ was sure he could take them out easily.

Next, he would finish off Blue Eyes laying at his feet. He may be unarmed, but he was far from innocent. He wouldn't view it as murder. DJ would view it as a simple correction. Finally, he would retreat back around the corner of the bar for cover as he would then engage Ballcap Boy at the opposite end.

He wasn't sure how that last part would go down. Would Ballcap Boy use the fleeing patrons as human shields? Would he take one hostage? Would he wait for them to move so he could get a clear shot? Or, would he flee for his life after seeing his comrades go down without much of a fight?

Guess DJ would have to wait and be surprised.

DJ took aim on the staggering Scarface to start the process, and it was going to be an easy shot. The target, the man's shocked face, presented itself in front of his sights. His finger was already on the trigger, pulling backwards.

His name was shouted above the sudden clamoring chaos of the room. It was sharp and clear. It was a familiar voice raised above the commotion of the small crowd starting to flee. The shout of Special Agent in Charge Brett Foster drove its way through his focused purpose of killing everyone in here with a gun.

He halted his pulling of the trigger at the last possible instant, pivoting the muzzle of the Glock upwards towards the ceiling. If Brett was here and shouting at him, these were not Shark Bait's men, but FBI Agents serving under Brett. He would never willingly go to jail for righting a wrong, but he would never kill one of the good guys either.

Of course, he considered to himself. *I might wing one if necessary...*

He turned his head towards the front entrance to the bar and located Brett, hands over his head and a look of panic on his face. "Everybody stand down," he ordered his Agents.

Everyone, including the guests, all stopped where they were and focused on DJ. It was like the whole room was waiting to see what he would do.

"You here to finally put the cuffs on me?" DJ asked Brett.

"I'm here to help you get the guy that killed Mary. You have my word you'll never have to worry about being arrested again. Maybe." Brett appeared to think about it moment more. "Well, let's just say I have a plan I think will work to keep you out of jail. Right now, I promise we're on the same side. You need my help, and I need yours. Will you trust me?"

No one in the entire room moved while DJ thought it over. It was like they all thought him larger than life. From his perspective, the whole thing was kind of funny. Minus the fact he almost killed a few of them.

DJ ejected the magazine from the Glock he stole from Agent Blue Eyes, then racked the slide rearward to eject the round in the chamber. The unfired 9mm ammunition tumbled and twirled into the air. DJ caught it in mid-flight, then dropped all of it on the counter behind him. He extended his hand down to Agent Blue Eyes on the floor, offering to help him back up. The agent grudgingly accepted.

Once on his feet, DJ asked him his name. "Cash. I was one of the men that picked up your in-laws this past summer."

"Oh. Sorry about that, then," said DJ pointing at the man's lip. "But you should have just announced yourself when you walked into the room. All that sneaking around almost got a bunch of you guys killed."

"We weren't sure how you would respond to a sudden announcement. My job was supposed to work it into the conversation casually."

"Casually, huh? The condition of your lip would indicate you failed."

Cash smiled at him through blood covered teeth. "I'm a firm believer in payback."

"You know, for a tiny little thing that just got a beat down, you sure are feisty. Let me know how that works out for you, Blue Eyes." DJ winked at him and gave a fake return grin.

The agent's reply was laced with sarcasm. "You'll be the first to know."

DJ laughed out loud and turned to Brett still standing over by the doorway. "The Mouse here is a keeper." DJ pointed a thumb at Cash. "So, what's the plan?"

"How about we talk about this up in your room?" Brett answered.

"Fine, but I hope you're wearing body armor. Abbi's going to hit you with the mother of all hugs."

DJ walked over across from the bartender he had been dealing with. He dug his new Jeep keys out from his front pocket and handed them to him. "Take care of that for me for a few days. I'll be back for it. I'll pay you for your trouble. I have a feeling I'll be leaving with these guys instead. And, leave everything in it alone."

He turned and headed for the door. Brett stepped out of the way and the others brought up the rear. Probably to make sure he kept going in the direction he was supposed to. Suddenly he came to a halt, and everyone else followed his actions. All but Brett reflexively reached for their sidearm.

DJ shook his head. Turning back to the bartender he said, "Almost forgot, toss me that bag of beans."

"What did you say these were called again?" the young man asked, tossing it across to him.

"The full name is Hacienda La Minita, Tarrazu. But most just call it La Minita. Best coffee in the world."

Chapter 11: Ambush

DJ relaxed on one end of a couch located along the fuselage of Brett's private jet. He sat stroking the ebony hair of Abbi as she lay there with her head in his lap. All around the cabin of the aircraft, people were sleeping wherever they could find a spot. It reminded DJ of his time in the Navy. Soldiers, no matter the branch, could sleep anywhere and in any position when afforded a few minutes of downtime. The airplane was no different for this bunch. Three of them gave up the couch so Abbi could take a nap. They were laying in the aisles and in between seats to catch as much shut-eye as they could.

He checked his watch. It was a little after 1 a.m. local time and they were on final approach to Boston. While he should be trying to catch some sleep himself, his brain was just too active. He couldn't help but think about his conversation with Brett back at the hotel room, nor trying to plan a course of action for when they landed.

After Abbi almost took Brett to the ground with a rib crushing hug, they sat down to share everything each one of them knew. Thanks to DJ, Brett knew exactly what Shark Bait looked like. He would take the full description and add it into the El Gran Blanco file, then kick it back up to active status. Because of Brett's rank within the FBI, he'd have no trouble taking over the case either.

DJ also told him of his rough draft idea to somehow set a trap for the assassin in Boston. He told Brett of the conversation he shared with Shark Bait before he had any idea who he was. He let him know about how DJ informed the killer of their plan to visit MIT, and how Shark Bait would have no choice but to stake out the place looking for them to show.

That's when Brett informed him about the murder of a man in the Bronx that seemed to be in the fake ID business. He told him of how the forensics team was able to pull up a purchase by an out of country shell company for two burial plots in Colorado. This gave Brett a hunch the man was somehow connected to DJ, and that DJ used the hacker to somehow switch the burial location for Henry Jackson. He suspected Abbi had already started the same process for Mary.

Brett was right, of course. And it explained why Beaver Nuggets was not returning any of Abbi's calls. He was dead. Shark Bait killed him.

It was also obvious Shark Bait had not followed the first assassin, who was really the illegitimate son of Charles Kaiser, in order to track DJ down. He got the information from torturing Beaver before killing him. He just happened along when Big Chuck's son was about to shoot the girls, and murdered the man for trying to horn in on his kill. After all, this wasn't a contracted killing for El Gran Blanco. It was personal. He was offended by DJ pretending to be him. The killer told him as much.

And if the assassin found out where DJ was hiding in Kentucky, then it would explain how the man caught up with him back at the diner. It was an accident, true. But Shark Bait was traveling to Boston because he already knew of the house DJ purchased there, thanks to torturing Beaver. They just happened to be following the same route when they ran into each other.

And if Shark Bait knew of the house near MIT, all they needed was to get there ahead of him and wait. It's why they were on the private jet now about to land in Boston. They would get to the house and work out a plan to trap him as he came in for the kill. They were only up against one man, and Brett had two additional agents with him along with a well-armed Tactical Team. All of them were counter sniper trained. And with a complete description of El Gran Blanco in their possession, they could just shoot him the first instance they saw him.

Ten against one were good odds. No, make that eleven, DJ thought to himself. He could not leave out Abbi. He had to find a way to include her in the trap-making process.

Additionally, DJ had an ace up his sleeve for a backup plan for luring in the assassin should this attempt fail. On a completely different set of ID's, DJ purchased a piece of property in the neighboring state of Vermont. It was two hundred thirty-eight acres of rolling hills nestled in the heart of a National Forest called "Green Mountain and Finger Lakes".

There was a small house there. Along with a storage building of sorts. It would likely be low on the list of targets for Shark Bait. But if the first location failed, and they needed a second chance, DJ could always fall back to that. It was isolated, heavily wooded, and DJ could wait there for months until the killer grew impatient and ventured in. He would not tell Brett and keep that to himself for now, however.

The original plan for the property was to build a weekend retreat for him and the girls. Mary really liked working in the garden and there was no way to have one at the Boston location. Plus, he really liked to play with his guns, but Massachusetts was not very friendly to those with firearms. The property in Vermont would be better suited for both, and was in driving distance for a weekend getaway and summer retreat while Abbi was enrolled in MIT. He would build a simple home suitable for them all once he surprised them with the house in Boston.

A surprise that never happened because of Shark Bait.

A flash of heated anger rose in him. He wanted to kill the guy in the worst way for what he did. But, if DJ was going to do this, and be at his best in the process, he could not let that anger show itself again. It would cloud his judgment and control his actions.

He shoved the emotion away. It was unnecessary in a moment like this. He needed to fix the problem. And the fix was straight forward from here. Land, head to the house, set up a sniper team with roving spotters, and kill the guy before he got close enough to do any more harm.

After being surprised by Brett in the hotel bar, the most nagging question in DJ's brain was, how did Brett find them? Turns out the answer wasn't exactly a legal move. Brett made a phone call to his old boss Tim Neville. Tim had a friend in the NSA. The NSA had the ability to tap into just about every internet connected security camera in the entire United States. And they could do it without requesting for a normal warrant.

Just feeding DJ's picture into the search parameters was not enough, however, because the computers just could not process that much information all at once. But give it a narrow search area, and it could do a much better job. Brett knew DJ was at the diner in West Virginia. He also knew DJ was headed to MIT thanks to the cryptic message he left on the bridge with the cop. And there were only so many routes to be taken from one location to the other. This narrowed down the search parameters considerably.

As soon as DJ and Abbi checked into the hotel, the prying eyes of the NSA supercomputers caught him and notified the user doing the search. That user called his friend Tim Neville. Tim called Brett who was already in the air headed to Boston. Eight minutes later the FBI jet was landing at the University Airpark in State College, twelve minutes away from the hotel located downtown. After a sixteen-minute wait on a called-in favor with the local sheriff's department for a lift, Brett and his men were all sitting in the parking lot discussing how best to approach DJ without him going all Rambo on the whole team.

The plan they decided on almost got people killed.

Now, here they all were, about to land in Boston well ahead of Shark Bait, attempting to set up a hasty ambush and finally take the notorious assassin out for good.

DJ considered their options for an ambush point. It would be tricky as there would be lots of opportunity for collateral damage with innocent bystanders potentially in the line of fire. It would take finesse and careful execution.

DJ's house was across the Charles River from MIT in a historic district of Boston. Beacon Hill was a closed group collection of small shops and multistory houses, seemingly all connected and touching one another and constructed of similar looking vintage red brick. Storrow Road, with its busy six lanes of traffic, ran parallel to the river marking the western edge of Beacon Hill. Branching off of Storrow was a short dead-end street called Charles River Square. It was only about 150 feet in length.

The thin street was a suburban canyon of sorts, lined on both sides with tall three-story row houses sitting close to the street. There were no front or back yards, and they were only separated from the street by a sidewalk. They wrapped all the way around the dead end to form a red brick "U" if viewed from the air. It had a narrow strip of grass with three elm trees evenly dispersed down the middle of the street. So small was the street, it lacked the width to even turn an econo-car around at the end without having to back up. Despite this, most of the owners had at least one vehicle parked along the curb.

The houses were virtually identical to one another in appearance. They all possessed matching white framed windows set in the red brick, floor to ceiling ones on the main floor, and a variety of sizes on the floors above. Large, shiny, black raised panel doors set on top of a small three-step concrete stoop, marked the matching entrances to all the homes. Shiny doorknockers with the address listed below on a matching brass plates were mounted in the middle of each one.

The houses all had a basement as well, and roof access up top. Each roof-top was divided by a high brick privacy wall. Many home owners set up chairs and tables to form lofty entertaining areas in the absence of back yards.

Outside of the main entrance and exit off of Storrow Road, there was a small tunnel near the seemingly closed off portion at the very end of the "U". It was a side entrance wide enough for pedestrians only. It appeared to bore right through one of the houses, leading to a side street. In fact, the owner had a bedroom right over the arch. DJ remembered thinking how odd it was. A weird example of what people did to shape their houses in a crowded and claustrophobic city.

Those two entrances to the tiny neighborhood were the only way in or out. It was surrounded by Storrow Road to the west, Revere Street to the south where the pedestrian archway was, a single lane darkened alley to the east, and a tree covered small park to the north.

The park was owned by the next set of row houses down the street, and contained no entrance or exit for their neighborhood. The alley to the east divided the back of the houses on that end, from the back of shops on the street behind them. There was no way to enter their neighborhood from the alley, unless you broke a window to climb through the back of one of those houses and then exited through the front door.

It was a perfect spot to defend with few entrances and crowded lines of sight. And since he now knew he had nine FBI agents and guns to do it with, he had a solid plan on how to set it up. He would go over it with Brett after they landed.

The corporate jet slowed in the air as it prepared for its descent onto the runway. One by one, awakened by the change in speed, the occupants stirred. The dead coming to life once more. Everyone here was running on precious little sleep, but in no time, the thought of what awaited them on the ground would pump adrenaline into them. With the exception of Abbi, every soul on this aircraft had served their country in some capacity. They were serious shooters, and in a moment's notice, despite little sleep, they would be back on their "A" game.

Within just a few more minutes, the plane touched down at Boston Logan International. Once on the ground, Brett informed the flight crew to prep for exit, and then to remain on the plane until he called them from their final destination. Ever cautious, Brett was obviously thinking of contingencies. He wanted to include a hasty retreat if needed. There was little chance Shark Bait could have beaten them to the house in Boston, but Brett was leaving nothing to chance. It was one of the things DJ respected about the Agent. He may be considered too young to run a field office, but his brain was as sharp as DJ had ever seen in a leader of men.

Brett rented three nondescript, four-door sedans to blend in at DJ's suggestion. They could be parked in random locations once they arrived. DJ's house was at the very end of the "U", and looked down the street. There was space in front of his house to park one of those vehicles. He could put another in the alley behind them, and the third could be parked on Revere Street near the arched pedestrian tunnel.

This would cover the two main entrances and keep anyone from sneaking in through a back window. It would only leave the small park to the north to sneak in, but one would need an extension ladder to come in through a back window of one of those homes. DJ just didn't see one man trying to sneak through any of those in order to get to him. The risk of exposure would be too great.

DJ expected either a frontal assault through the front door, or an attack on the rear of his home as the back wall ran along that thin alley. There was one other chance, though it would be difficult to pull off. If Shark Bait could make it to the roof of the shops behind, he might somehow make it across the narrow gap between buildings and over the alley to make a rooftop assault. Clearing a building from the top down was typical tactic taught in many combat circles, so DJ couldn't rule it out.

At this time of the morning, it was only a short thirteen-minute ride from the airport through the tunnel. Beacon Hill sat on the other side of Boston Harbor from the airport, and there were two tunnels providing access from that side. With no planes coming in during this time frame, the roads were clear. Beacon Hill as well, was a virtual ghost town. But it would not stay this way for long. By 4:30 a.m. things would start moving. The morning rush was in full swing by 6 a.m. And, it only slowed somewhat after 10. Boston was a far cry different pace than Ritner Kentucky where DJ and Abbi had been living.

Brett, DJ, Abbi, and Agent Cash formed the lead vehicle. Four of the Tactical Team took up the middle. Agent Hall and the two remaining team members occupied the rear.

DJ sat in the passenger seat and directed Brett where to drive. From the exit of the tunnel, they met up with Storrow Drive and circled the outside northwestern edge of Beacon Hill.

Once at the neighborhood, DJ lead the processional past his dead-end street and turned on Revere Street instead. There was an open spot across the street of the pedestrian tunnel leading in from the south side, so DJ instructed the next car to park there. Brett ordered two of the Agents to remain with the vehicle, and the other two to head into the tunnel and clear the street and the front of DJ's house first.

The last car with Agent Hall and the two remaining Tac Team members, DJ directed into the single entrance alley behind his house. Agent Hall said he would clear the alley and the street on the other side of the shops the next street over, and then come along and help Brett, DJ, and the two other Tac team members, already in front of DJ's house, clear the home before allowing Abbi inside.

Of course, there was no chance Shark Bait got there ahead of them and was waiting inside to spring a trap, but procedures would always be followed when it came to the FBI. DJ was pretty sure they probably had one just to use the bathroom.

By the time Brett circled the neighborhood, turned onto Charles River Square and pulled up in front of the house, Agent Hall and the two Tac Team members were waiting on the doorstep with guns drawn.

DJ shook his head. "Brett, is all of this really necessary?"

"Look," Brett replied. "You don't know who this guy really is. I told you one story about his past to help you sell the impersonation to Charles Kaiser. But the file we have on this man takes up more than just a folder in a file cabinet. It takes up the whole cabinet. All six drawers. And two other file cabinets to boot. He has hundreds of kills under his belt. Some quite elaborate in their execution. Some just hours after another kill far away. It shows very efficient planning. This is not just your normal everyday assassin. This man is nearly mythological in his reputation.

"And I'll tell you something else. You've walked away from two encounters with the man. He's twice failed to kill you. Accident, poor planning, I don't know. But something like this has never happened before. You can bet whatever he does for his third attempt will be to settle once and for all just how big and bad he really is. Word will get out about his failure with you, and that is knowledge he simply cannot allow to sit. He'll need to do something big to correct it. And quickly. Normally he could take his time and plan something special for you to make his point. But, now you're hurting his business."

DJ considered everything Brett was telling him. Maybe he wasn't giving the killer the proper respect he deserved. Until now, he was thinking they were on equal footing. DJ was looking at Shark Bait as if they were on the same level. But Brett reminded him the murderer had been perfecting his craft for years. Plus, he wasn't just your run of the mill criminal as the Senior Agent pointed out. There was a special kind of ruthlessness to him. A dark foulness was deep-seeded into his soul. It had been grown and nurtured into its own vicious kind of evil that DJ could probably never wrap his head around.

"Well," DJ said to Agent Hall standing near the front door. "I guess you can lead the way." He dug deep into his front pants pocket and fished the keys out to hand to him.

The Agent climbed the three steps to the top of the stoop and stood to one side. A Tac Team member stood to the other with a Sig Sauer MCX assault rifle. Another one readied himself at the bottom of the steps and to one side, to follow them both through. Agent Cash stood to the opposite side to follow them all in. Brett would bring up the rear.

DJ turned to Brett once more. "I'm familiar with the place, so I'll go in with them. You stay out here with Abbi."

Brett hesitated before replying. This was not something they would normally allow to happen, but DJ wasn't a normal witness that needed to be protected. He was as lethal as any agent here, and Brett knew it. After a second, Brett nodded but spoke a condition. "Fine. But you're in the rear. Let the other four do their jobs."

Hall unlocked the door cautiously and pushed it open. His partner with the rifle flipped a light on the end and aimed into the black void at the same time. Seeing that side of the room was clear, he stepped through the doorway in the same direction, and Hall followed immediately behind him to clear the opposite side of the room. The next team member charged through with Cash right on his heels, and DJ bringing up the rear. With the exception of DJ, there was a practiced order to it all.

As a Corpsman in the Navy, there was ample opportunity for DJ to witness Marines clear a building. There was a method and routine to the whole affair to not only clear it with efficiency and speed, but to make sure they did not accidentally shoot each other in the process. It was a practiced and well-rehearsed art. As DJ watched from the back of the line, he could tell these men were as good at this as he had ever seen.

A Corpsman attached to a platoon of Marines was trained in this as well. But it was more to simply familiarize yourself with the routine so you kind of knew what was about to happen. This was so you could get to a fallen comrade without crossing a fellow soldier's line of fire. DJ did not possess the hours and hours of training perfecting this job as these men did. Hanging out in the back of the line was the best course of action for everyone involved. And, it was a position he was familiar with.

Across from the front door was a stairway leading up to the floors above. It was perfectly in line with the front door, and wrapping around behind it was another leading down to the finished basement. It was set up as a live-in Au pair's suite. DJ planned to use it as his own personal apartment, allowing Mary and Abbi to take over the rest of the house until they could get married.

The basement had a small landing at the base of the stairs with a door leading into the rest of the apartment. It was partitioned out into a good-sized bedroom, full bath, and an open concept kitchen and living room. To one side of the landing at the base of the stairs was a large laundry room to be shared by all, a laundry chute and dumb waiter, the heat and AC unit for the whole house, plus a tankless water heater that took up the rest of the space. There was also a storage room DJ planned to turn into a small workshop.

The main floor where they stood now was very spacious. To the right of the door was a large living room with a fireplace. It was large enough to easily be divided in two sections with furniture. He hadn't purchased any yet. He knew better than to pick out furniture for two women without their involvement. He would only have to send it all back as soon as they laid eyes on it. He remembered the looks he got when he tried to help pick out furniture for the farmhouse in Kentucky. As a result, this building was an empty, echoing cavern of spacious rooms.

To the left of the door was a formal dining room in the front of the house. A short hallway in the back corner of it led to the chef's kitchen in the back, completely outfitted with brand new appliances from the recent makeover in preparation for the sale.

The one downside to the house was there were only small windows along the rear of the home to let in a little light. The back wall ran the length of the alley behind their private neighborhood, and there was simply not much to look at and enjoy. As such, the kitchen was decorated with vintage brick, raw timbers, and creative lighting to try and provide a cozy, romantic feel. It was nice, but DJ would have really enjoyed big windows with a view. A price he had to pay to get something this close to MIT for Abbi.

On the second floor above their heads was a large suite with its own bathroom and ample sized sitting area overlooking Charles River Square below. There was also a powder room off of a den and entertainment area. It could also make for a nice play area for kids.

DJ smiled at the thought. Would he be fortunate enough to have children again?

The third floor was entirely dedicated to a master suite fit for a king. There were two fireplaces. One for the bedroom, another for a small living room area on the other side of the building. There was a huge walk-in closet split in two for his and hers sections. A large bathroom included a whirlpool tub, and a massive walk-in shower with skylight.

Above that was the roof with a deck area for outdoor relaxing when the weather was right.

DJ stood on the first floor watching the stairs while the rest of the team cleared this level. He continued to remain on guard while they all went down to clear the basement next, with DJ describing what they would encounter below. Once this was finished, they gathered at the foot of the stairs to clear their way up to the roof. DJ told them the layout to expect in hushed tones, then Agent Hall started the procession upwards.

Pistol raised, he advanced one step at a time, but by now it was obvious to them all that the only people here were them. They had indeed beaten Shark Bait to the house. And, this put them in a great position to ambush him when the man came for DJ. Especially considering the assassin had no idea DJ was working with the FBI.

DJ watched Agent Hall make it all the way to the top step with the rest of the crew in a line. The man stopped and tried to peer through the open doorway leading into the den on the right, ignoring the closed door leading into the large bedroom on the left of the landing.

Suddenly the agent's head snapped back, and DJ caught a glimpse of blood spraying outward from the rear of his skull in the illumination of flashlights. It painted the wall behind him with red ichor. For a second the dead man stayed upright, unmoving and stiff with his unseeing eyes looking at the ceiling. Then, his muscles relaxed, and he collapsed at the top of the stairs.

There was another Tac Team member just a few steps further down on the stairs. His head was higher than the landing, and he was in a good position to see their assailant, but with his rifle, he could not swing past the railings to engage. He seemed to spot something, and then both ducked and leaped backwards and down into the other team member behind him. The move saved his life as bullets tore through where he was and into the wall on the left of the stairs. It also started a domino effect of falling bodies downward. The other team member lost his balance and fell backwards into Agent Cash. Cash kept his feet but staggered under the collision of bodies.

DJ missed the whole train of movement by stepping to the right just a fraction. As he did, he moved his weapon from a ready position to aiming up the stairs. Whoever started the bloodshed on the second floor did not want anyone to escape, so he charged into view with a silenced assault rifle of some kind, seizing the moment while most were falling and trying to recover their balance.

DJ was ready and put a round through his face. Just like poor Agent Hall who was only there to defend DJ and Abbi, the man's head snapped back and he went down in a pile to join the agent in death. In the flickering movement of reflected flashlights, DJ could see the man he killed was not Shark Bait. The man had friends, apparently. And where there was one…

"Multiple contacts!" DJ shouted over his shoulder to Brett through the still open door behind him. He had a choice. Stay put and wait to see what happened in front and behind him, retreat to protect Abbi, or take over and lead a charge upwards to kill everyone on the floors above. Behind, Abbi was safe. Ahead was the danger and the challenge. There was only one choice, then. Besides, retreat was not in his programming. Not now.

DJ darted around the collection of Agents, but before tearing up the stairs, he jerked to a halt and aimed straight above him, right at the edge of the hole in the second floor that was the stairwell. Sure enough, another dark figure was just now hanging a silenced assault rifle over the banister and preparing to rain bullets down on any who dared to try and move their way up. DJ was faster and expecting the move, putting three rounds through the banister rails into the mass of his body. The unknown soldier jerked and twitched, falling backwards out of view and taking the rifle with him.

14 rounds left. A spare mag in his coat pocket.

DJ could clearly make out what the soldier was armed with as he pulled it back over the railing. SCAR-16S. A product of FN costing nearly three grand on the civilian market. If these were full-auto versions, you could double that. And if they were black market items, you could double it again. If these men were friends of Shark Bait, and he had to assume they were, they were very well financed with some seriously deep pockets.

The proper way to ascend the stairs was slowly with his weapon aimed in the direction of the threat, but DJ threw caution to the wind. He needed to catch them off guard. He sprinted up the stairs three at a time, then dove and spun sideways over the dead bodies at the top.

This view let him see in through the den area doorway. It was clear for the moment but he could not see all the way into the room. Above him was the bottom side of the stairs leading to the third floor. No one was hanging a weapon over the rails in that direction. Down the hallway, looking past his feet and the corpses, the man he shot was still alive, lying on the wooden floor, but trying to swing his weapon into position. DJ put a round just under his left eye, and the man stopped moving there at the base of the next stairway.

13 rounds left. One spare mag in his coat pocket.

DJ scrambled to his feet as two figures popped into view. One was barely visible as he brought his SCAR to bear over the stair railing, the other slid sideways into view at the end of the hall. He had either been hiding in the powder room at the foot of the stairs on this level, or he had been waiting on the stairs the whole time. Either way, this man was now in position to shoot DJ, and DJ was defenseless as he tried to get to his feet.

He pushed hard and catapulted his way head-first and sideways in through the den's doorway, praying there was no one waiting for him. Bullets split the air around him, smashing into the frame of the doorway, and tugging at his jacket as he went through. One of the rounds impacted something hard in his pocket, and whatever it was shattered and broke apart in the folds. He felt heat and a sharp biting pain in his left side, but he did his best to ignore it.

There was someone waiting for him in the shrouded corner of the den. A man-sized bit of shadow in an otherwise dark room.

Still sliding sideways across the polished oak floor, DJ put two rounds into where he imagined the man's chest was, followed by a third into the black mass at the top of the form he knew to be the man's head. Bullets tore through the floor in front of DJ's face before the shadow died from a bullet-smashed brain, and DJ knew he had been lucky.

DJ could smell smoke, and the burning at his side was becoming more intense. He catapulted to his feet and tried to find the source of the burning pain. It was then he noticed he was on fire. Or rather his jacket pocket was. The spare mag… A close round must have destroyed the spare magazine in his coat pocket and ignited the gun powder. It was burning, and setting his jacket on fire in the process. He dropped his weapon and ripped the jacket off as fast as he could.

As the garment cleared his shoulders, a man stepped through with a weapon searching for him. DJ hurled the jacket as hard as he could at the man, a trail of flame and sparks leaving a flickering path behind through the air. It was the perfect distraction. He reached down for his pistol and rolled to his right. Before he could bring his gun up and engage this new threat, a single bullet exited from the soldier's face and he pitched forward onto the oaken floor. Cash dove into the room over the dead body as more bullets smashed the doorframe seeking him out.

DJ lurched forward, unclipped the SCAR from the combat sling attached to the dead soldier, and found it to be a full-auto version. He shoved his pistol into his waistband, and raising the weapon, stepped closer to the door.

"Cash, talk to me."

"I got winged. I'm OK though." The Agent spoke through clenched teeth as he got back to his feet.

The jacket was continuing to burn, causing orange flickering light to chase away the shadows of the room and the hallway beyond. DJ could just make out a Tac Team member trying to advance backwards up the stairs, pointing in the direction of the other landing around where Cash had been shot from. Bullets drove him back down the stairs, narrowly avoiding becoming another casualty in the process. DJ thought he could make out the closed door of the bedroom at the top of the landing start to slowly swing open. He put three rounds through the sheetrock wall to the left of the jam, right where he could envision someone standing. The door stopped its movement, but DJ kept aiming just to be sure.

A few more bullets from back around to the left passed through the wall to the left of the door. Exactly where DJ would have been if he was standing close to the frame.

"How bad are you hurt?" DJ asked the now-standing agent behind him.

"Tore a chunk out of the top of my shoulder. I could use a pressure dressing but I can still shoot. We need to get out of here. You and Abbi are our primary witnesses. We need to get you both clear."

"No!" DJ barked in reply. "This ends now! Help me take the stairs to the third floor."

Unsilenced gunfire erupted outside the house on the street. DJ knew it could only mean Brett had engaged targets at the front of his home. It also meant Abbi was in the direct line of fire. They were now pinned down from multiple angles. On the stairs and above his head were untold amounts of armed assailants. Out front were unknown numbers of other soldiers shooting at Brett and the woman he loved. They were trapped.

DJ was suddenly angry, despite knowing full well how emotion could affect his performance and decision making, and despite warning himself to steer clear of any emotion over and over again. It crept up the back of his spine anyway, and seized hold of his reason. In reaction to the sudden flame of fury sparked alive in him, he wheeled about and planted the toe of his boot deep into the side of the corpse at his feet. Twice.

Cash grabbed a handful of shirt and shook him. "Is there another way out of here?"

DJ shook his head in reply. He knew time was his enemy now, as well. Whoever was shooting at them knew they had only a few minutes before the police started answering 911 calls of gunfire. They had DJ's group pinned down with nowhere to run. Any second they would press in and try to slaughter them all. The only choice they had was to try and hole up on the ground floor and outlast the onslaught.

DJ racked his brain for a solution to their problem. Below him on the ground floor, he could hear Brett shouting orders. The man had abandoned the street and moved into the first-floor area for shelter. Fleetingly, DJ wondered about the other four Tac Team agents stationed outside of the neighborhood. What had become of them? Had they circled around to offer support and been killed? Where they out there right now pinned down as well? Were they waiting for orders before responding?

A way out suddenly dawned on DJ like a hammer hitting a nail.

"The back of the living room has two small windows facing the alley," he told Agent Cash. "It's the only choice. One of our cars is in that alley. The other is around the corner. If they're focused on the front, we might be able to sneak out the back. Can you run?" Cash nodded in reply.

DJ switched the selector lever on the SCAR to full auto, and started firing before he even made it through the doorway. He swung the weapon towards the next stairway landing and stepped forward just enough for Cash to bolt past. Around the banister of the stairs, the agent darted, then stopped at the top of the stairs to cover DJ's retreat. It would allow DJ to leap-frog past.

There was no one for DJ to direct his fire towards, and bullets rattled out in a steady stream impacting nothing but wood and sheetrock. Whoever used to be there and shot Agent Cash, was gone. They no doubt retreated to the third floor for a better defensive position.

The SCAR emptied its magazine, and DJ dropped it where he was, retrieving his trusty P320 from his waistband. He tore past Cash and down to the first floor. Before he even made the bottom step, what he saw caused fear and dread, with talons of razors, to snatch at his heart and begin to squeeze.

The four remaining Tactical Team Agents from outside the home had made it around to the front, and were now standing in the living room to his left. They were shooting at unknown targets through the windows facing the street. Brett stood at the base of the stairs looking back through the open doorway, shouting and waving at someone to stay low.

That someone was Abbi Jackson, the living embodiment of every good and decent thing in his life. The death grip of fear around his heart threatened to shred it in two. She was looking right at him. Horror etched across her face as an endless barrage of gunfire pelted jacketed bullets into every surface around her. She was hunkered down into a squatting position behind the edge of the rented car they arrived in. From somewhere high up and behind her, more than one enemy sent round after round through the top of the car, punching through the metal surface as if it were only paper.

It was clear now what the Tac Team was shooting at from the living room to his left. They were trying to offer her cover fire so she could sprint into the building, but it was having little effect.

Her eyes locked to his, and he understood there was only one choice for him to follow. He would bolt through the open doorway, grab her up, and shield her body with his as he brought her back to safety. He would die, of course. There were too many bullets flying for him to have much of a chance at survival. But she would live, and that was all that mattered. If his last act would be to save the woman who had allowed him to find joy again, then it was a fitting end to a life.

He was not sure why Brett chose to leave her on the street. And right at this moment, it was all he could do to keep from shooting the man in the back of his head. The instinct and reaction to do so was born from the flash of anger that still burned in him. He recognized this, and understood there had to be some sort of explanation for Brett's actions. But emotion was at war with reason and logic right now. Reason was winning, but just barely.

Brett is a good man, he thought to himself. Maybe the closest thing he had to a personal friend since the death of Henry. So, DJ would ignore the fact Brett had left her there defenseless on the sidewalk. He would race into the hail of bullets, gather Abbi into his arms, and bring her to Brett. Brett would care for her now. He would shield her from harm and protect her as if she were a treasure, for she surely was. And then, once Brett took care of all the bad guys in the immediate vicinity, he would find the man responsible for all of this. Finding the bad guy was something Brett seemed to excel at.

All of these thoughts were processed in a micro-second as he hurtled down the stairs. It was amazing how time could slow down in all of the chaos to allow him to think through things and make decisions. Like the decision to head through the front door and sweep Abbi into his arms.

He silently willed himself to pick up speed, as he shot past Brett standing just below the last step. *Hang on Abbi*, he said to himself. *Help is on the way.*

Cody Hamell loved his job. He got to kill people for a living. And, there was nothing more challenging or fulfilling in this world than taking the life of another with ruthless skill and precision. He was in charge of a ten-person mercenary team which got most of their work from a broker out of Boston. Usually their team worked alone, and outside the US. But today, they were attached to two other teams in a hastily put together ambush for some high-profile target. And they were going to do it right here, in the heart of Boston.

His group was supposed to secure the rooftops in the ambush. They would act as spotters and provide covering fire, along with applying direct force if needed. One of the teams would occupy the target's house and spring the trap when the man and his entourage entered, hoping to contain the kill zone within the confines of the home. The third team secured a range of vehicles stationed around the boxed-in neighborhood. They would provide an exfil strategy for both teams once the kill was complete. They were to leave no one standing if possible, but above all else, the main target needed to die.

It was not common to work with this many teams. Nor was it common to not have several days to observe and research out a solid plan. But there was apparently a timing issue, and they were called on to act immediately. The broker they worked with set up the plan, and was paying out a fifty percent bonus for the short notice. Within two hours of first contact, they met up with the two other teams in an abandoned business park, looked at some satellite photos to familiarize themselves with the area, and worked with the other teams to fine tune a set of responsibilities.

They were told the target was an under-the-table contractor who double crossed the people he worked with. He was fleeing to a safe house no one was supposed to know anything about. There was a girlfriend, and some well-equipped body guards.

Despite the lack of at least a week's worth of planning and recon, it promised to be a pretty easy kill. Especially considering the insane amount of firepower three mercenary groups would be bringing to the party.

Cody's team had been complete with no new members for the last three years. They were very familiar with each other, and had fine-tuned their communication and execution down to the letter.

He had no working relationship with the other two teams, but the lead team chosen commanded a pretty good reputation. They even completed contracts for the CIA in a few hotspots around the globe.

The group chosen for exfiltration and exit was the least experienced group of the bunch. But still, between the lead team currently taking up space on the second and third floors of the target's home, and Cody's team nesting up high on a few of the rooftops, this plan would likely go off without a hitch. The target would never know what hit him until it was too late. And if it looked like things were getting out of hand, well, Cody brought along a few surprises guaranteed to set things right.

His team was dropped off just after 7 p.m. near the side entrance to the neighborhood. A couple of them carried duffle bags with gear, and all of them were dressed in coveralls. They split into two teams on the north and south sides of the street right by the entrance on Storrow Road. They both knocked on the doors pretending to be city workers needing to do an emergency inspection on a reported gas leak. Both teams were let in with no issues.

They then killed all of the occupants with silenced, small caliber weapons making barely a sound. This allowed them access to the rooftops across from one another, securing the west end of the street, and setting up that end of the ambush.

Cody was then able to hop from roof to roof until he made the top of the target's home. He forced the door and let himself in. He cleared each room one by one just to be on the safe side, then opened the front door from the inside.

The lead team arrived a moment later after he made a phone call, and they started setting up that end of the trap. Cody went back up to the roof of the target's safehouse to man what would be an observation point, and a key hub for intel when they sprung their trap.

Whomever requested the job had key information on their target's movements. At first, the target was supposed to be coming in via car and there was just the main target and his girlfriend. Only Cody and his group were offered the contract at that point. But then, only a few hours later, things had changed. The contact was coming in via private jet a lot sooner, and he had himself an armed escort of nine seasoned hitters. Their broker brought in two extra teams, assigned a different one to be lead, but offered a substantial increase in pay.

Cody didn't care. Money was money, and more of it was better.

Now here he was, peeking over the edge of the target's roof, staring down on the man's girlfriend trapped in place behind a car next to the sidewalk. He could take her out easily, but Cody had a different idea. It was explicit in the contract for the main target to be killed. Everyone else was secondary. So, he was using her as bait to get the man to show his face and try to rescue her. On his command, his men would make sure the target died as intended.

The team inside had sprung their trap, but it did not go as smoothly as expected. One of them jumped the gun and engaged a guard because he felt he had a clear shot. Cody heard it all go down over the radio plugged into his ear. It was a rookie mistake, and the idiot was told not to engage just yet. He did anyway, and here they were, shooting up an entire neighborhood with precious little time left to complete the mission before the pigs showed up.

If he got his count right from listening in to the team below battling it out with the target and his men, three or more people from the lead team were already dead, and that meant Cody and his bunch were going to have to do something to turn this around before it ended up being a complete failure. Failure meant no payday, and that was simply unacceptable.

Initially, when their planned victim first arrived, Cody could have taken out the man easily. He was directly above their front door on the roof. He had him in his sights and might have even have been able to take them all out. But, the plan was to allow them to all make it inside first in order to ensure containment. Had this been his operation, he would have called an audible and finished the man right then and there. But it wasn't. His team was relegated to second. If Cody broke protocol and jumped the gun, then he may never get the opportunity to work with this broker again. And this broker had some of the better high paying ops available for merc groups.

So, Cody watched and radioed the team on the inside that the target was about to enter. But then, instead of their victims all going inside, they split up. The target with most of the group entered the building, and a lone guard and the girlfriend waited for them on the street.

Shortly afterwards, gunfire erupted below his feet, and chatter over the radio told him things were not going to plan. He leaned across the lip of the roof to go ahead and take out the guard and the girl, but four more guards came through the pedestrian tunnel. They must have parked around the corner and avoided initial detection. They saw him up there on the roof and started shooting. He had to duck back down to avoid being turned into a pin cushion.

He called to his men located on the roofs at the end of the street, to go ahead and engage in order to drive their targets inside. Then, he would introduce them all to his surprise problem solver.

His men did as he instructed, pouring ammunition at the guards and girl below. Cody peered over the edge to see all of them disappear inside. Just before he was about to key the mic and order his surprise to be delivered, incredibly, the girl darted back outside to retrieve something from the sidewalk next to the car.

He ordered his men at the end of the street to continue shooting and keep her pinned down. They did, and he stood and aimed below at her, waiting for the boyfriend, their actual main target, to come to her rescue. If the man did, Cody would shoot him to ensure mission completion, order his surprise, then he and his men would rappel down off these roofs and disappear using his backup plan for exit. After all, he never trusted anyone else's planning. This is why he brought along his little surprise.

Right now, high up on a roof with an excellent vantage of the victim's three-story row house, one of his men was looking through the sights of a Russian made RPG. The rocket launcher would reduce the front of the house to rubble. It possessed a blast radius guaranteed to kill everyone within a twenty-foot circle. Inside the building or out. It might even take out a few friendlies on the second and third floor. But, they were the ones that screwed this whole operation up anyway.

The other two teams were on their own. Cody would get the job done while everyone either died, or got caught by the cops who were probably already on their way. He and his men would ensure they never sat second-seat ever again. Like they should not have had to sit second seat this time.

"Come on out," he said out loud to no one. "Show me your ugly little face, whatever your name is."

He aimed below at the girl trying to hide from the hail of bullets being thrown around by his men. He smiled at the poor helpless girl as she twitched and cringed from bullets impacting everywhere near her.

She was the perfect bait. The perfect lure for his little trap. She was like a scared, bleating goat tied to a stake while the hunters waited for the lion to appear.

Cody smiled at the thought. "Here kitty, kitty, kitty."

Abbi caught sight of the small velvet bundle as it fell from DJ's pants pocket when he handed the keys over to the agent standing by the front door. DJ missed it, of course, but she saw it fall. For a moment, she almost said something to bring his attention to what he dropped. But then a flash of hopeful recognition as to what could be in the small bag, made her pause and her heart leap into her throat.

It looked like… Could it possibly be… Was that a ring bag?

She said nothing, silently hoping he would miss it. She glanced at Brett, but the agent didn't appear to see it. He was scanning the street behind them. *Please, no one notice*, she prayed.

And DJ, you better NOT step on it or you're a dead man! She fixed the back of his head with a glare of flaming daggers, silently moving him forward by the sheer focus of her will.

The man did not notice her glare, like he failed to notice the fact he dropped the small package to the ground. Thankfully, he did not step backwards onto the small bundle and crush it under foot either. Instead, he moved forward to one side of the door to follow the agents in to secure the home.

It was his home, purchased in his name. A fake one to be sure, but his nonetheless. But was it to be the one he took a knee in and made hers? Would this be the house they shared a room for the first time? Would their bed be somewhere above in the master suite?

The Agent opened the door and all of them filed through to make sure it was safe. She was to wait out front with Brett until they got word the coast was clear. She stole a glance at Brett again. He watched them go through, then he took to scanning the rooftops all the way around the street. As soon as she saw her opportunity, she bent down quickly and plucked the small package from the concrete.

He didn't seem to notice, or if he did, he didn't seem to care. She held it next to her side in her right hand, and rolled it around trying to learn its contents from the feel of the outside alone. It was a soft pouch. Maybe velvet? And she could feel a drawstring on one end. She rolled the thing around in her fingers and squeezed. A single lump attached to one end of a circle of metal.

It was! It was a ring! An engagement ring held tightly in a small velvet drawstring pouch. Her heart soared. Tears formed at the edges of her eyes and she turned her back to Brett lest he realize what was going on.

She brought the bundle up in front of her, held it at her waist, and with both hands began to carefully undo the string securing the contents. It was stubborn and knotted in some fashion she couldn't figure out from feel alone. She held it up then, studying the knot to figure out the best way to get inside.

"I bet you were the kid that always looked for the presents prior to Christmas morning." Brett spoke the words softly behind her, but he might have been shouting it through a bullhorn. She started and almost dropped the small velvet pouch again.

She closed her eyes in shame, and hesitated before replying. "I was," she begrudgingly admitted and turned around to face him.

"Why don't you give that to me? I'll tell him he dropped it and he'll never know you found out." The agent's eyes stared her down with no emotion in the light of the street lamps.

She stuck her chin out in defiance. "I will do that, but first help me with this knot."

Brett cocked his head to one side. "If he was ready for you to see it, he would have dropped to his knee instead and handed it to you. This was an accident and you know it. Why not wait to be surprised?"

"Open it for me right now, or so help me, I'll take you down right here in the middle of the street. And you know I'll do it too!" She wagged her finger and took a step closer to stare up at him in anger. She wanted to see what was in the little pouch, and she was not going to be denied.

Brett didn't move, but just looked at her. For a moment, she wondered if she could actually bring herself to follow through with the threat, but then she saw Brett's will buckle. He snatched it from her fingers and made short work of the knot. With a frown of disappointment, he handed it back to her. She pried the mouth open on the velvet bag and hastily dumped the contents out in her other palm.

She froze like a statue, and her breath caught in her throat. A simple gold band with a diamond the size of a Skittle glittered under the street lights. It was a beautiful promise, symbolized in perfect beauty lying there in her hand. She wanted to race up the steps with as much speed as she could, screaming "yes!" at the top of her lungs. She wanted to find the man, shout the words, "I DO" and drag him off to the bedroom. She didn't even care if there was a bed or not. He had told her the place was empty with no furniture. But she didn't need a bed. She just needed him.

Still staring at the small piece of jewelry, she asked Brett a serious question. "How soon can a justice of the peace do a marriage?"

Brett stammered. "I… Umm… I'm not… Abbi, I just don't know the answer to that question."

She looked up at him and beamed. "Will you be my maid of honor? I mean I know you're a dude and all, but I don't have anyone else… NO WAIT! Walk me down the aisle! You have to!"

Brett gripped her shoulders with both of his hands. "OK, you need to calm down. Put that ring back in the pouch and hand it to me. He cannot know you found out! I mean it. Calm yourself and put it away."

She looked back down at the ring in her hand and sighed. Brett was right, of course. She could not deny the man the right of asking her the question. She must let him plan it all out and make it perfect. But the truth was, she was dying inside. She wanted to scream at the top of her lungs that she was marrying DJ Slaughter.

As she dropped the ring back into its pouch, she couldn't help but think of her mom and dad. And right then, her joy and happiness at this new revelation suddenly melted into grief and sadness.

She was crying then. All at once. Losing her father had been bad enough. But she only lost her mother this morning, and that wound was wide open and fresh. Neither would be there to see her get married. Dad wouldn't be there to give her away, and her mother wouldn't be there to help her pick out a dress.

Holy crap, a dress... How was she supposed to pick out a dress? The closest thing to a dress she most recently wore was the cap and gown a few years back at her high school graduation. She was strictly a jeans kind of a girl, and now she was going to have to pick out a wedding dress all by herself.

There was no one to guide her into marriage. No one to explain what the transition was going to be like. No one to turn to in order to help her figure out the nuances of a more intimate relationship. No one to lean on while planning a life together with a man who couldn't even understand camouflage was not an actual color.

With one hand, she gripped the small golden band with its shiny diamond, with the other she grabbed a hold of Brett's lapel and just buried her face into his chest. She wept openly and unrestrained. She was suddenly very overwhelmed. She should be slapping herself into being calm and calculating, instead she was bawling like one of those girls she had always made fun of.

Gone was Little Miss Independent. Here was just a small, frightened girl in desperate need of her daddy's strong arm and calming voice. But all she had was a very confused, and openly shocked, FBI agent. So, she buried her face into his starched white shirt and cried with everything she had in her.

For a moment, Brett just stood there with his arms wide, daring not to embrace her. But seeing she would not let up, he wrapped his arms around her and held her close as she blubbered.

She needed to pull herself together. She knew that. Any minute DJ and the rest would finish checking the house. She could not afford to let the man see her like this. Her mom was right. She needed him to be the strong, capable man he was. They all did. Or this was never going to be over. She could not afford for him to be consumed with her well-being. She had to stop this. She had to stop it right now.

But she couldn't. All she could do was cry. And all poor Brett could do was hold her.

Gunshots then, from in the house. But there was no way the assassin could have gotten ahead of them. He should still be miles and miles behind them.

She heard DJ shout about multiple contacts, and then Brett was shoving her down onto the sidewalk. He knelt over her with his gun drawn. She could see him searching first the open front door, then the rooftops. More gunfire from inside. Then more shouting. Brett started speaking into a handheld radio about backup to his location. He searched all around them looking for more enemy. He helped her up into a kneeling position while he looked.

"We may need to run. Be ready!" he told her.

She prepared herself and was now suddenly scared. She laughed out loud despite the feeling and Brett gave her a look of concern for a moment before returning to his watch. She certainly was running through the full range of emotions one could feel in a short amount of time. Joy and happiness, deep grief and sadness, and now a stabbing fear.

There was supposed to be only one person they were looking for, but DJ, and now the squawking radio, declared multiple enemies. She was now very worried for her man. She had never really been scared for DJ before. She always considered him to be a man all the bad people in the world should be afraid of. She put him in a category that said he was almost invincible. A hero of heroes.

But now… Now she held in her right hand a small velvet drawstring pouch with a diamond adorned ring. Now it was different. Now she was concerned for his safety. Only with child-like fantasy had she ever imagined a man kneeling before her, presenting his hand and a ring. But now… Now she was so close to it actually happening, fear was racing through her brain telling her the moment might never appear. The specter of death was threatening to steal the moment from her.

More gunfire, but this time from out in the street.

Oh no.

They were surrounded.

Brett seemed to sense her concern. "Our guys are coming," he told her. "When they get here, we will either be leaving in this car, or we're headed inside. Get ready."

Two of them ran up seconds later, shooting at the roof over her head. For whatever reason, Brett decided inside the house was better than driving back down the street. Maybe there were more on other rooftops and Brett figured they would be easy pickings headed down the narrow corridor of houses. He put his arm around her and half lifted her into a standing position, driving her forward up the steps at the same time.

An agent tried to help by grabbing her other arm. The one holding the ring. Her hand banged his leg and the small velvet pouch slipped from her grasp, tumbling to the cement beneath her feet. Then they were all up the steps and inside. She could hear more gunfire from upstairs, and couldn't see DJ. He must be up there locked in battle above her. The others fanned out across the living room and started firing through the windows. Brett released her and took a step towards the stairs with gun raised. He started asking questions and barking orders.

Abbi turned back to the open doorway searching for the ring pouch. She spotted it there next to the car by the sidewalk. She had to get it back. There was a sudden urge to rescue the pouch like it was a small child in danger.

Before she knew it, and without a concern for her own safety, she was running back down the stairs for the small package. She dove to the ground as bullets began to impact all around her. Gathering up the precious bundle, she knelt there next to the car. Bullets struck the roof of the sedan inches from the top of her head with the sound of metallic hail. She was trapped.

She looked back towards Brett waiting for her inside. She could see him, waving and shouting for cover fire. She screwed up, she realized. In the biggest way possible.

Then she saw her love. DJ was racing down the stairs two at a time, pistol in hand. Their eyes locked, and suddenly she knew despite the danger she just placed herself in, he was coming for her. He was going to race headlong through the barrage of gunfire, sweep her into his arms, and get her to safety. There was no way he could live through something like that. But he wouldn't care as long as she was safe.

She would not allow him to do that. She would have to try for the open doorway to keep him from sacrificing himself. If she died for her foolishness, then so be it. But she couldn't watch DJ run to his death because of her stupidity.

She bolted for the front door as hard as she could, eyes locked on his. He wasn't slowing, though. He would meet her, she realized. They would die together on the front doorsteps of the house they would never know as their home.

To her amazement, someone tackled DJ from behind, driving him to the ground. It was Agent Cash, she saw. He had been running down the stairs behind DJ and dove on top of the man before he could kill himself. DJ would live at least. And that was all she could hope for at the moment.

As her left foot connected with the first doorstep, she heard a loud pop from somewhere back behind her, followed instantly by an insane hissing noise screaming rapidly in her direction. As she drew even with the open doorway, whatever it was raced past her with incredible speed, right over her left shoulder. She felt the heat of its passing, and heard it's angry buzzing as it flew past her ear. It just missed Brett standing next to her tackled boyfriend, travelling at a slight angle and racing into a room on the left-hand side. It narrowly missed the edge of the wall running alongside the stairway. Into the dining room perhaps?

There was a bright flash. A consuming light enveloped her in a glow of red, orange, and white. For the briefest of moments, she caught the sense of being in flight. But it didn't last. In an instant her universe vanished, blasted away in a heated rush of compressed air, blinding light and driving noise.

Chapter 12: I Got You

It was like a memorized scene from a bad movie. He knew every sight and sound. But it sickened DJ to no end to hear it, smell it, feel it, and yes, even taste it. The rush of it all yanked him out of the here and now, and catapulted him into the world of yesterday.

He flashed backwards in time to an uneven and rocky hillside. He was paused there on the steep slope to adjust the pack on his back. Gone was the wet cold of Boston. Here was only the dry heat of northern Iraq.

And the flies. There were always flies here. You could never get away from them in this country. One landed on the bridge of his nose, and he waved it away as he focused on his pack.

He was going to have to figure out a new way of positioning the contents inside the heavy rucksack. The straps were digging into his shoulder and causing a sharp pain in his neck. There had to be a way of redistributing his load to make it more comfortable to wear over a long haul.

As a corpsman attached to a squad of marines, he carried many of the same things they did, but also had the added weight of the tools and supplies for his job. Not only was he currently outfitted with a few hundred rounds of ammunition, an M4 rifle, several litters of water, and all the other requirements for a three-day patrol, but he also carried an entire arsenal of gear to fulfil his role. It was his sworn duty to patch these Marines up and keep them alive if they were to come under fire. It required a lot of extra stuff to carry. The heaviest of which were those stupid IV bags. Necessary, to be sure, but it added a lot of weight when you had nearly a gallon of extra fluids in your bag.

He was at the tail end of a line of Marines as they weaved their way up the slope headed to a ridgeline. Their three-day patrol out here on the outskirts of Soran was only really getting started. They were dropped off via Blackhawk helicopter only hours before. Their orders were to make a large three-day loop through these steep hills looking for any signs of enemy movement or hideouts. They would then hold their positions, radio their findings, and allow heavier firepower to do the rest from the air.

After a few hours of hiking from their drop off point, DJ realized his loadout was going to kill him if he didn't make some changes. As he paused to readjust and flex his muscles, the patrol kept moving, creating a gap between him and the back of the line. He could catch them with no problem, but first he needed to move these straps around.

From somewhere towards the peak of the ridge above him, he heard a loud pop, then a rapidly approaching wooshing noise. Like air escaping from a punctured tire. Only a lot louder. He wasn't sure what it was, but he instantly knew they were in trouble. A split second later, an explosion tore into the tail end of the Marines. Right near where he would have been. Bodies and debris flew everywhere. Despite the distance, a bit of shrapnel lodged itself in DJ's upper-left thigh.

The pain was sharp and swift, causing him to curse under his breath. But now was the time when his squad needed him the most. Now was the time for him to do his job. He ripped the heated shard of metal from his leg. He paused for just a moment as recognition told his shocked brain it was a piece of a canteen cup. It must have belonged to one of the dead or dying Marines in front of him.

Duty and training snapped him from his frozen state, and he started running for the closest bodies, ignoring the pain in his upper thigh. The wound wasn't too deep, and he could leave it until he got the others patched up and stable. Up ahead, his comrades finally located the source of enemy up on top of the ridge, and began to lay down fire. The familiar sounds of M4 rifles firing at their enemy broke through the air as DJ arrived at the first body.

The man was sprawled face down and unmoving. DJ landed next to him and flipped the man over on his back to find the wounds. The man's face was missing, his exposed brain had been pounded into mush and was falling out of the front of his skull.

He recoiled from the scene, scrambling backwards from unmitigated revulsion. This was not DJ's first rodeo, but it was the most horrific scene he had witnessed to date. He was not weak-stomached, yet he was forced to choke down bile at the horror in front of him. He closed his eyes and silently prayed for strength.

On his knees and immobile, DJ was exposed. He heard shouting from his men, and a bullet tore through the very top of his helmet. The force snapped his head over to the left, and if his neck was only sore before, it was positively screaming now.

The blow rolled him to his side, and the weight of his pack finished pulling him all the way over. He scrambled back to his hands and knees, and then bolted for the safety of a large boulder just ahead. On the way, he reached down to yank the dog tags from the dead Marine. If they were forced to retreat out of here, he would at least have the tags of the man to identify him and send to the family.

Bullets impacted the front side of the large rock as he dove in behind it. He reached for the straps of his helmet and ripped it from his head. He could clearly see where the heavy caliber round tore a chunk out of the top. He was lucky to be alive.

Further up the column of Marines, the sound of an M249 Squad Assault Weapon started laying down suppressive fire, and the line began to advance directly towards the enemy in short bursts of movement. They were being assaulted from higher ground, and if they were going to turn this ambush around, they would need to take the top of this hill. Otherwise they were probably all dead.

That was *their* job. DJ's was to render medical attention. He looked around to locate the other fallen Marine. He spotted him partially concealed behind another large rock, but he saw an arm move. The man was still alive.

Without thinking, he leapt to his feet and sprinted towards the wounded man. Behind him, beyond the line of Marines working their way upwards, another loud pop and instantaneous whizzing noise. DJ recognized it now. RPG. Rocket Propelled Grenade. The weapon had a larger than life reputation on the battlefield. He had been shown how to fire one, should the need ever arise, but had never got the chance to squeeze the trigger on a live round. He had been told at the time he only needed to hear it fired his direction once to give him nightmares for the rest of his life.

They were right.

The rocket passed through the line of Marines and impacted somewhere close behind him. This time it was so close he could feel the outward rush of heated air as more shrapnel peppered the back of him. Most of it going into his large medical pack, but some drove their way into his legs and buttocks. It tipped him forward violently, causing him to lose his balance.

He held a fleeting thought of regret for not putting his helmet back on. Then, he was tumbling, end over end, cartwheeling down the steep hill. The sound of crunching bone in his right arm carried to his ears. Next, a sharp piercing pain in his forehead. It drove into him with a fierce intensity. It was the most focused pain he ever felt in his life. It made the pain from his now-shattered right arm seem like a skinned knee.

And then all went black.

Eighty-three days later he awoke from a coma, lying in a hospital bed with his arm in a sling, and the sight of the most beautiful woman in the world reading to him out loud from a cooking magazine. Her name was

Cassie according to the name badge on her blouse. And when she saw him stir, she looked at him with pulse-stopping green eyes.

Then she smiled, and she was all he could focus on.

"Where am I?" he asked, clumsily.

She flashed a knowing grin at him. "Oh, you know where you are."

He looked at her with a blank expression for a minute before replying. "I don't understand."

Tilting her head to one side, "Are you sure? Are you sure you have no idea where you are?"

"A hospital, but where? And what happened to the others?" He tried to push himself into a sitting position with his good arm, but his muscles where lethargic and weak.

Cassie stood up and walked over to him. Sitting down next to him on the bed, she placed a hand lovingly on his cheek. "Think about it, DJ. You know where you are, and you know everything that happened to those men on that hillside." The expression on her face was one of patience and understanding.

And deep love.

He did know, he realized. This was all a memory. But not a real memory. It was mixed with something else. It was somehow real, but not real. It was like his brain was painting the here and now with fragments of his past, combining the two into something else.

"I'm in Boston, aren't I? Someone fired an RPG at us. It exploded in the dining room to my right." He looked to his right as if he expected to see damage and destruction from the rocket. "But, the explosion was bigger than what an RPG normally is."

"Correct," she replied. "It struck the back wall. There is a gas line to feed the kitchen back there. The house is on fire right now, so we don't have long." She leaned over to kiss him on his forehead.

"But I don't understand. Why are you here? Why am I here"

"Because, silly, you're still kind of broken. Despite everything that's happened, despite meeting someone else to help you through the pain of your loss, there's still a piece of you that will always be broken." She seemed to think about it for a moment. "At least for a while longer. But not forever, though." She bent over again and kissed him on his nose, and then winked at him while still in close. "Broken people need a helping hand from time to time."

He was confused. He knew all of this was some sort of weird PTSD induced flashback brought on by the RPG narrowly missing them all. But he could not understand if he was conscious and had lost his mind, or if this was some bizarre dream. Maybe he really was lying in a hospital bed. Just not this one. Maybe he was suffering from some sort of psychosis.

"You're not crazy," she seemed to read his mind. "I'm here for two reasons. To get you back on your feet, and to tell you to stop feeling guilty about loving someone else."

Shame and the fear of betraying his dead wife flooded his thoughts. She was right. He did feel guilty.

Her smile vanished and she placed his face in both hands. "Stop that! Stop that right now! There is living, and there is death. And you will never truly get to live again if you don't stop thinking about the other."

"But I love you," DJ declared with a wavering voice.

"And you also love her. And there is nothing wrong with that. In fact, it's necessary for you to move past us and give yourself completely to her. Trust me. I approve. You're not betraying me. I promise."

"But…"

"I said, I approve. It's settled. So quit holding back. And while I'm at it, quit treating her like she's made out of glass. She's not. In fact, very few of us women are. Oh, and another thing. She knows precisely who you are, so you just go ahead and be yourself."

DJ was stunned at what was happening. In fact, he didn't understand *what* was happening. It was bizarre, and he was confused.

"Now." She stood up and moved over to the door on the far side of the room. "You have a job to do." She opened the door and stood to one side.

Through the open doorway of the hospital room, DJ should have been looking at a hallway. Instead, he was looking at Abbi laying on her back at the foot of the steps. The same steps of his row house in Beacon Hill. Instead of seeing the hallway outside of his room door, he was looking from this weird construction built of his bizarre psychosis, out onto the street in front of his home. It made no sense whatsoever.

He could tell Abbi was alive. He could see her chest rise and fall with her breathing, but she was unconscious. The smell of smoke and burning wood wafted in through the open doorway.

"Get out there and do your job, DJ. You're good at it. She needs you. And you need her. So, go do what you're good at."

He looked into Cassie's eyes. He was torn. He loved Abbi. He long ago stopped doubting those emotions. But here now was his dead wife, somehow having a conversation with him, and telling him she gave DJ her blessing to go have a new life and a new love. It tied his emotions into a complex knot of feelings.

"Don't worry," Cassie said. "We'll see each other again. I promise."

"But when?" he asked her.

"That all depends on you. Now get off of your lazy butt and go save her."

DJ turned his eyes to Abbi through the doorway, waiting for him to come rescue her. He tried to move, and he did actually manage to swing his feet onto the floor, but nothing was working right, and everything hurt. Cassie walked over and draped his good arm around her neck to help him stand. Once he was upright and facing the door, she stepped around behind him and placed the palms of her hand in his back.

"Go now!" she shouted, and shoved him hard. He staggered and stumbled his way forward, and he instinctively placed his hands out in front of him. When he did, he noticed his gun still in his right hand. His grimy, bloody hand. The cast and the sling were gone.

Then, he was through the doorway, tumbling on top of Abbi, and rolling onto his back next to her.

There, up on the roof above his head, a man was peering over the edge with a surprised look on his face and a rifle held at his side. Without a thought, DJ fired at him. Chunks of brick exploded along the rim of the roof, and the assailant stepped back out of view.

His muscles were moving quicker now, and he rolled over to pick up Abbi with as much speed as he could muster. Despite whatever PTSD breakdown was going on between his ears, he was firmly aware the safest place to be was on the other side of this building, away from rocket propelled grenades. The plan right now was to get her into the house, and then somehow through one of those small windows at the back of the living room.

Clearing the doorway with Abbi cradled in his arms, he could see Agent Cash dragging an unconscious Brett away from the dining room and into the living area. From his viewpoint at the entrance, he could see a massive hole in the back wall of the dining room. Cassie was right. The explosion tore open a gas line in the wall. The pipe was severed and spouting a jet of fire towards the ceiling. That wall and the ceiling above it were now fully engulfed in flames. Smoke rolled across the ceiling in every corner of the ground floor, and they didn't have long before this whole street was going to be on fire.

The Tactical Team were now all back on their feet and aiming out of the windows looking for targets, but they had stopped their firing. One of them seemed to have the same idea as DJ and was busy knocking one entire window loose from its frame, hammering away on it with the butt of his rifle.

DJ hurried his way to the back wall of the living space with Abbi. He wasn't sure exactly how she was injured as he had no time to examine her. He only knew she was still breathing and unconscious. But this was the second time in only hours she had been knocked out. That was a bad thing. At the very least, she had a concussion. At the worst, she could have bleeding on her brain. She would need medical attention beyond his skills if that were the case. First, however, they all needed to get out of here.

And then there was Brett to worry about.

"What's wrong with Brett?" DJ asked Agent Cash.

"You tell me. You're supposed to be the doctor," Cash snarled his answer. He was clearly angry. And it was understandable why. The man lost a fellow agent, he had been shot himself, and he was dragging his boss through a burning house after being fired on with an RPG. If it weren't for DJ, none of this would be happening.

"Look him over for blood. Tell me where you find it. The rest of you." DJ turned his attention to the others in the room. "One of you stand guard on the door. There could still be others out front waiting to come in. The others need to help with those windows. They're our only way out now. And if we don't get through them quickly, we're all going to be roasted alive."

DJ wasn't in charge. Cash was, now that Brett was out of commission, and they all knew it. But the instructions DJ gave made a lot of sense. As such, no one corrected him on their chain of command. They just moved to execute. They made short work of the window, and one of the black clad figures checked out the alley before jumping through.

"I've got no blood here," Agent Cash stated. He was down on one knee, bent over his boss looking for wounds.

"He was ten feet away from the concussion of the explosion," DJ pointed out. "He's probably fine. Just knocked out is all. We need to go."

On cue, three of the Tactical Team went through the windows. They cleared the alley quickly, and one of them stood watch, aiming down towards the opening, but kept glancing at the roof. The other two caught first Abbi, then Brett as they were lowered through the small windows. Everyone save Agent Cash and DJ filed through.

"We can't leave Agent Hall behind," declared Cash standing in the open window, as clouds of billowing smoke poured out into the alley.

DJ looked the man in the eye and considered it. The spark of anger he witnessed in the man only moments before was gone, replaced by careful calculated determination. He knew if he told the man how foolish it would be to go back after the dead agent, the man would simply turn around and disappear back into the flames and smoke. He focused back on the men waiting in the alley, and loading Abbi and Brett into the waiting car they had left there. "Don't wait for us. If we're not back in two minutes, you need to get them to safety."

One of the tactical agents, probably the lead one, started to balk at the suggestion they should leave, but DJ turned away with Agent Cash and headed back to the stairs. The way was clouded with thick, choking smoke and breathing was becoming a chore. The smoke bit into the lining of his lungs and sent alarm bells ringing in his head. There were precious seconds left to try and retrieve the body at the top of the stairs. After that, there would be too much smoke to breathe and they would both lose consciousness.

Flames were crawling along the ceiling near the opening to the dining room, and heat was moving in waves through house. Just before they wheeled around the banister to head up, DJ grabbed Cash's shoulder from behind and pointed to the ground. He dropped to his belly and found a thin area of breathable air down next to the floor. The agent followed suit.

"Three big breaths, and then hold. We go up and get him together." Cash nodded, they breathed in deep three times, then jumped to their feet and darted up the stairs. The wall next to them was radiating an intense heat all the way up, as it was likely on fire from the other side in the dining room. In fact, the overall heat was now becoming unbearable. DJ knew the fire, slowly radiating outward from the dining room, was about to rapidly expand. They only had one chance to get the fallen Agent.

Cash made the landing first and grabbed the man under his shoulders and lifted. DJ was right behind him and bent down to pull the body over his shoulders in the classic fireman's carry. Cash was wounded, after all. While DJ could feel a sticky, bloody mess on his side and was wounded too, he was still in the best shape to carry the man.

Down the stairs they went with Cash leading. The smoke was burning DJ's eyes, and his lungs were begging him to breathe because of the added exertion. But to do so now would be a death sentence. Downward he went, the heat off the wall next to him told DJ it was about to explode in flames. The fire was even now crawling its way across most of the ceiling in the living room. Smoke clouded his vision in a haze of thick, flickering orange fog, burning his eyes. Had he not been this way before, he might have gotten turned around and lost.

Finally, the window was in front of him. He could make out Cash crawling through, then vanishing into the alley beyond. DJ could risk nothing elegant for an exit. His lungs were now screaming at him. His vision was blurred from tears brought on by the heavy smoke.

He fell head first through the window with the dead man still draped over his shoulder. He expected to face plant into the pavement of the alley, but instead, strong arms caught him and the agent. They lowered him gently to the ground, and the breath held in DJ's lungs exploded outward, followed quickly by desperate gasps for air.

He lay there breathing deep, but with his vision still blurry from tears. Off in the distance, his ears could make out the sounds of sirens. The cavalry was finally arriving.

"Are we waiting for the police to arrive?" It was Abbi speaking from somewhere above him, though he still could not see her.

"No," he heard Brett reply with a groggy voice. "I don't trust this city or anyone in it now. You five, get the other car around the corner at the end of the alley. Head to the airport. Stop for nothing. We'll be right behind you."

Someone helped DJ to his feet and ushered him to the waiting car. With the sound of sirens approaching and his house on fire, whoever ambushed them was likely long gone, or rapidly scrambling away from the scene of the crime.

Someone shoved DJ into the waiting car as the sedan fired up. His vision was starting to clear. He could see Abbi already inside and waiting. She was looking pretty rough, though. He grabbed her head in both hands and pulled her close to look into her eyes. Sure enough, in the glow of the dome light, he could see her pupils were dilated. If she didn't have a concussion from hitting her head back at the bridge, she had one now. How bad, he was unsure.

They were all in need of medical attention, he realized. Agent Cash had a round pass through his upper shoulder. Brett and Abbi were probably both suffering from concussions. Abbi for sure. He had some shrapnel damage and burns on his side from where the spare mag in his coat pocket exploded. They could all use a trip to the ER, and he told Brett as much as they pulled onto the street and began to race away.

"We don't have that luxury!" snapped Brett. "We have to leave this city now."

"But if we wait for the cops to get here, won't we have added protection?" DJ asked.

"We just got shot at with a missile! How safe do you think we're going to be just because a few cops show up? Your friend wants you dead so bad, he hired an army to take you out just now. They managed to destroy a section of Beacon Hill trying to do it. No. We're getting back on that plane and heading to the only place I know for a fact we'll be safe."

"How come I don't like the sound of that?"

"Because you're smarter than I would like to give you credit for," Brett declared. "We're headed back to the Colorado Field Office. I am going to put you behind a high fence, armed guards, and all the guns I need in order to keep you both safe."

DJ's heart sank. He was hoping as soon as they managed to get Shark Bait, he and Abbi could slip away at the first available opportunity. Instead, he was headed to the one place that threatened his freedom the most. He trusted Brett, for sure. The man said he had a plan that might keep him out of jail. Maybe. And he was sure Brett would do his level best to keep his word. But hanging out with a bunch of FBI agents, especially after one of them just got killed, didn't seem like the smartest thing to do. He was trying to stay out of jail. Hiding in a building that might as well be a jail seemed a bit stupid.

DJ closed his eyes. He still needed to know why Brett left Abbi outside on the street to be a sitting duck, but a little still voice in the dark corner of his brain had said to trust the agent back on the stairs. There was an explanation to what happened. Now he was going into an FBI field office after one of their own was murdered. He would logically be a perfect scapegoat and recipient of any fallout over the man's death. But, that little still voice said to trust Brett.

He took in a deep breath and let it out slow. Fine. He would trust the man for now. But trust was not an easy thing to hang onto. Especially when self-preservation was at the top of the list of priorities.

As if Brett could read his mind, the agent turned to him from the front seat and flashed a smile like nothing bad had just happened. Like an agent hadn't been killed. Like another hadn't been shot. Like historic Beacon Hill wasn't on fire right now. "Trust me, DJ," Brett smiled. "I got you."

Chapter 13: Judas

Thomas made more than one call before leaving the old man's cabin. As soon as he was able to let the anger dissipate over his conversation with the Russian, he reached out to a contract broker in Boston. He was in no condition to go one on one with Slaughter again. Not to mention he didn't have time to stake out the man's home in Beacon Hill. He needed to board a private jet and get to France as soon as possible. If he did not meet his contract obligation with the Russians, then he had no doubt he would have the mother of all contracts placed on his own head. Besides, everything was in place. He just needed to be there as a backup contingency if the first plan somehow fell apart.

Which it wouldn't. Thomas spent over four months planning every last detail of the Paris mission. He just needed to get to a big enough runway, have the private jet meet him, and wing his way to France trapped inside the flying sardine can of death.

God, how he hated to fly. It wasn't the height. He could handle heights as long as he felt in control. It's when he felt he had no control that the thoughts of falling to his death seemed to overcome him. Whenever a plane hit turbulence, he would break out in cold sweats. If there was a way to travel the globe quickly without flying, he would do so. Flying was truthfully the only thing that really frightened him. There were plenty of things that made him cautious or concerned. But flying? Flying had him popping pills to help deal with the panic attacks that would ensue at the first sign of a bumpy flight.

While Thomas would love to hang around and deal with Slaughter, he was out of time. He needed to meet his contract obligations. Afterwards he could focus on a way to kill his employer. Sergei Romanoff knew too much about him. The man had leverage over him, and this could simply not be allowed to continue.

Slaughter must die, of course. He had been insulted by the man. But, he could not afford to spend any more time on him. Calling in some freelance mercenaries to kill the man with overwhelming force seemed the smartest way to get things back on track.

Negotiating a contract for a hit team to execute a strike in the heart of Boston was pretty easy. Most of the independent teams and groups on the East Coast worked out of Boston. How Boston ended up being a sort of home-base for mercenaries, Thomas had no clue. It had been the norm since well before he got into the killing business. It may have had something to do with the old mafias that used to control the city. Maybe it had something to do with the ports and number of private air strips in and around the area. For whatever the reason, if you needed mercenaries, Boston was the place to get them. No matter where you wanted them deployed. And the feds had always steered clear of them because the CIA would use them from time to time. They were given a wide berth so long as they didn't get caught red handed on anything local, or get any civilians killed.

After securing a team of them and feeding them a story on the parameters of the terms, Thomas picked a suitable airfield and arranged for the jet to meet him. Next, he cleansed the house of forensic evidence, gathered any related materials into the living room, doused the whole thing down with gasoline, and lit the place on fire. Finally, he loaded up in the old man's truck and wheeled his way east. After swapping out the plates, of course.

Then, somewhere after sunset as he was taxing down the runway, he decided to reach out to a high-level contact he had cultivated in the FBI. After all, they would obviously be working the Slaughter case. Maybe he could get some intel to pass on to the merc team setting up for Beacon Hill and Slaughter's pending arrival. As soon as the man on the other end of the phone said he didn't know anything, he knew the informant was lying through his teeth.

Thomas told him as much and reminded his informant about what could happen to the man's family for withholding information. Not to mention his squeaky clean political reputation if he didn't tell Thomas everything he wanted to know.

The informant begged and pleaded, then. Slaughter was being protected by agents. He simply could not put the lives of fellow agents at risk for Thomas's personal vendetta.

It was either those men he barely knew, or the lives of the man's children. His choice, Thomas explained. After a few minutes of hemming and hawing, the traitor came clean.

Slaughter was, even then, boarding onto a private jet himself with a small tactical team and a few other agents. They were headed to Beacon Hill as the informant spoke, in hopes of setting up an ambush for El Gran Blanco. Slaughter was supposed to be the cheese for the trap.

Thomas yelled at the man then. He explained in detail what would happen to him if he held back information from Thomas ever again. He hung up the phone and immediately called the Broker in Boston. He told the man on the other end plans had changed. The contract needed to be amended. But he didn't want to back out. He wanted it done tonight. Bring on as many other teams as required. He would pay the premium for such short notice, but he wanted to make sure the best hitters were assigned to the job. And, he promised the man a huge bonus if Thomas could read about the whole thing in all of the morning papers. Thomas didn't care about collateral damage either. And he wanted to be informed as soon as it was done.

Then, hours later, somewhere over the dark Atlantic Ocean, his phone rang. It was the broker in Boston, and the news was not good. The contracted teams were the best, Thomas was told. But, despite their willingness to not let collateral damage get in the way of fulfilling the contract, Beacon Hill was on fire and their mark had vanished into the smoke. They were seen fleeing away from the house. They were followed in order to see where they were going and maybe make another attempt, but they entered Logan International Airport through the private terminal entrance. It could only mean their target fled the city via the same private jet he had arrived in.

Thomas didn't say anything at the bad news. He just hung up the phone. Maybe he was finally returning to his old self where careful planning ruled his decision-making process. Or, where an adherence to the rules meant life, freedom, and the success of the mission. Or maybe it was the little purple pills he popped whenever flying anywhere that had robbed him of emotion. In either event, he did not throw something violently across the cabin in a fit of blind rage. Instead, he contemplated his choices.

First, he could drop the whole matter. He could forget Slaughter's offense at taking his name. He could go on about his business like nothing ever happened. He could move on. He could move forward.

No, he decided. Out of the question. It was too late for that now. If there was one thing Thomas learned from a life of crime, it was that criminals gossiped more than a bunch of old ladies at a hair salon. Word would get out about how Slaughter pretended to be him. They would learn the infamous El Gran Blanco tried to do something about it but failed. Then he just slunk away with his tail between his legs like a whipped dog.

That would be extraordinarily bad for business.

Second, he could put all of this on the back burner. He could fly to Paris as planned, kill a politician, making it look like Muslim terrorists did it like ordered, then track Slaughter back down again and do all of this slow and methodically. It was how a true professional should execute all of his schemes and plots.

No. Out of the question as well. The longer the idiot breathed, the greater chance word would get out and Thomas was back to the same issue as before. It would be bad for business if people learned of his failures. Besides, he would have to start plotting the demise of Sergei Romanoff as soon as possible.

Third, he could try to hire more people to take out Slaughter and continue on to Europe. Kill two birds with one stone.

Except he had just tried that and it didn't work. He was already out a lot of money because mercs always got fifty percent of the contract even if they failed at their job. After all, it was very dangerous work being a mercenary.

Additionally, some of the mercs he just hired got killed in the process. Quite a few of them. This meant if he tried to hire more to kill the same mark, the contract price would be at least double because of the perceived danger. Money wasn't really an issue. Thomas had it pouring out of his ears. Murder was a lucrative profession. But it would be stupid to just keep spending money without assured success.

Plus, again, word would get out he was spending a dump-truck load of cash to kill one man instead of just doing it himself. It would make him look weak. Again, a horrendous business move.

Fourth, he could roll the dice and just turn the plane around. Everything was in place for the Paris mission. He had planned it down to the smallest of detail. And not only was it in place, it was being executed as he sat here on this plane. It was going down whether he was in Paris or not. Being there in the city was an agreement he made with Sergei as a way to quell his fears of something going wrong. Nothing would. Thomas was sure of it. But since Sergei was paying top dollar for it to go off without a hitch, he was instructed to come up with a backup plan. So, he did. And, if it was required, Thomas would have to be there to make it happen.

What he must consider before following through on this plan, was the annoying fact Sergei Romanoff was somehow tracking him. And Thomas needed to figure out how. The Russians had known he was in Kentucky. From there, they knew he migrated to West Virginia. Someone could be assigned to follow him physically, but Thomas doubted it. He would have spotted a tail long ago. More than likely the Russian figured out who he was from when he accepted Sergei's first job offer. The Russian had someone tail him back then. Once Sergei knew what he looked like and maybe a few other details about him, he could have somehow spiked his phone and been tracking him electronically ever since. Someone would have only needed to get within ten feet of him with the correct software on a laptop to have been able to pull it off.

That had to be it. He changed identities so often there was no way he could have been tracked using the digital footprint of an alias. Every few days he was someone new.

The phone. It must be the phone.

If that were the case, and it was the only plausible solution he could think of, then he should be free and clear now. The phone was destroyed by water and laying underneath the river out behind the old man's cabin. Sergei Romanoff would have no idea Thomas turned the plane around and went back after Slaughter.

So, did he roll the dice? Did he chance it? The only way the Russian would find out he wasn't in Paris, was if his well-orchestrated plan failed in some way, and Thomas wasn't there to trigger the backup into happening. If that happened… Well, he had better hope he could kill the Russian before the Russian could find him.

Thomas managed to torture quite a few people over the years, but he had never been tortured himself. That would all change if the angry man, who had a lot riding on Thomas pulling off this mission, got his hands on him. And this little fact made Thomas ask the question out loud to himself.

"Roll the dice? Risk the wrath of Sergei Romanoff?" He was silent for a long while before he made his decision.

Finally, he lifted the cabin phone from its receiver again and hit the button to call the captain. "Turn the plane around," he told the voice on the other end. "We're headed back to the US. I'll have a new destination for you in a few minutes." He felt the plane bank to the left as it started its slow U-turn in the air.

Next, Thomas dialed a number from memory. He needed to know where Slaughter and his FBI friends were headed to. He prepared himself to put the fear of God into the man he was about to talk to. Correction. Not the fear of God. After all, El Gran Blanco was far deadlier than a mythical being.

He might have served a lifetime in the FBI, but he was never under more stress than he was right now. And that was saying a lot considering the countless cases he had worked over the span of nearly thirty years. Beads of sweat decorated his receding hairline, and he felt sick to his stomach. Even though he already threw up once. For the first time in a long time, he had no idea about what to do with the problem he now faced.

As it stood right now, he imagined this is what Judas must have felt like after betraying Jesus with a kiss. That man hung himself from a tree over his guilt. Would this become his own fate too?

He sat alone in a regal, wood adorned hotel suite sipping aged scotch from the expensive mini-bar. It was rare for him to touch the stuff, but he needed something to take the edge off and help him deal with his situation. As he sat there, he reached for the tumbler one more time. His shaking hands caused the ice to make a tinkling sound. It was a happy sound normally associated with good times, especially to those not aware of what was going on in the secret side of his life. If any outsider were to see him drinking, they would think him celebrating what was happening a few miles across town. The truth was, he was drinking as a way to deal with his overwhelming guilt and shame.

His wife and children should be here waiting with him for the official good news, but he had requested privacy at this time. He told them it was so he could truly focus on the magnitude of the honor that was about to be laid at his feet. The truth was, he could not bear to look them in the eye and feign happiness while the weight of his traitorous act bore down on his conscience.

But what choice did he really have?

He spent a lifetime dedicated to fighting criminals and putting thugs and bullies behind bars. Nearly three decades of his existence was spent defending the underdog and the little guy. He stood up to corporate monstrosities who thought themselves above the law, all the way down to the local gang leaders who sought to prey on the helpless.

They were all the same, he knew. The only thing that ever changed was how well they dressed and where they held their meetings. Faded jeans or silk suits, they were the same. Conducting their dealings in the shadows of slums, or the well-lit boardrooms of high-rise glass monuments to power, they were the same. His life had been committed to taking them all down. They were the scum of the earth.

But now... *Now what was he?* He had now joined the ranks of the same criminal swine he had worked so hard at putting behind bars.

He began this journey so long ago, travelling down this pathway of his own failed humanity. It was done for noble reasons with his back to the wall. It started out as nothing more than a simple effort to save his family.

El Gran Blanco had singled him out because he was running a division for the FBI out of DC. His men had several investigations going at any one time, but one of them was focused solely on taking down the notorious assassin. That is when he got a package addressed to him at his office with no return address listed. Inside were photos. All of them pictures of his wife and children.

There were photos of his kids at school, playing on the playground. One of them even showed his oldest son, ten at the time, eating lunch in the school cafeteria. Meaning it had to be taken within the school. There were plenty of his wife running errands at the supermarket, or through the window of the kitchen preparing meals. One of them even showed them making love in a hotel room while they had been on vacation over six months ago.

Whoever had been following them all, had been doing it for some time. They obviously knew everything about he and his family. A simple typewritten note inside instructed him to remain silent or suffer the consequences. The sender said he would know if he told anybody. Witness protection would be no protection at all, he was promised. A smaller envelope inside contained crime scene photos. They were from the US Marshal's database of murdered informants who had been admitted to the Witness Protection program, proving the mysterious stranger's point. Whoever it was had resources inside the US Marshals. And that was a scary concept. The sender of the package promised to be in contact soon.

A few days later, he got a call across his private cell number for work. A number he never shared with anyone outside of his wife. It was El Gran Blanco, the voice on the other end told him. All he had to do to avoid the death of his family was simply feed information about the open case to him whenever the assassin called. After all, why should he care who El Gran Blanco murdered? They were always criminals themselves of some sort. On top of that, the man might need information on certain people the FBI would have the resources to find out about. Again, always criminals, so why should he care?

It had been an easy choice to make. Until now.

Earlier tonight, a different set of demands came his way. The man wanted to know if he knew anything about the DJ Slaughter investigation currently kicked into high gear after the attack on the fugitive and his loved ones in Kentucky. He told the assassin, no. The man on the other end instantly knew the response for a lie.

The assassin screamed at him for withholding information. He vowed to make him pay. The crazed man wanted him to choose a child to be sacrificed for his penance. He begged and pleaded with the killer for forgiveness. He explained how DJ was in the protective custody of agents, and how he just did not want to be responsible for the accidental death of good men only doing their jobs. He also explained how one of them was the new head of the Denver Field Office, and how killing that particular person would result in a manhunt for the assassin the likes he had never had to deal with.

The man was enraged beyond caring. He wanted all the information on where they were going and why. He did, however, promise to 'do his best' to not kill any agents. He backed off his vow to slay a child as payment for his transgression, but the assassin claimed he would not be so forgiving in the future.

Then, the unthinkable. He had gotten a call from SAC Brett Foster. There had been an attack. The man had been injured in an explosion and probably had a concussion as a result. Beacon Hill was on fire when he left and the man was unsure of how much had burned before the fire department arrived to start doing battle with the blaze. He also had no idea at this point if any innocent bystanders suffered in the attack. And, to make matters much worse, an agent had been killed and another shot in the shoulder. He asked their names, but Brett had avoided answering.

Brett informed him they were headed back home because it was the only place he felt for sure he could keep Slaughter and his girlfriend safe. He did not trust the city of Boston. They were attacked by obvious mercenaries, Brett explained. And as everyone in the FBI was aware, Boston was a central location for hiring those groups. Brett was concerned they wouldn't be safe anywhere close to the East Coast.

When he hung up with Brett, he walked to the bathroom of the posh DC hotel he was staying at, and threw up. Then, he pulled himself together, if only for a moment. Walking out of the bathroom with a painted smile on his face, he told his family gathered in the living-room of the high dollar suite, awaiting the late-night news sure to come from across town any minute, that he needed some privacy. He would like to consider the position and title about to be bestowed on him in quiet reflection. They were stunned, of course, but it was the only lie he could come up with.

He went down to the desk and asked them if there was an unused suite he could borrow for a few hours. He needed to be alone while he awaited the news. The manager, knowing now who he was, was only too happy to oblige.

Now, here he sat, looking out of a DC window at the Capital building, lit up and glowing through the branches of bare elms, drinking expensive scotch with trembling hands. How could his life exist in such an insane duality?

On one hand, he was about to receive incredible news and have a once in a lifetime honor bestowed upon him. His family was all gathered together to celebrate his good fortune. One he earned for a lifetime of dedicated service.

On the other hand, he was a secret traitor to his country. He had now betrayed not only every citizen of the United States, but his family, the oath of his office, not to mention...

His cell phone rang, and he spilled his drink trying to pull the thing from his breast pocket. "Hello?" he stammered.

"Please stand by for the President of the United States," a lady said on the other end.

A moment later the familiar voice of the man he had come to know over the past few weeks greeted him. "I wanted to be the first to congratulate you. Outside of your family, that is. I'm sure you were watching the news a second ago as the vote concluded. Sorry it was such a late-night affair, but you know how politics is."

He faked a laugh in response and tried to put as much confidence into his voice as he could muster. "Yes, sir, I do. So, what's next?"

"There will be an official swearing in a couple of days. I'm making it a big deal. Thinking we fly in every available agent we can and present you to them properly. The media, love cameras, the works. I'll say a few words, and then how about you give a short speech as well. I am sure you already have prepared remarks?"

"Yes, Mr. President."

"I don't want you to take any questions right now, the news media will want to use the opportunity to turn this into something political after I fired the last one. They've already been going on and on about how a civilian should be sitting in the position for accountability to the people, and I don't want you caught up in that narrative just yet. Anyway, I'll have someone call your staff with details. Now go celebrate with your family. You've earned it."

"Yes, sir. I will."

The line went dead, and a knock came at the door a split second later. Who in the world could know where he was, other than the hotel manager? He made his way to the door with his stomach tied into knots. He opened it to find his wife. She had a huge smile on her face and an oblong box wrapped in red shiny paper and tied with a blue bow.

"You really didn't think I wouldn't find you, did you? The night manager tipped me off," she said demurely. She handed him the box and placed a hand on his chest, shoving him backwards into the room.

"I just needed a moment to think. It's a bit overwhelming all of the sudden," he replied sheepishly.

"Well, how about you open that gift, then I take your mind off of all of this for a few minutes." She started unbuttoning her blouse as the door swung closed behind her. "After all, we have a hotel room all to ourselves. I'm sure we can find good use for it."

He faked a grin and started unwrapping the small box. Inside was an ornate wood and glass desk name-plate announcing his new title and his name. "FBI Director Timothy Neville."

His stomach suddenly rolled again, and he found himself sprinting for the bathroom door. A second later and he was hurling violently into the toilet once more. His shocked wife was right behind him, first rubbing his back, then wetting a washcloth as he hung over the bowl for a minute.

After letting the nausea subside, he finally looked up into her concerned eyes as she stood over him. He simply shrugged at her. "I told you, I feel like the weight of the world is on my shoulders," he said, half being truthful.

Before his wife had a chance to respond, the phone rang once more. He fished it out of his pocket again while still down on his knees. The caller ID told him the number was blocked, and he felt a moment of sickness wash over him again. He knew who was on the other end. He silently debated with himself over whether he should answer or not. But the consequences of not talking to the assassin were too great. He looked up into the eyes of his wife again. Yes. Definitely too great.

He swiped the virtual button on the phone's surface and answered. "Hello?"

"Congratulations on your new promotion," El Gran Blanco stated. "I do have to say, I never imagined I would have the director of the FBI working for me. So, this is quite an accomplishment for the both of us."

Tim looked up at his wife and smiled. "Thanks so much for that. It's quite an honor." He silently prayed his wife wouldn't ask who it was. He was all tapped out in lying to people for the moment. She would read right through him.

"Now I have some more questions for you," the man began.

"Can you hang on one second, sir? My wife is in the room. I need to go someplace more secure." He put the phone down and covered the mic with his hand, looking at his wife expectantly.

His wife lifted both hands, palms out, and whispered quietly, "Say no more. But get yourself upstairs soon. We have celebrating to do."

Tim waited until he heard the door close before talking into the phone. "I can't give you anything else," he started.

"Oh yes you can," the assassin interrupted. "And you will. Or your new job will suffer the shortest tenure of a director ever. It'll be the biggest scandal to hit Washington since Watergate. I will make sure every news outlet in the city knows everything you've been doing for me for the last twenty years. After all, every single conversation we have had has been recorded for just such an occasion as this. Can you imagine how damaging this will be to the new president? He'll be the laughing stock of Washington.

"And you'll go to the same prisons you have been responsible for putting so many people in. Eventually, they will kill you. But not before I start picking off your family members one by one. Your friends, too. Everyone you know, for that matter. If I think you care for them at all, I will torture them and kill them for the world to see.

"So yes, FBI Director Tim Neville, you will tell me precisely what I want to know with no reservation whatsoever. And you will do so now."

"But you don't understand," Tim pleaded. "My best friend in the whole world is on that plane with Slaughter. He saved my life. I can't do this to him. He has a wife." He was feeling sick again.

"Oh well," the assassin proclaimed with sarcasm. "You can make a new friend. Who knows, maybe he won't be around when I kill this Slaughter guy. We can always hope, right?"

Tim was going to do it, he knew. He would sacrifice his friend for the sake of his family. And with this new understanding now lodged in the pit of his soul, he promptly dropped the phone to the ground and started dry heaving into the toilet all over again.

From the phone's little speaker, he could clearly make out the sound of laughter coming from the man. Yes, Tim thought to himself hanging over the porcelain bowl. This must be exactly what Judas felt like at the end.

Chapter 14: Opposites Attract

DJ was worried about Brett. Things weren't going so well for him, and he selfishly couldn't help but wonder what it meant for him and Abbi. Since arriving at the Denver Field Office, he had only seen the man twice. But both times revealed a red-eyed man with a few more worry lines above his cheek bones. DJ imagined he must be dealing with the loss of the agent under his command, which was surely a tremendous load for any leader to carry. Plus, he must be under serious criticism and scrutiny from those over him for everything that happened over the last twenty-four hours.

On entering the FBI compound around seven in the morning, he and Abbi were shown to a hotel room of sorts. Brett explained they were used for housing witnesses or visiting dignitaries from time to time. It should not have alarmed DJ at all. It should have made him feel safer, considering there was a man out there willing to do anything to kill him. Except, there was an armed guard stationed outside his door. And DJ had the feeling the man wasn't there to keep the bad guys away. He was there to make sure DJ and Abbi didn't vanish into the night. To quote his old Chief in the Navy, it made DJ feel like a long-tailed cat in a room full of rocking chairs.

When he confronted Brett over it, he was told he wasn't under arrest, but he was definitely being detained as per protocol. But don't worry, Brett assured him. He had a plan. Problem was, the man refused to reveal just yet what those plans were. And being in the middle of an FBI compound, while still sitting on the same institution's current most wanted list, was doing nothing for DJ's nerves.

Abbi didn't seem worried at all, and was quite content to trust Brett blindly. DJ wasn't so sure, and he immediately began plotting their escape should the need arise. If he had to, it wasn't going to be too hard. The room only had one entrance and no windows. But, he managed to get a look at the facility from a satellite view on his phone before they arrived. And it was a good thing, too. There was no cell service in the room.

On the western end of the property, over a short wall topped with a row of pointy bars, was one of those big-box department stores in a large shopping center. Seemed like a weird location for an FBI field office, but

DJ thought it might be the easiest place to lose pursuit if it came down to it.

Their FBI hosts did not bother to search them, or relieve him of his backpack for some reason. He was sure Brett was trying to make them feel free for as long as possible. Until, of course, the man was left with no other choice and the shackles were snapped into place.

DJ was thankful for still having the pack. Buried inside was cash, and another set of IDs and credit cards. Not to mention his trusty Sig Sauer P320 and suppressor. If needed, he could grab the bag, and he and Abbi could go over the wall and escape this place. He was pretty sure they could both incapacitate the lone agent standing outside his door. It would be a straight shot to the back of the compound after that. But now was not the time to bail on Brett. Not just yet. He would give the man a chance to work on his own plan. If it was one thing DJ understood about Brett Foster, the guy was pretty smart. Nor had the man ever lied to him.

But would he? Especially if Brett felt it necessary to achieve his own goals? DJ wasn't so sure. He wanted to trust Brett, but his own paranoia was getting in the way.

There was an inhouse doctor waiting for them when they arrived. Aside from some bumps, bruises, and a few required bandages, they were examined and pronounced healthy. Agent Cash was ushered off to a hospital somewhere, and Brett said it was likely they would not ever see him again.

The next time Brett showed up, he had clean shirts for the both of them he scrounged from around the office. He also carried a brown bag full of burgers and fries for lunch. He even brought along a lightweight jacket for DJ since he had lost his own back in Boston. Brett still had not come up with a solid plan for them for the time being, other than sitting cooped up in this make-shift hotel room. But don't worry, he reassured once more. It would all come together soon.

Well, at least they had managed to catch up on some much-needed rest, DJ thought to himself. It had been sorely needed by the time they arrived here. Brett, on the other hand, was still looking ragged and worn, and DJ felt sorry for him.

They were uninterrupted until around 6 p.m. when a knock came on their door. Standing next to the man on guard duty was Agent Cash, his arm in a sling. DJ was surprised to see him and said as much when he opened the door.

"I'm not really supposed to be here," Cash told him. "Brett told me he didn't want to see my face for at least thirty days. I told him there were few people he could trust. Besides, this is just a flesh wound. The bullet missed anything important."

"Any chance we can get out of here and maybe stretch our legs?" DJ asked. "We've been cooped up in here so long, I was about to knock a hole in that back wall just to see the sky."

"That's why I'm here. Brett wants to see you." He looked over DJ's shoulder to address Abbi standing behind him, shivering in the wind whipping into the room. "You too. He wanted to tell you both what's going on. But, we can take the long way to let you stretch your legs. I'll give you a tour of the place along the way. Plus, he ordered Chinese take-out. Hope that's OK."

DJ and Abbi went back for their jackets. The guest quarters sat in a separate building and the room doors faced an outside covered walkway. Standing there with Cash in the open doorway a moment ago with snow flurries spinning in the air and a chill wind tossing his hair around, made DJ wish for a heavier jacket than the one Brett gave him.

He paused when he saw his pack sitting next to the lightweight coat on the bed. Inside that pack was everything he needed for him and Abbi to make an escape. The longer he stayed here, the more convinced he was going to need to slip away before he was officially handcuffed and charged. If he slung it over his shoulder right now, however, Cash would likely be tipped off to his planned escape.

He sighed and followed Abbi out the door, pulling the jacket on as he did. True to his word, instead of leading them all back to the main building, Cash turned right to head towards the back of the compound. Before getting out of earshot of their guard still standing by the door, Cash told him to go find some coffee. They would be back in about thirty minutes.

Running parallel to the hotel-like suites, of which there appeared to be about five, was a three-level parking garage for all of the agents and staff. The top level looked to be covered as well. Either to keep the snow off the heads of everybody required to park on the roof, or to help prevent prying eyes from looking in via drone or satellite. DJ was unsure which, and didn't bother to ask Cash.

At the end of the building and the parking garage was more open parking lot ending in fence. On the other side of the fence was the back wall of the department store DJ spotted on his snooping before arrival. The lot they were standing in was empty of any cars, and this prompted to him to look closer at the garage. It was largely devoid of vehicles as well.

"I know it's a weekend, but shouldn't there be more people?" DJ asked.

"We're on a skeleton crew right now. The senate vote on the president's pick for our new FBI director was early this morning. Like 2:30 a.m. or something. Along with a bunch of measures and laws. Anyway, the president wanted to show him off to as many rank and file FBI as possible. It's a way of saying we are going to start getting back to the business of enforcing the law, instead of cherry picking who to prosecute due to politics. At least that's the message he is trying to get out there. He's a politician himself and who knows if he really means it or not. Most cases were shoved onto a back burner. Ninety percent of every office is flying off to DC to some Air Force base for the speech tomorrow. It's going to be quite the media spectacle."

"Seems like a bit much," DJ commented.

"Well, usually presidents appoint someone that's never been an actual agent. In fact, I can only recall one of them who came up through the ranks as a regular agent in the last thirty or forty years. They almost always appoint directors from outside the agency. They're attorneys, litigators for the DOJ, and predominantly politicians in some way. So, it's pretty rare. At least in the modern era."

"Who is it?" DJ asked.

Agent Cash came to a direct halt, causing DJ and Abbi to pass him up before realizing the man stopped. "You're kidding me?" Agent Cash asked, staring at DJ with incredulity.

"Sorry, but I seldom watch the news. Should I know who it is?"

"It's Brett's old boss. The same man who helped you both by supporting you guys with a handful of loyal agents during the Big Chuck ordeal. One of them being me. Our new director is former SAC of the Dallas Field Office, Timothy Neville."

"Oh," replied DJ. "I hadn't heard."

"Yeah, well you owe him a lot. In fact, if Brett is able to keep the both of you from spending the rest of your lives in prison, it will be because of that man. And now…. Now he has more power than ever. But if he uses that power to help you out… *again*… it will come at substantial risk to himself and Brett."

Agent Cash stepped forward and put his finger in the middle of DJ's chest, seemingly unaffected by how he was several inches shorter than the man he was confronting. DJ didn't move, but just looked down at him. "Both of those men have stuck their neck out for you," Cash said with an edge to his voice. "On more than one occasion. And they both mean something to me. So, understand I am dead serious when I tell you this. I know you have a gun in that rucksack of yours. I know you probably have cash and another identity for the both you to disappear on. But if you try to vanish on Brett now, after everything that's happened, and after everything he and my... my former boss have risked for you, I will hunt you down and shoot you myself. Even if staying around means you go to prison for the rest of your life. Don't you destroy those two men's careers after everything they've done for you. You owe them both."

There was a long pause as both men stared into each other's eyes. Tension was building between the two. DJ could feel it. There was about to be an altercation. DJ was not sure anything could stop it from happening. Brett was his friend, but friendship only went so far in a situation like this. He could end all of this right now, DJ knew. He could knock Agent Cash out, grab their gear out of the unguarded room behind them, and be over the wall before anyone knew it. He should do it. He should do it now.

But just then, Abbi intervened. She did so as only a woman could. She stepped forward, and reached up with both hands to place her palms on the agent's cheeks. There was a tenderness in her eyes, and a sincerity neither men could dismiss for acting. DJ watched as Abbi and Cash's eyes locked in the midst of swirling snow. The soft simple flurries had transitioned to puffs of white floating cotton.

Lit by the glow of the parking lot lights, she spoke to the man. "Brett means something to me, too," she told Agent Cash. "I promise you that. And you mean something to me as well. What you did back there for us, for your fellow agent who lost his life, I cannot tell you how special that makes you. You have my word, Special Agent Cash. Even if it means a lifetime of prison, we will not violate that trust."

DJ looked on with wonder and a growing love for this woman. She was truly something else, and he could not believe how blessed he was to have her in his life. She made it worth living. But it was more than that. Her presence challenged him to be a better man.

A second before, as he had been restraining himself to keep from punching the man in the nose, he was planning their escape. It didn't matter if Brett lost his job or not. DJ was not willing to go to prison for doing nothing more than taking out the proverbial trash. The people he killed up till now had been some of the most evil and despicable low-lives on the planet. They were murderers who would have kept on murdering if he had not ended them. There was not one ounce of remorse or regret in him, and DJ would not spend a lifetime behind bars for it even if it meant

Brett losing his career. Brett would bounce back. He would recover. DJ and Abbi would not. Life in prison was exactly that. Life. In prison.

But now, after seeing the woman he loved do what she did, and hear what she said, his own bent moral compass got its needle straightened back out. She was right, and he knew it. So, he was with her in this decision. No matter the cost. Honor meant something. But more often than not, it required a price in sacrifice.

"But I now have to know," Abbi asked the agent. "That Neville guy… He's more to you than just your old boss, isn't he?"

Cash looked at her for a moment as is if debating how to respond. Finally, he spoke only one word. "Yes," he said. Then, he stepped around them both and continued on as if he wasn't concerned if they would follow.

DJ and Abbi looked at one another, and then back to Agent Cash as he walked away. Abbi's look of surprise turned into one of stubbornness, and she squinted after the agent. DJ had seen the look before and knew what was coming.

She charged after the man and grabbed his arm, pulling him around to look at her again. "You really don't think you're getting away with that answer, do you?"

"I think you've stretched your legs enough," he replied. Agent Cash's face had gone back to an emotionless rock of granite. "We need to go."

"We will. But only after you tell me just why this Neville guy is so important to you." Abbi's back was straight and her hands were now folded into fists and planted on her hips.

Yep, DJ thought, *she's about to get her way*.

The short, blonde agent did an about-face and walked again, leaving Abbi and DJ standing there once more. Calling over his shoulder, the agent said, "We're going to be late."

Abbi was now standing a pace or two ahead of DJ, but he didn't move. He chose instead to watch and see how all of this played out. The last thing he was going to do was get in her way when she had her mind made up on a direction.

Abbi hated secrets. With a passion. If she caught a hint of one, she would worry over it and mess with it until she broke it apart to learn what was inside. Her curiosity would allow for nothing less than a total surrender of the truth.

Besides, now DJ was curious too.

Abbi watched him walk away from them for a full three seconds more before responding. "FBI Director Timothy Neville is your father, isn't he?" Abbi blurted out, hands still on her hips.

Agent Cash lurched to a halt, unmoving. He just stood there frozen like a statue in the snow. Then, he wheeled about again and marched straight up to her. DJ wasn't worried for her in the least. In fact, he found it comical. Besides, she could probably tie him up in a pretzel before the unsuspecting agent knew what hit him.

"Now you listen to me carefully," the young man began. "You say one word of that to anyone and so help me I will shoot you in the knee." The agent was only a little bit taller than Abbi, so both were looking at each other eye-to-eye. One of them was glaring his best menacing agent-stare. The other was smiling broadly and practically bouncing in place with joy, like she had just unwrapped a present.

Abbi dove forward and wrapped the man up in an embrace. The man's eyes went wide in complete surprise and shock, and his mouth hung open a bit. He looked directly at DJ with an expression DJ could only smile at.

Hugging him tightly Abbi said, "Oh, it's going to be ok, Agent Cash. Promise. Your secret's safe with me." She let go, then turned him about and shoved her arm into his, walking him back the direction they were supposed to go. "I never tell any secrets. Well most of the time. OK, to be perfectly honest I almost never keep a secret. I don't think a Christmas has gone by that I didn't tell everyone I knew, exactly what they were getting ahead of time. But, I don't think I have ever had a secret this big to keep. I am almost sure I can keep this one. Besides, it's not like I know a lot of agents to blab to. Other than Brett, of course. Oh! Brett! He knows too, doesn't he? Well, of course he does. He would have to know. I bet *he* can keep a secret, being in the FBI and all. I bet he has some really big secrets locked up in that head. Anyways, I promise I won't tell yours. No crossed fingers or nothin'. Lips are sealed. But, I have to admit, that is a *huge* secret. It's going to be, like, trying to crawl its way out of me every time a see another agent dude. I mean, seriously, how have you not told anyone yourself?"

Abbi and an overwhelmed Agent Cash just kept walking away. Abbi was babbling away like teenaged girl walking down a high school hallway, and Cash was in shocked silence. He was obviously dumbfounded over what was happening. *I'll bet*, DJ thought to himself, *they never train you for encountering an Abbi Jackson at Quantico.*

He watched them walk away for a second or two more, snow swirling and becoming thicker, a smile stretching across his face. God, how he loved that girl. Here, surrounded by uncertainty and the chaos of recent events, when worry and gloom should be dominating the moment, Abbi had somehow managed to paint in a rainbow of joy in the midst of the storm that threatened them.

With the love for Abbi reaching a crescendo of sorts inside of him, he reached down to pat the small ring he planned to give to her buried deep in his right front pocket. While he had changed his shirt and taken a shower, he still only had the pair of jeans he had been wearing since yesterday morning. It should still be safe and sound in the bottom of his pocket.

But it wasn't. It was missing.

And just like that, the smile ran away from his face. It was gone.

There was nothing there but the small penknife he always kept with him. In the space between heartbeats, the peace and joy Abbi gave him only seconds ago, like a present wrapped in shiny paper, vanished away in the wind. He must have reached into his pocket at some point, and when he brought his hand back out, it came out as well and tumbled away. That loss came as a physical blow.

It wasn't the money he spent purchasing it that caused sudden sadness to prick his heart. It wasn't the hours agonizing over the right style that made him feel tragically empty all at once. It was everything that little reflective rock on that thin band of gold represented to him. Its disappearance symbolized everything that had gone wrong in his life. It seemed he could find joy one minute, only to have it ripped from his grasp like a bully stealing a kid's ice cream cone the next.

It was just a ring, he knew. He would easily buy another when this was all over. He closed his eyes and turned his face to the heavens, trying to send the negative emotions away from him.

Wet snow collided with his face, stinging him with freezing condemnation. *You're to blame for all of this*, the darker part of him declared. *This is all your fault, and you don't deserve happiness.*

NO! He screamed at the negative side of him to shut his hole. He did nothing wrong! Shark Bait was responsible, he told himself. That man was turning into an annoying fly buzzing around his brain, frustrating the very thoughts of his own mind. No matter how many times he would swat at it, the thing wouldn't die or go away. It seemed to exist only to drive him crazy.

DJ dropped his gaze to his feet, drew in a deep breath, and sighed. He shook his head to try and focus. It was so hard to try and stay positive when there was so much negativity swirling around him.

Positives and negatives attract, he thought to himself. It seemed that for DJ, if something good was happening, you could bet that something bad was headed his way. It would suck itself to him in a weird polarity attraction of good luring in evil.

Frustrated, he set off at a trot to catch up.

Chapter 15: Ethereal Wisps of Smoke

As soon as DJ was shown into Brett's office, his blood pressure was sent spiking through the roof. Brett was there as promised, and he had Chinese takeout arranged on a nearby conference table. But there were also two large private security officers, hired to handle guard duty and regulate access to the building, standing to one side of the room. One had his hand resting on his weapon. The other was holding a taser gun in his hand.

Additionally, all the gear and clothing DJ and Abbi left in their room now sat in a chair in front of Brett's desk. Including DJ's cherished backpack. He knew the pistol once hidden inside was no longer there, however. He could see it in the center of Brett's desk.

It was obvious in an instant as to how his bag and gun ended up in Brett's office ahead of their arrival. Agent Cash had not been offering to let them stretch their legs as he claimed. He was lengthening the amount of time it would take to get to the office so someone could go behind and confiscate their belongings. Agent Cash had been distracting them. And there could only be one reason.

They were about to be arrested.

DJ felt betrayed and was suddenly furious. A quick glance at Abbi showed she wasn't too happy either. They both came to a halt just past the entrance, and DJ quickly analyzed the best way out of here. Behind him offered the most expedient escape route as only Agent Cash stood back there blocking the way with his arm in a sling. DJ felt he could mow over the smaller agent with no issues, but they would have to be quick. If they weren't, the guard with the taser gun already out would shoot him from across the room. If those prongs went into DJ, any fight he had would be stolen from him in an instant.

The real question was, what would Abbi do? She would certainly back his play. But, any move he made right now must be considered with what her move would be. Their actions might conflict with one another. Or worse, they could cause her to be harmed. The wheels in his head were spinning trying to come up with a plan. And he'd better do something now.

Sensing DJ's intentions, Agent Cash spoke up behind him. "DJ, you better look behind you before you do anything stupid." DJ and Abbi both turned around slowly as suggested. His heart sank at what he saw. Four more guards had appeared out of nowhere in the long hallway, and snuck up behind them. He never heard a thing. They must have been hiding in a nearby office waiting for them to pass. All four held taser guns at the ready.

It was over and he knew it. He turned back to face Brett. The man had both hands up and his palms out, the universal signal for: Hang on just a second. But DJ was having none of it.

"This?" DJ began, sweeping his hand to gesture at all the muscle waiting for him. "This is how you tell me you're placing me under arrest? I thought we were friends, Brett. What happened to your stupid little plan? What happened to you telling me to trust you? Is this how you get your man? You just act like their friend and then stab them in the back?"

"All of this," Brett began. "All of it was to give you no choice but to listen to what I had to say. If I started telling you what was about to happen without this contingency in place... Well, let's just say I have a healthy respect of what you are capable of. Now I need you to hear me out. I am still telling you to trust me. I think I've proven you can."

For a moment, no one moved. Everyone was waiting to see what DJ would do, and he was trying to decide exactly what that was.

In the end, it was Abbi who made the first move. "I gave my word, Brett." She turned around then to look Agent Cash in the eye. "And no matter how bad I want to kick Agent Cash here in his little man parts, I will keep my word." Casting a sidelong look at DJ, she added, "And so will he. Isn't that right sweetheart?"

DJ looked back at her and shrugged his shoulders. "You're not the boss of me. Truth is, I haven't made up my mind yet." He ignored the glare from Abbi and turned back to Brett.

"Hear me out," Brett asked. "I really do have a plan. But... it will require patience and trust."

"I'm listening," DJ said flatly.

"Then come in and sit down."

DJ stepped over to stand across the desk from Brett. "I'll sit down when you have all of your trained monkeys put their cattle prods away and leave the room."

Brett sighed and stared at DJ for a second or two more. The bleary-eyed and worn look was back. DJ could tell the man was being crushed by too little sleep, an abundance of guilt over what happened in Boston, and just all the pressure of the situation. But he didn't care. He was mad. If Brett wanted him to relax, he would have to back off with his goons.

"Fine," Brett replied. "Cash, you stay. The rest of you, outside." The hired security all seemed disappointed they weren't going to get to shoot DJ with about fifty thousand volts of electricity.

Well, this wasn't over yet, DJ thought. The night is still young. They would probably still get their chance.

The room cleared and Cash closed the door. Brett pointed at the table. "So, are you two hungry? Can we sit down and discuss this over a meal?"

DJ didn't move, and considered whether he wanted to sit down and eat with the man who was now all but promising to put him behind bars.

Brett reached down and picked up the Sig Sauer on his desk. He looked at it thoughtfully, then tossed it over to DJ. The move surprised DJ, and as it arched through the air, he began to process this new development by trying to decide who he would shoot in the knee first. Brett, or Cash at the door behind him? But it was the scolding look he caught from Abbi as soon the gun touched his palm that kept him from cycling the slide backwards and racking a round into place.

Brett's voice cut through the office with a sharp edge. Gone were the placid tones attempting to persuade DJ. Here was a stony commitment to how things were going to be. "The truth is," Brett said. "I could have just had Cash taser you when you opened your room door. We could have cuffed you without a fight and drug the both of you down to the holding cells in the basement. But I chose to treat you with more respect than that. You saved my life this past summer. You pulled a bullet out of my gut on a kitchen table for crying out loud. You did everything you could to free my wife, and you made the hard choice to go after Big Chuck by yourself to keep us all safe. I am one hundred percent on your side, you big idiot! But if you can't see that, then just do what you're good at. Just shoot your way out of this room without any consideration of the wreckage you'll leave behind. But know as soon as you do, you and I are done. You will have officially drawn the lines. And I promise you, you better kill me when you point that gun at me, because I'll be trying to do the same to you the next time we meet."

DJ was torn. Emotions churned inside him with blender-like fury. He was angry at Shark Bait for bringing him to this point, hurt because of a sense of betrayal by Brett, guilty over his desire to punch the same man in the mouth, sadness over putting Abbi through all of this, and there was even a sense of desperation at facing prison. Yet, here the man was, telling him to ignore all of those emotions and fears and to just blindly trust him. He was being told to allow handcuffs to be placed on his wrists, and lead willingly away to a cell somewhere.

But truthfully, how could he not? The man let him go once before. He'd had ample opportunity to cuff him and place him under arrest since the hotel yesterday. Plus, he had been allowed to run around with a gun Brett surely knew to be stolen from the Big Chuck incident this past summer. And here he was holding it again after Brett just tossed it over to him as a sign of trust.

Up till this moment, DJ knew Brett Foster to be calculating, thinking three moves in advance. He knew him to be calm and cool under pressure. He knew him to live a life dictated by common sense, and a strong moral code. But above all of that, he knew the man to be honest and honorable.

His brain flashed back to a moment when he was just a boy. He was standing there looking into the eyes of his father. The man was smiling at him in a knowing way, counseling him over something DJ could no longer recall. But the words the man would speak that day would live with DJ forever. "Son," his father stated. "The most valuable asset a man will ever own is his integrity. Lose it just once, and you may never get it back."

DJ blinked at the agent who had become a friend out of desperate times, standing across from him now in his wrinkled suit and his worn-out demeanor. The question was simple. Had Brett lost his integrity with DJ yet?

No. No, DJ did not think so. The pistol he held in his hand was proof enough. Only a man of integrity would have made that kind of risky move. A man of integrity would risk his own life, trusting in a friend to make the right call and not use the weapon he just freely gave away.

There was only one choice then. Trust him. Trust him to somehow flip this all around despite how bad it may look.

DJ felt his shoulders sag under the surrender of trust, and he turned his eyes downward toward the desk separating them. "Fine," DJ said. "You win. I trust you." He held the gun back out to Brett. The man looked at him a moment more, then seemed to acknowledge DJ's acceptance of the situation.

Brett took the Sig Sauer back from DJ, sat it back on the desk, then reached down and picked up a large satchel. It was the kind professionals might use in lieu of a briefcase. He laid it down across the desktop, patting the side of it reassuringly. "Now," he said with a genuine smile. "Here is my brilliant plan to keep you out of jail forever."

Thomas Huntley, AKA El Gran Blanco, was really rolling the dice right now. Not only had he abandoned his trip to Paris, defying the contracted agreement he had with one of the world's biggest crime lords, but he was about to launch an all-out attack on the FBI. He was already on their top ten most wanted lists. But this little move, if the truth were ever uncovered, would land him squarely at the top. Forever.

It didn't matter, because he had never been caught. Nor had any law enforcement agency on any continent ever come close. And he wasn't going to get caught now. Oh, to be sure, a few people were bound to get caught. Some would probably die along with it. But no one would ever be able to tie El Gran Blanco to what was about to happen. The blame would be cleverly laid at someone else's feet.

Thomas started doing internet searches and making video calls before the plane even got turned around good. He reached back out to the broker in Boston for more people. This time, he specifically asked for a Red Level contract.

Reds were always messy. They typically involved high level hits on complex targets. The probability of people dying or getting caught was higher than normal. So, they tended to be pricey.

The way any contract worked was an efficient process ensuring anonymity between parties, fair prices charged to competent hitters, and good intel provided to the shooters ensuring a higher success rate. First, the hitters would have to submit themselves to the broker announcing what level of contracts they were willing to take. And there were three levels: green, yellow, and red.

Greens were easy and presented few risks to the hitters. Of course, anything could happen in a live-fire situation. Plus, they represented the lowest level of pay. Greens were where everyone started. Some even chose to stay at this level, enjoying the ease in being able to get the job done without the risk involved with other contracts.

Yellows were a bit harder and held a higher threat of both getting killed and caught. Many were willing to take the chance because it paid better. However, one could not be considered for a Yellow contract without having a substantial number of completed Greens under their belt.

Red contracts were extremely risky, typically involving geopolitical hotspots around the globe. They were contracts against rival drug cartels in third world countries, or hits from one tin-pot dictator on another. Sometimes, they were used by the CIA when they needed to shield the US Government from culpability.

Reds paid very well, but you could not be considered for Red unless you had successfully completed several Yellow contracts. For Red contracts, the employer had to disclose all details of the mission in advance to the Broker. The Broker then determined risk and assigned an initial price. They would then present the offer to eligible groups. The groups could come back with counter offers, and the broker would then function as a go-between for bartering until an agreement was reached.

For any level of contract, if the employer ever lied about the complexity, or did not disclose all relevant information, they were charged a substantial penalty. They also risked never being allowed to do business within the system again. Since working outside of the system was fraught with fraud and substantial risk on both sides of the table, no one really wanted to chance getting placed on a black list.

Very few knew who the Brokers were. Contact was made through the same clandestine web location fronting as a porn site that Thomas used back at the old man's house. This method always worked and had never been infiltrated. Plus, no physical contact was made with any individual. It was all done across the internet.

When Thomas made contact with the Broker asking for the Red contract, he was informed since he did not disclose all the information on his first contract, in that his target was being protected by FBI agents, there would be a costly financial penalty. He was warned if this ever happened again, he would be blacklisted permanently.

Thomas countered by claiming he never knew of this detail. Plus, the hitters themselves bore some of the blame because they jumped the gun on execution. A fact the Broker already disclosed to him, having obtained this information from one of the other two groups who managed to get away clean. The broker conceded this, and reduced the amount of the penalty.

Thomas then informed him of the details for the Red contract request, and the Broker never balked. True, there had only been one other contract issued against a target in FBI custody, and inside a Federal building. That had gone down in Oklahoma City, and had been covered up using a patsy. It was made to look like an act of domestic terrorism, and also resulted in killing quite a lot of innocent bystanders. It was one of the most expensive contracts to date. Attacks against governments across the globe were routine, however. Just not on this scale, and not using this kind of manpower.

The attack in Oklahoma City involved explosives in a rental van and almost collapsed the entire building, an efficient and less risky endeavor on the part of the perpetrators. Since then, new construction took truck bombs into consideration.

The Denver Field Office was of newer construction, and getting close enough for a truck-bomb to kill all the targets inside was next to impossible. There was a barrier fence keeping vehicles from getting too close, along with a guard gate one would need to have proper paperwork and identification to gain entrance through. The building was wrapped in glass for aesthetics, but it was of special design and considered blast resistant. It would not withstand a very large truck bomb like the one in Oklahoma City if it got close enough, but that is what the wall was for.

Because of those precautions, this attack would involve a direct assault with at least two teams. One would go through the front gate. The team would just pull up to the guard shack in a van, shoot both guards from the window, then hop out and hit the button to cause the gate to slide open. The second would take advantage of a vulnerability at the back of the compound. They could simply back up to the fence behind the adjacent department store with a large box truck and hop on over.

For exit, both teams could leave the way the first entered. They could just waltz right through the open and unguarded front gate. After everyone with a badge and any prisoners in the holding cells were dead, of course.

A third strategy would be employed by attacking the facility's capability of communication. First, they would kill all phone and internet lines into the entire block. Then, sever the surrounding cell tower connections to the communication grid. Both could be done with small, remote triggered explosives. Finally, they had to combat the large radio antennae on the roof. Thomas would handle this himself using a well-placed shot from a fifty-caliber sniper rifle from a half-mile away. This would isolate the entire area and prevent anyone from being able to communicate about the attack. It would buy them the time they needed to get the job done.

Thomas organized the plan down to the detail, and then relayed it all to the Broker. The Broker was momentarily stunned when he told the man he would be participating in the attack. It would be from a remote location outside the combat area, to be sure. But employers never pulled triggers themselves.

The Broker provided an initial price, and it was staggering. He would still have plenty in reserve, but it would surely cost him. Thomas didn't care. In the end, leaving this Slaughter character breathing was going to cost him much more in lost business. The man needed to die. Besides, if Thomas ever chose to, he could announce this was all his own doing, and it would make him even more expensive to hire. It would show the world there was nothing he was not willing to do to get the job done.

Despite the danger of the mission, one team took him up on the job. No one else did, but that was OK. This team possessed enough manpower to get the job done, he was told. And, it was one of the same teams who helped out on the Boston job. This concerned Thomas, but the broker assured him this team had not been a part of the lead shooters. They had only been in place as support. Besides, this team managed to almost turn the whole thing around by launching an RPG at the target. They also had no problem with killing innocents as they had taken out two families in setting up the ambush in Boston. Those two things showed Thomas the level of commitment he was looking for.

The window to get all of this done was short and would have increased the price somewhat. But that was offset with a unique opportunity which would decrease the risk to the shooters. After talking to the new FBI director, he knew the place would be a virtual ghost town tonight. Most of the occupants were headed to DC for the speech the president was wanting to give.

That had to be a costly endeavor, Thomas thought to himself. But no one could spend money quite like a politician.

Director Neville begged Thomas for his friend, Brett Foster, to be allowed to live. Thomas offered no guarantees, but said he would try. A complete lie, of course. Thomas gave orders to the invaders who were, even now, poised to strike the facility on his order, to slaughter every single person who showed their face. He gave them ten minutes to kill everyone they saw, with the specific plan of making their way to the holding facilities in the basement, and the guest-wing sitting out back. They were to search those two areas and murder anyone there. This was a priority. The only real priority.

Thomas was uncertain where Slaughter and his girlfriend might be, but Director Neville told him he had ordered Agent Foster to put them in the holding cells. However, the man informed him, it might be an order Agent Foster chose to ignore. In which case, they would be in the guest rooms in a free-standing building by the parking garage. To make sure, Team 2 would enter from the back of the compound and sweep through those rooms first. They would then move up the parking garage stairs and enter the building from the top floor. They would clear down and meet up with Team 1 on the ground floor and exit the facility.

Team 1 would enter the front gate, killing the two guards located there. They would then pull up to the front entrance and walk right through the front doors. There was another security station with a metal detector to one side. They should be able to surprise the lone guard with no issue. They would clear the ground floor, then a pair of them would guard the stairwell and elevators for anyone coming down or trying to flee the building.

The rest of Team 1 would head down to the basement, moving towards the holding cells. They would kill anyone along the way, and anyone who might be in those cells.

Thomas would take out the radio antenna on the roof, as well as serve as spotter and over watch support with his sniper rifle. The whole thing should go down quickly and with little resistance.

One final piece of the assault would steer any investigation afterwards to a different perpetrator all together. It was a little something he cooked up for another job earlier this year, and never chose to implement.

He paid a person with olive complexion to dress in middle-eastern attire, and record a video claiming responsibility for a generic attack on a well-known Muslim extremist group. His paid actor ranted a bunch of political nonsense to the camera, and made claims more attacks would follow.

Of course, Thomas was going to use it to throw off the scent on that other attack, but it would work for this one as well. The previous hit he intended to use the video for ended up going down completely different. He saved the video anyway, figuring it would still come in useful somewhere down the road. After all, the actor did a very convincing job, and there were no specifics on the attack mentioned. Too bad the actor had to die once he completed his work.

He sent the video to his paid hitters via the Broker and requested it be placed on a thumb drive to be left at the scene. It would effectively ensure the FBI placed all of their investigative efforts in a different direction.

Thomas was currently on the top floor of a two-story residential in a neighborhood half a block away. He knocked on the door, shot the person who answered in the head with a single silenced round, and entered. Despite having to limp his way through the home thanks to his stab wound, the family inside offered no real threat, and he put them all down quickly. Including the infant he found in a crib. He could not risk it yelling over a dirty diaper or needing fed. Besides, it was wrong to have the child grow up in foster care. He knew full well what it meant to be raised by crappy parents. Better to put it out of its misery.

He set up his sniper's nest in an upstairs back bedroom. From this location, he owned a clear shot across an open field and into the FBI compound. His angle of view was not direct. It was off to one side at a pretty good angle, but it still possessed a commanding overlook of most of the front. He could clearly make out the front gate and guard house, along with the entire front of the building and guest parking. He could even see through the ground floor windows, and make out the lone security guard sitting at a desk and leafing through a magazine. Despite the snowfall, with his high-power scope, he could even make out the image on the cover. The bored guard was into cars.

Both teams were split up and in position awaiting his order to move. But Thomas wanted to do a quick sweep of the area with his scope first. If he spotted anything of importance, he could radio the two teams and alter the plan. He was wearing a headset mic, and as he panned around with his scope, he could hear the others doing last minute checks on equipment.

The sun had long set, and the overcast sky and snow blocked out any chance of moonlight. The shrouded darkness helped to make every office in the four-story building that was occupied light up like beacons. Each one was an illuminated rectangle of floor to ceiling glass.

There were only three occupied offices he could see from this side. One of them commanded his attention immediately, however. It was on the top floor, and on the corner nearest the guard gate and furthest from him. It seemed to be one office much larger than the rest. Its location and size suggested to Thomas this was likely Foster's office. Zooming in with the scope showed three men standing in the office and facing the door.

He didn't know what Brett Foster looked like, but considering all the circumstantial evidence, he was betting the man standing behind the desk was him. Foster was a white guy dressed professionally with sandy colored hair. He couldn't see his facial features as the man was facing the opposite side of the room. He could make out a partial profile, however.

The other two were dressed like part of the private guard team securing the building and the front gate. *Odd*, Thomas thought. *Why would Foster have guards in his office just standing around?* It almost looked like they were waiting for something.

The office door opened and in walked his target and girlfriend.

Slaughter… The mere sight of him sent a wave of heat crawling up the back of Thomas's neck. Adrenaline coursed through him in an instant and his hands started to tremble with anger. He impulsively clenched his jaw, and he could feel his eyebrows clinging together as silent fury rolled through him. He was always one in complete control of his emotions. But there was just something about this man that caused him to abandon intelligent thought, and toss his precious rules of survival out the window like a discarded fast-food container from a car.

The man's existence did not merely infuriate him. Anger was an emotion that lived in brevity. It was here one moment, then fading into memory the next. This was deeper. There was hatred and loathing burning in his heart for the man.

A part of him wanted to leave the rifle where it was and charge across the field below him with nothing more than his bare hands. He wanted to radio the waiting small army about to descend on the compound, and tell them he would storm the gates all by himself.

He closed his eyes and took in a deep breath. *Tantrums are for babies*, he reminded himself. But it was a shame he needed reminding.

Looking back through the scope and zooming in, Thomas set about trying to read lips. It was a useful skill he picked up over the years. He could only catch a few words here and there from Foster, but mated to the replies coming from Slaughter and his girlfriend, he could tell there was some serious tension going on. It looked like only now was Slaughter being informed he was going to be placed into a holding cell.

He was suddenly glad he had not yet given the order to move to the men about to attack. A Slaughter running around loose in a building full of weapons was the last thing he needed.

A sort of standoff was happening for a moment, and he could tell Slaughter was weighing his options. Thomas held his breath. Was it possible this would all resolve itself and the guards would end up doing his job for him? Thomas was both hopeful and fearful of this at the same time. Part of him wanted to be the one responsible for the demise of his enemy. The other part didn't care how the man died.

Just die.

Suddenly, Foster gestured to the two guards, and they begrudgingly left the room. Only one other agent hung back by the now closed door. A short guy with piercing blue eyes.

Then Slaughter approached the desk with a clenched jaw and stubborn look in his eye. There was even more tension, and Thomas again wondered if a fight were about to break out. Finally, after a long pause, Foster picked up a weapon that had been sitting on the desk. It was a silenced job, which meant it wasn't exactly FBI issue. He tossed it through the air to Slaughter, who caught it in his right hand in a manner that said he was about to use it. His palm was high up in the beaver-tail and his finger was along the slide. His hand gripped the weapon in a perfect ready position.

The move was as much of a surprise to Thomas as it seemed to be to Slaughter.

Then, Foster appeared to go into a rant about something he couldn't quite make out from the angle. Whatever he said seemed to take all of the energy out of Slaughter. His adversary's shoulders slumped a bit, and then he handed the gun back. Foster placed the weapon back down on the desk and started talking again. The agent reached down and picked up what looked like a briefcase-bag. He set it on the desk and apparently began to talk about the contents. Slaughter seemed to be shocked by what he was hearing. The man looked to be in a sort of daze for a moment. Then, he walked around the desk to stand facing the windows while he continued to listen to what was being said to him by Foster.

With the zoom maxed out on the scope, Thomas could see Slaughter in perfect close-up detail. He could make out a jagged V-shaped scar above his right eyebrow. He could tell the man had not shaved in a few days. And, there was a look of contemplation on his face like he was trying to decide on something. Like he was weighing a life changing decision.

As Thomas watched, about to key the mic and radio the two teams to alter the plan and head straight to the top floor office, Slaughter turned around. He was addressing Foster still standing at the desk with whatever decision he had come to. Slaughter's head aligned perfectly with the illuminated crosshairs of his scope. Beyond his adversary, he could see the girlfriend looking her beloved in the eye. He could see the love she held for Slaughter, and suddenly the wave of heated fury was coursing through him once more.

Thomas imagined pulling the trigger on the heavy caliber rifle. He envisioned the massive round exploding his target's head like a stick of dynamite obliterating a pumpkin. He could almost see the look of unmitigated horror wash over the girlfriend's face as Thomas would provide her an image she would live with for the rest of her miserable life.

The .50 caliber rifle exploded to life in his hands, and the view through the scope vanished in an instant. The roar of the round launching from the barrel became his whole universe. It filled the small bedroom with volume, and a concussive blast causing photographs to jump off the wall and crash to the floor. For a split second, Thomas did not even realize what happened. He was completely taken by surprise.

But then he knew. He had screwed up yet again. In his emotion-filled state, his dream of pulling the trigger translated into action. Thomas jerked the weapon back on target. He needed to know if there was any chance the armored piercing round actually burrowed its way through the thick, blast-proof, transparent composite pane. Was this nightmare now officially over?

His stomach knotted from what he saw through the scope. There, staring in momentary shock at the spiderwebbed section of window, was an unharmed yet seemingly invulnerable Slaughter. His eyes were transfixed to the bullet now frozen in the middle of the pane, perfectly in line with where his head had once been.

There was still a chance, Thomas thought. The blast-resistant material was now weakened. A second round might be able to punch through. Faster than thought, he aligned the cross hairs once more, and sent a second round hurtling towards his target.

Again, the composite pane did its job. The round was stopped cold and suspended in the material. But this time, Slaughter was not frozen in disbelief and failed understanding at what was going on. This time he was a blaze of movement, and so was everyone else in the room. Foster grabbed the messenger bag from the top of the desk with one hand, and tossed the silenced weapon he had placed there back to Slaughter. Slaughter caught it in mid stride as he raced for his girlfriend. His girlfriend was darting to one side, and scooping up a backpack which had been sitting in a chair. The agent at the back of the room near the door was swinging it open and waving them to hurry through.

The man was escaping his grasp yet again. Thomas moved his left hand to key the mic just long enough to shout at his men to move, and to relay the current location of the target. Then he was firing a third round. Then a fourth. Then a fifth and six. With blazing anger, he looked on helplessly as the composite pane of transparent material did its job over and over again. This was not glass, Thomas thought. It was a force field. And it could not be breached no matter how hard he willed it.

They were gone then, slipping into the hallway and through his fingers like ethereal wisps of smoke.

Chapter 16: The Vomit Hole

One minute, DJ was sitting there listening to Brett tell him the most insane plan for making him and Abbi right with the law. And it truly was insane. Was it possible Brett Allen Foster was not the intelligent, calculating, Special Agent in Charge he thought he was? Because as he listened, the man sounded like he had been smoking up a bowl of Colorado's best weed when he hatched this hair-brained idea. The next minute, something hit the window behind him with a deafening *smack*.

DJ sprang forward and away as an involuntary reaction. When he spun about, what he saw fascinated him for a split second. The glass pane, a solid piece stretching from floor to ceiling, was far thicker than he at first thought. In front of his face, fractured patterns rippled through the foot-and-a-half thick wall, expanding outward in radiating circles. It reminded him of what a windshield would look like if it was hit with a hailstone or baseball. Only this was far more extreme. And what sat suspended in the middle of the circular pattern sent a chill reaching up his spine with the spectral fingers of death.

A bullet the size of a small missile sat encapsulated about three quarters of the way through. It burrowed into the wall at an angle. Someone just tried to shoot him from somewhere off to his right. A someone who could only be El Gran Blanco.

Shark Bait found him once again. Was there no end to the man's reach?

A second bullet struck the wall with a heart-seizing smack, creating an identical pattern a bit further to his right. This time, DJ felt the vibrations through the soles of his boots as the impact carried through the floor. Part of him wondered what kind of glass could capture armored piercing rounds like a pebble in Jell-O. The other part of him screamed to get moving.

So, he did.

DJ spun around, the safety of Abbi foremost on his mind, but she was already a blaze of motion herself. She snatched up his backpack and turned for the door. At the same time, Brett shouted his name and tossed his Sig Sauer to him. DJ caught it in mid-air and followed in line behind

Abbi. Brett was right on his heels with satchel in hand. Agent Cash stood at the door waving at them to hurry. Waiting in the hallway, he could see the faces of four of the security guards Brett previously dismissed. They were still sticking around because they had apparently been ordered to wait by Agent Cash. Their faces indicated confusion, but a shouted order from Brett behind him sent them all scurrying.

"Secure the parking garage! Now!" Brett screamed, a touch of panic in his voice. "Radio to the rest we're under attack." The guards, still not sure of what was going on, responded anyway. After all, the man who gave the order was in charge of the entire facility. Their confusion and questions could be dealt with later.

The hallway ended in a "T" intersection. Right branched off into open office space. Left tunneled through the building past the elevators, and bore further into the heart of the fourth floor. They all turned that direction, but one of the guards slowed down to talk to Brett. There was no one answering the radio from the front gate, he announced. Brett ordered everyone to a halt, dropped his bag to the ground, and snatched the radio away from its owner. First, he called out to the gate, but was met with silence. He called out to the downstairs desk, but received no response from there either. Next, he called out for anyone to answer. Nothing.

DJ used the pause to dig out the two spare mags for his Sig from the pack, and then slung his arms through both straps. He slipped the magazines into his left back pocket with the bottoms up. This way he could quickly change one out if he needed to. And he had a feeling he was going to need to.

A door opened across from DJ, and he placed the gun to the head of the figure revealed there without even thinking. The person sucked in air in a frightened rush, and DJ held off dropping him. It was just an FBI technician of some sort in a white lab coat. The thin black man with geeky glasses and pizza hanging out his mouth looked like he might pass out right there.

Brett reached out and pushed DJ's weapon to one side. "We're under attack," Brett told him. "Get under a desk and hide." Turning to DJ and Cash, he said, "If the gate and front desk aren't answering, we have more to worry about than a sniper. And I need you and Cash to help me out. I need to get to the guest rooms down by the parking garage. The rest of these guys need to stay here and protect whoever is on the fourth floor."

"Why?" DJ asked. "We have all of our stuff right here."

"When I heard about the attack on your home in Kentucky, I had my wife brought here for safe keeping. I thought it might have been some of Big Chuck's guys seeking revenge. She's still here. She's staying in the room at the end of the building you were in. Two doors down."

DJ blinked in response, then turned to the four guards. "Get us to the garage access on this level. Then you guys need to collect any personnel on this floor into one room and hole up. We're headed down the back way to get his wife."

The men looked at him like he had a hole in his head, then turned their attention to Brett. Brett just nodded his approval, and the guards seemed to accept the plan then. He had to remember he was not the one in charge here. This was Brett's house, and he was just a guest. Actually, maybe "guest" was too intimate a title.

He turned back to Brett and addressed him again. "Do you think we can barricade ourselves in her room?"

Brett shrugged. "The walls are thick enough, but we need to consider something else. You're who they're after. If we can get them to chase you, the rest of this building will cease to be in danger. Most of the people here are just analysts and lab rats. All of the actual agents are gone. They can't defend themselves. We only have a handful of guards here, and most of them were just supposed to watch you and the gate. We don't have enough firepower to repel invaders. We need to lure them away using you as bait."

"You know another way out of here other than the front gate or over the wall?" DJ asked.

"Well, there is a side maintenance entrance, but I have a better idea."

"What?"

"First, we get to my wife." Brett gave no other explanation and jumped to the head of the line with the guards, and started them all moving further into the building. DJ decided to take up the rear in case anyone came up the elevator or stairs behind him, ushering Abbi to move along ahead.

He heard the chime of the elevator after moving only a few feet. Instead of continuing down the corridor after the others, he reversed directions and charged towards the elevators. He had no idea where the stairwell was. He had not noticed a sign marking the entrance. However, he could at least defend the elevator, making sure their enemy did not take them all out while running down the hallway. With no options for cover, anyone with a fully automatic weapon could mow them down with little effort. Besides, taking the fight to the enemy head on was more his style.

"What are you doing?" Abbi cried out.

"Keep going!" DJ yelled back at her, still rushing back to the elevator. "I'm coming. Promise."

He made it to the sliding doors just before they opened, and it was a good thing he did. Three men with rifles and full combat gear were waiting inside. DJ's Sig was eye level to the first one he saw, and he never hesitated. The gun bucked in his hand and the man dropped into the floor, his brain pulverized from a 9mm slug.

Sixteen rounds left. Two full mags in his left back pocket.

He swung right to engage the next. This one tried to duck out of the way, but he wasn't fast enough. DJ's round ripped through one side of his skull and it was lights out for him as well.

Fifteen rounds left.

The last guy proved more of a challenge. His rifle was pointed at the ground because his buddy had been in front, between him and the doors. But when his comrade dropped, the man quickly tried to swing his weapon at DJ's middle. DJ countered by swinging his left palm down and out, blocking the rifle. With his right, he tried to aim at the man's head. His enemy, however, did some blocking of his own. He released the left hand supporting his rifle, and flipped it up and away from his body, halting DJ from swinging the Sig to his head.

DJ pushed in, then. He took a quick step forward with his right foot, then brought his left knee up hard into the man's groin. He followed that up by smashing his forehead into the bridge of his enemy's nose just like Abbi had taught him. The nose was a sensitive area, she had pointed out. Even a glancing blow would make a person's eyes water. It would render the person vulnerable to more lethal strikes.

As she instructed, it took all the fight out of his adversary. DJ finished him off by swinging his gun back to the man's temple and squeezing the trigger.

He stepped back out of the elevator and searched for Abbi's group. They were all rounding a corner at the far end. He waved at her to keep going. She hesitated, but did as she was told and vanished from view.

DJ returned once more to the elevator to survey the equipment of his enemy. All three were using short barreled and silenced AR variants with a red-dot sight mounted on top. The brand was unfamiliar to him, but nowadays there were about a million companies making competing versions of the AR15.

All three were also wearing tactical vests. The armored kind. DJ was unsure of the level of protection they offered, but it was better than running around with just the windbreaker he wore. He would love to remove a vest and claim it for his own, but he didn't know how much time he had before reinforcements arrived. If there were three that took the elevator, there had to be more coming up the stairs. It's what DJ would do. Divide forces to cover every exit from the fourth floor.

But where were the stairs?

First, DJ stuffed his pistol in his waistband behind his back. Next, he unslung a rifle from its tactical sling around a dead guy's neck, along with plucking a spare mag and a radio from a pouch. He really wanted one of those vests, but this would have to do. He shoved the rifle mag in his waistband and dropped the radio in his jacket pocket.

The radio had a short earbud connection just long enough to stretch from a high-up mounted position on the chest or back. He would have to figure out how to listen to any exchanges later. With no vest, the cord was too short to reach his ear. And, if he unplugged the earpiece, he could no longer try to be stealthy. Anything said across it would be broadcasted across the small speaker.

The AR15 was not full-auto modified, but the red aluminum trigger announced it was not exactly stock. A closer glance confirmed his suspicions. A tiny engraved kicking mule on the front of the trigger, declared this was an "Angry Mule" variant. Angry Mule was a company specializing in three position trigger packs for AR15 rifles. Three position triggers fired a round when pulled, and a second when released. It made for a very fast firing system that could take the place of a fully automatic version, yet yielded far better control. It made double-tapping your target a breeze. DJ smiled at his new discovery, and put his head through the sling.

Now, where was that stairwell? It had to be around here somewhere. He was pretty sure building codes required stairs to be located within so many feet of elevators in case of fire. Swinging his head left and right towards both ends of the hallway showed no signage marking the stairs. He backtracked around the corner towards Brett's office, and sure enough, there the door was. They had passed it while they fled.

DJ returned to the corner and drew aim on the door. From this position, he had a good view of both the elevator doors and the stairwell entrance around the corner from one another. The elevator doors were locked open as there was a dead guy in the way. It was sounding a buzzer indicating it could not close the doors, and someone needed to come take care of it.

As he watched, the stairwell door cracked open a sliver and held there. DJ waited for a good target. He didn't want to take a chance shooting a lab-tech sneaking up the stairs looking for a place to hide. It held that slightly ajar position for a minute more. Someone on the other side was likely listening for movement in the hallway. But, the only thing they would hear was the buzzer of the elevator from around the corner. Finally, it opened and an armor-clad, gun-toting figure popped into view with a weapon raised. He saw DJ too late and caught two between the eyes. His head snapped back and his body followed it over to the ground.

DJ dropped to a knee and continued to aim, waiting for the next idiot to show his face. From back to his right, all the way down around the corner Abbi and his group had gone, he heard gunfire. A lot of it. Abbi was in danger and he could no longer hang out here. He needed to put a few rounds through the door and then beat a hasty retreat.

He never got the chance. The unmistakable sound of a spoon flying free from a grenade could be heard from the doorway. It meant either an explosive device, or a concussion grenade. Either way, he was in a deep pile of stinky stuff.

He launched himself into a sprint toward Abbi. Behind him, something smacked against the wall and dropped to the floor with a thud. He dropped the rifle to flop around from its strap, slapped his hands over his ears, and closed his eyes, all while in a full-out run. Two seconds later, an explosion ripped through the building behind him, and he felt the sharp sting of shrapnel. One in his upper right shoulder, another in his lower left thigh.

DJ staggered from the impact and concussion, but managed to keep his feet. He grimaced in pain and but kept pushing forward, swinging the rifle up into both hands so he could run harder. He had to clear the next corner or he was a dead man.

Twenty-five feet. Twenty. Fifteen. Ten. He pumped his legs as hard as he could. The promised safety of the corner was just before him, but an internal clock was ticking away in his head. How much time would it take for his pursuers to clear the immediate area outside of the stairwell door, then advance to the hallway he was sprinting down? Five seconds? Ten?

He was out of time.

He dove into a slide, simultaneously rolling onto his left side as he slid along the polished floor. A chorus of gunfire exploded behind him and bullets tore through the air above his head. Not aiming for precision, but merely for effect, he double-tapped the Angry Mule trigger and sent four rounds screaming back down the hallway. He saw a figure stagger to one side in response, and the gunfire paused. Had he hit him, he wondered?

He scrambled around the corner and to his feet. There were bloody red streaks on the floor from his wounds. How bad was he hurt, he wondered? If the wounds were severe, he would start to feel the effects of too much blood loss in a second. Or maybe they weren't so bad, he hoped. Either way, there was no time to find out. He had to get to Abbi and the others. Their gunfire was louder now after rounding the corner, and it seemed as if it were Morse code calling out to him for help.

He popped back around the corner and let loose with four more rounds for effect, and then took more careful aim. One man was dragging a wounded comrade back around the corner. Another was aiming around the edge at DJ. His enemy let fly with a few rounds of his own. The first was so close to his cheek, he could feel the wake of its passing. The next punched through the sheetrock on the corner and continued through to the wall behind him. The first four rounds from DJ were fired blindly, and he was unsure where they went. The second two were focused and precise. He drilled the man dragging his friend. The first bullet took him through the neck. The second connected with the top of his skull. Both rounds painted the hallway red behind them.

DJ darted back around the corner. He closed his eyes and did a mental count again. Eighteen rounds left in this mag, a full mag at his waist... Crap! The spare mag was gone, he realized. It must have fallen out of his waistband while sliding around on the floor. He did a quick look and spotted the full mag sitting in the intersection on the hallway floor. Well, he wasn't going back after it. He no longer possessed the ammo to make people duck for cover. He now needed to make every round count.

He could spare two rounds, however. He pushed the rifle around the corner and let two go just to keep his enemy from charging down the hallway. Sixteen rounds left.

He bolted in the direction of Abbi as hard as he could. Rounding yet another corner, he saw an open area just ahead with a set of glass doors to his left. As he got closer, he saw it was a landing of sorts. A spot for people to pause as they entered the building from the parking garage. The sign to the right of the door confirmed his hunch, indicating this was Parking Garage Level 4. The sporadic gunfire from Brett and crew was louder here. They must be just beyond on one of the lower levels. But now he had a problem.

If he proceeded through these doors, he would undoubtedly find his group and be able to provide some assistance. But he would also be leading the men following him right to them. His group would be sandwiched between two enemy forces. The odds of them all coming out of this unscathed were nil. He had to find some way to quickly even the odds or this fight was going to be over soon. And, he did not have long. The men following him would be moving along slowly lest he jump out and ambush him, but they would still be coming.

Across from the exit to the garage was a break area. It was a large rectangular room filled with round tables for workers to enjoy a meal. Along one wall was a trio of refrigerators and two electric stoves. On the counter next to them, were four microwaves. Inspiration struck him and he tore across the room in long strides. He ripped open the cabinet doors above the stove and was instantly rewarded with what he was looking for.

Sonny had been serving on Cody Hamell's mercenary group for almost two years. It was a larger group of nearly fifty guys, and they just received Red certification this year. It was a good bunch of men to work with. They made decent money, and no one ever got hurt. If they ran into a surprise on a mission, some threat they had not accounted for, Cody seemed to always have a surprise of his own.

Sonny was impressed with Cody's intelligence. The man was smart about how he ran his organization. He would often sell a mission on a specific number of guys, only to show up with more than needed to get the job done. And his men accepted splitting the payout between more shooters for the peace of mind it offered. He always had alternative plans in place despite the intel and assurances provided by the customer. In fact, he usually had a backup to the backup.

He organized his group into teams of eight. Each team trained and functioned with its members almost like a family unit. They slept together, ate together, and trained together. Each one was familiar with how the other operated, and could anticipate how their teammate would function. When more than one team was assigned to a job, Cody functioned as an informational go-between for all of them. And, more importantly, he went on every single mission serving as a ninth member, ensuring he was familiar with the habits and capabilities of each member of his group. Plus, Sonny mused, his boss could definitely pull his own weight.

This was the first time all of them were on a mission together.

True to Cody's style, he agreed to the mission only as a four-team operation. Two teams would breach the front as required by the customer, and two would come in over the wall in back. According to information provided by the customer, the place should be largely empty. Only a handful of actual agents and armed security guards were all they should have to worry about. It should be a cake walk. But this was a federal building, and his boss left nothing to chance. For this mission, it was all hands on deck. Nearly fifty guys were participating, but the customer didn't know it.

Cody assigned the rest of his men to function as support groups staged nearby should they need it. They were set up to not only rush in and lend a hand, but they could intercept any local law enforcement who might somehow show up to defend the compound.

Cody, on the other hand, was on a special mission of his own. He wanted to know exactly who they were working for, and he was out snooping right now trying to find out.

This was the second mission they were running for the unnamed contract bearer, with the same target as the goal. The first went south thanks to bad intel. Had Cody not brought along an RPG to even the odds, maybe some of their own group would have perished in the fiasco of Beacon Hill. Now they were running a second mission for the same man less than seventy-two hours later. This was also against the same target, but this time being held in this FBI compound. Plus, their customer was also taking part as a sniper and providing over-watch support to ensure the mission was completed successfully. The customer participating was a condition of the contract.

This sent up all kinds of red flags for Cody, and he wanted to know who this guy really was. So, while Cody was nearby, his self-imposed mission was to locate the man and try to figure out his identity. To this end, he had already surveyed the area to determine the best locations for a sniper to set up for over-watch on the front of the compound. His boss was out there now using three small quadcopter drones, outfitted with thermal cameras and GPS equipped acoustic shot locaters. They would help him both find their employer, and provide aerial reconnaissance for his teams should they need him.

But that was Cody's mission. Sonny's was to lead his team through the front entrance and down to the basement. Another team would enter the front gate with him and setup on the ground floor as a support unit. At least that was the original plan before it all rapidly changed.

The man who paid for their services called a last second audible just before they were supposed to breach the gate. He apparently spotted the intended target on the fourth floor in a window. With the man's heavy caliber sniper rifle loaded with armor piercing rounds, he decided to see if he could penetrate the bullet proof glass and end this thing with one quick pull of the trigger.

Sonny heard the shots go off just before the man's failure was broadcasted to the entire group over the radio. Sonny hoped Cody would have pulled the plug right then, but overwhelming force clearly still had them with the advantage, and the job would pay them a lot of money. Besides, if they completed this contract, killing a high value target located inside an FBI field office, they would have more work thrown at them than they could handle. Completing this mission was going to be absolutely wonderful for business.

His team, designated as Alpha, with the support of Team Bravo, went through the front gate with no issues. They entered the ground floor entrance to the large glass structure quickly, and the rent-a-cop at the check point presented no threat either. While he had his gun out, he seemed too scared to even try and use it. Despite their idiot contract holder blowing their surprise entrance, they encountered no real resistance.

Then, they hit the fourth floor and everything changed.

Sonny had spent serious time with his team. They were well trained. They were seasoned. At no time had they ever suffered any serious setbacks. But then they ran across one lone man on the fourth floor of this building, and he single-handedly cut Sonny's team in half in less than two minutes. The stranger was probably one of the few actual agents left behind, not winging his way to Washington DC.

The lone agent capped all three of Sonny's guys he sent up the elevator. The man must have been waiting at the sliding doors with his gun drawn and ready. It was something that would have never happened if their employer had not started shooting at the building. If he would have only called in the updated location of the target, Cody's group could have done what they did best. They could have been in and out of the facility, and accomplished their objective, in under five minutes.

Then, while coming up the stairwell behind the elevator, the hero agent took out the first guy through the door. Sonny had tossed a grenade into the hallway and sent the man scampering like a scared bunny. But it didn't end there. When they rounded the next corner, the man got in a lucky shot and wounded another one of his guys. And when they tried to drag their wounded teammate back around the corner, the agent killed another one. With one of their own weapons, no less.

Sonny was torqued. One man managed to take out most of his team. He was down to himself and two more, plus his wounded man. And he didn't think the wounded teammate would live beyond the next few minutes. The bullet went through the throat and he was bleeding out as

Sonny stood here fuming in the hallway. He was no longer concerned with the mission and killing their high valued target. Whoever was running around the fourth floor taking out his guys was his priority now. To commit himself to this new goal, he reached up and unplugged the radio from his ear.

His last two remaining men looked at him like he was nuts. They could do what they wanted, he explained, but he was going after the man who decimated his team. They did what he expected them to. They simply nodded in agreement and removed their earplugs as well. Team before mission. It tended to be the mindset of most people working in this seedy industry.

Besides, it sounded like one of the teams coming in from the back, ran into their intended target on the second floor of the parking garage. The target was pinned down, and in a couple of minutes this would all be over. The fourth team entering the back had already bypassed and moved to the front for exit, based on assurances of the team who had cornered their target.

Sonny raised his weapon and led his remaining team forward, leaving their dying friend behind them. They couldn't save his life. They could only avenge his death.

He approached the next turn with stealth and caution. Before he got there, silenced gunfire broke the silence in short bursts. Two shots. Two more. Then two more after that. With each set of two, the hallway around the corner grew dimmer.

Their lone hero was shooting out the lights. He was setting up an ambush point. And it was obvious.

When Sonny reached the corner, his listened first. Hearing nothing, he reached into a vest pocket and retrieved the small mirror on a telescopic stick he always carried. Mechanics used them to see around the nooks and crannies of engine compartments. Sonny used it for checking corners. It was something the first guy who died should have done. Sonny was not going to make the same mistake.

He could see the man. A dark form was paused in an alcove halfway down the next section, watching for them to stupidly stroll around the corner and get ambushed. But Sonny still had three more grenades left, and this looked like a great time to use one.

Suddenly, the man was aiming at the corner Sonny was hiding behind and firing. He must have spotted the mirror. Sonny kept watching the mirrored surface and reached for a grenade. Before he could pull it free, the agent stepped out from his doorway. He continued to retreat further down the hall, firing with every step. Then, just like that, his stolen rifle was empty. The man looked down at the weapon, and then he just chunked the rifle down the hallway towards them. A heartbeat later he was fleeing from them, head down and sprinting hard.

His enemy was out of ammo. He was completely defenseless.

Sonny popped around the corner and drew aim just as his quarry vanished around the far end. He fired a couple off, but knew he missed the moment he let the rounds go free. Then, he and his men were bounding down the darkened tunnel like hounds after a bunny. There was no way he was letting this guy get away. Sonny threw caution to the wind and really stretched it out, running for all he was worth. With his enemy out of ammo, Sonny decided against shooting him. Instead, when he caught up, he would gut the loser like a fish.

Halfway down the dim corridor, just before the alcove where his enemy had been hiding, Sonny realized he made a fatal mistake. He unwittingly fell straight into the stranger's trap. His feet hit a super slick spot on the linoleum floor, far slicker than it could ever be on its own without help. With the lights in the ceiling shot out, he missed seeing what caused the floor to suddenly become so treacherous. His feet shot out from underneath him, and for a moment, he hung there in the air. He was as helpless as a small child and was instantly overcome with an overwhelming sense of foolishness.

There were two incredible collisions then. The first as he crashed to the floor on his side, caused something to snap in his elbow. Rapiers of pain thrust through his arm and shoulder, all the way to the base of his skull. He would have screamed were it not for the second collision. Both of his men, hot on his heels, descended on him with nearly five hundred pounds of combined weight. A sickening crunch sounded in his ears, and all the pain from the first collision ghosted away from him in the blink of an eye.

His spine snapped like a twig, paralyzing him. His head twisted around in a severe angle. He could hear himself struggling to breathe from a partially collapsed airway, but he was unaware of the sensation of the struggle. All pain, all feeling, all everything, was replaced by a persistent numbing sensation that felt like his whole world was slightly buzzing.

He wished he could move and fight. He wished he could shout at his men to watch out. Their enemy was not the rabbit running in fear he pretended to be. Rather, he was the lion in the darkness about to rip into them from the shadows. But mostly, he wished he could die facing this nightmare killer, instead of laying on the floor in a broken heap of shame and regret.

There were two shots, then, and he knew the last two remaining members of his team were dead. Both shots were close together and possessing the muffled clap of a suppressed 9mm round.

Now what agent would have a silenced pistol readily at his disposal?

The answer was none, of course. And if his adversary was not a lone FBI agent running around on the fourth floor, then who could he be?

Could it be the Slaughter character they had been paid to kill? But he was supposed to be in custody and defenseless, at least according to the intel provided by their employer.

Suddenly, Sonny's biggest regret was not leading his whole team to be bested by a single man. It was being fed bad intel by a bumbling idiot who ruined their surprise assault.

He could hear his enemy approaching behind him. He wanted to turn his head and at least be able to look the man in the eye. He wanted to spit his last breath of hate at the mysterious stranger. Instead, all he had was this awkward view of the floor, looking into the alcove where his killer only moments before had stood. He watched it grow darker from the shadow of the man now standing over him. His last view of this world was going to be staring into a corner at a piece of discarded trash. A beautiful metaphor for how he felt.

What a shameful ending.

Wait. That was not simple discarded refuse haphazardly kicked into a corner. That was an empty plastic container of vegetable oil. So that's how...

Darkness.

DJ burst through the swinging doors marking the exit into the parking garage, and a blast of cold air nearly took his breath away. This was the rooftop level. And while it was covered to shield employees from the elements, it did not keep the winter wind from sweeping through. He instantly wished for something heavier than the lightweight windbreaker he wore.

After finishing off the three guys in the hallway, he forced himself to take a moment and remove his fallen enemy of a vest and all three rifles.

He also swapped out the mag for his Sig so he now had 18 rounds of 9mm ready to go. One in the chamber and a full mag in the well.

As he came through the doors, the gunfire from somewhere down below came to an echoing halt. The sudden silence made his heart sink. Had the bad guys just taken them all out? Had his delay with removing weapons and gear cost them their lives?

There were two ways down from here. A stairwell just to the right of the door, and one further away at the far end of the garage. He chose that one. Taking those would cause him to end up straight across from the end of the guest suites. If he were Brett, it's where he would have gone. It would have been the most direct route to his wife.

DJ launched into a run. At the entrance to the stairwell, he paused in the open doorway to listen. Hearing nothing but the wind brushing past his ears, he started his way down. He paused again on the third level and peeked through the opening. Nothing. He wound his way carefully down to the next, and peeked again.

There they were. Brett and crew were holed up on the other side of a cluster of nondescript sedans. Not that he could see them. They were all keeping their heads down. But he could make a good guess by what he *could* see. He took it all in, and ducked back around the corner.

Six enemy combatants were aiming across a concrete divider intended to funnel cars one direction. They were aiming at the cluster of shot up cars, government issue by the plates on the front. In between them were two dead bad guys and one dead guard from Brett's group.

DJ had been wondering what happened to those guards. They were instructed to secure the fourth floor. He was unsure what changed the plan. From the look of it, they either refused the order to keep their boss safe while he went to rescue his wife, or Brett changed his mind. But Brett would never do that and leave the rest of the facility at risk. Risk himself, of course. But DJ just couldn't see Brett ordering them to protect him instead of the innocent lab rats running around the building.

Before he could decide on a course of action, one of them called out. "Make this easy on yourself. We only want you, Slaughter. All you have to do, buddy, is stand up nice and straight. I'll put you down quick. You won't feel a thing. I'll let the rest of you go. Come on out and take it like a man."

Abbi's voice reverberated through the garage, echoing through the concrete structure, and causing DJ to grin from ear to ear. "Why don't *you* drop your gun and come over here and face his girlfriend? *You* won't feel a thing. Come on, now. Come and take it like a man!"

"Wow, Slaughter. You gonna let your woman do all the talking? That's sad, man. Look, I know you're almost out of ammo and I got two more teams on the way. One of those guys will have a couple of grenades. I'll just blow all of you up. You really want me wasting your girlfriend like that? Do the right thing, brother. Stand up and let's get this over with."

DJ had finally taken a moment to appropriate a vest from the last men he killed in the hallway. In the vest he was wearing was a couple of grenades. He grabbed one now. Pulling the pin, he let the spoon fly with a metallic "chink". Typically, grenades were set on a five second delay. So, he counted to two, leaned around the corner, and slung it underhand at the group.

He could have risked it and just come around the corner shooting. He was certain to end two of them with no issues. But they would start scrambling and shooting back in short order. These guys were all seasoned combat veterans, and there was no guarantee he could take them all out without being hit. Besides, the man said more teams were on the way. DJ was pretty sure one of those teams was who he encountered on the fourth floor. That meant another one would be here any second. He didn't have time to get in a shootout and hope for the best. The leader before him made a great suggestion. Just blow them all up.

The grenade did a slow arc through the air and hit the cement about six feet behind them. DJ whipped back around the corner and cupped his ears. He caught someone begin to shout the word "grenade," but they never got the entire word out of their mouth. It went off with a thunderous clap, made even louder by the cavern of concrete. He stepped quickly back around the corner and raised his confiscated rifle as he went, looking for survivors.

Hollywood always misrepresented the fragmentation grenade. They depicted it going off with an incredible fireball, and with such destructive force that it sent everything within twenty feet cartwheeling through the air. Doors were blown off of hinges and turned into flying debris. Bodies were sent sailing through the air. But none of that was true. Instead, there was a simple flash of light, a puff of smoke, and it was over. Blink, and you might even miss the flash.

No one was ever blown apart by a grenade going off close by. Unless they were holding it when it went off, of course. Instead, there was only enough shrapnel for one to hold in their cupped hands. And it only exploded outward from the source with enough strength to rip and tear into bodies nearby. All of it was largely captured by whatever unfortunate body part happened to be in the way. Plus, within a twenty-foot circle, one might have the ear drums ruptured. Chaos and bleeding out were where a grenade did its most damage.

"Hold your fire!" DJ called out to his group as he stepped out of the stairwell. But DJ didn't listen to his own commands. One of his targets moved, and DJ put two through his ear. Another tried to roll over slowly, and DJ ended him as well. He scanned all of them, a broken and bleeding row of bodies scattered about behind the concrete barrier. A hand moved, accompanied by a groan. DJ finished him too. "I think I got them all," he announced. Brett and Cash eased their way out of the group of cars, weapons at the ready.

Wait, DJ thought. There were only five bodies here...

The sixth jerked up from the other side of the barrier and hastily swung his rifle DJ's direction, but DJ hesitated. He had the drop on the surprise enemy, but Cash was directly in his line of fire on the other side. His rounds were capable of ripping through eighth-inch steel like it was butter. His enemy's body would not stop the rounds from passing all the way through and hitting Cash.

In desperation, he dove to his left. The two extra rifles slung over his shoulder were sent flying. He was a clattering collection of gear, weapons, and body parts. He knew his move was futile, and he could only hope the two FBI agents on the other side could take the guy out as DJ vanished from view on this side of the barrier.

He felt the twin, back-to-back blows of 556 ammunition ram into the center of his chest from his enemy. It drove the wind from his lungs with the intensity of a mule kick. He was pretty sure he took them in the protective plate mounted to his stolen vest. But he was still in trouble. The hits took all the fight out of him, and he was moving slow. The next two rounds would be right through his vulnerable head.

There was an explosive chorus of gunfire, and DJ involuntarily winced. It was over for him, he acknowledged. He closed his eyes, trying to breathe past the pain in his chest, and waited for the end to come.

But it didn't.

And then he felt utterly ridiculous.

The shots he heard were not from his enemy punching holes through him over and over again. They were from Brett and Cash firing simultaneously at his would-be killer. Laying there on the cold concrete, DJ patted himself looking for holes, but there were none. Granted, he was hurt, to be sure. He had shrapnel dug into his shoulder and the back of one leg. He probably had bruised ribs and a sternum. But he was alive. And as soon as he got his wind back, he could shoot as well.

There was another team on the way, he reminded himself. That sudden understanding sent him rolling over and pushing himself staggering from the ground. There was still work to do. They had to get to Brett's wife, and then beat-feet out of this place.

In his haste to get down to Abbi and help out, he never tried to listen in on his enemy with the radio mounted to his vest. He did so now, shoving the ear piece in and switching the thing on. Why was it even tuned off to begin with, he wondered?

Brett, Cash, and two security guards were moving towards him. Only two guards, he noted. Abbi suddenly appeared, shooting out from between two cars and sprinting past them all. She hurdled the barrier and wrapped him up in a hug, almost taking him to the ground again. He groaned in pain, and she quickly stood back and looked him over to see what was hurt.

She started to ask the question but DJ silenced her by holding up a finger and pointing to his ear. There was conversation from a leader to team leads. He was telling someone he had positioned two drones overhead for observation, but the heavy snowfall was interfering with the thermal cameras.

Two more teams were bad news, DJ thought. Drone support was bad news as well. But it turned out this snow storm was a blessing in disguise. It would help to conceal their movements.

Then the voice on the other end called out for location updates, and the first voice answering had DJ reaching for another frag grenade in his vest. The advancing team had circled around to the back stairs of the parking garage, and they were almost to the second level. DJ knew his group was out of time and needed to move. His sudden intensity surprised Abbi, and a look of fear descended across her face.

DJ pulled the pin and tossed the grenade into the stairwell behind him. Then he reached down and scooped up both discarded rifles by their straps, and started shoving Abbi back towards the barrier with his free hand. "We've got company!" DJ shouted.

There was a shout of surprise from inside the stairwell behind him. Then the grenade went off. This time DJ did not have his hands over his ears, and despite most of the volume being muffled by the enclosed concrete stairwell, the explosion was deafening.

Brett reached the barrier and grabbed both extra rifles from him as DJ and Abbi climbed over. Cash and the two guards were busy removing weapons and ammunition off the dead men in the middle garage. DJ briefly wondered how difficult it must be for them to be yanking ammunition from their fallen comrade.

"Where is the other guard?" DJ asked Brett, handing him the other radio he had slipped into his windbreaker pocket. His friend just shook his head, and took to aiming at the stairwell as he moved backwards. DJ let him cover their retreat and motioned to Cash at the wall they had been hiding against. "We need to jump. There's a squad coming up the back stairs, and another moving through the building on the first floor. It's our only way out." He handed off the other rifle to one of the guards. The same guy, only a few minutes earlier, held a taser ready to electrocute DJ until he pooped himself. Now they were both fellow soldiers fighting for their very right to live.

Agent Cash pointed to DJ's vest. "How many more of those grenades do you have?"

"One," DJ replied.

In mass, with Brett watching their six, they moved through the group of shot up vehicles and started over the wall. The second floor was quite a drop to the ground, and Cash instructed all of them to hit and roll to avoid injury. A guard, the very same one DJ handed a rifle to, went first. DJ took the man's weapon, and then dropped all the rifles down for him to catch.

"Wait," Brett interjected. "My bag too."

DJ looked down against the wall and saw Brett was referring to his messenger bag with all the files in it.

DJ understood why he wanted the thing. Inside represented Brett's plan to free him and Abbi. But DJ questioned whether it would even work or not. Especially considering what was happening right now. No matter, DJ did as he was asked, and dropped the bag down to the waiting guard.

Brett started shooting. And someone was shooting back. It was unclear if anyone had been hurt by the grenade DJ tossed, or if it just gave them a few extra seconds to try and escape. But there were obviously survivors, and they had advanced to the point they could exchange gunfire.

"Move!" Brett ordered. No one waited around to argue. Everyone bailed over the wall at this point, with Brett firing a steady volley of bullets at the stairs in order to keep them from rushing through.

DJ hit the ground and rolled, coming back to his feet quickly. But the drop sent a shockwave through his sternum. He hadn't been the same since Big Chuck hit him with that table leg back in the summer, and taking two bullets to the chest a moment ago only served to aggravate the old injury. He grunted from the pain, and Abbi appeared to look him over. Surprisingly, his shoulder and leg were not hurting at all. Either the grenade in the hall only caused superficial damage, or the adrenaline pumping through his veins was covering up the injury.

Abbi had a concerned look on her face. "You're not OK."

"No. I'm not," DJ replied. Then he flashed a quick smile. "But there will be time for you to nurse me back to health later." He turned to Cash who was helping guard number two stand. "Get to Brett's wife. I'll cover his retreat." Cash nodded, and the three of them set off for the end of the guest building. Abbi was choosing to stay with him, and DJ wasn't arguing.

Brett stopped firing and hurdled over the wall, his empty rifle left behind. He dropped into the snow beside DJ and Abbi, and Abbi helped him scramble to his feet on the slick pavement. They started after the others, with Brett favoring his left foot. He must have twisted it from the fall, DJ thought. DJ covered their retreat, walking backwards while aiming at the place Brett dropped from, looking for the enemy to show their face. A good ten seconds passed without him seeing a thing, and DJ risked a glance backwards.

Brett had left him and was at the last room already. He watched the agent grab the hand of a long-haired brunette. "Move it," Brett hollered at him.

"Just go," DJ replied. "I'm right behind you." He didn't want to just turn around and run with Abbi to the safety of the corner. He had the sneaking suspicion if he turned his back, that's when the enemy would poke a gun over the wall. He kept backing up and did not wait to see if Brett and crew would listen. Abbi stayed right behind him, her small hand resting on his right shoulder, stepping backwards with him as quickly as she could.

He spotted the first one, then. Their enemy did not advance to the outside edge of the parking garage where DJ jumped from. Instead, their pursuers elected to head back down the stairs and come out at the end of the structure. DJ panned right to engage while still moving towards the corner, but the first man was already firing.

Abbi went down in the snow behind him with a soft squeal, and DJ lost his mind.

His whole reason for living had just taken a bullet because of him. Rage descended on his self-control like a load of bricks, crushing it underneath. Kill them, he thought to himself. Kill them all without mercy.

He changed direction, choosing to advance instead of backing away. He moved right at them, firing two rounds at a time. Gone was his practiced discipline of counting every round fired. Here was a man blinded by hatred and grief, incapable of rational thought. When he ran out of bullets for the rifle, he would switch to his friend the Sig. When he was out of rounds for the Sig, he would rip their throats out with his teeth.

In the middle of his advancing and firing, two rounds with each step, he could hear screaming coming from somewhere. Not a feminine scream, like it was maybe Abbi in pain, but a solid male voice. And, it was not a scream of someone wounded. Rather, it was filled with boiling hot passion. It was hatred in its purest form.

It was him, he realized.

The first man fell before his onslaught, twin rounds through the bridge of his nose. The second man fell, two red holes connecting above his left eyebrow. The third staggered backwards into the shadows of the stairwell, two more rounds planted just below the Adam's apple.

Kill them. Kill them all.

"DAVID JOHN!" Abbi's angry voice snaked through the snow like a braided whip, securing him steadfastly in place.

She was alive. He snapped around to stare at her. She stood there with hands on her hips, wind tossing her hair to one side, and a glare cutting laser beams into his heart. She was perfectly fine. She must have just lost her balance and slipped in the freezing concoction covering of the pavement.

A bullet split the air to his left, causing him to focus on the source. It was not from behind at the end of the parking garage. It was not from off to his right, back towards the main building where he expected help would be showing up from any second. No. This shot came from behind Abbi. It came from over her shoulder by Agent Cash. The man was standing off to one side, and shooting just past them at some target behind DJ. It was a risky shot to take, and there was only one reason to take it.

DJ wheeled about with weapon raised, only to see another figure drop to his knees just past the open doorway to the stairs. He locked eyes with the dying man for a second, as the man desperately wrapped his hands around his own throat. It was a futile effort. Blood squirted out between his fingers from the gunshot wound provided by Agent Cash.

Cash called out through the frigid, swirling snow. "Quit playing around! We gotta go!"

DJ ran for it, snatching Abbi's hand as he raced by. The snow was falling at its heaviest now. As DJ and Abbi cleared the side of the building, it drove into them at a ninety-degree angle, driven by a biting wind. Flakes the size of fifty cent pieces plastered the sides of his head with wet, stinging kisses. It drove into his eyes, obscuring his vision even more. The world was a white, freezing mess, and he had no idea where he was going.

When he reached Agent Cash, he could finally see their destination in an obscurity of white. A tall, narrow, cement box stood like a sentinel in the snow. Brett was in front of it, holding a steel door open and waving at them to hurry. There was a light source somewhere inside illuminating the interior, and DJ could make out both remaining guards and Brett's wife. None of them were wearing jackets, and Lisa had her arms wrapped tightly about herself. As cold as DJ was in this flimsy windbreaker, they had to be freezing.

Why were they headed inside a concrete cube with no way out save the door marking the entrance? It was foolish. Somewhere out there in the snow storm were more guys with guns. And probably more grenades. Being trapped in a box hiding from the world was not where they needed to be. They needed to be hopping the fence and getting out of here under the shielding cover of the storm.

As soon as he and Abbi crossed the threshold of the giant block, Brett slammed the door behind them with a metallic clank. There was no wind inside, but the cold air made it feel like an icebox. Understanding flooded his chilled brain, and he knew now why Brett chose this spot. It was not to hide. It was to escape.

In the center of the room was a raised platform of circular concrete. In the middle of it was a smaller circular steel hatch. One of the guards was already unlocking a large padlock with a set of keys that were tethered to his waist with a retractable leash.

Brett bolted the door from the inside and turned to the room. "The entire property runs over a main sewage line. When they built this place, they set up this access point right at the end of the parking lot. For security reasons, we hold copies of the keys. When I first took over, I grabbed some hip waders and went down to check it out. It leads directly past the shopping center behind us. About half a mile from here is another access point. We can get out there."

"Won't it be padlocked from the outside too?" DJ asked. "How are we supposed to get out?"

"That one has a different locking system. There is an emergency release latch on the inside of all of them in case workers need to exit from any point in the network. This one was different because we didn't want people accessing a federal building without our control. There's just one problem."

Brett's wife spoke up through chattering teeth. "It's filled with crap?"

Brett nodded, but continued. "Worse. There is a security camera right there," he said, pointing into an upper corner.

Every eye in the room followed his finger to see a camera aiming at them all.

"So," DJ commented. "If any of our bad guys are looking at the security feed on the first floor…"

"Right," said Cash. "We'll get visitors any minute. Our only choice is to run and hope for the best. Even if they're watching us right now, there's no way for them to know where we are without someone with a knowledge of this place explaining to them. Now," he said turning to the room. "I hope none of you are fond of the clothes you're wearing. Because you're about to be knee deep in sh…" He stopped himself from completing the sentence as he seemed to consider the women in the room.

DJ smiled inwardly. Apparently, chivalry was not completely dead. Some men still watched their language around a lady.

Abbi stepped over and patted Agent Cash on the cheek, smiling like she was proud of him. "I think we all know what you meant. Now let's all go for a swim, shall we?"

"Wait," said DJ. He reached up and keyed the mic on the radio on his vest. "I would like to speak to the man in charge, please."

For a moment there was silence. Then, "Speaking," came the reply.

DJ was hoping Shark Bait would have been the one to answer. While it was only a one-word sentence, DJ could tell this voice belonged to someone else. "I'm the guy who just killed a bunch of your men. Let me see… I think the count is somewhere close to sixteen. Of course, my friends got a couple of them too, and I should probably give them credit for that. Anyways, sorry about your men, but the guy who hired you really should have given you more information about me."

Silence for a moment more, and DJ was starting to think the other person had simply turned the radio off. Then, "Well why don't you tell me now. Just who are you?"

DJ keyed the mic and laughed before answering. "I know it sounds a bit cliché', but how does 'Your Worst Nightmare sound'? The real question you should be asking, is who is the person who hired you? And I'll go ahead and let you in on that secret because I am sure he didn't bother telling you his real name. The man who hired you is none other than the infamous assassin known as El Gran Blanco. He hired you because he can't seem to kill me himself. Every time he goes up against me, he ends up limping away. Just like you and your team will tonight. Just to make sure we're on the same page, have you heard of El Gran Blanco?"

"I have," came the answer. The voice was flat and even and DJ couldn't make too much from of it.

"Now that you know who hired you, I wonder... I'll bet you he has plenty of people who would pay top dollar to have his head served to them on a silver platter. Bet someone could make a lot of money off that deal. Probably a lot more than killing little ole' me.

"Anyway, if you see him again, tell him he not only failed at killing me for the fourth time in a row, but my girlfriend was wearing a vest when he shot her. He screwed that up too. Tell him, I think it's time for him to retire. Tell him I'll be the one to retire him. Tell him... he can stop trying to track me, because as soon as I get all of my friends safe, I'm coming for him. We'll be seeing each other real soon. For your sake, I hope you're not there when I find him." DJ switched the radio off, unplugged the mic from his ear, and shoved the cord down into the pocket on his vest.

Brett nodded his approval. "Nice job on telling him who hired him. You think there's a chance he'll actually go after the man himself?"

"I have no idea," DJ shrugged. "But after losing so many men, he's got to be angry. I just wanted to give him something to think about."

With that, DJ flipped on the small tactical light mounted to the end of his rifle, and started climbing down the ladder into the worst smelling place he had ever been in his life. "Oh, God!" he exclaimed, choking down bile. "This is horrible!"

Brett snorted. "You should have been down there with Cash and I this summer when it was hot. It was twice as bad. Agent Cash gave it a nickname afterwards. He started calling the place, 'The Vomit Hole'. Would you like to know how he came up with it?" smoke.

Chapter 17: Trio of Calls

"Whatever you do, don't lose him!" Cody commanded the young man in the passenger seat.

"I'm doing my best," Digger replied with his thick British accent. "But do you have any idea how hard this is?" His afro-covered head was down, dark eyes glued to the glowing screen of the tablet computer in front of him. His forehead wrinkled in concentration, and his fingers furiously worked the flight controller of the drone somewhere overhead, invisible in the night.

Cody turned back to focusing on the road and the snow. It seemed to be coming from everywhere. At moments the wind would drive it from the left. Then the right. Or it would plummet straight out of the sky like lead-weighted cotton. Right now, it was swirling in circles, making it nearly impossible to see where he was going. Honestly, at this point, not being able to consult the GPS, he had no idea where he was or where he was headed. He was clueless, but he didn't care. The only thing of importance right now was tracking the man responsible for all of this.

For a moment, he considered what all had led him to this point. Three complete teams were dead. Twenty-four men in the space of about ten minutes. They were people he knew. They were people he liked. Some were people he was close to. Now they were gone, and his business had suffered a staggering blow because of a huge mistake by their employer.

Their first mission for the man was conducted in Boston. That one went south for two very specific reasons. Number one, they were told the target was protected by security guards. In reality, they were FBI. This alone was not a big deal as the element of surprise was on their side. That and overwhelming numbers. The second, was because a shooter jumped the gun sooner than he was supposed to. He was a newer recruit to an opposing group, and his mistake resulted in the trap not being sprung according to plan.

Cody could write off those mistakes to mere accidents. Stuff like this happened from time to time in the line of work he was in. Especially if you were working with other teams.

But this time…. Oh, this time was a far cry different. Everyone knew the windows of this facility were blast resistant. Everyone. It was all over the internet when they did their location assessment. There were countless news stories talking about it. All of them pointed out how, even though the building was designed to be wrapped in aesthetically-pleasing glass, it was actually state of the art construction engineered to defeat truck bombs. The glass was not glass. It was a two-foot-thick compound of nano-polymer layered resin, with microscopic threads of reinforced Spyder Series Kevlar.

The stuff was the love-child of the US Government's own DARPA project, and a tech billionaire intent on colonizing the solar system. It was as advanced a material one could ever hope to build anything out of. After all, it was designed to defeat hurtling space rocks speeding through the solar system. What was the idiot thinking by shooting at it with a gun? It would take a tank round to punch its way through.

The shot warned their adversary of the attack, and Cody should have pulled the plug right there. However, the claims by the contract holder of the place being empty with very few actual agents tempted him to continue with the mission.

It still should have worked. Surprise was once again in their corner. Defenders were few. Cody's group functioned with well-seasoned shooters, and the place would be cut off from outside communication preventing any call for help. Plus, the mother of all winter storms was blowing in. Despite the change, the mission should have still been a success.

But it wasn't. It had turned into a colossal cesspool of defeat.

Aside from the incredible mistake of their employer shooting at the building, the man had also omitted one huge piece of information. Their target was no ordinary rich criminal in the custody of the FBI. He was a shooter himself. And a good one, it turned out. A shooter that was not actually in the custody of the FBI, but walking about freely and having conversations with the head agent running the facility. In the man's office, no less.

The whole thing reeked. This was not a hit on a high-level FBI informant like they were told. This was a hit on a Tier 1 level shooter for the US Government. Had to be. He was either a spook for the CIA, or an operator for some dark government agency not even on the books. Nothing else could explain what was going on. And trying to kill someone like that was inherently connected to a shipload of repercussions. Not only was the man skilled, and therefore requiring a more thought out approach, but he was attached to resources capable of tracking Cody down and ending them all if they failed.

To make matters worse, Slaughter informed him over one of his own radios that their employer was really the legendary hit-man known as El Gran Blanco. A man who, if his identity were to be believed, could not manage to kill Slaughter on his own. He was uncertain of those claims. But if anything, it solidified his commitment to tracking their employer down and holding him accountable.

When Cody made the decision to show up with his entire team, he even included his in-house tech wizard everyone lovingly called Digger, or Diggs. Bayllen Diggery was a recruit he discovered on a mission to South Africa. The ebony skinned young man was wickedly smart, and a natural when it came to anything involving tech. Cody recognized talent and potential when he saw it, and added him to his team without much of a thought.

And he was thankful he did.

When they needed the internet scoured for information on people or locations, Digger produced all they needed quickly. If something required hacking, or they needed access to locations guarded by high-tech security, Digger made it happen in short order. He could even build his own tech to get the job done if something could not be purchased off the shelf.

It had been a no-brainer to include Diggs and a few of his custom drones on this mission.

Long ago, Diggs came up with the idea of modifying his fleet of drones with shot locaters to pinpoint both friendly and enemy combatants. It was a pretty ingenious set-up. Each drone was equipped with a small microphone tuned to lock onto sharp spikes in noise volumes. Gun shots. They sent this information wirelessly to Digger's computer. As long as at least three drones picked up the signal, they could use triangulation to locate precise longitude, latitude, and elevation of the shot. The system could then overlay this information on a digital map. It would geo-locate any shooter in range down to a five-foot radius. It could even tell you what floor they were on.

Digger could then order the on-board camera to aim in that direction automatically for the operator to see it on a screen. And the camera could see in three modes. Standard color, infrared, and thermal were all options.

Diggs built six of the things, and could control them all from one controller. He loved them so much, he even named them after famous video game characters. He was truly a king among geeks.

They brought along three of the things to provide aerial surveillance for the strike. Using thermal imaging, Cody would be able to keep an eye on all of his teams, and call out issues they needed to be aware of. In addition, using the shot locators, Cody would be able to zero in on their employer. The man was supposed to take out the radio antennae on the roof with a fifty-caliber rifle. When he did, Cody would know right where he was. He could then track him as he left the scene.

While their employer did not take out the radio as intended, he did still give away his position to the drones keeping watch overhead. And then, he bolted out of there just like Cody expected he would.

They had been following the man's SUV for just over fifteen minutes with a quadcopter named Brucie. Ten of those minutes were filled with a constant stream of failures coming in across the long-range digital radio. Cody had been torn between heading in to help his friends, or continuing the pursuit of their employer. In the end, getting payback over his lost comrades jumped to the top of the priority list.

He issued orders for the guys to bail on the mission and get out of there. They would head to a predetermined rally point and await further orders. Diggs dropped two of the drones into the courtyard of the FBI compound, and the remaining team members scooped them up on the way out.

Right now, he and Digger were driving far faster than they should be in a blinding snow storm on the outskirts of Denver. He was in the middle of a full-fledged white-out, and could barely see anything through the windshield.

A stopped truck appeared out of nowhere, and Cody jerked the wheel to the left, narrowly avoiding the collision. It was only after he was even with the other vehicle, Cody could see the growing red signal of a traffic light through the driving snow. He gritted his teeth, braced for an impact, and charged right through, praying no one was coming from the side. Thankfully, most people were choosing to stay inside on a night like this. No one T-boned their truck, and he continued on.

A beeping tone blurted out from the passenger seat next to him, louder than the defroster going full blast. "What is that?" Cody demanded.

Digger silenced it with a tap on the screen. "Wind alert. We are flying in higher winds than we're supposed to."

"Diggs you better keep that thing in the air!" he ordered.

"I'll do the best I can, but it's getting real tough to keep the bird on path. Plus, we are wearing out the batteries at a much higher rate. The wind and cold are killing this thing. If that guy don't find someplace to park quick, Brucie will be out of battery in less than six minutes."

Cody slammed his fist against the steering wheel in frustration. Tracking this guy was the only bright spot in this otherwise dark day. If he lost him because of a battery failure…

"It's worse, boss," Digger continued, never breaking his concentration from the screen. "There's so much snow in the air, the thermal's having trouble seeing through it all. I had to drop the altitude to less than fifty feet. That's high enough to clear traffic lights, but most everything else is taller. I'm trying to keep in the middle of what I think is the road, but if I'm wrong, I'm gonna smack a tree, or telephone pole or something. The object avoidance sensors just can't see through all of this snow."

Cody's knuckles were white, gripping the steering wheel. In part to ensure he maintained control of the speeding vehicle. But mostly from frustration. Half his team was dead, and he could not wait to wrap his fingers around the man's throat. Super assassin or not. "You know what? Just keep your mouth shut unless you have something good to tell me."

"Course change!" Digger shouted. "Target turned left. Make your turn in one hundred meters."

Cody squinted into the wall of white, desperately looking for a street sign or some indication of a crossroad. He mentally started counting distance, calculating how far he already traveled since Digger called it out.

There! In the snow were tire tracks making a left-hand turn, and the distance seemed about right. It must be from his target. He turned left as well, following in the tire tracks he now guessed to belong to his planned victim. He silently prayed he made the right decision, or this little trip would be over in short order.

"Stop!" Digger commanded. "Contact's pulling in on the right. He's stopping. Hang on and let me see if I can get a better picture… I see a sign…"

Cody came to a halt right in the middle of the road. There was no one behind him he could see, but visibility was almost non-existent. If anyone was following along behind, they wouldn't see him until they were on top of him. He kept his eyes glued to the rearview mirror, looking for headlights, ready to take off and avoid a rear-end collision.

"It's a motel," Digger said. "Not a retail chain. Looks like a privately-owned place. He pulled up in front of some rooms. He's getting out…" He sucked in air through clinched teeth then and eased back on the control.

"What happened?" asked Cody with tension in his voice.

"I told you I was pretty low. I think he heard the rotors. He looked right at me. He didn't take off, though. He may not have been sure what he heard. It's pretty windy right now. I can barely make him out now. There! He's gone inside." As if on cue, another alarm started sounding and Digger tapped the screen to shut it up.

"What was that one?"

"Two-minute alarm on the battery. I gotta land now, boss. Stay put and I'll drop it outside my door." Cody nodded and Digger worked his remote. A few seconds later and the sound of the electric motors of the drone could be heard faintly over the defroster and the wind outside. The drone lowered even with the passenger side window and then hovered there. Diggs lowered his window and reached out and grabbed the thing. The rotors shut off and Digger brought it inside, rolling up the windows immediately after.

The drone resembled a shoebox with four short arms on the corners, supporting the small helicopter style blades. Scrawled across the side with a yellow paint pen was the word "BRUCIE" in all caps.

Geeks and their toys, Cody thought to himself. "What game was Brucie from again?"

"GTA. Grand Theft Auto. Desensitizing the world's youth to violence since 1997," Digger said with a grin. "But the Brucie character is from the 2008 edition." While Cody watched, the young black man with his trademark horned-rimmed glasses swapped out the large battery that took up most of the body. He then rolled the window back down, held the drone out at arm's length, and sent it back off in the night.

"Alright," Digger proclaimed a moment later. "Brucie is back on station. Got him on hover mode watching the door. In this wind we have about twenty-two minutes. And.... Yep. I just saw a thermal move past the window. That was probably our boy, unless he's got a friend in there too. So now what?"

"Now, we get the rest of the team over here and decide what we're going to do."

"We're going to kill him, right?

"Oh, he's going to die. But not before we verify who he really is, and decide on what's the most profitable pathway forward."

"As long as he dies."

"Yeah, I agree. As long as he dies. Now, here's what I want you do..." Cody started the vehicle moving forward again while he began to give Digger instructions. Digger set to work right away, eager to fulfill his roll. Cody pulled into the first small parking lot he found, and pulled out his phone to start calling the rest of his team.

The phone rang in his hand before he got a chance. This was likely a team member anxious to know what they were going to do about the fiasco at the FBI compound. No doubt, every one of his team was going to be thirsty for blood at this point. It was going to Cody's job to get them to show some restraint for now. First, he needed to figure out how to turn lemons to lemonade. If the man really was El Gran Blanco, he was worth a ton of cash. If he could somehow get paid off of this deal, it would go a long way to making up for the fact half of his team was dead.

He answered. "Hello?"

As soon as DJ escaped the sewer, emerging from a matching concrete shack, he knew they were in trouble. There was already over a foot of snow on the ground, and the drifts were far deeper. And, it was bitterly cold. Too cold for people who had been wading around in ankle deep water and sewage to withstand for long. Frostbite was going to be a serious issue in just a few minutes. A problem Brett pointed out a second after crossing through the doorway and into the wind.

"We need to get out of this, now," Brett stated. Both he and Brett began combing the area looking for options. They quickly agreed on the only one that seemed available. There was a used car dealership across the street. They couldn't tell from this distance if it was opened or closed, but in either event, the heat was on. And, with the outside of the building surrounded by glass windows, it would be easy enough to break in if the place was locked up.

DJ ordered everyone to jog to keep warm blood circulating into their feet. He then pointed to the guard he labeled "Thing" to lead the way. It was what he started calling the largest guard with the muscles, crewcut, and the single eyebrow that stretched across his forehead. The other man was equally muscled, but could not have been more than five feet, five inches. He reminded DJ of a boulder with feet. Mighty Pebble, he thought to himself, grinning at the notion. He could call him MP for short.

He took up the rear to try and focus the stragglers. They set off eagerly trying to generate heat in their body. But Lisa, he could tell, was struggling. The cold and wet was sapping her strength at a rapid pace, and was now beginning to show on her worse than the others. She was being dragged along by Brett and was openly crying now. Finally, the agent paused to sweep her into his arms.

"No!" DJ barked. "She needs to keep her body moving. He then turned his attention to Lisa and began to yell. "Move, woman! Move! Don't give those people the satisfaction. You're almost there. You can do this. You get yourself in that building and *then* you cry all you want. Now pump those legs and get your backside in gear!" DJ was doing his best to channel his old drill instructor. He wasn't sure if he was pulling it off, but Lisa managed to nod her head through her tears and move quicker.

The sharp crack of a gunshot broke through the shifting driving snow in front of them. Both men aimed instinctively in the same direction, with Brett stepping in front of his ailing wife. DJ's concern for Lisa evaporated like mist, as fear for Abbi prioritized its way through his biased brain.

"Let's go!" Thing called out. The guard was standing there with gun in hand, waving them on, holding the front doors open. He must have put a round through the lock to gain access, DJ thought.

MP, Abbi, and Agent Cash were first through the door. Brett ignored DJ then, and picked his wife from the ground, breaking into a jog for the front door. DJ did a quick glance around to see if they were being pursued before following.

They seemed to be right next to the shopping center area behind the FBI field office. They had made their way through a corner of the parking spaces wrapped around the side of the large retail complex. From there, they drew a ragged line across the empty snow-covered street, and into the outer edge of the used car lot. Visibility varied as wind swept clouds of thick snow across his vision. Sometimes he could see a hundred yards or more. Other times, fifty feet was all he could manage. But aside from his group now making their way into the building behind him, the entire white world seemed to be devoid of all human life.

DJ turned and jogged for the open door. His feet were tingling and growing numb, and each step sent stabbing pain up through the soles of his feet. He couldn't feel his lips or nose. His ears felt like they were being poked with needles, and his fingers were now robbed of most of their feeling. He needed heat in the worst way. They all did.

He passed through the door and Thing pulled it closed behind him. Inside the showroom floor, DJ began to appreciate the apparent size of the place. The sign out front read "Buckee's Rides". The name suggested a dive of a place. The kind he would normally steer clear of. The kind of place where salesmen would all but tackle you to the ground and steal your wallet. But inside told a different story.

It was sleek and modern with an expansive showroom, including newer models under spotlights. There were rows of offices in the back with floor to ceiling glass for buyers to negotiate and sign papers. Off to one side was a snack-bar area for potential customers. Over all, it was a really nice place.

It should have been a priority to get the alarm shut off, and then try to get wet clothes off of people and warm them up with whatever he could find. But there were no alarms sounding.

Probably because MP held a stranger to the floor face down, with a knee in his back and a gun to his head. The guy was blubbering a plea to not be shot, and promising he could give them any car they wanted. He obviously worked here, and was the reason the alarm was not on.

Brett barked at the shorter muscle-bound guard to get off of him right now, and MP begrudgingly followed orders. He still held his side-arm in the ready position and looked willing to raise it at the slightest provocation.

Brett helped the employee from the floor and flashed his badge, asking him if anyone else was around.

"No… I'm the only one. I swear. If you're really cops, why did you have to shoot the lock? You could've just knocked on the glass." DJ instantly believed him. For whatever reason, while every other employee had run for the safety of their homes as the storm rolled in, this man had stayed behind. And now he was trapped here with the rest of them. DJ could find out later why the man was still here. Right now, he had a medical priority he must deal with.

"Do you have any blankets here?" He asked the man. The man was somewhere in his late fifties, and the embroidered name and title on his long sleeve polo told DJ he was the Facilities Manager. The name simply read, John.

The manager nodded his head as he answered. "Sure. The owner has a room set up with emergency supplies. We've got enough blankets for an army."

"Great," DJ replied. "You're going to take me to them in just a second. And does your boss keep any of those hand warmer packs around?"

He got another nod in reply.

"OK," DJ said addressing the room. "I need everyone to listen to me and do exactly what I say. All of you are going over to that waiting area." He pointed to a waiting area off to the side. "Get your shoes and socks off as fast as you can. Then I want you to sit in a big circle and start rubbing each other's feet. It's going to hurt. Maybe a lot. Do it anyway. Do it now!"

As he talked, he sat himself down on the floor and began to remove his own boots and socks. He got back to his feet as fast as he could, and then told the manager to lead the way. His own feet were tingling and smarting with every step, but he tried to keep his toes wiggling as he walked.

The manager walked quickly just ahead of him, but kept looking at the gun in DJ's hand with nervous glances. He decided to try and talk to him and alleviate the poor man's fears. Maybe he could encourage the guy to help them willingly.

"So, you're a manager here?" DJ began.

"Yeah. The dealership manager," he nervously responded.

"Why are you still here? Why not head home with the rest of the employees?"

"Well, I'm salary. I thought I could use the extra time to get some paperwork done. I've been backed up. I was almost finished. I was about to finally leave when that guy shot the door open."

"You were going to try and leave in this? There must be close to two feet of snow on the ground and almost zero visibility. Do you have a death wish?"

"Naah." He stopped at a single door in the hallway and produced some keys. As he sorted through them, he continued. "I'm a bit of a gear head when it comes to cars. I have a truck that'll eat this stuff for breakfast."

DJ shook his head but kept his mouth shut. Everyone who owned a four-wheel drive seemed to think they were equipped to take on any environment. But a friend had once told him something he never forgot. The only thing a four-wheel drive was good for, was getting you stuck two miles deeper in the woods. Nothing beat skill, understanding, and maybe a winch. It was a statement DJ had come to believe over his lifetime. He had seen many a four-wheel drive off in a ditch due to over-confidence.

He once saw an old Marine Corps deuce and a half mired in a muddy ditch. The driver had radioed for a wrecker to come and get him when DJ happened along with his patrol. His Lieutenant took one look at the situation, and told the driver he just didn't know what he was doing. The LT clambered up in the thing, and sixty seconds later had it pulled back up on the road. DJ watched the man work in amazement.

"I'm from the deep, dark part of Alabama," the LT told the stunned driver. "We know a thang r' two bout' muddin'." DJ sure missed that LT. Many officers had their heads full of classroom taught leadership. But that old Marine Lieutenant of his was a leader and a doer.

The door opened and DJ snapped his attention back to the here and now. What he saw made him appreciate the intent of the business owner, and DJ asked the manager about it. The room was filled with stacks of foldable cots, shelves of blankets and pillows, dehydrated meals, and even stacks of clothing sorted by size. Along one wall was an area just for kids and infants. It held playpens, stacks of diapers, dry formula mix, and even boxes of toys.

John The Manager explained how the owner had built a chain of dealerships by focusing on giving back to the communities in which they resided. This included, in part, emergency preparedness in being able to respond to disasters like hurricanes
and tornados. The maintenance bay in the back could be converted to emergency shelters in order to help those in need. Each dealership was constructed to include larger than necessary bathrooms with shower stalls. And, even kitchens to support feeding a couple hundred people if required. There was now a Buckee's Rides in all fifty states. Each one could not only support their immediate community, but could truck out these supplies to a neighboring state should there be a need.

DJ was impressed. In fact, he was more than impressed. He was downright thankful. Stumbling into this place had not just been fortunate, it was an outright blessing. He grabbed an armful of blankets, and then turned to John The Manager.

"OK, scratch the hand warmers. I need access to those showers. And I guess I need to fill you in on who we are, why we are here, and why I desperately need you to keep your mouth shut about it all. Do you know the FBI building behind the shopping center over there?" DJ asked motioning in the general direction with his head. John The Manager nodded in reply.

DJ then began to weave a tale about how the place was attacked to kill him and Abbi. The reason for this, he explained, was they were key witnesses to a crime involving the last remnants of associates affiliated with Big Chuck. A look of recognition flashed across John The Manager's face at the mention of Big Chuck. Since the summer, it was all the local media could talk about. If you were from the Colorado, you knew who Big Chuck was, and what all had happened this past summer.

"So," the man asked him. "You're not an agent yourself? You were bossing those guys in the other room around."

"I was a Corpsman in the Navy," DJ explained. "When it comes to first aid and triage, I *am* in charge." He smiled at the man. "Now show me those showers. We've got work to do."

Two minutes later and DJ was shuffling people into warm showers. The idea was, the warm water would quickly raise the temperatures of the exposed areas of skin in danger of frost bite. Before jumping into a shower himself, he examined each one of them carefully looking for evidence of irreparable damage. Gratefully, he spotted none. But the shower also served to wash away any biological material that might have caused them sickness after walking around in raw sewage. Cholera and E. coli were the two most dangerous things he could think of, but there were probably a host of others. Getting clean as soon as possible was a very real need.

After each one finished their shower, they wrapped themselves up in blankets and made for the emergency storage room to find clothing. Thankfully, not only did John The Manager help find things to fit for every one of them, but there was an assortment of coats and jackets as well.

An hour later, sitting inside the showroom with the lights turned off, DJ and Brett sipped hot chocolate and looked out at the snow. Abbi found plenty of instant mix packets and made them all steaming cups. Right now, she was back in the offices help setting up cots for people to catch some rest. The news informed them this snow would proceed well past midnight. Brett informed them all they were not going to do anything but stay right where they were, hidden from the world, until at least morning.

Brett also confiscated everyone's cell phones and made sure they were turned completely off to avoid being tracked. One of the guards was married and seemed to be concerned he was not being allowed to call home and tell his spouse he was safe. Brett assured him that word would get back soon enough that he was one of the ones who escaped with the SAC. And, if he risked calling her, he might place her safety into question by whoever was after them. Thankfully, John The Manager was not married. So, they did not have to worry about an anxious spouse concerned over his safety.

While the others prepared to get some rest, Brett and DJ used the opportunity to talk about their situation and maybe devise some sort of plan. They sat sipping hot chocolaty goodness in a couple of cushioned chairs, and looked out through the tall glass panes into a world gone white. If he allowed his mind to go blank and forget about the threats pursuing them, DJ could almost enjoy the moment. Thin panes of transparency separated them from swirling balls of ice, illuminated by the parking lot lights seen dimly through the thick cover of the storm.

While the winds were not blizzard strength in intensity, the amount of snow descending from the heavens was staggering.

Brett interrupted his momentary focus on the storm, and brought his attention back fully on to their problems. "I'm going to have to report in soon so they know for sure we got away cleanly."

"Won't security video show us escaping through the sewers?" DJ asked him.

"Sure," Brett replied. "But they won't know what happened to us after we left. For all they know, we could have been ambushed and kidnapped after we exited."

"You can't," DJ stated flatly. "There is obviously somebody in the FBI leaking information out to Shark Bait. How else could he have known I was being held back at your offices? How else could he have known the place would be virtually empty? One of your friends gave us up."

"You think I don't know that?" Brett shot back with venom in his voice. "I am painfully aware. Right now, there are only two agents I trust. One of them is in the other room preparing to get some sleep. And he happens to be the son of the only other agent I trust." Brett stopped short, the look on his face telling DJ he just realized he said too much. He wasn't aware Abbi had uncovered the secret only a short while before.

"Mr. Neville is Agent Cash's dad," DJ said bluntly.

Brett blinked in response. Then, "How…"

"Abbi figured it out," DJ shrugged. "She hates secrets."

Brett just shook his head in overwhelmed surprise. "Regardless, I know we have a leak. Someone has found themselves on the payroll of El Grand Blanco. I'm just not sure yet who. There were a handful of people who knew you were brought to Denver. My second in command, for starters. Plus a few more. We know for a fact there were plenty of agents on the take when my predecessor was running the show, because of what we dealt with on the Big Chuck case. So, it's likely a leftover we haven't caught up with yet."

"Well," DJ said. "Let's start working backwards. How many people both knew about me being in Denver, *and* knew we were in route to Beacon Hill to ambush Shark Bait?"

Brett seemed to process that, and then looked over his head back towards the offices before answering. "Just the people who were on that plane…" He trailed off as he thought about it.

DJ realized where the man's brain was going. Could his trusted confidant Agent Cashin be passing information to the enemy? It was certainly possible. He could have easily phoned Shark Bait when no one was looking and tipped the assassin off.

DJ though back to this past summer. Abbi had hacked the phone from Big Chuck's son to help set up a plan of attack on getting back his in-laws. Could she do the same thing to Agent Cash's phone? Could she explore her way through the dark digital closet of the agent's cellphone to find out who he had been talking to? Was there some secret app for communication sitting on his phone like Big Chuck's son had used?

DJ quickly outlined his thoughts to Brett, and they put together a hasty plan to find out. DJ headed to find Abbi with her laptop bag of tricks, and Brett went to find Cash and keep him occupied. Abbi quickly agreed to anything involving use of her skills, and fished the agent's cell out of the bundle of phones they stored in Brett's messenger bag. She set to work on it while DJ went to find Brett and let him know.

What he saw when he rounded the corner of the small office Cash staked out as his temporary bedroom caused him to pause in the doorway in shock. There, standing in the room with his weapon pointed at Agent Cash's head, was a Brett Foster he had never seen before.

Agent Cash was still lying down on his cot. Brett was bending over him. One hand held his service Glock to the forehead of the junior agent. The other clenched the man's shirt in a tight knot just under his chin, and Brett was speaking through clenched teeth.

"My wife was there!" Brett fumed. "My wife! You're the only one I can connect the dots to. The Tac Team members were all brought in from the Dallas office in the transition. We sent the other ones here out to other agencies just to make sure we didn't have any corrupted ones. They were guys I trusted. Guys I worked with."

"You trusted me, Brett," Agent Cash replied in measured tones. "You worked with me as well. Why question my loyalty over them?"

"Because you were the only one who knew DJ would be in my office when the sniper attacked. And just last week, you made the comment that my office wasn't secure enough because a sniper could take me out through the windows. You said it like you were joking. The phone on my desk rang right then, and I never got the chance to explain what those windows were made of. You didn't know they were bullet proof. You didn't know. You sold me out, didn't you? And worse, you endangered my wife. My wife! You brought her into all of this! Now tell me what that assassin has on you to make you sell me out."

"Brett…" the younger agent began. But Brett cut him off to accuse him even further.

"Are you telling me it was all a coincidence you were not only at both locations, but that a sniper tried to do exactly what you had pointed out only days before?"

"Brett…" Cash started to speak again. But again, Brett cut him off to continue his rant. Spittle flew from his mouth as he pressed the muzzle of his weapon harder to Agent Cash's skull, pushing the man's head back further into his pillow. DJ had a profile view and could see Brett's finger pulling the trigger all the way back to the break point. An ounce or two more of pressure and Brett would shoot the man.

Brett was exhausted and running on little sleep. DJ and Abbi were both rested up since arriving in Denver. But Brett continued to stay busy the entire time, coming up with an insane plan to keep them out of jail. Plus, the man was working contacts and combing through any leads to be had from other agencies, along with Interpol, trying to get ahead of Shark Bait.

DJ knew Brett to be a person who seemed to be able to connect the dots. He was a natural investigator, able to peer through the proverbial fog of information to determine the truth. He also knew him to be cool under pressure. Even if the life of his wife was in jeopardy. But apparently the events of last summer, along with the feeling of possible betrayal by a friend, combined with the loss of sleep to push Brett over the limit.

Brett was probably right, DJ thought to himself. Agent Cash was very likely the mole in Shark Bait's back pocket. But the evidence was circumstantial at best. It was unlike Brett to simply jump from the realm of possibility, to condemn another to death. Especially one he seemed to trust so much.

But then again, this was the second time in less than a year his wife had gotten caught in the crosshairs thanks to the betrayal of fellow agents. Going on as little sleep as he had, maybe it was simply too much for the man to take without exploding.

Cash had saved DJ's life back at the field office. The man had calmly fired a bullet right past him in order to take out a would-be killer. He could have easily planted that round through DJ's skull. It didn't seem to add up. Cash might be the mole they were looking for, but the man deserved the benefit of the doubt until Abbi finished going through the phone. And if he didn't intervene now, Cash would be dead. If found to be innocent, Brett would never be able to live with himself.

No. He had to stop Brett before it was too late. He did the only thing he knew would end this before Brett could pull the trigger. DJ did not attempt to reason with his friend. He did not jump and try to wrestle the gun away. He did what he did best. With lightning speed and practiced precision, he drew his own weapon.

The range was close. Less than ten feet was all that separated him from Brett. DJ's well-rehearsed skill came in to play as easily as breathing. He was extremely confident there was no way he could miss.

The gun bucked in his hand with familiar feel, as DJ sent the round screaming towards his friend

---

He was a traitor. There was no other way to define himself. He wore a mask for the world to see and judge him by. He could live out what the mask portrayed to others. He could act the part. He could carry himself appropriately to enforce the lie. But that's all it was. All *he* was. A lie. Timothy Neville was a walking, talking, betraying lie.

He smiled for the cameras and answered questions for reporters with all the skill of a politician. Part of being a Special Agent in Charge, and leading a field office for the FBI, was learning the art of politics. Mostly this meant negotiating the power players at the top of the agency. But now, now with his promotion to the office of Top Cop, his political prowess was being turned to maneuvering his way through the world of senators, congressmen, and the Washington elite.

So, he smiled. He shook hands and played the part. He carried himself with an air of leadership for the cameras turned his way. He interviewed one by one with all of the big media outlets ahead of the official swearing in ceremony, wearing a slight grin of knowing authority, and the cloak of self-assurance.

But the simple truth was, he was a living, breathing lie.

Funny thing was about becoming a traitor, the more you jumped over the line to perform your nefarious deeds, the easier it was to shove those feelings of guilt aside. The reasons you told yourself for justification of your actions, slowly morphed into your own weird version of the truth. But buried deep inside your soul, the real truth was always there. It could never be fully eradicated or erased. It would always resist being changed or altered. The truth was persistent, forever burrowed into the depths of your heart, and pricking at your conscience with all the annoyance of a thin splinter.

Prick… Traitor. Prick… Deceiver. Prick… Betrayer.

Word had finally filtered its way through official channels that the Denver Field Office had been attacked. People were dead. Brett was missing. Video of him and his wife escaping under the protection of a couple of site guards, along with three other yet unidentified people, showed his friend had somehow managed to get free.

For this, Tim was thankful. But he was also filled with dread. He was quite sure that one of the two unknown males were none other than DJ Slaughter. And this meant El Gran Blanco would be calling him again soon, asking where Slaughter had run to.

Slaughter… He wanted nothing more than to shove him off of something really high. It was his fault all of this was happening. True, Tim found himself entangled with El Gran Blanco long before Slaughter showed up in the picture. But that only involved passing information along to keep the assassin safe. Now though, Tim had been transformed into a two-faced turncoat in a three-piece suite, actively putting his best friend's life at risk.

And his wife. Let's not forget his wife.

These thoughts rolled through him as he sat on a comfy couch in a green-room, backstage of yet another national all-news channel. He was to record an interview for the Sunday show to be aired tomorrow morning. It was late. He was tired. And this would be the final interview of the day. He could only hope his interviewer had not got word of the attack in Denver just yet.

He instructed the guys on site to keep it under wraps as much as possible, but he knew there were always a few people dying to tell what they knew to a reporter. Blabbing about secret stuff had a way of making people feel important. But, if he could make it to Monday before the news found out, the swearing in ceremony would be over. He could stay on topic and keep putting forth the message the president wanted to convey. Luckily, there was a severe winter storm in Denver dumping mountains of snow on the city, and miring everything to a standstill.

If not, if they somehow already knew, and if he was asked, he already had a spin to the story in place. He would tell them the investigation was just getting started. He would point out that this would be the second major event that had happened to his mismanaged agency in less than a year. This is precisely why he had been appointed to this position. And, he was looking forward to getting the agency back on track and restoring it to its previous sterling reputation.

His phone buzzed in his pocket, and the caller ID on the screen said, "Blocked". His heart stopped as he knew this was the call he had been dreading.

He answered.

"You already know what I want," the familiar voice of El Gran Blanco said on the other end. "Give it to me now."

"I do. But I don't have what you need yet. Brett isn't answering his phone. It's going straight to voicemail. I can only assume he turned his phone off because he suspects a mole in the agency, and he's trying to avoid being tracked. I'm pretty sure he would never expect it was me, however. He'll reach out soon enough. I am probably the only person in the entire FBI he trusts right now. When he does, I'll milk him for information and call you back. I just need a way to contact you."

There was silence on the other end for a moment. Either the assassin was seething with anger and unable to speak, or he was considering whether Tim was lying or not. If the man even suspected a lie, his family would all start dropping like flies. He wasn't, of course. He was going to willingly throw Brett to the Shark a third time just like the previous two. And the sad thing was, it got easier and easier each time.

He bit his lip and waited.

Finally, "I will contact you every hour on the hour, until you give me what I want."

"You can't do that," Tim pleaded. "Somebody will get suspicious of all those phone calls."

"Then you better figure something out. I don't care. Get me what I need." The phone went dead.

Tim looked at the blank screen for a second more, then slowly returned it to his breast pocket.

He thought then of his son. The son few people knew about, and now serving some unknown post in the FBI. Where was Bradford at right now? When the young man had come to him while they were both still at the Dallas office, Bradford told Tim he had put in for a transfer. He wanted to make it in this career on his own. He demanded Tim not ask questions about where he was going so he couldn't check up on him, and use any influence he might have over the new post he would be taking.

Tim had grudgingly agreed, only because he had a good idea where the young man was going. There was a new department for Special Crimes being spun up in Los Angeles. It was in line with what he was already doing in Dallas. There were a lot of openings there, and Bradford had once told him he would like to eventually make it out to either the East Coast or the West Coast. It's where all the fun stuff happens, he explained. It only made sense Bradford would be heading to LA.

But now with everything that had happened, he wondered... Could his son have instead transferred to Denver to work alongside Brett? Certainly, Brett would have tipped him off if that were the case.

Right?

Tim thought about the fact there were three other unidentified people with Brett as he made his escape. Two males and one female. One of the men had to be Slaughter. The girl must be Abbi Jackson. There were two guards and Brett's wife. But who was the other male?

It probably wasn't Bradford. Tim was probably right about LA, but he had to know for sure. He snatched his phone back out. He would call his assistant and have her track down the agent for him and tell him where the man was assigned. He wouldn't tell her who he was, of course. And he knew it would be breaking his promise to his son, but he had to ease his mind. If he had also put his son at risk... Well, that was not something he could live with.

A knock to the greenroom door came before he could dial the number. A kid of not more than twenty poked his spikey-haired head around the corner, wearing a headset. Some sort of production assistant, Tim assumed. The kid smiled at him and asked if he was ready to record. They were all set up. They just needed to get him into make-up for about five minutes and they could start shooting.

"How long is this going to take?" Tim asked. "I am expecting a phone call in less than an hour. When it comes, I'll have to excuse myself and take it."

"No problem," the youngster said with a grin. "It's all being recorded anyways. If you get your call in the middle, we can just edit that part out. Unless you think it may make you have to leave?"

Tim considered that option before responding. It would be an easy way to finally end a long day of tedious interviews. No, he decided. He needed to finish this day strong. In the world of politics, the longer you could stay on message, the better. "It shouldn't take me away." He reassured. "That'll be fine."

He stood to follow the assistant to a make-up chair down the hall. After all, even traitors had to look their best on camera.

Chapter 18: With Friends Like These

The target was small. Only a little over an inch would mean the difference between missing completely, or causing serious bodily harm. But DJ was not hoping for serious bodily harm. Quite the opposite. He was aiming for the gun held in Brett's hand. Specifically, the top part of the service pistol. If he was too far left, the 9mm slug would rip through the front of Agent Cashin's face. Too low, and he would punch a hole through Brett's hand. Too high, and he would miss completely. But, the gunshot would likely cause Brett to flinch and finish pulling the trigger. So, either hit the target or very bad things would be the result.

DJ didn't miss. At this range it was almost an impossibility for him. DJ practiced trick shots like this just for fun.

The round smashed into the metal slide of Brett's service Glock, ripping it from Brett's hands, and destroying the pistol in the process. They picked up an extra pistol from the dead guard in the parking garage, so Brett still had one to fall back on. Plus, they had two AR15's and rounds to go along with them. Still, it didn't make DJ feel too good knowing he just reduced the amount of available firepower down by one full gun. Had he thought the thing all the way through, he might not have done what he just did. But then, DJ admitted to himself, he tended to be more of a shoot first, think second kind of person.

It was a trait which could have disastrous consequences if he wasn't careful.

The look of stunned surprise instantly carved across both agent's faces was priceless. It seemed to take both men a second to process what just happened. At first, they were staring at each other with grave intensity, only one thing occupying their thoughts. Living or dying. Traitor or friend. Murder or justice. The next instant, they were staring at where Brett's pistol used to be, and then back into each other's eyes in confusion. DJ would have laughed out loud were it not for the severity of the situation.

Then both heads turned his way, and DJ focused in on condemning Brett for his actions, choosing to press his advantage over the moment. "Have you gone stupid?" DJ asked Brett. "You were just telling me this man was one of only two agents you could actually trust. And yet you were just about to split his brain in two."

Brett stood upright, releasing Agent Cash's shirt, and leveled a finger at DJ. "I'm getting real sick of you firing rounds my direction."

But DJ would not be diverted off course. "I agree there is some circumstantial evidence pointing at short-stack here, but why not let Abbi do her job and tell us for sure?"

Agent Cash blinked in response to the news he was being investigated by Abbi. Then, "Wait… Are you letting that girl hack her way through my life right now?" He directed the question to both Brett and DJ, swinging his head back and forth between the two.

DJ shook his head. "Not your whole life. Just your phone. If you've been talking to someone you shouldn't, she'll know it. Deleted an email or text? She'll resurrect it. No matter what sneaky little app you have installed. I think she said something along the lines of never being able to erase or a hide a digital footprint. It's always there if you know where to look. So, got anything you want to tell us now? Been to any websites you're ashamed of?" DJ smiled.

DJ heard Abbi clear her throat behind him.

"What do you have?" DJ asked over his shoulder.

"To be honest," she answered. "I'm not really sure."

"Well I kinda need to know if we need to keep pointing a gun at him or not," DJ said with a touch of frustration, turning to look at her directly.

Abbi merely shrugged in response, and seemed unsure of what to say. Behind her were both guards, now dressed in civilian attire, but still wearing their gun belts. Both were standing with hands on their sidearms, alerted to the situation thanks to the muffled gunfire of DJ's silenced Sig. After all, they were only in the next hall, and silenced guns were seldom ever silent.

DJ pointed at Mighty Pebble and said, "Let me see your handcuffs."

"I don't think so, buddy," the short man sneered.

"Now!" Brett's command cut through the air with hard edged authority, and MP willingly tossed his handcuffs over. DJ, in turn, tossed them to Brett, and the senior agent then commanded Cash to stand and turn around.

After handcuffing Cash with his hands behind his back, they all three followed Abbi back to where she set up her laptop. The guards dutifully tagged along behind. On the screen was a spreadsheet, and she plopped down in front of it to explain what they were seeing.

"This," she said, pointing to a column of numbers on the left, "is every number he has called in the last six months. Most of them are grouped together into three groups of numbers. One of those is yours, Brett. But, I am not sure who these two belong to," she said pointing two phone numbers out.

Brett leaned over to look closer. "One of those belongs to our automated switchboard. Dial that number and say the name of the person you want to reach, and it connects you to whatever agent or site personnel you're looking for. Numbers change all the time, as do section leaders. This makes it easier to reach whomever you need. That last number belongs to his father."

Abbi nodded and continued. "There are only 18 other numbers showing up in the last six months. I ran them through an internet search and most of them are all various takeout places around town. No red flags there. These four came up as unlisted, but they all have the same first three numbers. 689."

Brett nodded before replying. "Those are all assigned numbers to agents. Just probably people he works with."

"So then," Abbi concluded, "there are no other numbers for the last six months. None. No friends or family. Except, of course, for his dad's number. On the whole, that seems a bit odd for someone to only be calling work or takeout places to eat. Additionally, he has a banking app. It requires facial recognition to get in, but I went past that with no problem. He has no large deposits or transfers indicating someone was paying him off. No red flag there, either. However..." She stopped and looked over at Cash. For a moment she seemed embarrassed she was snooping into the man who was standing in the same room with her.

"What?" Agent Cash asked.

"Well," she turned back to face the screen. "It's just that there's no other apps on the phone. None. Only the ones that come with the phone, one other for checking his security cameras at his home, a banking app, but that's it. The history shows only a game being downloaded a few months back, but it was deleted less than twenty-four hours later. And that's just... Well... It's just weird."

Brett and DJ both just looked at each other for a moment, and then Abbi's reasoning seemed to click into place.

Brett spoke the conclusion first. "You think this makes him look like he has a burner phone. Like he keeps everything for work on this one, and everything else on another we don't know about."

"Well…" Abbi replied. "Yeah. Exactly. It's weird for someone to not have any apps on their phone. It's just not normal."

Brett smiled and then called for the cuff keys from Mighty Pebble. As he uncuffed Agent Cash, he reassured Abbi. "You have to have known Agent Cash here for a while, but then you would understand. There is nothing more important to Cash here other than the job. The FBI is his life. It's all he's known since he was old enough to not wear training pants. He looked up to his father. He was either pretending to be a G' Man when he was a kid, or working on his grades to make sure he got into Quantico. He's never had a girlfriend for longer than… I don't know. I think the record was three weeks. He doesn't have a burner phone. It's just who he is."

Brett then turned to look Cash in the eyes, and held out his hand. "Cash," he said with humble sincerity. "I'm sorry. I should have given you the benefit of the doubt. Instead… Well… I'm sorry. Please forgive me." Both men looked at each other for a minute before Brett got his response.

Agent Cashin took his hand and simply shrugged. "Probably would have done the same thing. But we need to quit wasting time and come up with a real plan. One that involves figuring out who stabbed us all in the back, and lets us get El Gran Blanco at the same time. We can't waste any more time just sitting here."

And in the blink of an eye, it was apparently over. DJ doubted the younger agent would truly ever forget what just happened, but it did certainly seem like Cash flipped a switch and moved on. True, men tended to do this far easier than women. In general, of course. But he never saw someone just instantly be willing to move on as quickly as Agent Cashin just did. He was definitely a next-chapter kind of guy. If it had been DJ with a gun pointed to his forehead, he would have punched Brett in the throat first before just letting it go.

Agent Cash was right, though, DJ thought to himself. Despite what had just happened, they could not afford to waste any more time in coming up with a plan. Brett desperately needed some rest, but they all needed to sit down, put their heads together, and come up with a strategy. Right now, with snow falling from the sky by the truck load, and no one with a clue on where they disappeared to, they were safe. They could focus on a course of action. Abbi, now connected to the dealership's free WiFi, discovered the storm should end its assault around four in the morning. They had enough time to design a plan of attack, and then get a few hours of much needed rest before they left the safety of this place and ventured out.

Brett nodded and called everyone together into the waiting area by the service department. Including John the Manager. Probably more to just keep an eye on the man. They pulled the chairs into a makeshift circle and started discussing. Lisa focused on making more hot chocolate and coffee for everyone, with DJ preferring the latter. He even broke out his precious and dwindling stash of La Minita to share.

At first, the conversation focused on theories about how Shark Bait could have learned the location of DJ and Abbi, and who could have sold them all out. But Brett, despite his exhaustion, was the one who focused them into a plan. It was rough, at first, with people poking holes in it almost instantly after he concluded. But, slowly it began to morph into a solid course of action. It took a turn for the better when DJ produced additional information about all of his secret holdings on the yet unused alternate identity. It really took off then, giving them a way to set a trap, and make sure everyone stayed safe.

The entire time they talked, John the Manager listened in. DJ could not see locking the man away in an office somewhere after all he had done to help them. And, at one point, Brett pointed out directly to the man that if he breathed a word of any of this, he would probably be killed by the same people pursuing them. They would first torture him to make sure the information was solid, then they would just put him in the ground somewhere. Brett added that right now, no one knew who he was. If he kept his mouth shut, no one ever would.

The poor man seemed like he was about to pee himself over everything he heard anyway. At the possibility of torture, he turned positively white with fear.

Good, DJ thought. *The more scared you are of all this, the better.*

As Brett introduced his idea, he pointed out a number of people could have tracked down DJ being transported back to Denver. For one, a flight plan would have been logged as per FAA regulations. The system could have been hacked, and then simply looked to see where an FBI registered jet was heading to in route out of Boston. By the same token, his second in command could have been checking in on him the entire time to see what he was up to. The pilots were FBI personnel, and would have reported on their flight plan back to the Denver office. His A-SAC would have had access to this information. And who knows who she could have blabbed to prior to departing the field office with most of the agents in tow for DC?

The more Brett thought about it, the surer he was that this information could have been shared easily across the entire office.

Whoever the mole was, would have likely been long gone when the hit team showed up to finish DJ off.

Bottom line, it could have been anybody.

Knowing this, they sat around and devised a plan in an attempt to ambush their adversary once more. It was rough at first, with various people pointing out holes as they talked through it. But gradually, as they all worked together, a well thought out plan began to materialize. It was complicated, but it would work like a charm if all of the pieces were put together just right.

In order for it to work, they would need to let someone in on the plan. In fact, without the assist of another player, there was no way it *could* work. This other person had to be someone who had authority and access to resources and personnel. It needed to be someone Brett had a deep history with, and could trust completely.

There was only one person who fit this description. Newly appointed Director of the FBI, Timothy Neville.

Trust is a powerful asset, DJ knew. They were all lucky to have someone with such power and influence they could count on. They were fortunate to have the head of the entire FBI as an ace up their sleeve.

And Brett was blessed to have such a friend.

Chapter 19: Tigers, Pickles, and Cash

The motel room door burst inwards with a great, wood splintering force, bringing with it a blast of frigid cold and stinging snow. Thomas caught a glimpse of a shadowed figure wielding a sledge hammer before it vanished from view, slipping back behind the damaged frame. As he rolled off the opposite side of the bed, shooting pain driving through his buttock, his Glock seemed to find its way into his hand all on its own. He quickly drew aim on the shattered opening, looking for a target that would assuredly present itself. In a just a second, a flash-bang grenade would be hurled in through the gaping hole that used to be the door. It would go off with intense noise and light designed to disorient, then his enemy would enter.

He would fight, of course. But he would lose.

He had considered himself safe. His retreat through the storm should have concealed him. The motel room he rented was paid for in cash. The identity he used had never been used before. He should have been safe to nurse the wounds of his most recent defeat in solitude and peace.

This would be a fitting end to an increasingly long list of pride-wrenching failures. He had been caught, quite literally, with his pants down. He had been sulking on the bed, wearing socks, undershirt, and his boxers. Then the door was almost ripped from its hinges, and the last final fight of his life was now upon him.

And he would fight. With everything in him, he would fight. In his socks and underwear, he would fight. He would lose. But, he would fight. He would fight with the heart of a winner that he still believed lurked somewhere deep within him.

Despite his recent stumbles.

A whirring sound could be heard over the blast of wind. Louder, it grew. Something was coming closer. Rapidly. Not a man like the sledgehammer-wielding shadow glimpsed moments before, but a machine of some sort. They were too scared to face him head on. They knew his reputation of killing. So, they were sending in some sort of mechanical beast. And judging from the angry buzzing swiftly approaching, he had a hunch he knew what it was.

Let it come, he thought. Let it come.

He let go of the Glock with his left hand, his right still drawing careful aim on the opening. He reached across the surface of the now disturbed bed, still holding the warmth of his laying there, to place his hand on his new weapon of choice. An unlikely weapon to be sure. But a weapon none the less. After all, everything was a weapon.

Everything.

For a fraction of a second, he caught the first glimpse of his robotic enemy as it materialized out of the darkness and snow. He acted then, standing, and hurling his pillow like it was a deadly missile, and not the soft memory foam sleep aid that it was. Halfway to its destination, Thomas was able to confirm his suspicions on what the buzzing contraption was.

A drone. A quad-copter. Either flying with use of artificial intelligence, or guided by the hands of its owner, he was not sure. Nor was he sure of what the drone was ordered to do once it entered the room. But one thing was certain about small drones. Almost anything could knock them out of the sky. Pigeons, a thin wispy tree branch, or even a pillow thrown in haste could render them into nothing more than expensive garbage.

Because of this, any quality drone was equipped with sensors and software for avoiding obstacles. The more expensive, the better the avoidance capability. But Thomas knew he had the storm on his side to aid him. Meaning, the thick driving snow would interfere with the drone's radar/sonar. It would have difficulty detecting a rapidly approaching pillow hurled by an angry half-naked assassin from fifteen feet away.

The drone saw the obstacle all too late, and tried to both brake and climb out of the pathway without success. The pillow struck it a glancing blow and sent it cartwheeling out of view. He could hear the electric motors whine even harder to try and correct its flight. He heard the drone crash into something metallic, probably a parked car, then its mechanical buzzing ceased to exist.

More than likely Thomas could have just shot the thing out of the air. But why waste a perfectly good bullet on something that didn't even have a heartbeat? Any second now, he was certain to need every bullet he had for things capable of bleeding. He knew he had a precious few moments before his attackers refocused their efforts, and he used this opportunity to retreat further back into the room. Peeking out from around the corner headed into the tub area, he watched for a target to present itself.

They wanted him alive. He was sure of it. If not, he would have been dead already. They could have shot an RPG through the window. They could have tossed a few grenades through the door. For that matter, they could have just driven through the wall with a commandeered garbage truck. There were about a million ways his enemy could have gone about killing him. But they didn't. And that meant they wanted him alive.

This narrowed down the possibilities of who was out there in the snow, contemplating on how best to get to him now that their drone was out of commission.

The cops?

The cops would certainly want him alive. It wasn't in their playbook to kill first. They needed someone to prosecute. It was always capture first, and then kill if there was no choice left. Even for someone like El Gran Blanco. But there was little chance law enforcement could have tracked him down to this cheap, cash only motel room. And little chance they would use a drone to get him. Possible? Yes. But a slim chance at best.

Then who else?

Before he could spend more time in theory, a familiar voice called out from the darkness beyond the door. "If we wanted you dead, you would be dead. All we want is to renegotiate the terms of our deal." Thomas recognized the voice as belonging to the leader of the mercenary group he had hired to attack the FBI compound.

They would be understandably furious at him for blowing their element of surprise. Some of them were dead because of that mistake. Renegotiating terms was not high up on their list of things to do right now. They wanted payback. They wanted blood. The only question was, why was he not dead already?

He needed to find a way out of this. He needed time to figure out a plan. Right now, the only way out of here was through that open door. He didn't see charging out into the snow wearing boxers and a wife beater, and facing untold numbers of angry mercenaries, as much of a choice. Best to just keep talking until he could find a pathway forward.

"I'm listening," Thomas called out.

"We know who you are," the leader replied. "You were probably out of coms range at the time, but the target told us all over radio who you were. You're El Gran Blanco."

"Who?"

"Don't play dumb. You're the famous assassin. And despite being pretty upset with losing a few of my best hitters, I know you probably don't work alone. There is no way you could have accomplished all of those jobs without having some sort of team in place to assist. And you and

I both know this was not the first time you farmed out work to people in my profession. So… We could allow our emotions to control our actions and just blow up the whole building in order to kill you, but then we know what the results of that would be. Your team would just turn around and kill us later. Am I right?"

"That sounds reasonable," Thomas answered with a grin on his lips. He finally spotted a way forward from here. "What did you have in mind?"

"We team up. Again. I have friends that have died because of this mission. Someone needs to bleed for that. Slaughter needs to bleed for that. You obviously have some way of tracking him. As far as I'm concerned, we're still both on the same mission."

Thomas considered that. Maybe this *was* a negotiation. "I'm not paying you any more money."

"Look, I'm going to step into the room now. Just me. Swear." As Thomas watched, an open hand appeared around the door frame. Then another. Slowly, a figure stepped into the room with his hands raised. Thomas knew he was now face to face with the leader.

"What's your name?" Thomas asked him, the sights of his weapon aimed right between the man's eyes.

"Cody. Cody Hamell. What's yours?"

Thomas cocked his head to one side. Did the man really think he was going to go on a first name basis with him? Thomas asked as much. "You don't really think I'm going to be honest with you, do you?"

"Of course not," the man answered. "But we can't walk around calling you Mr. Shark, now can we?"

Thomas actually laughed out loud. Partly because of the question, and partly because of how stupid these guys really were. These idiots still wanted to work with him. It would be their undoing. After all, he was an assassin. Killing people without anyone knowing what you really looked like was a trademark of the craft. If these moronic shooters thought he was going to allow them to walk around knowing who he was, they were stupid.

Typical grunts.

Fine, he thought. *They could have their deal. For now.*

Right now, he was like a tiger at the circus. He would perform his tricks for the audience to watch, and work with the guy holding the whip and the chair so the fans could cheer. But in the end, tigers do, what tigers do.

They eat people.

"Henry," Thomas said. "You can call me Henry. Now how about I put some pants on and we can get out of here. By the way, what exactly were you planning on doing with that drone?"

"We figured you would shoot first and ask questions later if we just approached with a simple knock on the door. The drone was armed with a taser. We figured on stunning you first, and then trying to talk to you. It has a bullet-deflecting housing. We thought you would just shoot at it. We never figured on you trying to take it out with a pillow. Simple but effective, by the way. Never saw that coming."

"You were really going to taser me?"

Cody nodded with a grin. "And to be perfectly honest, I would have enjoyed it too."

Thomas laughed out loud again. *Yes*, he thought to himself. *And you're going to be the first person I eat.*

Bradford Cashin scrolled through the call history on his phone as a way to get to a frequently used number. Finding the switchboard number for the office, he tapped the screen and put it to his ear to listen. It rang once before picking up, and the prerecorded voice of the digital assistant on the other end prompted him to speak a name to be connected to. "Alice Manafort," he spoke his response quietly.

Alice was the Assistant Special Agent in Charge for the Denver Field Office. She was the second in command under Brett. It was Bradford's understanding from talking with his father, she had officially placed her hat in the ring for the position Brett now held. Under normal circumstances, she probably would have gotten it. She possessed seniority, and already served as an A-SAC for two years in LA. She had commanded a meteoric rise through the ranks most of her career, and the timing was right for the promotion.

And then it wasn't.

Politics and imaging for the public, along with a black eye in the news, came in to play during the aftermath of the Big Chuck case. Brett, through no intention of his own, was labeled a rescuing hero. They offered him any post he wanted, and he chose to run the Denver office. It didn't hurt that Tim Neville was his close friend, and Tim rubbed elbows with the people that mattered when it came to making those sorts of decisions.

Politics and circumstance intervened to block Alice from her natural progression into the position. Bradford wasn't positive, but he felt

Alice was a bit perturbed over the situation. In fact, he was reasonably sure the only reason she accepted a lateral move to Denver to serve under Brett was because she felt he would eventually fail at his job. When he did, she would be in a perfect position to step in and save the day.

Those feelings were why Bradford chose to call her.

A few rings later and someone picked up. Though, it wasn't his A-SAC. It was her personal secretary, Priscilla McMasters. If pickle juice had a personality, it would describe Priscilla to perfection.

"Alice Manafort's office," the voice on the other end stated curtly.

"This is Agent Bradford Cashin. I need to speak with her ASAP."

"I'm so very sorry," she answered unconvincingly. "She has instructed me to hold all calls unless they are considered critical. She's trying to coordinate the investigation into the attack in Denver. She's headed back there now. I can take a message."

Bradford imagined Priscilla's hair in rollers and a mudpack on her face, grossly out of sorts for having to screen calls in the middle of the night for her boss. There was a bit of a bite to her voice. More so than usual. And that was saying something. Bradford was just another pesky nuisance she had to deal with.

"Priscilla!" He barked at her through clenched teeth. "I am one of the agents that was in Denver during the attack. I was with Special Agent in Charge Foster when we came under siege. We escaped, and I'm with him now. Now connect me to her immediately. Trust me. She is going to want to take my call," he whispered emphatically.

There was silence on the other end for a moment while Priscilla "Pickle Juice" McMasters, seemed to weigh the validity of what he just said. She probably didn't even know who Cash was, but she did know of the attack and why her boss was headed back to Denver in the middle of the night. "Your name again?" she asked.

"Agent Bradford Cashin."

"If you're with the SAC, then why doesn't he just call her directly?"

"Because he doesn't know I'm calling in. He wants me to keep silent and say nothing. But I've lost all confidence in SAC Foster's leadership. I need to report in to someone I can trust. I need to update the *real* leadership in Denver about what's going on and get instructions. Now connect me to her right now. If you don't, and she learns you blew me off, I can promise you won't have a job by morning."

"Hold one…" The phone went silent and he knew he had been placed on hold. She was no doubt calling her boss and filling her in on what she had been told, and asking for instructions. Should she let the guy through?

After what seemed like an eternity, Alice popped back on the phone. "Are you still there?" The voice on the other end contained thinly veiled venom and contempt.

"Yes, Pickle.... Yes, Priscilla, I'm still patiently waiting to report in." Bradford shook his head in disbelief. He could not believe he just called the woman "Pickle".

"Connecting you now," came the short reply.

He heard a brief series of clicks as he was connected. There was no ring on Bradford's end to indicate he was now calling the Assistant Special Agent in Charge. She was just suddenly there. "Who am I speaking with?" Alice's voice was melodious and calming. She was the very antonym of her secretary. He was pretty sure it's why so many people liked her. Her demeanor was always uplifting and positive. But while he had never seen it himself, his father explained she was quite the cunning little shark. She circled through her co-workers, and the criminals she pursued alike, until she saw an opportunity to take a leg off.

"Agent Bradford Cashin," he replied with a steady voice. "I'm one of your Team Leads in Special Crimes."

"So, *you're* the other person on the video we saw escaping through the sewer. We were in the process of doing a head count to figure out who you were. Are you OK? Are you injured?"

"I'm fine, ma'am." He hesitated a moment before continuing, seemingly unsure of how to continue, and she used the opportunity to jump in.

"Why haven't you reported in? What's up with all the secrecy?" The tone in her voice conveyed genuine concern.

"Well, you see… Well… Actually, that's why I'm calling you now. I'm… I'm just not really sure how to say this…" He stammered and stalled through whispered tones.

"Out with it, Agent. You can speak to me with complete confidence," she reassured. "I just want to help you. I want to help you all. We need to get you safe. But in order to do that, I need you to just tell me what's going on."

Agent Cash took a deep breath and then plowed forward. "SAC Foster believes we have a mole in the FBI. Ever since he uncovered a few in the Denver office back over the summer, he has been concerned we didn't find them all. He thinks what happened in Boston was the result of a leak. I told him that whoever is after Slaughter, probably had all of his aliases staked out, waiting for him."

"I see."

"And that's another thing," He stated with exasperation. "Slaughter is everything his name implies. He's a ruthless, soulless killer. He's not the good guy caught up in a bad circumstance that SAC Foster believes. He should be prosecuted. In fact, I believe he may actually be connected to another mob group who was at war with Big Chuck. I think that's why everyone is after him. But Foster doesn't. He let him wander around our facility completely unguarded! Plus, I've seen the guy kill. He's just too good at it. There's no remorse or hesitation in him. He dispassionately kills anyone in his way. I'm telling you, SAC Foster is wrong about him. He's dangerous." His voice rose with passion as he talked, and he forced himself to pause and just breathe.

"It's going to be OK, agent." Her voice was smooth and calming. Bradford could almost picture her with a pad of paper in her lap, sitting in a wingback chair, and listening to him while he lay on a couch telling her his problems. Bradford didn't like her. He didn't trust her. But he needed her none the less.

"You see, ma'am," he continued. "He thinks a mole in the FBI revealed where Slaughter was and that the facility would be practically empty. He thinks that's why they attacked. But I have a different theory," he said with a touch of sarcasm in his voice.

"What is that?"

"SAC Foster put the guy up in a guest suite out back. He let him have access to the phone system. And, Foster never took away his own phone. I believe the idiot called someone. That someone probably sold Slaughter out, and that's why we got attacked. The imbecile brought all of this on himself, and got some of our own people killed. Plus..." He paused again.

"What is it, agent?"

"In his effort to find a fictitious mole, SAC Foster... Well... He put a gun to my head and tried to force me to confess. He blamed me. *Me!* It was a miracle he didn't actually pull the trigger. I'm lucky to be alive."

"Wait a minute," the voice on the other end said, her tone changing completely. "Are you seriously telling me Special Agent in Charge Brett Foster pointed a gun at another fellow agent and threatened him?"

"That is exactly what he did. He's out of control. That's why I'm calling you." Bradford found himself breathing rapidly from anger into the receiver, and forced himself into a state of calm.

"Where are you now?"

"We're headed south. To Slaughter's old ranch. We commandeered this giant four-wheel drive to get through all of this snow. The ranch is still under federal control and Brett figured it would be the best place to hole up. He wants to stay hidden from the world until he can figure out what to do next. He's going to call in a favor from our new director and his old boss. He seems to think newly appointed Director Neville can help us set up a trap, but I'm not so sure. As you may know, I worked in Dallas for him too. But he's always seemed like one who would circumvent the law to accomplish his own goals."

"Really?" came the simple reply.

"Look, I don't have much more time. We stopped for a pee break and I'm in the bathroom. But can I level with you?"

"Of course you can," she replied reassuringly. "I just want to get you safe."

"Let's just say that Director Neville and I go way back. Way, *way* back. I know him quite well. I used to think he was a role model. But now... Let's just say I am concerned over this new promotion."

"OK, agent. I need you to listen to me carefully. I am going to let Brett have his space like he requested. But I am going to start working to get you rescued and this Slaughter guy arrested. But it's going to be tricky. There are politics at play. So, I need you to sit tight and play along with whatever scheme SAC Foster has come up with. But when I call you, I may need you to do something risky. Something you may be uncomfortable with."

"What's that?" he asked the calming voice on the other end.

"When I need you to, I may need you to take SAC Foster into custody. Can I trust you to follow the law and make that happen?"

Agent Cashin paused and considered that. She was asking him to violate any trust and friendship he may have with Brett and actually put him in handcuffs. The serious significance of just such an action was huge. It would be career-ending, or career-making. He was silent for a moment more while he weighed her words and what she was asking of him.

"Agent, are you still there?" she asked him with a slight hint of uncertainty in her voice.

"Yes," he replied. "Yes, I can."

"Good," A-SAC Manafort stated. "I'm counting on you."

"Understood," he whispered into the phone. "They're coming. I have to go." Agent Cashin didn't wait for a reply. He simply punched the button to end the call and took in a deep breath. He smiled outwardly then, and looked up. "She bought it," he told Brett. "Hook, line, and sinker."

"Yeah?" Brett asked, standing next to DJ in the small office of the dealership. "I almost bought it myself."

DJ agreed. "And you thought I had a natural gift for acting," he told Brett. "Now we need to find ourselves a ride out of here."

Phase one of their plan was now in place, Cash thought to himself. Now on the way to phase two. But first, he needed to take care of a few things.

He had to find a way to get Abbi alone.

Chapter 20: The Beast and Lines of Blue

DJ was actually quite impressed. He might have underestimated the claims of John the Manager. The man said he had a vehicle that would eat whatever the storm managed to dish out for breakfast. DJ blew him off when he said it, thinking he was just another four-wheel drive owner possessing embellished visions of grandeur. Turns out, he actually knew what he was talking about.

DJ stood in the maintenance bay of the dealership with opened mouth amazement. Crouched before him like a great hulking beast, was quite possibly the meanest looking truck he had ever seen.

It started life as a standard four-door, crew cab, heavy-duty pickup. The kind with twin sets of tires in the back for hauling heavy loads. Then it had been lifted, stretched, and outfitted with everything a redneck would love. Instead of four doors, it had six. Instead of having four tires in the back, it now had only two. But they were each wider than two tires combined, and covered in mud and snow eating ridges of rubber. It provided a massive surface area to keep the truck moving forward through soupy and ugly conditions. Conditions like what awaited them for their trip.

The truck was wrapped in massive black steel bumpers, and contained a winch in both the front and back. There were lights everywhere, and pointing in every conceivable direction one might imagine for scoping out rough terrain in the darkness. There was a snorkel system enabling the huge thing to ford deep water, or for getting fresh air above dust clouds generated by dirt roads.

John the Manager stood there like a proud father displaying his son for crowds of adoring fans to witness. "I call it," he proclaimed with glowing pride, "the Beast."

"Yeah," DJ responded, taking it all in. "I can see why."

"It has four-wheel steering," John the Manager continued. "It has a super tight turning radius for such a big vehicle, but I can also make the whole thing track right or left. It has a state of the art all-wheel drive management system. It automatically funnels power to the wheels that need it most. I can lower the air pressure from inside the cab to help provide even more traction. And then, raise it again when you're back on the black top. It has cameras everywhere to help you negotiate rough terrain. Plus, I can even climb out of the cab and stand off to the side so I can get a better view of what I'm trying to get over or through, and then actually drive the thing with the app on my phone."

"What?" DJ asked. "You're kidding me."

"Yep. It allows me to see precisely how to angle my wheels for those real tricky maneuvers. It's got an over one-hundred-foot range. It'll even operate the winches and lights."

"Wow," DJ managed to spit out. "That's… that's quite a truck."

"That's not a truck," John the manager exclaimed, turning to DJ full on to emphasize his point. "That's a Space Station." The man was smiling so broadly it nearly split his head in two.

"Right… Um… Got it. Star Trek reference."

John the Manager's countenance fell with a crash. "Star *Wars*. Not Trek."

"Star something. Whatever. I get it. You have one awesome truck. Now, will you let me borrow it?"

"Oh, of course not! Not a chance! Are you crazy?" John shook his head in disbelief at the very notion.

"But you said…" DJ started to respond, shocked at the rug being yanked out from under him.

"You asked," John the Manager corrected, "if I had something that could get you through all of this snow. I said yes. And I do. No question. The Beast will get you anywhere you want to go on the entire globe. But I'm not letting you take it from me. What I am prepared to do is drive you to where you need to go."

DJ shook his head. "Look, man. There's a chance the people after us will be staking out where we're headed. It's too dangerous."

"And I don't profess to be the bravest thing in the world, either. But no way I'm just letting you take my baby."

DJ stood up a little straighter and his eyebrows locked together in serious focus. "Well then I could just take the keys from you."

John the Manager appeared to physically back down a bit, but his resolution remained firm. "You could try, but this doesn't have a key. And I'm not telling you the secret to make it work for you either."

There was a standoff then. DJ adorning his most menacing and imposing glare. John the manager mostly looked at his shoes, but still refused to concede defeat.

"You don't need to beat him up, sweetheart." The familiar voice of Abbi spoke up behind him. "We'll just take his phone, I'll get into the app he uses to start the thing, and we'll be on our way."

Both men turned to look at her. She stood there behind them, arms crossed across her diminutive body, wearing a playful yet sarcastic grin on her face. She looked directly at DJ and addressed him. "When are you going to learn that not everything needs to be solved with bloodshed or bullets? And when are you going to see that I'm a bigger asset to you than you think? We're a team, you and I. And the sooner you get that through your testosterone filled brain, the better. Maybe you should ask my opinion on things before you just lock and load on whatever problem stands in front of you."

"Umm…" DJ really wasn't sure how to respond. First of all, it never occurred to him that Abbi could just hack her way into the truck. Not sure why. She seemed to be able to hack into a lot of things. It was just not a solution that jumped out at him.

Secondly, he really was trying to include her in everything. At least he thought he was. She had made her stand about being part of the solution to bring down Shark Bait quite known. And, he had backed down like a good little boy. After all, it was better to try and work with her in an effort to keep her safe, than to see her run off and try to do it all by herself.

"You can't break into my truck!" John the Manager was beside himself at the notion of someone just hacking their way into his pride and joy and stealing her.

"Actually," Abbi replied. "I think there is little you can do to stop me. Especially with captain trigger finger here standing next to me."

"Wait," John the Manager begged. "Please! Don't do this. I don't have a wife. I don't have kids. I have my truck. It's the single most important thing I own. It took me over two years to get it to where it is now. You can't just take it from me."

"Well, it would be better off than seeing you die," DJ replied calmly.

Brett was there then. DJ didn't know when he walked in, but he was back by the doorway, listening. "What's going on?" he asked.

"You see this big, glorious machine here?" DJ asked him, motioning behind him to the colossus parked in the maintenance bay. "John the Manager here says it can ford through four feet of snow and get us to where we need to go. But he doesn't want to just hand over the keys. He wants to drive us."

"Then let him drive us," Brett said simply.

"Have you been drinking?" DJ asked, looking at Brett like he had lost his mind. "What if they've staked out the airport waiting for us to try and fly out of here. He could die. You want that on your conscience?"

Brett looked at John the Manager and addressed him without responding to DJ. "OK, let's be clear here. We're headed to Denver International Airport. Specifically, the terminal for private charters. It's the same terminal where the FBI parks their jets. Since I am in the FBI, and since our enemy is tracking all our moves, it would be logical that they may have the place staked out. They may try to ambush us there. In which case, this whole carefully laid out plan of ours is going to collapse into a pile of bloody bodies. If you volunteer to drive there, you could very well end up at the bottom of that pile. Are you sure you want to do this?"

John the Manager blinked back and forth between all three of them. "I…" He stammered and seemed unsure of what to say next. Then, all at once, his back stiffened and a stubborn resolve began to wash over him. "Yes," he said. "Yes. This is my truck. And this is my store," he gestured to both. "I became a part of this when you blew the lock off my front door. And… And I have a confession to make." He looked at them with all the appearance of preparing to unveil a huge secret.

"I… I am…" John the Manager stuttered. "My name is John Crafton. I am the owner of Buckee's Rides. This is our home office and why I was still here doing paperwork. It's also how I can afford a custom truck build like The Beast, here." He looked at them one at a time. DJ caught the impression that this news somehow should have changed things for them all. To be honest, though, DJ couldn't see how.

"OK," DJ said. "Umm… nice place you have here? Thanks for taking us in?" He looked at Brett and Abbi to see if they had any clue why this was an earth shattering revelation. Their blank response confirmed they were just as stumped as he.

John shook his head, realizing his point was not clear. "You don't understand. I've billed this place as a nationwide used car chain that believes in and supports community. I put emergency preparedness centers in all of my dealerships and try to help out with things like natural disasters and such. When Christmas rolls around, we do big toy drives in every state. And all that is well and good. But, to be honest, lately it's been feeling like just a big gimmick.

"This…" John said looking at each of them with passion filled eyes. "This is *really* helping out. I mean, you guys go out and fight crime every day. Right now, you're staring down death and still continuing to press on. Plus… I'll be honest with you. I was one of the people Big Chuck was extorting money from. Offering you a law enforcement discount on a used sedan seems like the biggest joke ever. This is an opportunity to really give back. To really do something that matters. And to say thank you at the same time. So… So, I want to do this."

DJ and Abbi swiveled back to look at Brett, both waiting for a swift rebuke. For DJ, he kind of understood exactly what the used car dealership owner felt like about being taken advantage of by crooked people. But this guy wasn't a fighter. He was grossly out of shape. He probably couldn't hit the broadside of his own building with a shotgun at close range. He just shouldn't be allowed to continue with this. He should be handcuffed to a chair and told they were sincerely sorry for inconveniencing him. Then, they should steal his monstrosity of a truck and barrel off into the snow.

But, on the other hand, DJ *did* understand the desire to do something and make a difference. How could he turn the guy down when the risk was not extreme? After all, the people after them would have trouble getting to the airport as well.

Unless they were already there. Nope. Handcuffed to a chair it is, DJ thought, flipping his opinion back the other way.

"Then I don't care," Brett said. "Drive us if you want. Just as long as you know you could end up being shot repeatedly with automatic weapons and dying a fruitless death for doing nothing more than becoming an Uber driver. But whatever. Happy thoughts." Brett turned back to the door. "Whatever the decision, I'm too tired to fight with anyone anymore. And we're leaving in ten."

DJ was surprised at Brett's decision, but he decided not to try and override him. To do so would just create more drama. And like Brett, he was tired of the arguments. No, it was best to just load up and start forward on their plan.

They decided that fighting a well-connected assassin with deep pockets and a team of mercenaries with only limited resources was foolish at best. They only had two agents, two security guards who had very little combat experience and training, two civilians, and a Navy Corpsman who had been medically discharged. It was time to let someone else do the heavy lifting while they hid themselves away using DJ's enormous pile of cash and an alternate identity.

They would head to the private charters terminal. There were a couple of services there that always had pilots and planes on standby. They were right now, sleeping away in special quarters just a few feet away from parked planes in hangars. Those charter services made their living by waiting for the next corporate big wig or rich playboy to come along and book a private flight to New York or LA.

Even though it was the wee hours of the morning, the storm had all but ended with only light snow now falling. Denver International would probably already have crews out clearing runways and de-icing planes. They would want to get as many back-logged planes gone, and as many delayed entries landed as possible.

The city had a plan for events like this when it came to road clearing. Those crews were out all night plowing main thoroughfares and the highways. All DJ and team needed to do was get to one of those roads and make their way in. Abbi had already found an updated map online showing where those crews were focusing their efforts. By her estimates, they only needed to make it two miles through a sea of snow and they would be good to go.

Those two miles, however, had drifts as high as five feet or better. It blanketed everything with such thickness, it would be hard to tell where the roads even were. Plus, there were cars out there buried and stranded, and hiding under what looked like simple mounds of white. This is why they needed a vehicle like the Beast. It had the weight to keep its momentum, traction to keep moving forward, and a winching system to unstick themselves.

Once on a plane, they would head east using DJ's alternate identity to book passage. They would leapfrog the storm that just passed over them and land in Albany, New York. They would pick up a couple of SUVs, cross into southern Vermont, and head to his remote get-away in the woods. The small hunter's cabin had access to well water, fireplaces, and one of the bedrooms was converted to a bunk room and would sleep six.

They would pick up supplies and hide in the thick forests of Vermont until all of this had blown over. More importantly, DJ had hidden some weapons and ammo there when he was dividing up his apprehended stash from Big Chuck. They wouldn't need them, of course. But it was always prudent to be prepared. Best of all, only one person would know where they were, and Brett trusted him with his life.

It was a good plan, DJ thought. All they had to do was get in The Beast, get on a plane heading east, and call FBI Director Tim Neville to inform him of what they were doing and how he would play his part. Brett was convinced he could persuade his boss to participate, especially with the plan already enacted by informing his A-SAC they were going to hide somewhere else.

Shark Bait would find out through his sources they were all headed to DJ's old ranch outside of South Fork. Tim would fly in a few teams from Dallas to set up an ambush, and when the assassin and his friends showed up to kill them, they would end up being trapped in the same boxed-in canyon that DJ had been trapped in only months before. There would be nowhere to run, and the FBI could hopefully apprehend them all.

If for some reason Shark Bait did not show up with his team of hitters, and instead left them to do the job on their own, Tim could offer immunity to the first one that coughed up any details leading to the arrest of the assassin. One of them would surely tell all they knew in favor of freedom.

Meanwhile, DJ and the rest would sit comfortably in the woods, allowing themselves to be snowed in by the same storm that had just passed over them. They would grill steaks, watch movies, and hunker down next to a roaring fireplace in complete comfort and solitude while those they trusted in the FBI used their unlimited resources and connections to wrap this all up.

It was a great plan. And, it would all be over in 72 hours.

DJ was positive Shark Bait would not sit this one out. The assassin was enraged by not having murdered DJ yet. He would be on hand to issue the killing blow at DJ's old ranch in southern Colorado. Only, DJ would be a few thousand miles away enjoying ribeye next to a fireplace, and cuddling close to Abbi.

DJ turned and patted the side of The Beast and then looked at John the Manager. "Fine. You win. Now let's load up in this Beast of yours and see if you can actually drive this thing."

John smiled back at DJ and merely nodded.

———————

There was no ambush set up at the airport. At least not one they happened to stumble into, and Brett was eternally thankful. But while he may have been exhausted, and the results of that exhaustion prompting him to put a gun to Agent Cash's head, he now had his superpowers functioning at 90 percent. What happened with the young agent was just a momentary failure. Brett was able to get in a small power-nap and he was now back on his game. His ability to see through the fog of details and connect the dots on a case were back to operating at near full strength.

It was why he didn't mind Mr. Crafton driving them in his giant obviously-compensating-for-something monster truck. His super-powers told him that the bad guys would have cleared out as fast as possible. And while he was sure they would be back, they would want to lick their wounds and develop a clear course of action first. One that was a bit more detailed than the attack on the FBI field office. One that offered them a greater chance of success.

Had their attackers done their due diligence in researching the building prior to their assault, they would have never attempted a sniper shot through a hardened window. If they would have just left that part out, and simply started with shooting the guards out front with suppressed weapons, they could have owned the entire compound and accomplished their goals in under five minutes.

It was a huge mistake on their enemy's part. The next attack would surely be more thought out.

At the time they had come up with this plan, sitting around the dealership drinking hot chocolate, Brett was certain the leak in the FBI was somehow associated with his A-SAC running her mouth. That, combined with a few undiscovered holdovers from the Big Chuck era, could be the only reason El Gran Blanco could have learned of their plans. So now, all he had to do was bait them with some false information and let his old boss take care of the rest.

But now here he was, sitting in an overstuffed captain's chair flying towards upstate New York at over 600 mph, running through all of the details and evidence in his head for the fifth time in a row. And why? Because his brain itch was back.

Something was off. Something didn't make sense. The dots he thought were connecting quite nicely a few hours ago, were now signaling him something was wrong.

When working a case, his brain would try to assemble all of the facts and clues together like puzzle pieces. In his head, he saw all of this like glowing pictures of file folders, rearranging themselves in random order. Each folder was a collection of facts about the case, or a random bit of useless information that didn't seem to belong but happened into the mix anyway. When an order was established, signaling a possible conclusion, interconnecting lines appeared between them all. If the arrangement told the story incorrectly, the line would pulsate a vibrant red, wink out, and the process would repeat.

If the interconnecting lines glowed blue, it meant that the series of events and facts leading to this conclusion were possible. He then mentally stored this possible conclusion off to the side, and tried again.

If, somewhere along the way, all the pieces glowed a bright green, he knew he had his answer. He would then pursue this connection until he could prove it out.

If none of them ever glowed green straight away, eventually only leaving a collection of blue connected facts with probable conclusions, he would turn each one of them over and over again in his brain. It simply meant that the combination was wrong, or he was still missing a key bit of seemingly irrelevant evidence.

But something was going on that had never happened before. His group of facts and conclusions pointing to his A-SAC running her mouth and inadvertently leaking information, had at first instantly glowed a bright green. He then hatched a rough plan together to set another trap for El Gran Blanco, and smoothed out the rough edges by consulting his friends.

That was all before his power-nap back at the dealership.

Now, sitting on the plane about to call his boss to put the final piece of his trap in place, he decided to look at his group of facts and circumstances together once more. He did so because his brain itch had returned, telling him something was wrong. When he re-examined his concluding folders, the green glowing line linking the pieces together, suddenly, right before his mental eyes, flipped from a pulsating green to a twinkling blue.

His truth was no longer a truth. It was back to being nothing more than a possibility.

Before his power-nap, he had been certain. But somewhere enroute to the airport, his brain-itch showed back up. He ignored it because he was focusing on looking for an ambush. He knew it would not come, but he had to be vigilant none the less. Once he was safely on a private jet screaming through the skies, he decided to focus in on his brain-itch to see what the fuss was all about. Now winging away across the great blue expanse of a new day, staring at his collection of facts that had changed colors, he was suddenly no longer sure of himself.

Because of that color change, there was now a grapefruit sized knot in the pit of his stomach. It wasn't just his own life at risk, depending on him making the right call. There was a whole crew looking at him and trusting him to get it all right.

For starters, there were the two guards. They certainly seemed committed to their job and helping him out, but they didn't really belong here. This was not their fight. They did not take an oath of office to work for the FBI, nor did they have any real training to speak of. Their one true purpose was to stand in front of an FBI facility, look menacing, and add a layer of protection against possible terrorist attacks or a lone wolf assault. It was a layer of protection always meant to be more psychological than physical.

But here they were. And he could tell by looking into their eyes they were both very worried, and weirdly thrilled at the same time. This was the adventure of a lifetime they could tell their kids they were a part of. If they lived. They seemed to be occupying this existence in a duality. Partly a brash and masculine thrill ride. Partly a harsh brush with reality that made them realize just how frail their own existence was. Brett had seen it before. He had experienced it himself.

Getting them both home safe was a heavy burden pressing into his shoulders. If they had been true agents, it might have been different. But they weren't.

Then there was Agent Cash to consider. If Brett didn't get him out of this alive, he was not sure he could ever look Tim Neville in the eye again. His old boss and friend didn't even know where his son was serving, as per Cash's request. Brett imagined what kind of blow it would be suddenly realizing his own son had been in such serious harm's way the whole time. He wondered if Tim could ever forgive him if something were to happen to Cash.

He shot a glance at the young agent. The man was glued to Abbi's laptop looking through case files on El Gran Blanco. He had her hack into the FBI database to pull everything ever discovered about the assassin. He could have just used Brett's credentials to gain access, but that would have created an electronic trail that could be tracked. Cash had thought it prudent to keep his research secret for now in case of a mole. Right now, he was pouring over all of the old details, and reading every comment ever provided by every agent that had been assigned to the case.

He was a good man, Brett thought to himself.

Then there was DJ and Abbi to think about as well. Brett felt a strong connection to them both. They had gone through a tragic and complicated ordeal over the summer. Abbi had lost her father back then. And now she had lost her mother. All she had left was the scruffy looking ex-Corpsman sitting on the couch across from him, as she leaned against him and tried to get some sleep.

Poor DJ was called into service and forced to become a life taker instead of a life saver. His past was horrific in losing his wife and children. But now he had Abbi. He deserved a second chance at life with her. Brett was nearly overcome with the pressure to make sure they both made it out of this alive.

He turned his head to look at his wife. She was already smiling back at him, waiting for him to make the call to Tim with the phone already in his hand. There was a blind trust and faith sparkling in her eyes. She was sure he could make all of this happen. He was her hero. He was her knight in shining armor.

He mentally glanced at all of the facts once more, the ones that falsely told him the source of the leak and sent him down this pathway. For the sixth time in a row since boarding the plane, he could see they were still linked together with glittering blue cords. Only a possibility. Something important was missing.

He quickly considered the ramifications of being wrong.

If Alice Manafort was not the source of the leak, intentional or not, then El Gran Blanco and his team of mercenaries would never know where they were headed. His call to Director Neville would still put the ball in motion for an ambush, but their target would never enter the boxed in canyon to be trapped and eventually captured. They would end up having to camp out longer in DJ's wooded retreat in Vermont. They would be back to square one.

He could see no downside that put them in any more danger than they were already in.

Brett took a deep breath and dialed the private number for his friend, FBI Director Tim Neville. It was so strange calling him that. They had spent so much time as coworkers and friends, he just never really thought of him as anything else. He started his relationship with Tim as his Section Chief. They became close working a case hunting down a serial killer. When everyone else blew off Brett's theories on the case, Brett took his ideas up the chain of command to the first person who would listen. That person was Tim.

Tim thought he was crazy at first, but decided to risk it. They pursued Brett's hunch after hours together, with Tim admitting later that his plan was to let Brett follow his gut to failure. Brett would learn a valuable lesson and never go over his boss's head again. Tim would reprimand him, and young Brett Foster would be a better agent because of it.

Problem was, Brett ended up being right. They caught the killer, and Tim ended up getting a promotion because of it. Brett didn't mind, however. He was happy having been proven right. In the process of capturing the killer, Tim almost died. Were it not for Brett, Tim would be another name on the long list of victims for the killer. Tim was grateful to

Brett for multiple reasons as a result, and ended up keeping Brett close with every promotion he took.

His thoughts were interrupted by the hesitant voice of the newly appointed director on the other end. "Hello? Brett?"

"One and the same," Brett replied.

"Where in the world are you?" he said hastily. "Do you realize what your disappearance has done? Everyone is freaking out right now. Are you all OK?"

"We're all fine. But you mean no one has contacted you about me at all? You haven't heard anything from A-SAC Alice Manafort yet?"

"No... Why? Have you already reported to her? Because she should have called me immediately afterwards. Her reputation suggests she is better than that."

Brett smiled a bit at this news. Tim was correct. Alice had information on him that had been provided by Agent Cash nearly five hours ago. At least his hunch about Alice being vindictive and opportunistic was correct. So far, so good.

Brett then informed his boss about everything that had transpired. He told him about his current working theory on the leaks, even though the lines were back to being blue, a point he did not even mention to his new director. Then, he outlined his plan for ambush. He gave him all of the details Tim would need to make it happen.

He explained how Tim could use tactical teams from both Dallas, Texas and Albuquerque, New Mexico to isolate information away from the Denver Field Office. He sent him screen shots of a digital map of DJ's old ranch, and explained how there was only one way in and out unless you had mountain climbing gear to ascend the canyon walls. He informed his boss of the fire trails used by the forest service which would allow a few team members to circle around the property from behind, and set up sniper spots on those same walls as over watch. It would make sure no one could sneak out. Plus, they could use drones launched from the New Mexico Air National Guard to provide aerial reconnaissance over the valley.

The FBI would stay back and use those drones to watch for entrance into the valley by El Gran Blanco and his men, then swoop in and close off all retreat. It was just a waiting game after that. Until they gave themselves up, or stupidly tried to shoot their way out.

Tim was stunned into silence at the level of preplanning already done by Brett. He promised to get moving on it ASAP. But he needed to know where they were going in case something happened. Someone needed to know where the Special Agent in Charge of the Denver Field Office was hiding. Brett agreed and gave him the address.

Was there anybody else who knew of these plans, Tim wanted to know.

Sure, Brett informed him. He then told his director about their angel disguised as a used car salesman back in Denver. How the man had done everything he could to help them out and give them shelter. How he had overheard everything, and at some point, after this was all over, they should present him with a special FBI Commendation for Civilian Service.

Tim readily agreed.

Was there anything else Tim should be informed of, his boss asked? Brett glanced over at Agent Cash for a moment and considered. Should he tell his boss the man's own son was with him? No, he finally decided. There should be no more risk to the young agent. The worst should now be over. Best to keep his boss in the dark.

They hung up then, and Brett focused on closing his eyes and letting everything fade into the background. He could sure use some more rest. Problem was, as soon as he closed them, all he could see were file folders of facts and details connected by thin, pulsating lines of blue. He couldn't help but rearrange those folders a couple of more times, looking for the missing connection. But no matter how many times he shuffled them around, the lines continued to remind him he was acting on nothing more than a possibility. Just a hunch he was now following blindly.

And then, he felt himself fall into real slumber. Aware of it, yes. But firmly embraced by it. Finally.

Chapter 21: Digger's Cake

John Crafton exhaled with relief once he finally arrived back at his home. But he was too pumped up with adrenaline to just simply climb into his bed. He needed to get his brain into a more relaxed state. Right now, his mind kept turning over the events of last night, again and again. To think, he was actually able to help the same FBI agent who was celebrated a few months before for taking down Big Chuck and putting an end to his vicious empire. The same Big Chuck who extorted thousands from him every month.

It was crazy to think of.

There were no bullets whizzing past his head, or white-clad ninjas leaping from the snow drifts on the ride to the airport, but his heart had been pounding as if they were all under a full-scale assault. He had done nothing heroic or brave. He had only sat behind the wheel of the Beast and helped them get to the airport. The agent had been right. He had done nothing more than perform the functions of an Uber driver.

But it had still been nerve-racking anyway.

It had taken him nearly two hours to make it from the airport to his home on the city limits. The main roadways leading into and out of the airport were clear, having received constant attention from the city. But after that, he had to ford through hip deep snow, and negotiate stalled out cars. A few times, he saw other cars try to fall in behind him as he deftly picked his way through Denver. But despite leaving a clear path in his wake, they were not equipped for these conditions like he was. They quickly fell behind, stuck in the snow.

He considered helping some of them, and he certainly possessed the tools to get their cars and trucks unstuck, but there was no way to help them all. And even if he did help out, they would only be stuck again seconds later. So, he ignored them and plowed his way home.

By the time he pulled up in front of his garage, the sun was well up. He was surprised to see the Home Owners Association had been able to keep the neighborhood streets cleared. But then, he lived in a snooty, upscale neighborhood and paid extraordinary monthly fees.

He jumped out of the truck into snow that came past his belt buckle, and forced his way to the front door. As he jumped and pushed his way through the white freezing fluff blocking his way, he wondered where his new friends were. By now they should have been in the air for over an hour or more, assuming they were correct with their belief that there would be pilots on standby sleeping at the hanger. They were probably right now settling in for some overdue sleep in the expensive leather recliners that doubled as airplane seats.

Which gave him a good idea. He would turn on his fireplace, kick back in his own recliner, and maybe watch an old black and white movie. Something with John Wayne in it. It was a bit early for a drink, but a good scotch would help him settle his nerves and serve to relax him. He would relax to the Duke play alongside some of Hollywood's greats in "The Sons of Katy Elder." He hadn't watched that one in a while.

John smiled at the notion.

His love affair with the iconic actor went all the way back to his youth. Few people in today's society even knew who John Wayne was. If they did, they probably had never seen a single movie the man starred in. A number that almost reached two hundred and fifty. His grandfather loved the man. His dad loved him, too. And his own love for the actor could not but help be nurtured along, considering how many Saturday afternoons were spent with all three generations of Crafton men eating popcorn in front of a TV.

In fact, John was named after the beloved Hollywood hero. He even had a dog named Duke at one time, the nickname the world knew for John Wayne.

His grandfather started a collection of movies and memorabilia devoted to John Wayne's legacy. His own father did the same, often engaging in friendly arguments over who had acquired the best stuff. When the older Crafton died, he left his collection to his son. By the time John inherited all of it, he could have started his own museum to the memory of the Hollywood legend.

There were original movie posters, bronze statues of the man in iconic poses from some of his most famous movies, autographed ticket stubs from a red-carpet event, and even collector plates that filled up an entire china cabinet. His house was decorated from end to end with it all, and every single piece precious to John. Not only did it celebrate the life of a famed actor, but it memorialized his father and grandfather.

The many beloved trinkets, posters, and statues were probably why he never married. Most women, on learning of the rabid-fan nature he had for the long dead actor, thought him too weird and eccentric to enter into a real relationship. He couldn't be looked at seriously.

Their loss, he often thought to himself. John Wayne was a man who other men should pattern their life after. He was a real man's man. It was one of the reasons John felt a connection to the heroes who invaded his dealership last night. They seemed like real men. Men who had never used skin moisturizer, or got a manicure. Men who fixed things themselves. Men who were quite accustomed to bruising their knuckles in trying to get the job done. Men exactly like John Wayne.

He was covered in snow by the time he made his way through the front door, having fallen twice trying to make it through. When his wet shoes hit the tiled floor on the other side of the threshold, he nearly went down again. He was saved only because one hand was still on the doorknob, and he was able to catch himself before he went down hard. He breathed a sigh of relief at his good fortune. Well past middle aged, a fall onto a hard surface could have hurt him badly.

He stamped his feet to dislodge as much of the snow as possible, then carefully made his way to his bedroom. A hot shower was in order. It would warm him back up, and get him into that relaxed mood he was looking forward to. Then, a little classic John Wayne in front of a roaring fire, along with a glass of aged scotch, should prep him nicely for bed.

He was standing in nothing but his socks, fiddling with the shower nobs, when the doorbell rang.

Now who in the world would be out on a morning like this? The storm was over, but the roads were mostly all impassable.

He wrapped himself up in his thick bathrobe and slid his feet into warm slippers. He supposed it could be a neighbor checking on him. Or maybe a co-worker? After all, he had his phone turned completely off since running into the FBI group from last night. He had forgotten all about it and hadn't turned it back on. Both his VP of operations and his personal secretary had probably been trying to reach him for a while now.

His VP lived a few neighborhoods over and owned a couple of those snowmobile things. His family liked that sort of thing. It would make sense for him to jump on one and ride over to check on him. He should have remembered to turn his phone back on after dropping off his new friends at the airport. For that matter, he should have called them to see how they had weathered the storm themselves.

He took a peek through the peephole to see a bundled-up gentleman with his arms crossed for warmth, stomping his feet a bit and rocking back and forth like he was trying to stay warm. John didn't recognize him, but he was wearing a hood and stocking cap for warmth. It was probably indeed just a neighbor. He opened the door a crack and poked his head through.

"Yes?" he asked the freezing figure before him.

"Hi," the man said, standing there shivering with his hands up under his arm pits to keep them warm. "I'm looking for John Crafton."

"What's this about?"

"Actually, by the look on your face, I can tell I have the right address." The man moved then, quicker than John would have thought possible. One second the stranger looked as if he might freeze to death. The next he was swinging a long black pistol up from underneath one of those armpits with one hand, and shoving the door hard with the other.

Panicked, John fell back and wheeled to run into the house. The door flew open behind him and he imagined a bullet would be boring its way through his brain just a heartbeat from now. Instead, he heard a crash and groan, and something metallic clatter to the floor. John turned the corner then, running for all he was worth in his slippers. His robe opened free, revealing his nakedness underneath, but he had other things than modesty to think about. He risked a glance behind him as he rounded the corner, and saw his attacker sprawled out on the still wet tile in front of the door.

John never slowed however, knowing his pursuer would be back to his feet in a moment, and John needed to use this opportunity to get away. But to where? Anyplace he could close a door to, his enemy would be able to just shoot right through. If only there was some way he could fight back.

There was, he remembered. John Wayne! John Wayne could save him!

Included in the many treasured items lovingly placed around his home, was a Colt 1911 pistol in a maple collector's box with glass top. It was a commemorative edition in tribute to the movie 'The Sands of Iwo Jima'. It was a working model of the pistol John Wayne used, decorated with gold inlay and featuring an etched likeness of the man, a fatigue clad warrior with a rifle slung over his back. He stood in his iconic pose with his hand on the pistol at his waist, and stretching the length of the pearl-handled grips. It included a chrome-plated magazine loaded with real forty-five caliber bullets with polished copper tips.

While the thing could shoot, it was never intended to be used as a real gun, but something just to admire on a mantel above a fireplace. Untouched, it was worth thousands. If a round were to ever be fired from it, it would be rendered un-sellable and worthless.

No matter, John thought. He would use it now.

He tried to turn the corner into his bedroom with such a head of steam, he shoulder-slammed the door frame heading in. He grimaced in pain, but soldiered on. Heroes didn't let a shoulder bruise stand in the way of a mission. And he was on a mission.

A mission to save his own neck.

Across from him, sitting on the nightstand next to his bed, the coveted maple box awaited him. It stood displayed next to a wooden carving of a John Wayne likeness matching the one on the pearl-handled grips. A thin brass tube stretched up from behind the small actor, supporting a lampshade above and casting a warm glow. Adrenaline coursed through his veins, and he practically dove across the room for the box, his open robe flowing out behind him like a superhero cape.

His fingers closed around the box and he fumbled with the clasp holding the lid closed, but his shaking hands failed to get the job done. In desperation, he slammed it to the floor, shattering the glass top. Remnants of the pane shot out in a circle, and he hastily bent to remove the gun. It pried free from the molded velvet background with ease, and he grabbed for the loaded magazine next. A triangular shard of glass still lodged in the frame nicked his palm in the process, and blood began to flow freely.

He ignored it. Heroes were undeterred by the sight of their own blood. And pain? What was the saying? Pain was just weakness leaving the body? At least that is what he imagined heroes saying.

He slammed the magazine home to the sound of heavy footfalls fast approaching behind him. There was little time left. He knew enough about the gun to know there was a safety on the thing, but he had no idea if it was on or off. He also knew he needed to rack the slide back to push a bullet into the barrel. He held the thing out at arm's length and pulled back on the slide hard with his left hand. There was a satisfying metallic *shlack* as he loaded his prized pistol.

He was out of time.

The door flew open behind him, and clinging to desperate hope, John spun about. With eyes closed and a shout of fear, he blindly aimed and pulled the trigger.

The gun exploded with thunder and recoiled with a tremendous force, yanking his arm upwards and to the right, twisting his wrist in the process. His eyes snapped open at the ear-splitting clap, and he was certain he failed. Heroes did not scream like a girl and shoot at the enemy with their eyes closed. They faced them head-on, driven to success by their commitment to justice. Well, at least he could look the man in the eye before he lost his life.

To his surprise, he saw his attacker staggering back into the hallway, and then collapsing to the floor in a lifeless heap.

He had done it. He had won. He had vanquished his enemy.

Oh no, he thought to himself with sharp clarity. *My friends. I have to warn my friends.* If this man tracked John down to his house, then they must already be aware of the trap being set. They thought they were running to a safe hiding spot, John concluded with horror. But instead, they were running into their own trap.

John spun around to face the nightstand once more, reaching for his cell phone sitting on the corner of the nightstand, and dropping the gun on the bed. He brought it to life and began combing through the list of contacts for every store. On learning where his new friends were heading, he offered them transportation from his dealership in Albany. He promised them whatever they wanted. They just needed to show, ask for a specific contact person, and they would be given any combination of vehicles they wanted. No questions asked.

John then called and left a detailed voice message for the general manager, giving him explicit instructions on how to handle the transaction. The Albany store would do a store transfer on the vin numbers back to Denver, and John would write them off to store use. His hero friends could use the transportation for as long as they liked, and return it when they were done.

Finding the number he was looking for, he poked at the contact and held the phone to his ear. It rang three times and then the general manager in Albany picked up the phone.

"Hi, Mr. Crafton," the voice began. "Got your message from earlier. We'll take care of it. They can pick whatever they want and we'll transfer them over. But are these new employees or something?"

"No," John said breathlessly. "I am doing a favor for…" he paused. He didn't want to spill the beans on everything that had transpired over the last several hours. The last thing he wanted was to say he was doing the FBI a favor. "Look, I can't tell you what's going on right now. Just know it's not illegal and I will explain it all later. Right now, I just need you to keep it all a secret. Handle this yourself. Don't pawn it off to someone else. When I tell you what's really going on, it's going to shock you. I just can't tell you now."

"No problem. I'll take care of it. They know to ask for me, right?"

"Yes, but listen. I need you to do me a favor. I need you to have them call me. Tell them it's very important. Don't let them leave without calling me."

"Yeah, sure. I can do that." The voice on the other end seemed a bit confused by it all, but he was in no way going to press the owner of the company for more details.

Then John heard another voice behind him, and it turned his blood cold. "Hang the phone up," The voice calmly instructed. "Or I'll blow your head off." The voice grated like two blocks of granite rubbing together. "Right now," he pressed.

John pulled the phone away from his ear slowly and hit the button to hang up. He stood frozen there for a moment. Then he shot a sideways glance at the Colt sitting on the blankets next to him. He wondered if he could reach it in time to get off a hasty shot. He got lucky once before. Maybe he could get lucky again. He should have known there would be more than one of them.

"Turn around slow," the graveled voice demanded.

John did as ordered, and his heart sank even further. He wasn't looking at the man's friend. He was looking at the same one. Remarkably, the guy was still alive. He didn't seem to be hurt at all. There was no pool of blood at his feet like there should have been from a .45-caliber weapon. And, he was pointing his long black pistol right at John's face.

But how?

As if reading John's mind, the stranger answered his question. "Here's a little tip for you. Don't shoot like a cop and aim for the chest. Your adversary might be wearing body armor." He pulled his coat aside to reveal a thick black vest of some sort, obviously the same body armor he had been referring to. "Always aim for the head. You'll end the fight quick."

John's world went haywire then. For a split second, things began to spin about wildly in a chaotic dance of motion. It was nauseating at first, but it was quickly over, replaced by shooting bright tinted hues. Every shade of the rainbow swarmed around him in buzzing comets of color. It was as if he were stuck in a bizarre globe of glowing tie-dye paint. He could sense nothing. He could feel nothing. His hands and feet were gone. He consciously tried to look at his hands but his body had disappeared, he found. Everything he knew had been replaced with a world of colored flashes and swirls.

And then it was gone just as quickly as it came. He floated along in a void of darkness for a time, and was oddly content to be there. Just floating along with not a care in the world. He was there for what seemed like a long time before he finally heard the voices call to him from somewhere beyond his vision. The voices were familiar. The voices were ones he thought he would never hear again.

The voices belonged to his grandfather and father. They told him they had been looking forward to his arrival. He could feel their presence then, though he could see nothing just yet. Just a deep blackness, darker than the darkest night.

Hang on, they said. This part of the trip was almost over.

Cody Hamell sent the hollow-point round through the bridge of the used car dealer's nose with rehearsed precision. Then he stood there watching as the man lay there convulsing on the ground. The last bit of information in what was left of the dying man's brain, fired across damaged synapsis, and caused his legs to jerk, and his arms to jump and twitch like a fish out of water.

Death was a strange thing when it came to a head shot. Most of the time the body just keeled over and lay there unmoving like it never possessed life to begin with. Like someone flipped a switch and just turned it off. Sometimes, like now, the dying twitched and flipped around like a weird marionette on invisible strings.

One day, Cody would die. Maybe soon. Maybe on this very job he was working. He wondered then what would happen to him. Would he just turn off like a broken toy? Or would he flop around like Mr. Crafton here?

Cody shrugged to himself. All he could do was keep moving forward one moment at a time and hope he made it to retirement. Part of him wished when his time came, it would be quick and over just like this. That someone would do him the favor of just flipping the switch for him and ending it all. It would be a far better way to go than lying in a hospital bed somewhere with tubes hanging out of him and a nurse visiting him with a bedpan.

He needed to ensure the man was dead. He was positive he was, but he would be derelict in his duties if he just left him twitching there on the ground. It didn't seem right to just leave him jumping about like that. Plus, he had seen men live and come back from injuries that should have killed them. He aimed and sent a second round through the man's brain pan. The businessman convulsed one more time and then ceased his movements forever.

Cody cleared his throat. He felt a little stuffy and was starting to lose his voice. He was coming down with a cold. He bent down to retrieve the empty casings from the rounds he just fired. Later, he would swap the barrel out on his gun making it nearly impossible to ever tie himself to this murder. As he stood back up, he couldn't help but groan. The man got in a lucky shot right to his chest. While the plate protected him like it was supposed to, it still would leave one nasty bruise. On top of that, he had slipped on the floor in the hallway and tweaked his back. There was a sharp pain now right between his shoulder blades, but he would be fine once he stretched it out.

Cody took a last look around the room and then turned to go. He retraced his path back to the front door and took a look around there as well. While he took a fall in the hallway, all of his body had been covered with clothing and gloves. There should be very little chance of DNA being left behind. He stepped out, pulled the door closed, took a sweeping look around to see if he saw anybody, then made his way back to the road where the two vehicles were waiting for him.

In the van taking up the rear, was the remainder of his team. Nine very upset men, armed to the teeth and demanding payback, sat seething inside. They all wanted to kill the other man in the front vehicle. It was El Gran Blanco's fault they suffered the losses they had. Had they received the intelligence they required, they would have approached the job differently. Had the man not jumped the gun and tried to assassinate the target through a hardened window, they would have had the element of surprise on their side.

Despite their need for blood, they fell right in line with Cody when he issued them orders to play nice. Cody knew he had a reputation with his team. He was almost always right, and his plan never failed to produce a nice payout in the end. That opinion did not change with them concerning this mission. They knew this was not his fault. Failure could be laid squarely at the feet of the assassin in the lead vehicle.

Cody climbed into the driver's seat next to Digger, spotting the look of nervousness on the techno-geek's face. He was obviously concerned with being left alone with the killer in the back seat. Digger had been the most vocal about not liking this plan when Cody put it all together. He wanted to just blow up the hotel room and be done with the man. He was exceptionally ticked off for taking out one of his drones with a pillow.

For a long moment, Cody considered following his young team member's advice. But the downsides would be far worse for them if they would have followed through with that line of thinking. Killing the assassin would have been an emotional response. Not an intelligent one.

"All done," Cody reassured the assassin behind him. "There is now only one other person who knows our targets are headed to Vermont. And you're sure your contact will keep his mouth shut?"

"Absolutely," the response came from the smiling figure in the rearview mirror. Cody would like nothing more than to knock the fake smile from the man's mouth, but the game must be played.

"Still don't want to tell me who that person is?" Cody pressed once more.

"Would you reveal them if you were me?"

Cody offered up an equally fake grin. "No, I suppose not. I guess all we have to do is book our own passage out of here and go kill our guy."

Digger cleared his throat. "Actually, I think we need to make a stop off at home first."

Both the assassin going by the name of Henry, and Cody looked at him curiously.

"Why is that?" Cody asked.

"I have a little something I've been working on that will make this job a breeze." Digger laughed out loud then. "Actually, it's a whole lot of little somethings." He laughed harder then, paused for a moment to look at them both, then laughed even harder. Cody was not sure what the private joke was, but he knew the young man enough to trust him.

"You want to clue me in there, Diggs?" Cody looked at him patiently while Diggs giggled at what was going on in his head. Finally, he stopped laughing and explained what he had been working on his spare time. Cody didn't understand the intricacies of what his geeky teammate was talking about, but he did understand the overall scope. Enough so to make him love Digger all the more. If the youngster was right, the next part of this plan would be a piece of cake.

Chapter 22: Transition

DJ was spooked. They all were. John asking for them to call as soon as they got to the dealership in Albany, but then not answering was peculiar. Considering everything that happened, it put up a big red flag for them all. In the end, though, with little more to go on, they proceeded with their plans anyway.

DJ was concerned John the Manager was the only other person who knew where they were headed. But the man didn't know specifically where they were going, and Vermont was a big state. Even if he had somehow been compromised, Shark Bait would not have specifics about where they were hiding.

He thought back then to the hacker who had set him up with all of his fake ID's. Beaver Nuggets would have had information about the other name DJ was using now, but he had not helped DJ buy this piece of property. That was done all on his own some time afterwards. He supposed, should the assassin have contacts within the hacking community, given enough time they might be able to track down the purchase and figure it all out.

DJ shook his head as he thought through it all driving away from the dealership with a set of all wheel drive vehicles. There was no way Shark Bait could have known about John the Manager. None. Zero. DJ was overreacting and just on edge.

Then again, there was one way to be sure.

As he made his way east towards the state line, he turned to Brett lost in thought and staring out of the passenger side window. "Brett, can you get Director Neville to check on our used car dealer?"

Brett turned to look at him. "That's bugging you too, isn't it?"

"Yep. We have a few hours before we arrive. If we can get an answer to that question, we can continue with our plan. But if not, then we need to consider something else."

Brett pulled out his burner phone picked up at the airport from a vending kiosk. "Way ahead of you," he replied. "I can have him reach out to locals and say he is a friend. Could they do a health and welfare check." He dialed the number and put the phone to his ear.

It was probably nothing, DJ thought. But better safe than sorry.

Abbi chimed in from the back seat. "Hey, we need to pull in to one of those outdoor stores for some supplies. I figured out a way to put up a wireless perimeter fence around your cabin. But I'll need a few things. If for some reason we are still being tracked, it will give us advance warning of someone approaching."

DJ smiled. She was indeed continuing to prove she was a part of the team. And just like that, DJ was overcome by a sense that everything was going to be alright. It was almost over. He might not be the one to put a bullet into El Gran Blanco's heart and provide Mary the justice she deserved, but it didn't matter. Justice would still be served one way or the other.

Everything is going to be alright, he told himself. He could feel the certainty closing about him like a warm comfortable blanket. All they needed to do was have a little more patience and faith.

His smile broadened deeper and he turned to Brett. "You want to find a grocery store so we can do a little shopping? I'm thinking we need to pick up steaks for grilling."

Brett glanced at the buzzing phone in his hand about an hour and a half later. They were approaching a critical time when they needed to make a decision about continuing with their plan. DJ, over in the driver's seat, seemed totally relaxed and unconcerned. It was like the man thought it was all officially over. But Brett was still a bit apprehensive. He still had not been able to connect all of the dots in such a way as to make those lines glow green, and the phone call in his hand might be just the missing piece he was searching for. The Caller ID told him it was the director, and he anxiously answered the phone.

"Good news," Tim said. "It looks like you saved the guy's life. According to the Chief of Police, Mr. Crafton suffered a heart attack. A couple of uniforms arrived in time to give him CPR. He's fine and resting comfortably at the hospital. He'll be under observation for a few days, but it looks like he's OK. I was able to talk to him myself."

Brett breathed out a huge sigh of relief. "Did he say why he wanted us to call?"

"He apologized for scaring you like that. Said he only wanted you to know that if you needed anything else, just give him a call."

"And the local PD doesn't know anything about this?" asked Brett.

"As far as that's concerned, they think he's a close personal friend of mine. They were more than happy to do the new director of the FBI a favor. But now thanks to that, I've had to promise I'll go fishing with the Chief the next time I'm in town."

Brett laughed. "He apparently doesn't know what a menace you are to anglers everywhere."

Brett continued to talk for a few minutes with his boss concerning the ongoing setup of the trap for El Gran Blanco. Things had progressed at a rapid pace, and everything was already in place. They were just waiting for the assassin to wander in to DJ's old ranch and be trapped.

Brett relayed everything to the rest of the group, and then began to relax. Everything was finally going their way. They would follow Abbi's direction and set up a perimeter. They would arm themselves with the stashed weapons DJ claimed to have hidden on the property, a surprise revelation to Brett. They would be careful and take precautions, but it looked like everything was finally going exactly like they hoped. In fact, it appeared the only worry Brett and crew had at the moment, was deciding what type of steak to grill for dinner.

He glanced at his watch in anticipation of dinner, and with sadness saw it was only just now past lunch. Oh well, he thought to himself. He would suggest they pick up a quick fast-food bite before pulling in to DJ's backwoods retreat. But he, for one, would eat light. He would prefer to save room for a hot steak and a steaming baked potato.

He shoved that nagging brain itch aside, finally. He was not sure why it was annoying him or what was missing in order to connect all of those dots, but this would not be the first time he was able to close a case, only to find the missing pieces after the bad guy was locked behind bars. It was rare, true, but it happened. It just didn't happen much.

Whatever, he thought to himself. I am tired of stressing over it. I am going to relax with my wife in front of DJ's fireplace, eat the steak the man bought for me, and let my boss handle the heavy lifting for a change.

And then, when this was all over, he was going to present his rather brilliant plan for keeping DJ and Abbi out of jail to the new director. Once the man conceded, Brett would then gladly tell his A-SAC Alice Manafort she could have his corner office. He was just not cut out for running an FBI field office. He was sure she was going to be thrilled, and he really hated that part, but it was what need to happen in order to make him happy.

A change of pace was definitely in order.

Chapter 23: How Times Change

Cody looked at his watch. He was getting closer to being able to get his vengeance on the infuriatingly cocky assassin standing across from him, sipping coffee from a gas station's disposable cup like he had not a care in the world. But according to the time table, the blessed moment was still a ways off. Oh, but what a sweet moment it was going to be when Cody could see the look of betrayal on the man's face.

The longer he spent with the man, the harder it was to play his part in this little charade. When El Gran Blanco split his own face with his fake smile, Cody wanted to split it with the butt of his rifle. As he glanced around his group, he could tell they were having a hard time with this as well. He just hoped they all could keep convincing El Gran Blanco long enough to make it all work out.

One thing was certain in his mind, however. When he did spring his trap on the killer, they would have to be careful. Cody had instructed Digger to uncover everything he could on the man. What his techno-teammate discovered, was the man was as sneaky and dangerous as a black panther in the night. It was certain the assassin did not trust them and was looking for a trap this entire time. When they slipped the noose around his neck, they would need to be cautious. His reputation said he could kill with ease.

They made the flight back to Boston in record time, and Digger, along with another teammate, ran back to the warehouse to pick up a few supplies. Diggs focused on his electronic toys, and his shooter concentrated on extra ammunition. They also gathered a few more grenades and their trusty RPG just in case. It was amazing how an RPG could quickly turn the tides of a battle. One moment you could be about to meet your maker, and the next you could be celebrating your victory.

Of course, if Digger was right, all of this would go off without a shot being fired. Until the very end of course. But there would be no hard-fought battle of supremacy. Geek power would rule this day. Sad, really. Cody rather enjoyed the sound of gunfire and the smell of spent ammunition wafting across the arena of combat.

Warfare was a new creature, he mused. Technology and software were becoming more critical to engage and defeat one's enemies. It was the primary reason he brought Bayllen Diggery into the fold.

And he would prove his worth on this job.

They waited on the tarmac in Boston for close to two hours while Cody's errand boys gathered their supplies across town. According to the pilots they hired, they should still arrive at their final destination ahead of the snow storm now barreling towards the East Coast.

And they did.

They arrived at the Deerfield Valley Airport, a privately-owned airfield just outside of Wilmington, Vermont, well after sunset. It was a skier's destination where the rich and famous in the upper New York area liked to hang out. They stepped off the plane with the first few flurries falling from the sky, and the pilots were in the air rocketing away before their passengers even cleared the airport.

From there, after procuring a couple of large vehicles, they drove another hour as the flurries turned into light snow. The storm's characteristics changed from when it tore through Denver. It was now larger, but less fierce in its scope. Right now, it was only gently dropping feathers of white from the heavens. There was just a light breeze, and visibility was still pretty good. According to forecasts, there would be no gale-force winds. Just a heavy dose of snow. No white-out conditions.

And now, here they stood under the shelter of pine boughs just off the road. Cody checked his watch yet again, anticipating both a satisfying revenge, and a profitable payout. The shark circling in their midst would hopefully never see it coming.

The finish line was in sight.

According to their intel, the Slaughter property was just up ahead beyond a bend in the road. A satellite map view of the area showed a long and narrow gravel drive barely visible through the trees. Several hundred yards long, it weaved its way through the woods, crossing a deep ravine via a small bridge, and eventually ending at a diminutive house. There was a small clearing out front, a large carport off to the side, and some sort of barn or utility building in back. All of it closed in and surrounded by dense forest. From appearances, it was a large property consisting of a few hundred acres, and there were no other dwellings even close.

The plan here was straight forward and uncomplicated, Cody explained to El Gran Blanco. The first move was to establish aerial reconnaissance with Digger's drones. Three of them would do a high-level flyover and scan the area looking for thermal signatures, then set up station on three corners of the house. Snowfall was not heavy for the time being, and they would be able to fly high up and out of earshot of being heard while hovering. The drones going by the names of Mario, Dante, and Lara Croft would be able to hover for nearly forty-five minutes before having to make a return trip back to Digger for new batteries. As long as the wind didn't start howling like what had happened in Denver, they should have all the surveillance time they needed out of the drones. If the wind picked up beyond ten miles per hour, the drones would start to eat up battery faster, trying to fight the wind and stay on point.

The next part of the plan was to get Diggs in close so he could use his newest creations to take out their targets. Digger called his new toys *Hornets*.

The Hornets were small drones capable of fitting into the palm of your hand, and Digger built ten of them. Each one was fast and nimble, and relied heavily on artificial intelligence to perform their tasks. The small drone's job, and the sole reason for heading back to Boston in order to pick them up, was to take out an enemy without ever having to place yourself in harm's way.

If you could import a clear enough picture of your target to the small onboard computers, along with height and weight of the intended victim, the Hornets could be released into an area to track down and attack the enemy. Using AI, it could differentiate the target from other people standing nearby, and swoop in with devastatingly awesome precision.

If you couldn't provide enough information in order for the AI to make a positive ID, like in this situation, they could just be ordered to attack whomever they made contact with.

The drone pilot stationed some distance away, need only establish a GPS fenced-in area for the kill-zone, and the drone would do the rest on its own. No real skills were required to fly them. You simply gave them some orders, and like obedient soldiers, they went out to accomplish the mission. There was no hesitation. No fear. No adrenaline flowing through flesh and blood veins and affecting decision making. They were perfect little killing machines.

The Hornet could be equipped with one of two weapons. The first was a simple, lightweight, 22-caliber bullet. The thing would function similar to the way a scuba diver would use a bang stick against a shark. On identifying the target, it would dart in with incredible speed and strike the victim in his forehead. The small caliber projectile would easily penetrate the skull, and then bounce around inside like a pinball machine, wreaking deadly havoc. Cody marveled at how clean and clandestine one could kill with one of these Hornets. El Gran Blanco seemed instantly fascinated by its lethal capability.

The second weapon, and the one they elected to use, involved merely incapacitating the intended victim. Instead of a bullet to the forehead, the tiny drone was equipped with a dart head designed to deliver a small dose of tranquilizer. The same kind typically used by zoos to put large animals to sleep. And instead of aiming for a spot above the victim's eyebrows, it quite literally went for the throat. The needle was long and thin, easily penetrating layers of clothing to deliver its payload. Yet it was not thick enough to accidentally kill the target.

The target would be sleeping soundly within seconds, and the effect would last for about fifteen to twenty minutes. Well enough time to move in on foot, secure them with zip-tie restraints, and do with them as they pleased.

At first, Cody pressed for the quick and sure option. Just kill everybody in the house and then leave. But the assassin insisted on the other choice. He wanted to look the man in the eye when he died. He wanted to make the man watch as the assassin took the life of his friends, saving the girlfriend for last. Then he would slit the man's throat and stand over him as Slaughter bled out.

It was all Cody could do to keep from just putting the man out of his own misery right then. Hearing him talk was grating on his nerves. However, choosing this route, while inserting extra risk, had the added benefit of dragging this whole thing out. Cody needed the extra time to finally bring everything to a close. He grudgingly agreed to the assassin's wishes.

The question Cody had for his techy friend was, how did they get the killer drones inside the house?

Digger had a plan, of course. The tech wizard owned six other drones. Three of them were going to be keeping over-watch from high above with thermal imaging cameras. But another of them was considerably larger than the drones they used for spying and keeping an eye out for threats. It was still small enough to be carried in the trunk of a car, and it could fit through an open doorway with careful flying, but it was large enough to carry a payload. The young man named it Big Daddy after a character from the 2007 video game "Bio Shock."

In the game, Big Daddies were very large, armored, bio-engineered creatures, Cody was told. And it was a fitting name Diggs chose for this drone. All of his other drones had four rotors. Big Daddy had eight. Each rotor had a bullet-deflecting duct protecting the blades, and a protective front snout guarding its nose. This allowed the heavy-duty drone to be able to bounce off of things and continue on, or receive gunfire and still be able to complete its mission.

There were modular attachments on the front for various missions. One allowed for a taser to be fired at an enemy. It was the fate chosen to incapacitate El Gran Blanco before he took the thing down with a well-aimed pillow. Another attachment mounted a 9mm pistol underneath with a fifty-round drum of ammunition. It was even capable of carrying a ten-pound payload, and it could do it for a distance of over ten miles.

Digger would crash Big Daddy though the living room window at full speed. The Hornets would follow through and start doing their work on the inside. Just in case anyone managed to escape through a back door, the surveillance drones would alert Cody's team. His men would be stationed in a circle around the house and ambush anyone trying to leave.

The goal here was not to kill anyone, but if their targets managed to break free, then taking them alive was off the table.

Additionally, the Hornets would only be given a kill zone of about fifty yards from the house. They didn't want to risk them accidentally homing in on one their own guys.

There was only one downside to the AI driven Hornets. Because of their small size, they only had enough battery power for about ten minutes. This fact meant they could not release the drones from where they were currently gathered. They would need to pack them in fairly close. Cody and his men were unfamiliar with the terrain. If Slaughter had set up any traps in the woods, they might not know about it until it was too late. They would have to proceed carefully.

In addition, the natural terrain meant they would have to sneak in with a fairly straight approach, right up the gravel road leading to the house. The ravine they needed to cross was only passable via the small bridge built for the driveway. They didn't have any climbing gear or ropes, so crossing from another location would be hazardous. Especially in dark, icy conditions and under the low visibility of night and snow fall. If they tried to come in around the ravine from the far sides, it would take them hours of hiking through the woods. Their targets were under the impression they were safely tucked away out here, so Cody decided to risk it. The three drones up above would be able to pick up an ambush with their thermal cameras well in advance.

With no one offering up any additional information or fears about the plan going forward, Cody instructed Digger to send up his three surveillance drones. The young man skillfully launched all three simultaneously from the cover of the trees they were hiding in, and then guided them out through the trunks and over the main road. From there, they shot straight up to about a hundred feet, and then followed the road to the entrance of Slaughter's property. The main road was lifeless, and the drones spotted no cars passing below. It was only just after nine in the evening, but most sane people were huddled up in their homes under the threat of heavy snow.

Cody peered over Digger's shoulder at the screen resting underneath the raised tailgate of one of the large SUVs. Sheltered from the snow fall, he watched Diggs direct the cameras for signs of life hidden in the trees and along the gravel road. But hunt as they did, no heat signatures showed up to point out people hiding in the trees. So far, so good.

From there, the drones moved slowly up the long gravel drive, a hundred feet overhead and peering through the canopy for hidden targets. In short order, they arrived over the house.

Against the colder background of everything else, the house was lit up like a Christmas tree. It glowed in various shades of red, yellow, and orange as the occupants sheltered all warm and toasty inside. Cody could see the long plume of smoke rising from the chimney in puffy shades of crimson and gold. It eventually dissipated and became the same temperature of the surrounding air, vanishing altogether.

Seeing nothing to alert them to a possible ambush, and detecting no one outside in the snow, Diggs left two of them high up, and used one to do a slow sweep around the house at a lower altitude. It circled slowly in a wide arc just above the tree tops, peering through the darkness. Occasionally, they could make out a person pass in front of a window. In the front of the house, something glowed brightly on the front porch.

"What's that?" asked the assassin looking at the screen from the other side, hands wrapped around his cup of coffee, and coat pulled up high under his chin.

Digger laughed. "That means this is all going to plan, and everyone inside has no idea what's about to happen."

The assassin stared his response without saying anything, questioning eyes lit up by the glow of the screen asking his silent query.

"That," Diggs reassured. "That is a barbeque pit cooling off on the porch. They've been grilling. And right now, they're all lounging around a fireplace, probably stuffed to the gills and sitting there with their pants unbuttoned like proper fat Americans." Diggs turned to look at Cody, giving him an approving nod that now it was time to head in on foot.

"Put Big Daddy on station over the house," Cody instructed Diggs. Turning, he gave orders to the rest. "Make a final check on your gear.

Jerry, you got point. I'll bring up the rear with Diggs and our boss here," he referenced the assassin. "Move slow, please. We'll have risky footing all the way to the target. I don't want to be slowed down by a twisted ankle."

"What about the RPG?" asked one of his men, holding the launcher over one shoulder like a lumberjack holding an axe.

Cody thought about it. "Too big and cumbersome. Just stash it. We've got a few grenades should we need them." He looked around the group and issued a final order. "This is our rally point. Should something go wrong and we get separated, we meet back here. We no longer have superior numbers, and we know our target can shoot. Don't get stupid. If this suddenly goes south, get yourselves back here and we bail."

Cody checked his smartwatch one more time and smiled at what he saw. Not too much longer, he thought with confidence. This would all be over soon.

DJ caught Brett looking at his phone. "Any word yet?"

"None," Brett answered. "I would have thought they would have wasted little time in invading the ranch once they had the information. I'm really thinking tonight or tomorrow they'll make their attempt." But despite the confidence portrayed in his voice, Brett's connected eyebrows told another story. He was worried.

"Then I wouldn't worry just yet," DJ said.

Brett had been a constant see-saw of emotions. One minute he would seem relaxed and unconcerned over what was happening back in Colorado. He carried himself with confident knowledge their plan was going to work. The next minute would find him brooding, the wheels in his head turning everything over and over trying to decide if this was going to be yet another failure.

DJ understood. They couldn't risk another failure. There had been too many encounters with their enemy where they managed to escape by the skin of their teeth. The only time where DJ almost ended up on top was back at the waterfall. DJ smiled at the thought. He was sure the stab wound in the assassin's butt cheek would leave him limping for some time to come. Of course, even then, had Abbi not thought to put on a vest...

Brett looked at DJ with concern. "We need to set up a guard duty. Just to be on the safe side. Just in case Abbi's make-shift perimeter catches movement."

"Well, I can tell you it *will* catch movement," DJ warned with a worried look. "And when it does, I'm not sure what to do about it. I guess we can throw some corn out in the yard and hope for the best."

Brett didn't get what he was talking about. DJ, acting like he heard something, jumped up and ran to the front door, swinging it open in a panic.

Brett was there next to him, gun drawn and ready, looking desperately out into the falling snow. "What is it?" The man showed ready to plug the first thing that moved.

DJ smiled at him. "Relax, G-Man. The game cameras are bound to go off several times tonight. But the only thing they're going to see is the hundreds of deer that call these woods their home." He reached down and opened a small trash can near the front door. Dipping his hand inside, he pulled out a handful of dried corn and tossed it all up and down the covered front porch. "They come right up and eat this in front of the windows. Coolest thing you'll ever see."

Brett shot a venomous glare. In hushed tones he reprimanded DJ. "Not funny. I don't think you understand. Something is off."

DJ scattered a second handful of corn and got serious for a moment. "What are you talking about?"

Brett continued, quietly. "I've been running this through my head over and over again. At first, I thought it all lined up. Our conclusions and the plan we put in place to finally catch this guy seemed to all make sense. But now…"

From behind them, the guard DJ referred to as "Thing" spoke up. "Close the door!"

DJ grabbed both of their coats from the pegs positioned next to the door. He handed Brett's off and then ushered him outside, pulling the door closed behind.

As they both zipped up their coats, DJ asked again. "What are you talking about?"

"I don't really know how to explain it other than to tell you it's the way my brain connects the dots on a case. Sometimes I can see a connection through all of the facts and details. I use what I see to decide how to proceed and act in an investigation."

"So, you rely on your gut to guide your actions," DJ concluded.

"Not exactly. I mean, yes, I rely on my gut feeling about things, but it's more than that. I kid everyone I work with that I have Special Agent Superpowers. But honestly, I really do have a gift with this sort of thing."

"So, if your Spidey Senses warned you something is off, why are we secluded out here in Vermont with no one to help us if we get in a jam?" DJ was getting perturbed now. At first, he was just playing along with Brett, thinking the man was over reacting. But now he was starting to think Brett may have placed them all in harm's way with a foolish plan. They were at risk of Shark Bait catching them with their pants down yet again. If Brett really did have a special intuition about this sort of thing, why were they out here?

"That's just it. At first, I was pretty confident about all of this. But now, not so much." He moved over to catch some warmth from the still-hot grill. "I feel like we're wrong about this. But I've turned the thing over and over again in my head, and I can't for the life of me figure out what has me spooked. I tried to blow it off, thinking I was just over-reacting. But the longer this goes on, the more I'm worried."

DJ stepped next to him, swinging the grill lid up and holding his palms out over the glowing charcoals. "Look, I know you to be pretty good with this sort of thing, but we're here now. So just what do you think we should do? Pack up everything and take off again? We can't just keep running around. At some point in time we have to make a stand and trust our abilities. Besides, no one knows we're here. Seriously. We've told no one."

Brett turned to look out into the darkness, seemingly looking for words to say. But just as he appeared to be about to say something, the door opened behind them quickly. They both spun to see Cash standing in the entrance.

"Abbi just got a hit on the bridge camera," the stalwart agent said.

Filing back inside and closing the door behind them, they all focused with expectation on Abbi. She stood by the fireplace in the corner, staring at the screen with concern.

"What is it?" DJ asked, coming to stand next to her and look at the screen as well.

She shook her head. "I'm not sure. The camera registered movement, snapped a picture, and then sent a text message to my phone with the attachment. But cell phone service around here is spotty. The time stamp said it happened over twelve minutes ago, so there's a real delay."

Brett spoke up. "What's the picture of?"

Abbi shrugged, still staring at the screen. "Don't know yet. It's taking its time loading. Sorry but the service here is really bad."

From the moment Abbi began speaking, Thing and Mighty Pebble stood, gathered up their rifles, and were now peering out of windows across the room. Cash shrugged his coat on, grabbed a rifle as well, and killed the lights. Next, he opened the front door and stepped to one side of the frame, searching the snowy darkness for signs of life.

DJ watched as Abbi's face changed under the glow of the flickering fireplace. "There," she blurted out. "It's loading now."

As quickly as she became alarmed, she reversed course and relaxed. Her demeanor instantly calmed and she smiled to the rest of the room. "It's only a deer," she reassured. "Look, it's running across the bridge. It must have heard something out by the road. Car, I guess. Look how cute he is," she exclaimed. She immediately ran over to Lisa and both women began to coo over the photo like they had gotten a new puppy for Christmas.

It was amazing to DJ how Abbi could be such a tomboy one moment and a complete girl the next. She was a complex creature, full of both youthful joy and carelessness, and serious aged intensity. One minute she was trying to learn a new martial arts combination to viciously bloody up an opponent, the next giggling like a schoolgirl over a new cute top she found at a department store.

Everyone in the room visibly relaxed, with Thing and Mighty Pebble leaning their rifles back against the wall where they were previously stashed, and making themselves comfortable back on the couch. They went back to watching the movie Abbi had loaded up on her laptop and connected to the TV.

Cash lowered his weapon as well, and moved around from the frame to stand fully in the open doorway, looking out into the night. He stood there with all the appearance of having spotted something. DJ was about to ask what, when Abbi spoke up from over by Lisa.

"Oh, here comes another," She cried. "Maybe we can get a closer look. There's such a bad delay. Sorry, everyone. I didn't account for such horrible service. I should have known my husband would buy a piece of property as far away from the civilized world as he could." She smiled at DJ with a playful grin.

DJ, Brett, and Lisa all stared back with open eyes and a painted-on blank expression. Not realizing what she had said, she glanced at them all in confusion. DJ, then, was overcome by a strong desire to look at his feet. He was suddenly very embarrassed. Seeing this, Lisa couldn't help but snicker a bit, and then looked at Abbi.

They *all* looked at Abbi. Brett and Lisa were having trouble stifling their smiles, wondering if she would figure it out.

Abbi placed her hands on her hips, and that chin jutted out in defiance. "Just what is so funny?"

No one answered for a moment. Thing and Mighty Pebble were completely clueless as to what happened, and Cash still stood in the doorway looking out into the snow.

Cash cleared his throat, "Guys…"

DJ ignored him. He could care less about cute little deer heading to his house for free handouts of dried corn.

"Again," Abbi demanded, "Just what is so funny"

"Guys?" Cash repeated.

Lisa spoke up then, placing her arm around Abbi's shoulder. "You just called DJ your husband."

Abbi's face went white. "No, I didn't."

Lisa nodded. "Yes… Yes, you did."

Abbi lowered the phone and her head. DJ felt bad for her, but he felt pretty embarrassed himself. But why? I mean they were all grown adults. And everyone in the room knew he desperately wanted to marry her. So why was his face flushed and back of his neck burning as if it were on fire? For the love of Pete, he wasn't in high school any more. I mean he was a widower for crying out loud.

Agent Cash repeated himself for a third time. But this time adding more details. "Guys, I hear something."

DJ blew him off again, still lost in his own troubles. "Just deer stomping their way through the snow. Close the door. We can see them through the window when they come up on the porch."

"No," Cash elaborated. "It sounds like… like… fans…"

Brett turned to look at the younger agent. "You mean like the hum of tires on a car back out on the road?"

"No," Cash replied, still staring into the night. "Like a fan on high. Or… or a weed-whacker. And it sounds like it's getting closer."

They were all staring at the agent now. Both curious as to what he could be hearing. As they watched, Agent Cash took a step back into the room and raised his weapon.

They were all on alert now, and both DJ and Brett drew their sidearms. They both stepped in front of the women, and the two guards scrambled off the couch for their rifles.

DJ could hear whatever it was now. It *did* sound like a weed-whacker, and it was getting closer. He wasn't sure what it could be, but it was bizarre. And it couldn't be a good thing. Now he was suddenly sure Brett was right about this plan not working.

"Close the door!" Brett ordered.

Agent Cash moved to do so, but it was too late. The large buzzing weed-whacker emerged from out of the night flying at incredible speed. It was moving too fast for him to see what it was, and Agent Cash partially blocked his view. But something large and loud flew into the man, propelling him backwards into them all. Like a human bowling ball, Cash knocked them all scattering into the room. Abbi went down, the phone in her hand clattering across the floor.

DJ rolled to his knee and trained his gun on the thing now laying against the far wall. But Mighty Pebble was already standing over it with his rifle and pouring rounds into the machine.

DJ could now tell what it was. An eight-bladed drone, almost four feet in width, was buzzing and trying to lift itself back up off the floor. Mighty Pebble leaped into the air and forward, landing on it with both feet and crushing it back down to the hardwood floor. Apparently seeing a vulnerable spot on its top, the muscle-bound short man emptied the remainder of his magazine in between his feet in an incredible show of sparks, smoke, and gunfire.

The loud buzzing of the giant drone winked out in an instant, but Mighty Pebble continued to stand on top of it with his empty weapon. The look on his face said, if it buzzed to life again, he would dismantle it with brute strength. With his small stature, bulging muscles, and his fierce look of determination, DJ was reminded of an angry dwarf from a popular fantasy movie he had seen a few years back. Were it not for the fact their lives were in peril, it would have almost been comical.

His ears picked up a chorus of buzzing out in the night. More drones, he concluded with panic. He had to get the door closed. He scrambled for it, but the guard he referred to as Thing had the same idea and got there first.

A split second before the big man's hand could close around the edge of the door, he recoiled and jerked his hands to his throat. DJ caught a flash of something small shoot through the opening to strike the guard just under his chin. He staggered back, yanking whatever struck him out of his throat and staring at it in horror. Whatever it was, was small, and concealed within the shadows of the flickering room and the guard's cupped hands. The lights were still off, and the room was only visible through the dancing warm glow of the fireplace.

The big man collapsed then, falling over backwards into the small dining table separating the kitchen from the living room. It collapsed under the weight of the giant guard, and caused a terrible racket.

The crashing of the table was not loud enough to cover up the sound of more buzzing from outside, however.

DJ again scrambled for the door, but he was too slow. A swarm of small buzzing things poured through the opening, spreading out with speed and agility his brain almost couldn't process.

Thing was the first victim, and Mighty Pebble was now next to go. MP swung the butt of his empty rifle like a bullet shooting flyswatter to no avail. Whatever it was they were now battling deftly ducked his attempt, demonstrating it had a mind of its own. It juked left, then right, and drove forward into the man. Like Thing's assailant, this one also went right at the base of the man's chin. Mighty Pebble brought his hand up to block, and whatever they were fighting impaled him in his open palm. MP screamed in pain and fear, and franticly shook his hand trying to fling the thing free.

The guard danced, spun, and staggered his way into the kitchen. He tripped over a piece of table and went down. He appeared to try and stand again, but then stopped moving altogether.

They're robots, DJ thought. *We are being attacked by tiny flying robots.*

One of them dove at DJ, and without thought, he reflexively fired from the hip. Despite the size and speed, DJ's practiced abilities saved him. The thing splintered in the air, reduced to flying bits and pieces, destroyed by the single hollow point round passing through it.

From the peripheral of his vision, he could see his friends falling victim from the crazed mechanical onslaught. One by one they were rendered into heaps of unmoving bodies, as the swarming things drove into them with unrelenting and brutal accuracy. But only one other person commanded his attention and focus.

Having sprung to her feet, Abbi slapped at one with an open palm. In a show of agility, she connected, though just barely. It went spinning past her ear, and she focused on the next one hovering and bouncing just out of reach. With horror, DJ watched helplessly as the one behind her corrected itself. Without emotion, the tiny robot dove in and planted itself right between her shoulder blades. It stuck there, and DJ finally realized their weapon. They were equipped with long needles. Probably delivering a lethal poison of some sort.

They were going to die, he realized. All of them were going to die. And not by the skilled attack of the elusive Shark Bait. By these… things…

He dove for her then, trying to catch her as she fell to the ground, and another of them streaked through the air for him. He ignored it. He didn't want to live in a world without Abbi. His life had been shattered and ripped apart when those villains of the past invaded his home, and murdered his wife and children right in front of him. He had found a way to cope and exist, somehow, but he was never complete. Then Abbi showed up in his life. She put him back together. She restored him.

Let them take me, he thought. *I cannot do this again.*

He felt the sharp sting of a needle bite into the side of his exposed neck, driven deep by the speed of the insect-like contraption. For a second or two, it buzzed beneath his ear. Then, like someone flipped a breaker, it turned off. His world spun and twisted by whatever poison was now swimming in his veins, and down he went. He could not make it to Abbi in time. Just like the rest of the room, he was now a victim of the tiny mechanical creatures.

As he lay there on the floor in front of the fireplace, just before all he knew did a fade to black, he could see the phone Abbi once held. It was propped up next to the brick comprising the hearth. On its still glowing screen, a photo presented itself as a mocking last image. It was a picture of armed men crossing the bridge to his home. The time stamp was now fourteen minutes old, he could read. Those men were who he should have been slain by. Not these robots.

Death by robot, he thought to himself. *My, how times have changed.*

And then, everything just floated away, replaced by nothing at all.

Chapter 24: Now It's Over

DJ wasn't sure how long he lay there floating in darkness, but he was awake now. He forced himself to keep his eyes closed and feign unconsciousness. His ears probed the surrounding area for signs of life, listening for someone talking or shuffling around the cabin. All he could make out, however, was the crackling of the fireplace in front of him. He could still feel the warmth of the flames on his front half, but his back half was painfully aware of the brutal cold creeping through the open door somewhere behind.

He risked cracking one eyelid open, just a slit. Through the fuzziness of his eyelashes, he could still make out the phone lit up with the image of the rifle-toting men crossing the bridge to his home. He also became aware of one comforting piece of information. His fingers were still wrapped around his Sig Sauer pistol.

He was still armed.

Somehow, he was not dead. Maybe the poison was not enough to kill him? Or maybe they had only been drugged in order to knock them all out? If so, they must have got their dosage wrong because he was now back to functioning normally. And since he heard no sounds of his attackers, then perhaps his enemy had not yet entered the house.

He moved then, with all the speed he could manage. Springing from the floor to his knees, he aimed into the center of the room, searching for a target to kill.

And froze…

The room was empty of enemy. It was also empty of his friends and Abbi. They were gone. Across the room, where Thing had flattened the table, he found it reassembled and back in place like nothing ever happened. The giant drone Mighty Pebble had slain was missing as well. He was all alone in a perfectly reassembled room, free of the chaos of moments before.

He climbed slowly to his feet and looked around with unbelieving eyes. It was like the events of the last few minutes were nothing but a dream. He was alone here in the dancing glow of the fireplace, looking around the undisturbed room as if he had always been the only one in it.

The only thing out of place was the snow drifting in through the front door to coat the entrance with light powder. That, and the cell phone near his feet with the image of their attackers still frozen on the screen. It was the only proof of what transpired.

What in the world was going on?

Through the window now, he became aware of more flickering yellow light. Like something was on fire out in front of the house. He darted to the door in response, desperate to learn what was happening. His heart burned with desire to know what became of Abbi and the others.

But mainly Abbi.

There, in the middle of the tiny snow-covered yard, someone had gathered firewood from where it had been stacked on the porch. The pile must have been doused in lighter fluid meant for the charcoal grill. A small bonfire was sending sparking embers high into the air, in sharp contrast to the falling snow. The glow bathed the encroaching frozen forest in yellow and orange shifting light.

But it wasn't the strangest thing he saw. Cassie was back, standing there in a white skiing outfit like she was about to go sledding with the girls. And from experience, he now knew what was going on. He was unconscious, and she was here to give him a pep-talk about what was going to happen.

There was no question he was madly in love with Abbi, but the sight of his wife filled him with memories and love for the woman who gave birth to his now dead twin girls. It was a strange sensation to love two different women, one living and the other dead, but he no longer felt guilty over it. Cassie's last visit somehow set his mind at ease about feeling ashamed. She told him she approved. She had given him her blessing.

He wasn't sure why he kept seeing his dead wife. Was it some sort of delusion or psychosis? Or had she really come back to him from the grave to prod him along and keep him focused when he needed it the most? He didn't know, but he no longer cared. He just accepted it for what it was.

She beckoned him from next to the fire. "Come over here where it's warm, you silly man. We need to talk again." DJ merely nodded and stepped off the porch. The yard was more of a small break in the trees, just enough of an opening in the canopy of evergreens above to allow the snow through. In a few steps, he was standing in front of his wife.

He couldn't help but hug her when he got close, and she readily embraced him. Her hug was familiar and soothing, melting his worries away. For a second, he just closed his eyes and rested there, soaking in remembrance of their time together.

Finally, she pushed him away from her gently, but with authority at the same time. She looked him in the eye and seemed to take him all in, with a warm smile curving her lips.

"Why are you here again?" DJ asked her.

"I told you I would see you one more time," she replied. "But after this, it will be a long time before I can speak to you again. So, this is the last time we do this. At least for a while." She reached up and stroked the week-old beard on his face. "I like this new look you have going." Her green eyes twinkled in the glow of the bonfire next to them.

"You said you always preferred me to be clean shaven."

She shrugged. "Everything changes." She patted his cheeks one last time and then lowered her hand, turning away to face the fire.

He shook his head and refocused. "Again, while I love the fact that I can still connect with you from time to time, I need to know why you are here."

"Change," she said. "Things change."

DJ blinked. "What exactly does that mean?"

"DJ, sweetheart, by now you know life seldom gives us a steady diet of any one thing. It is full of change. And, we have choices when those changes come upon us. We can embrace those changes and adapt to them, and still live out life to our full potential. Or, we can remain stubborn. We can hold onto the things we have, refusing to let go, and end up suffering emotionally when the change happens anyway. We end up flattened and run over by those changes when they proceed along without our approval."

"I... I don't understand."

She turned back to him and smiled. "Well, of course you don't, you silly man." She turned back then and wrapped him in another embrace, leaning her head into his chest.

DJ looked around the clearing that was the small cabin's yard, watching quarter-sized snowflakes fall from the night sky. To one side, he could see the shadow of their embrace stretching across the blanket of white. "For once, would you quit speaking to me in riddles and just tell me what I need to know?"

She pushed back from him again and looked up. "Fine," she said. "You've got it in your head of how things need to be. Add that to the very strong tendency you have of trying to be the one in charge, and you quickly fall into a dangerous spot. One where you won't trust the people around you to do their part."

"I trust them," he defended himself.

"Do you?" A touch of frustration coated her words. "Do you really? DJ, going forward from here I can only tell you the following: If you don't learn to trust the people around you to be part of your team, and to live up to their potential, none of you are going to come out of this. You've got to trust them. You can't just take it on yourself to be the hero of every dire situation. If you do that, you yourself will never live up to your own potential.

"You still don't trust Abbi. She is quite capable of taking care of herself if need be. She is also quite capable of making the right call when it needs to be made. If you would only trust her.

"You still don't trust Brett. According to everything he's been taught, he should have handcuffed you long ago and tossed you in a cell. But he didn't. He's been working this whole time to come up with a way to not only help you catch this guy, but exonerate you in the eyes of the law at the same time. And even though you now know what the plan is, there is still a part of you ready to run away and hide when this is all said and done.

"And what about Agent Cashin? He could have turned you in and set you up any time he wanted. But he didn't. Instead, he is blindly following Brett, and risking his own life over and over again just so you can walk free.

"Despite all of those facts, you trust no one. And that needs to change. Starting right now." She stopped talking then and just stared into his eyes. He could tell she was wondering what he would say or do with all of this information.

She was right, he knew. Right about all of it. The last few years had changed him. In so many ways. He was now capable of doing things he never imagined. He had transformed himself because of circumstance into something else entirely. In many ways, it was a good change. He could take charge of almost any situation and come up with a direction to fight in. He was no longer fearful or scared of what the world had to offer. He could face almost any situation head on, and not back down.

Until it came to Abbi, of course. When it came to her, he had a real weakness. When it came to her, he was a mere frightened little boy. And why? Because he didn't trust her to take care of herself. He didn't trust her to be able to think through a situation and make the right call. He didn't trust her to follow through with it even if she did.

It wasn't just a need to protect the ones he loved. Oh, to be sure, that was there. That would always be there. And that would always be his responsibility and commitment to her. But it was more than that. He simply did not trust her in serious situations to do what needed to be done.

He should be ashamed of himself.

It was one thing to take on the mantle of the protector of one's home. It was quite another to make Abbi somehow smaller than she was, and to place her in a testosterone-built box of chauvinism.

And when it came to Brett Foster, despite showing fierce loyalty to DJ, he didn't really trust Brett either. Deep down, he saw Brett as a by-the-book lawman who could not be counted on to see beyond rules and regulations. DJ couldn't help but believe that despite Brett's record to the contrary, at some point he would knuckle under and turn into a rule-bound cop with a badge, incapable of self-reason. When push came to shove, he would always follow the letter of the law, instead of relying on his own sense of justice directed by common sense.

But none of that was true.

And Cash? Well he didn't really know Cash at all. He never stopped to think about why Agent Cash was following along in this little adventure. He just assumed he was blindly loyal to Brett, and that was that. But there had to be more to it than that.

The more DJ thought about it, the more he became aware that Agent Cash was doing all of this because he believed it to be the right course of action too. Cash didn't seem to be the type of person to blindly follow anything.

DJ's shoulders sagged under the realization Cassie was one hundred percent correct with it all. In silence, he hung his head and looked at his feet buried in snow halfway to his knees. When it came down to it, he now understood, he didn't trust anyone other than himself.

Cassie reached up gently, took his chin in one hand, and lifted his face to look at her. "You're an amazing man. You're a leader. And finally, after all this time, you are becoming a man that this world has few of anymore. The only thing that is keeping you from stepping into your new role is the willingness to trust the people around you. I'm here to tell you to embrace your friends. Summon within you the willingness to take that final step and … change."

"But…" DJ hesitated, unsure of how to ask his question.

"What if she dies?" Cassie asked the question for him.

DJ could not bring himself to say the words, so he merely shook his head in response.

Cassie took a full step back, leaned over on one hip, and crossed her arms. "Let me ask you something, DJ. Do you think she wants to spend the rest of her life with you?"

DJ thought back to her referring to him as her husband this same night. "Yes," he declared. "I'm sure she does."

"Is she a stupid girl?" asked Cassie.

"What? Do you mean for choosing someone like me?"

"No. I mean is she intelligent or not? Is she smart, or is she stupid?"

It was a harsh question laced with a hint of exasperation, and DJ was taken back by the sudden assault. "No. She is one of the smartest women I have ever met. She was accepted to MIT, for crying out loud. Not that it's saying much, but she's way smarter than me."

"Exactly my point. Don't you think a woman who was accepted to MIT and can do complex math problems in her head, is smart enough to know what the risks are for wanting to be with a man like you? Don't you think she is fully aware of the dangers?"

DJ said nothing in response, finding it hard to come by words at the moment, but understanding where Cassie was going with this.

"And DJ, do you think the woman is fearful at all? I mean does she walk around jumping at her own shadow?"

Again, he thought back to how she attacked Shark Bait armed with nothing more than a milk shake. He thought to how she equipped herself for battle and tried to ambush the killer by waiting for him on the bridge. "No. She is definitely not scared of much," he said.

"So, you silly man, if she is smart enough to know what she is getting into with you, and brave enough to fight anything you both encounter head on, what is your problem? If she dies in the process of all of this, should you not focus on how she was willing to pay the ultimate price in order to spend a few days on this earth with your scruffy face?"

Just like back at his row house in Beacon Hill, DJ could not believe the weirdness of what was happening here. He was being given relationship counseling about his new love, from the ghost of his dead wife, after being rendered unconscious by a raging killer assassin. There was no doubt about it, he was crazy. He had lost his ever-loving mind.

But even still, he knew Cassie was right. Right about it all. He had to trust his team. Because that is what they were. A team. He had to trust Abbi. She made her decision. She knew what she was getting into with him, and she chose this path anyway. So, whatever happened, happened.

We only have a short time on this earth, he thought to himself. *Why waste it swimming around in worry and timidity?* He would trust his team. He would trust his soon to be wife. He would change.

Cassie nodded in approval. "That's my fuzzy-faced hero," she said, apparently reading his mind. "Now listen carefully. This is the last time you and I will talk for a long time. Honestly, I am not sure how long that will be. But know this, David John Slaughter: I will be waiting for you with breathless anticipation." She stepped forward quickly, and before DJ had time to react, she struck him hard across his face with an opened-palm slap.

He flinched in shock, closing his eyes and wincing to the sharp pain. When he opened them again, prepared to give her a piece of his mind, nothing was the same. That world was gone, replaced by one far darker. And way more intense.

He was staring into the evil grinning face of El Gran Blanco.

"There he is," the man declared, inches from his nose. The killer's breath was laced with the smell of coffee. For the briefest of moments, DJ thought of his custom roasted La Minita still stashed in his pack. He would enjoy a fresh cup after he ripped the man's throat out with his bare hands. He moved to do so now, and suddenly realized his hands were bound tightly behind his back. Zip-ties, he concluded in an instant.

DJ smiled inwardly. While the bulk of the population believed getting out of zip-tied restraints was nearly impossible, DJ knew differently. It was a misconception propagated by television and movies. In fact, soldiers on the field of battle often carried them to restrain captives. And for the most part, it generally went without a hitch. But DJ was aware, no matter the method used with the plastic bindings, you could generally break free without too much of an issue if you exercised the correct method to break them. He had even seen video of an eight-year old girl doing so with shoelaces.

He would be free of his bindings, he promised himself. But timing would, of course, be everything.

Shark bait stood, towering over him then, and DJ realized he was flat on his back in the snow. He blinked as a large flake landed on an eyelash. Blinking and turning his head, he quickly took in the situation around him.

He found it to be a grim one. They were in very serious trouble.

Much like his delusional moment with the shade of his wife, he was in the small cleared out area he called his front yard. There was a fire going in the middle of the space. Again, probably started by one of their attackers gathering firewood stacked up on the porch. He was stretched out on the ground to one side, with the cabin to his feet.

Above his head, the men of his group had been assembled. They were not bound as he had been, but were lined up facing the house with the fire between them. They were in a neat little row on their knees, mixed looks of anger and dismay stamped on their faces.

Closest to him was Brett. They shared a look. It said he was ready to spring into action at the first opportunity. But there was fear there as well. He had only seen that fear once before when the man's wife was in danger back over the summer. He was thinking about that now, DJ could see.

Next in line was Mighty Pebble. That fierce focus reminding DJ of the fantasy-world dwarf, was still carved into his face. He, for sure, was ready to pounce. Just give him a direction and a target.

Cash was next. Emotionless as always, he rubbed his stomach slowly and kept his eyes scanning the area on the opposite side of the fire. He must be bruised from the impact of the monster drone invading their cabin in the woods. Despite not being able to read his expression, DJ knew the man well enough to know he was already prepared to leap forward and fight.

Last in line was the giant guard known as Thing. There was no anger, nor a plotting focus in his eyes. He was just flat out scared. He was only thinking of his own hide right now. In his mind, DJ could tell, he was staring down an impossible situation. The only thing he was ready for, was to run at the first opportunity. He also kept one hand to his throat, presumably concerned over the damage the tiny, buzzing robot caused.

Great, DJ thought. *Can't rely on him for anything. And he's the biggest guy here.*

Continuing around the circle, he spotted a large group of rifle-equipped shooters. All of them were sort of clustered together, seemingly not at all concerned with having to defend themselves. Judging from their casual countenance, they were quite sure the four lined up on their knees would not try to attack them. They stood relaxed, with most having their rifles slung over their shoulders.

It was odd, to say the least. What was keeping his friends from attacking the group?

And then he understood.

As he continued to pan his gaze around, he got back to the cabin. And there, sitting on the edge of the porch, holding on to each other in the cold, were both Abbi and Lisa. Behind them stood three more armed men pointing weapons down at their heads. Brett and the others were not attacking, because doing so, would mean a certain death for the two women. His friends might as well have been shackled to a concrete wall. The threat of harm to the women on the porch kept them firmly where they were.

He turned back to look at Shark Bait standing over him, and became aware of two more men standing close. One of them was a thin black man in glasses. He had DJ's trusty Sig Sauer pistol tucked into his waistband, but no other weapon. Surrounded by his armored comrades, the man was an anomaly. He clearly looked out of place amongst the other grizzled warriors. Clutched in both hands, a tablet computer glowed, the screen casting a reflection in the young man's glasses. He kept turning his attention downward to what it was showing him. This must be the one responsible for all of the drones, he concluded.

Next to him was another soldier. And this one looked familiar. It took DJ a second to figure out where he had seen him before, but then it all came back in a rush. This was the man he spotted standing high on the roof of his house in Boston, looking down at him and Abbi on the sidewalk as they were being attacked. DJ had thrown a hasty shot at him, but missed and ricocheted the round off the edge of the building. From the way he stood there with authoritative confidence, this was a guy used to being in charge. He must be the one leading all the others.

This could only mean he was also the one DJ talked to over the radio back in Denver. Apparently, the information DJ provided to the leader was not enough to change his allegiance. This also meant, as soon as DJ figured out a way to finally take the life of the assassin towering over him, he would need to kill this guy shortly after.

The tactical advantage to any conflict involving groups of soldiers was to take out the one giving the orders first.

There was a whole lot of killing needing to be done, DJ mused. But the question was, how? The girls being held hostage on the porch made things incredibly difficult. He turned his eyes back to Abbi. He wasn't certain, but it looked like she gave him a wink as she whispered something into Lisa's ear.

Was she already planning her own line of attack? The three men standing over her had no idea how skilled she was in hand to hand. An attack by her would certainly be a surprise. But then what? It would take DJ a long moment to free himself of his restraints. Anything could happen in that span of time. And what of the others? What would their course of action be if Abbi turned on her captors?

They certainly found themselves in a very tight spot.

Shark Bait standing over him spoke with smug assurance. "That's right. Soak the situation all in. I want you to fully understand there is nothing you can do to get out of dying this time. But don't worry. I won't make you die all at once. That would be far too easy." He patted his back pocket. It was the same place DJ had plunged a dagger. "You've been a large pain right back here. In more ways than one. And, you need to pay for that. Slowly."

The obvious leader of the others wiped his nose on the back of a gloved hand before stepping forward. "On your knees, big guy," he ordered before sucking in hard through his runny nose, trying to keep it from dripping down onto his upper lip. He reached a gloved hand down and helped him to his knees, and DJ instantly assigned a nick-name to the man in charge.

Sniffles.

The snow was still coming down, but only barely. Just a thick tuft of cotton from time to time fell through the trees. They must be experiencing a small break in the storm, DJ thought. There was still over a foot of it on the ground, however. The forecast promised nearly three feet before it was all said and done.

Sniffles stepped back from him to stand over by the geek with the computer.

Geek, DJ thought. That's a good name for him, too.

DJ glanced at the Sig tucked in Geek's belt. If he could just wrap his hands around his old friend, he was certain he could do a lot of damage.

"What?" Shark Bait asked him. "I see those wheels in your head spinning. You actually think there's a way out of here, don't you? But there's not. It's over. And I am going to start taking things away from you bit by bit until you're nothing but a shell of the man you once were.

"I'll make a deal with you, though," he leaned forward a bit at this, pointing his silenced Glock at DJ's nose. "You suck it up and take it like a man, and I'll let your girlfriend live. How does that sound?"

DJ didn't reply, but turned his eyes away and looked downward. Right now, he needed to appear to be defeated. It might buy him enough time to find an opportunity to strike. Or Abbi, for that matter. She was up to something. He just wasn't sure what yet.

Shark Bait took a couple of steps back and gestured to the row of men on their knees across the fire. "All of your friends there are going to die, Mr. Slaughter. You know that, right? They're going to die right here in the middle of these God-forsaken woods, buried underneath the snow. They probably won't be found until spring. Because, no one knows you're here, right? And guess what. It's all going to be your fault. Your fault," the killer repeated, pointing the barrel of his pistol right at DJ's nose.

DJ kept looking at the ground, but tried to see what the others were doing out of the peripheral of his vision. If DJ tried to rush Shark Bait right now, it would only end badly. Brett and the others were nowhere close to anyone to make a difference. The only people within easy striking distance of an enemy was Lisa and Abbi. But even if Abbi struck now, causing a distraction for the rest of them to act, he was not certain they could flip the tables on all of this.

"How does it feel?" Shark Bait asked him from nearly ten feet away now. "What's it like knowing the blood of these men will be on your hands? Knowing that *your* choices are responsible for them not returning to their families?"

For a second the question hung there in the frozen air, but DJ was not contemplating the answer. He was looking for the opportunity to strike. He was looking for the chance he needed to become the lethal killing machine he knew he could be.

Shark Bait snapped his weapon up and fired, sending a round into the row of men on their knees, and DJ could not help but wince in response. Before he could turn his eyes that way, he knew instantly that one of them was dead.

But which one?

Across from him, he watched with dismay as the guard known as Thing stayed upright on his knees for just a second more, a bullet hole burrowed through his skull just above the man's right eyebrow. Then muscles relaxed in death, and the man fell face forward into the snow. The once white clearing behind the dead guard was now stained in crimson splatter.

It sunk in then. The nasty truth of what Shark Bait just said about him being responsible for the death of others drove into him. He realized he didn't even know Thing's actual name. He had been in battle with the man, and DJ could not even be thoughtful enough to learn what his name was.

He shot a look of dismay to Brett. And right away realized just how much of a friend the agent really was. The return look from Brett was not one of accusation. It was a look of reassurance. Brett was silently communicating with him that this was not DJ's fault. This was solely the fault of the ruthless killer standing before him. The assassin was responsible for countless lives being lost. He was responsible for the tears of so many family members of the slain. He killed not for necessity or justice. Shark Bait killed for money. Or in this case, vengeance and just to prove a point.

He just murdered a man to prove he was the biggest bully on the playground.

At the end of the line of doomed men, Mighty Pebble sat staring with horror at the back of his dead friend's head, skull blown outward by the passing of the bullet that claimed his life. He was in shock, DJ knew. Men in shock often failed to act when needed.

Great, DJ thought. Now I can't rely on him to help us out of here either.

He looked back into the eyes of El Gran Blanco, no longer able to hide his anger and disdain for the man. The assassin saw it and smiled. Lowering his weapon, he drew closer and leaned over to look DJ in the eyes, grinning from ear to ear with sick satisfaction.

Whispering, the infamous killer said, "I'll let you in on a little secret. I never planned on letting any of you live."

He had to do it now, DJ thought. Even though his hands were bound behind him, he had to make his attack now with the man so close. DJ would drive his forehead into the bridge of the man's nose, snap his bindings using the technique he learned the hard way from an insurgent in Iraq, then dive for Geek and the pistol at his waist.

But that is when Geek finally spoke for the first time, and everything got weird. "They just turned in, boss," he said, aiming his attention at Sniffles standing next to him.

Sniffles was not a small man. DJ judged him to be somewhere around six and a half feet tall. He was also on the hardened side. Meaning his size matched his strength. So, when he butt-stroked Shark Bait with his weapon, who was still leaning down from having whispered his promise to DJ, the assassin was hit too hard to recover. He wasn't knocked out, but he was surely having trouble remembering his own name. Sniffles hit him with everything he had.

As stunned as DJ was, he wasn't too shocked to not notice the man's weapon falling free from his grasp. But, before he could try to do anything about, Sniffles kicked forward and sent DJ over onto his side.

"Don't even think about it, big guy," Sniffles instructed. "Now get over there in line with your friends."

DJ made an attempt to do as ordered, but with his hands behind his back, it made it nearly impossible. He rolled over onto his face in the snow, and tried to get his legs under him and push up from the ground. He flopped around there for a moment or two, looking ridiculous he was sure, and then Sniffles reached down and pulled him up.

From his newly found upright position, DJ looked down at Shark Bait with satisfaction. The man had groggily rolled over onto his back, and was now looking up at him with a dazed expression.

DJ smiled down and spoke, "Man, you're having the worst week ever." He then turned to stare Sniffles in the eye. "And you? You should have made sure to kill me in Boston. Because I promise you this, you will not walk out of here alive."

DJ's bravado filled promise would be seen by most, he was sure, as extremely careless. But DJ had come to a few conclusions over the last few seconds. And they all revolved around the fact he and the rest were not dead yet. Geek mentioned someone had turned in just before Sniffles laid Shark Bait out in the snow. It could only mean someone was now coming up his drive. That mysterious someone must have given Sniffles orders to leave everyone alive. At least for now. So, DJ made his statement for one specific, and very tactical reason. He needed Sniffles to hit him.

And Sniffles obliged.

DJ saw the punch coming from a mile away, but he didn't dry to duck it. He did, however, try to roll with it and lessen some of the impact. He might have been willing to sacrifice his body for the greater good, but who in their right mind likes to get punched?

DJ staggered backwards from the impact, hearing Abbi gasp from the porch. He stumbled, in part from the actual blow. But also from a bit of impromptu acting. Backwards, he staggered in the direction of Brett and the remaining men. Just before he got there, he appeared to lose his footing and went down hard on his back.

The zip-ties binding his hands behind his back, made a bit brittle by the cold, and pulled tight against his butt, snapped under the sudden impact below him.

Mission accomplished. His hands were free.

Keeping his wrists together to maintain appearance, he slowly rolled over and fumbled around until he could make it to his knees like the others. "OK," he cried, awkwardly shuffling around in the snow. He spit a wad of blood onto the ground in front of him. "I get it. Shut up and get in line." Brett eyed him suspiciously, and Abbi shot flames of fire from her eyes across the clearing. She was hot over his being so stupid, he could tell.

He hung his head for a second and spit into the snow again, but then shot a quiet whisper out of the side of his mouth to Brett. "*My hands are free."* He looked back up and tried to act natural. He wasn't sure if Brett heard him clearly, but he dared not try to repeat himself.

From the amount of blood in his mouth, Sniffles had split his lip open. He gingerly checked to see if all his teeth were still there with his tongue. He found them intact. That was a plus. Despite having a busted lip, he now found himself in a much better situation.

He was unbound and lined up with the two men he knew he could count on to act when they saw their opportunity. And, he was across from the one woman he was sure would act. She would even act without him if necessary, he knew. Things were still looking grim. But at least they now had a fighting chance.

It would be enough, he reassured himself. His team could handle anything thrown their way. Just don't panic, and watch for opportunities.

Sniffles refocused his full attention on Shark Bait. Slinging his rifle over his shoulder and drawing his sidearm, the man currently now fully in charge, ordered the downed assassin to roll over on his stomach. He grudgingly complied. Next, Sniffles ordered one of the three on the porch to come over and secure their new captive's weapon, and to zip-tie his hands behind his back.

They were pulling him up to a kneeling position like DJ and the others, when the sound of a vehicle forging through snow could be heard. A second later and headlights could be seen casting penetrating beams through the trees, causing moving shadows from the trees and undergrowth. As it broke into full view, DJ could tell it was one of those expensive luxury SUVs from Britain. It pulled into the clearing of the yard and the driver turned the wheel. Whoever it was, chose to loop the vehicle around and point itself back out, instead of just pulling straight in and stopping. When it finally came to a halt, the driver's side was facing the group.

The driver's door opened, and out came a well-dressed man in a three-piece dark suit. He was of medium build with jet black hair slicked back on his head. DJ had no clue who the man was, but Shark Bait surely did. He shouted a desperate offer to Sniffles. "Kill that man right now and I will double whatever he was going to pay you!"

Sniffles, standing behind the kneeling assassin with his gun to the man's head, scoffed at the offer. "Money is not the reason I'm handing you over, you idiot. It's about following orders. Though," he turned his attention to the new stranger, "I am still getting paid, right?"

"Oh, indeed," the stranger said with a thick Russian accent. He pulled on a long black coat and a pair of leather gloves as he talked. "In fact, our man was able to successfully transfer all of the accumulated wealth from the many banks El Gran Blanco uses. My boss was quite insistent on erasing the man and his holdings from the earth. I am prepared to hand those accounts over to you at the completion of our business. You will be quite well rewarded for your loyalty."

DJ couldn't help himself. "I'm sorry, but what the heck is going on?" he asked out loud.

The Russian chuckled as he carefully stepped through the foot-deep snow, heading to the back door. "You are the man Slaughter, are you not?"

DJ spit another wad of blood into the snow before replying. "One and the same."

"You use no profanity when you talk. Heck instead of hell. I would assume a man of your reputation would have a different vocabulary. Why is that?" The Russian buttoned up the long coat as he spoke, and adjusted his gloves for comfort.

DJ shrugged. "I had a Drill Instructor once tell me the use of profanity was an indication of a lack of intelligence. If you can't articulate yourself with real words, you should just shut up. But don't be offended by that. Because of that advice, I spend a lot of my time not talking." DJ smiled at the man. "So, who are you?"

"Me?" the stranger replied. "I am nobody. But I now introduce you to the man for whom you can thank for still being alive. At least for now." He swung the door open and stepped out of the way. "Meet my employer. International Business man, Sergei Romanoff. The man who would have you dead, knows him quite well."

DJ shot a glance at Shark Bait, and was surprised. The man was genuinely frightened. Whoever this Romanoff guy was, they should probably all be worried if Shark Bait was scared of him.

Sergei stood and allowed his driver, or whoever the other guy was, to help him with his own large black coat. Likewise, he reached into the pockets and pulled out a pair of expensive-looking gloves. As this new man dressed, taking his time, he seemed to not pay attention to anyone else. It was as if he didn't even know the rest of them were there. In response, DJ took a slow panning look around the group. Almost everyone of their other attackers seemed nervous.

Odd, DJ thought. This Sergei guy didn't even appear to be armed. Yet the small army of men standing in the now increasing snowfall, seemed unsure of themselves. Some of them shuffled where they stood in a nervous manner, turning their attention towards anywhere but this new man. DJ cut his eyes sideways at Brett next to him, and thought he might even see recognition in the agent's eyes.

DJ didn't like the way things were adding up on this. Shark Bait was scared. The soldiers surrounding him were acting antsy and unsure of themselves. And, even Brett seemed to know who this guy was. The conclusion was, Sergei Romanoff was a man with a dangerous reputation.

Finally, Sergei spoke with his own much thicker Russian accent than his driver. Looking straight at the assassin and ignoring everyone else, he slowly advanced across the space as he spoke. "We had contract, you and I. We were making a history together. It was profitable relationship, was it not? I pay you very well, and you kill the people I tell you to. But you became blinded by your own ambitions. You placed your needs ahead of my own." He spat on the ground, and shook his head. "Such a shame."

DJ, turned his attention to the assassin once more. The man positively appeared to be shrinking into himself. He was petrified.

"Do you know how I have been following your movements?" Sergei asked the assassin. "Have you figured out how I know precisely where you are? I can see in your eyes, you do not. I tell you now, so you can know before you die.

"Two years eighty-three days ago, I send you on job. You positioned surgeon on call in case something go bad. It does go bad. You get shot in back. But you do not know surgeon works for me as well. I have him place small tracking device inside you. I follow you ever since to see if you live up to your end of all contracts. To learn all about you in case you decide to turn on me. After all, your loyalties lie with any who will pay you.

"It was gamble. If you go through scanning device at airport, you would know right away. But you don't fly with commercial. You fly private. You are scared of flying. Petrified. You take pills and drink whisky, and fly on private planes when you have no choice but to travel in air.

"Yes, Thomas Huntley," Sergei said, tapping a finger to his temple, still approaching in slow measured steps. "I know everything about you."

Again, DJ looked at the assassin. The man was positively shriveled up in fear, with his eyes on the Russian as if he were being approached by a monster.

"I give you big job. With this job, you can retire in luxury. Kill one man. Make it look like terrorist attack, and you swim in money the rest of your life. You said you could do it. No problem, you say. You promise me your plan would not fail. But even if it did, you would be there as backup and ensure job gets done.

"When I see you not even in the country, but out chasing your own target because you feel he insulted you, my man warns you to get to Paris. He warns you of consequences if you fail.

"Your plan failed. The target did not die. You were not there as backup like promised.

"And these men you hire? Do you really want to know why they would never take your money over mine? It is not because of my reputation they turn on you. It is not for money they turn on you. Have you ever wondered who runs brokerage in Boston? I do. My family has owned the Boston Brokerage for generations. As soon as I find out you turn on me, I find out which group you hired, and I call them. I tell them to, how you say, string you along until I get here.

"So, Thomas Huntley of Louisiana, I am here to show you are not above everyone else. You too, must follow rules or suffer. I am here to terminate our contract, and with it, your life."

Sergei then gestured around the clearing, and for the first time, he actually looked at DJ and the others. Now the Russian was standing only a few feet away from the shriveled-up assassin. "I will do you this one favor," Sergei said with a flourish of his arms, indicating DJ and the others. "I will kill them all for you. But not before they watch you die first." He then turned his attention to Sniffles. "Give me his gun. He will die from bullets he loaded himself. He will die by his own weapon. Symbolic of how his own choices have killed him." He faced the terrified assassin on his knees in front of Sniffles. "You cost me a billions of dollars with your failure. You now pay with your life."

DJ surveyed the situation one more time, trying to gauge the right time to move, as the snow fell from the sky with thick drifting flakes. To his front left were six soldiers in a loose group. Only one of them was actively aiming their weapon at DJ, Brett, Cash, and Mighty Pebble. The rest were standing there unconcerned, with their rifles slung casually over their shoulders. They could be charged, but DJ was pretty sure all of them could bring their weapons around and start firing before they were reached.

On the other side of the fire, standing over Lisa and Abbi, were two more soldiers with rifles at the ready. DJ was not sure how Lisa would respond to a sudden attack by him and his friends, but he was very sure he knew what Abbi would do. It would involve some fancy ninja moves, and if she executed them perfectly, he was sure she could take the two behind her by surprise. But could she do enough damage before she was shot? That was the question.

To his right front were Shark Bait kneeling in fear, Sniffles behind him, one more soldier who had come off the porch to help with Shark Bait, Geek, and now Sergei. The Assistant, the name DJ now assigned to the other Russian, was still standing by the expensive SUV. He had closed the doors to keep the warmth inside. He was standing there with his hands now buried deep in his coat pockets, waiting for it to all be over.

Impossible odds. An impossible situation.

With little choice left to him, DJ planned to move as soon as Sergei put a bullet into Shark Bait. Their attention would all be focused on the execution. He would have a split second to rush the Russian, but no more. DJ's sudden movement would bring everyone's focus on to him. The bad guys would try to kill him. The good guys would then make their move.

For added distraction, as he sprung from the snow, he would pass the edge of the fire illuminating the clearing. He could see a log poking out from the flames. Half of it was on fire. The other half, not. He would scoop it up as he passed, and hurl it into the midst of the Russian and his group. It might give just enough distraction for him to close the gap. Then again, it might not. If he reached the cluster of men in time, the group of six to his left would not fire on him for fear of hitting Sergei or Sniffles. If he managed to get there and still be breathing, he would go for Geek and his trusty Sig stuffed into the man's pants.

It was a longshot. But what else could he do?

DJ looked around, desperate to find something else that could help. If only he had a gun. The one blessed skill he seemed to possess was the ability to wield a firearm as if it were an extension of his will. With a gun in his hand, he was a superhero. Without it, he was just… A guy. On his knees. Being turned into a snowman from all of this frozen stuff dropping from the sky.

In his looking around, he locked eyes with Brett. Brett was staring at him with an intensity. Like he was trying to send DJ a message via telepathy.

What, DJ silently asked with his own eyes.

Down here, Brett said with a flicking glance towards his own knees.

DJ risked a quick look. And then he wanted to bellow with joy. *God bless Brett Foster*, he silently shouted to himself.

Apparently, his friend learned a valuable lesson from their adventures over the summer. The lesson? There was no such thing as having too many guns. Because what DJ caught a glimpse of when he looked down, was the fact that Brett had a backup strapped to his ankle.

And not one person searched him…

Maybe these guys weren't so dangerous after all. Maybe they had only previously focused on shooting at people, and spent very little time capturing people. They definitely searched DJ. His spare mags were gone. His knife was gone. Even his wallet was missing. They certainly saw him as a threat.

But what else had they missed? Was Cash packing a backup gun too? It was probably just wishful thinking, but it would be a game changer if he was.

He couldn't help but steal a glance back at the backup gun. This entire time, Brett must have been pulling his pants leg up. Slowly, ever so slowly, he had been exposing the small little thing on the inside of his left ankle. All DJ had to do was rock back slightly, pluck it from its scabbard, and get to making bad guys dead. He would have to shoot left handed, but at these ranges, DJ was almost as good with his left as he was with his dominant right.

He recognized the make and model in an instant. It was a stubby 9mm Glock with a double stacked magazine. The mag would hold ten rounds, but be reduced to nine with one in the chamber. Question was, did it have a round in the chamber? Or did the slide need to be cycled first? If the latter, it would add precious time to the sequence before he could start shooting.

Brett seemed to sense DJ's concern, and issued a soft whisper of assurance while keeping his gaze firmly aimed at the Russian. *"Eleven. Take it and go."*

Eleven. Awesome. It meant Brett had been exceptionally thorough. He loaded the weapon along with completely filling the mag. He really did learn some hard lessons over the summer.

Sergei took possession of the pistol, and turned to Shark Bait who was now almost in tears. "Move aside," he ordered Sniffles. Sniffles stepped over next to Geek.

The time was now, DJ thought.

"NO!" Abbi screeched from the porch, and the whole clearing turned her direction.

The Russian stared at her for a second. "You wish to take this man's place?" Sergei asked incredulously.

"No," Abbi corrected, with venom in her eyes. "I wish to kill him."

Her statement hung there for a shocking moment. DJ could not believe what he was hearing. He wanted to yell at her to shut up. He wanted to ask her just what was she thinking? But then the statement of his dead wife echoed through his memory.

Trust your team.

But taking the life of another was something that changed you. You were never the same afterwards. You were a darker version of yourself. It was like looking into a stained and tarnished mirror afterwards. He could not allow Abbi to do this to herself. It might have been different were she fighting for survival. But this? This was execution.

Trust your team.

DJ gritted his teeth and remained silent.

Sergei cocked his head to one side. "What has this one done to you to make you so angry?"

"He murdered my mother. He took her from me. She died in my arms. He shot her from a long way with a rifle like a coward. You want to humiliate him in his death? Give me a rifle like he used. Let this tiny girl blow his brains out from up close. Let me look him in the eyes."

Trust your team.

DJ did trust his team. But, he did not want Abbi to do something she might regret for the rest of her life. He knew she was tougher than she appeared. But was she tough enough to do this?

DJ didn't think so.

Trust your team.

"Don't, Abbi." DJ pleaded. "You don't want to do this."

"Oh yes, I do," She spat her angry words at him from across the clearing. She turned her head back at Sergei. "Give me a gun. Let me kill him."

"Abbi, please." DJ begged. "You have to trust me. Killing someone changes you."

Trust your team. The voice pushed the reminder through to the front of his thoughts. But he pushed it back just as quickly.

"Let it change me, DJ" Abbi shouted. There was cold anger in her eyes. She was fully engulfed in her passion, unwilling to think clearly. "Let it change me, then. I don't care. He murdered my mom, and I want justice before I die."

DJ tried to reason with her. "This won't be justice, sweetheart. It will be murder."

For a moment, she just stared at the assassin who had turned his head around to look at her. Then she quietly replied with a distant voice, barely heard across the clearing and over the crackling fire. "I know."

Sergei spoke up then. "Come, my dear. Your wish has been granted."

Still sitting, she turned to Lisa and clutched her hands for a moment, sharing a look. She pulled Lisa close and hugged her neck. Then she was standing and moving with purpose to Sergei, but staring with raging hatred at El Gran Blanco as she made her way past. The assassin made to say something to her. It was unclear what. But before the first words could truly form on his lips, Abbi lashed out and struck the man with a balled-up fist. The assassin recoiled from the blow. The two stared at each other for a moment more, and then Abbi continued on as the soldiers around them laughed.

Geek pushed his glasses up his nose and exclaimed, "Now that's the kind of woman I need." The comment caused DJ's blood to boil, but he fumed in silence.

Sniffles smiled at the younger man and replied. "I don't think you could handle a woman like that."

Abbi was there then, grim determination on her face. Sergei smiled. "You," he instructed the soldier standing near Sniffles. "Give her your rifle." There was a slight hesitation, and DJ understood. No shooter willingly gives up his weapon. Even if it's your boss giving the order. The hesitation was fractional, however, and the man held it out to Abbi with the barrel pointing away from them.

"Ever hold one of these before?" Sergei asked her. She shook her head in reply, staring at the thing and holding it gingerly.

Right away, DJ knew this was a setup. He had taken her shooting often. She fired his own similar rifle countless times, and loved every minute of it. True, she wasn't very proficient. But, she did nothing but grin from ear to ear as she blew up plastic soda bottles at his make-shift range back home.

Trust your team.

She was going to give him the distraction he needed. She was probably going to take out a few of them as well. But what exactly was her plan here? When should he move? Who should he aim at first? Who was the biggest threat?

Trust your team.

Yeah, yeah, yeah, he thought to himself. *I'm trusting my team. I'll just have to be ready to move.*

Sergei pointed at a spot on the weapon in her hands. "This here is safety. It is off. But," he paused as he considered another option. "How much damage do you wish to do to this man? How much do you wish him to pay?" Sergei was positively beaming with joy now. He was thrilled at how much mental agony he was inflicting on Shark Bait.

A quick look at the assassin on his knees showed a defeated man. He was no as imposing of an image as his reputation portrayed. It was over for him, and he knew it.

With a burning heat in her eyes, she answered Sergei's question. "I want his head to come off his shoulders. I want to kick it around like a soccer ball. Is there a button for that?"

Sergei laughed out loud at her bloodthirsty claim. "Yes," he assured her. "There is button for that." He reached down and flipped the selector lever to another setting, and DJ was sure he knew what it was. Full auto.

This surprised DJ. The previous versions of AR15 variants these men used back on the attack at Denver were not full auto versions. Apparently, after their failure, they allotted for more firepower on this attack. Full-auto weapons certainly had their place in combat. Most of the time, as shown by Hollywood, it was extremely over-rated and far less accurate. But in real life situations on the field of battle, it could certainly come in handy. DJ guessed they figured they might need the edge when attacking him again. The more firepower, the better.

Sergei patted her shoulder. "Aim at his face. Hold trigger until it stops making noise. You will get what you want." He then turned his attention back to the sagging assassin on his knees. "Lay down on your back, Thomas. Time to pay your penance."

Shark Bait didn't move. He just sat there on his knees, hands behind his back in bondage, staring into the snow. His lips appeared to be moving. He was talking to himself, DJ realized, but he couldn't make out what was being said. The killer was broken. There was nothing left of the assassin that was.

Sergei's increased in volume and intensity as he repeated himself. "I said lay down on your back!"

The man didn't budge. He sat there mumbling with hollow, vacant eyes. Mentally, the man was just gone.

Sergei, angered at the man's failed compliance, left where he was and stepped quickly to Shark Bait. He aimed a kicking shove at the assassin's chest, intending to force him violently to his back.

Shark Bait, with a seemingly casual effort, and somehow shockingly free of the plastic restraints securing his wrists, shoved the foot harmlessly aside. In one fluid movement, he came off the ground, wrenched his own gun from the hand of Sergei, twisted him around, and pulled the Russian's back into him with his weapon to the man's temple. He immediately began moving sideways in front of the cabin with his hostage, heading for the corner of the building, pulling Sergei along like a human shield.

When the assassin made his surprise move, DJ moved as well, plucking the small Glock from Brett's ankle and aiming at Shark Bait.

Everyone was aiming at Shark Bait. Even Abbi. They all focused on the hostage situation. And to DJ's joy, every one of them failed to notice he had a gun.

Shooting the Russian and Sharky was out of the question as Abbi was now in his way. Shark Bait's sideways movement had brought her in between him and his primary target. But, he had a lot of other options to choose from. He was making his mind up, when Abbi made it up for him.

"Now," she said in a calm, even voice. She swung her weapon left, aiming at group of six clustered on the far end of the clearing. They saw her aim, and probably could have easily taken her out, but she was also standing between them and Sniffles. They hesitated. Abbi, DJ, and Lisa did not.

Abbi fired a long rattling burst into the group, and the men tried to disperse from out of her line of fire. He wasn't sure, but from the corner of his eye, it looked like most of them had been hit.

Lisa, on the other hand, surprised him completely. He now understood what the hand holding and hugging were all about between the two women. Their captors must not have searched Abbi thoroughly either. Abbi kept a small assisted-open knife in her pocket. It was something DJ had insisted on long ago. Never be without a knife, he told her. From a common tool, to a lethal weapon, a knife was something you always wanted to keep close. She must have handed it off to Lisa when they held hands. When they hugged, she must have issued her instructions to be ready to move.

And move, she did.

Lisa turned and made two very hard, and upward thrusts with the blade that magically appeared in her hands. The first went into the groin of the man immediately behind her, a hard strike right into her captor's manhood. Her second jab aimed to do the same with the other soldier, but the man tried to both block, and move backwards at the same time. His open-palmed block only resulted with the blade pushing its way cleanly through his hand.

Both men staggered away from her. For DJ, they represented the most critical target. He needed to kill them before they retaliated against her. He placed a round into each one of their faces with little effort, and they were a threat no longer.

Nine rounds left.

DJ would have continued to shoot into the group of six, for Abbi had not killed them all, but both Cash and Mighty Pebble were charging into his aiming path. They were wading into the group bare knuckled to try and finish them all off.

DJ could only wish them luck, and he sprung from the ground, moving hard right. From the corner of his eye, he saw Brett charge for Abbi. He was going to save her and pull her down out of the line of fire, DJ thought.

So, DJ took another option. His goal was to move laterally to one side and get Abbi out of his line of fire. He would only need to take about three giant steps for her to be clear, then he could take out Shark Bait and the rest.

The assassin had other plans. He used the hesitation by his enemy, who were unwilling to risk shooting Sergei, to take out the most immediate threats in front of him. Swinging his weapon away from the temple of Sergei, he rapidly picked off targets from his left to right. Sniffles took one through the teeth, and that was the end of him. The leader jerked over into the snow, dead on arrival. The soldier standing next to him died next. DJ saw the round exit from the back of his head. His body stiffened and rocked backwards to the ground as well. DJ was unsure why Shark Bait felt the need to kill the harmless Geek, other than the fact he still had DJ's Sig tucked into his belt, but the guy took one in the throat and teetered over backwards, gurgling blood and grasping for his neck. His computer tumbled away from him into the thick snow.

Shark Bait continued around, ignoring Abbi and DJ for some odd reason, and put a round through the face of the driver still by the SUV. DJ watched the man drop a weapon he failed to notice from lifeless hands. The driver apparently had one concealed in the folds of his thick coat.

In the three steps DJ took moving right, Shark Bait killed four men with incredible speed.

Abbi swung her rifle back to Sergei and the assassin, but Shark Bait was faster. Thankfully for DJ, Sergei became involved then, jerking violently to try and free himself. Shark Bait's round went just to one side of Abbi.

From his left, DJ heard Brett groan. His friend had been hit.

DJ was clear of Abbi then. He ignored both the slumping Brett he could see from his peripheral vision, and the gunfire erupting on the far side of the clearing with Cash and Mighty Pebble. He couldn't help any of them. He must focus on what he could do in front of him.

Shark Bait was concealed behind his struggling hostage. So, DJ did the only obvious thing possible. He shot the defenseless Russian right through both knees, and Shark Bait's shield dropped out of the way.

Abbi seemed to sense she was in DJ's way, and darted to her left, moving as fast as she could pump her legs.

Shark Bait could see vulnerability and the threat DJ now posed. Abbi had presented a buffer between him and DJ. But that was gone now. Sergei's body had made a barrier between him and DJ's bullets. But the Russian was now lying broken at his feet. He ducked and wheeled around. He had been approaching the edge of the cabin, and because of the bright glow of the fire to DJ's left, beyond that edge was cloaked in black shadow. Shark Bait stepped into the shadows and vanished. DJ, desperate to end this, put a round into the mass of where his body should be.

But did he hit the man?

The hair on the back of DJ's neck raised, and a whispering voice in the back of his head gave him a silent order. *Move.* He did, diving sideways in the snow. He heard the first bullet whip past his ear. It was followed by a second just nicking his scalp with a stinging slice. He scrambled forward, trying to move laterally to the invisible shooter. The snow was too thick for a sprint, and down he went. In answer to his clumsiness, he felt the hot sting of a bullet rip across his lower back. He heard another shot, but it didn't connect anywhere close to him.

Ignoring the pain, he rolled to his side and fired into the darkness, one round after the other with measured breaks, until the slide locked back. He was empty. He was defenseless. He waited for an answering eruption of gunfire to end him.

It never came. Shark Bait was either dead or gone, vanished into the dark forest behind the cabin, running for his life.

Abbi ran for him then, dropping her rifle into the snow. He ignored her and tried to focus on the others. Brett was on his knees with both hands pressed to his belly. His shoulders sagged, and his chin was tilted to the ground.

Beyond him, still on the porch, was Lisa. She had freed a rifle from one of the dead men and was shooting into the group of six. Abbi had done considerable damage on that end of the small clearing. People were crawling on the ground, and Lisa was firing at them one round at a time.

Agent Cash was locked in a struggle with one man over the possession of another rifle, and as DJ watched, Cash spun and twisted the guy straight into the fire. Burning wood scattered outward and a shower of embers shot into the air. The man still had his rifle, and laying on his back in the fire, he began to shoot wildly. One of the errant rounds took Lisa in the leg, and she shouted in pain. She stumbled backwards and slumped against the wall of the house.

DJ was pleased to see the agent had come away from the struggle with the soldier's pistol strapped to his vest. He put one round through the skull of the man on fire, ending him. He spun to face the rest, advancing with calculation into those who remained.

The fire blocked the rest of the scene between them, and DJ had more concerns. First off, he needed to get to Brett. He shot past Abbi and slid down next to his friend, searching for the entrance and exit wounds. The bullet passed just below the man's navel, and exited out of his lower back. DJ found the exit wound easily. He was concerned, however, because without going in, he had no real way to control the bleeding. All he could do was apply pressure, pray, and get the man to an ER.

He looked up and around. Lisa had finally noticed her husband had been shot. Despite her leg wound, which DJ could see was bleeding profusely, she was back on her feet and headed their way.

"Abbi," he shouted. "Take her belt off and tighten it around those wounds. Make sure it covers both the one in front, and the one behind. Not too tight. Just tight enough to slow the bleeding." Without a word, she beelined to Lisa to comply. Lisa, however, shoved Abbi aside and kept plowing towards Brett.

DJ focused on Cash, and could finally see the rest of the scene on the other side of the clearing. Mighty Pebble was a site to see. His face was covered in blood, and held something clenched between his teeth. DJ wasn't sure, but it looked like a finger. He was staggering around, just at the edge of the bushes, struggling with two more men. Both of them were held in a head-lock with their backs to the stout guard. Each one was fixed tightly by a meaty arm, and MP was squeezing for all he was worth.

As DJ watched, one of the men found a dagger, and planted it in the leg of Mighty Pebble behind him. MP would not let go, however, and despite his injury, he seemed to squeeze even harder.

"Cash!" DJ called out. "Finish up. I need your help."

Cash responded by stepping close to the three struggling men in front of him. Without thought, he placed the weapon to the foreheads of each soldier being held by MP, and dispassionately killed both men. The bloody guard dropped both corpses, then looked down at his leg.

DJ shouted to the man. "Leave that knife where it is. Don't pull it out. You'll only cause more damage. Just stagger over here by the fire. I'll help you in a minute." He refocused on Cash. "There is a roll of duct-tape in the hallway closet. Get it now. And hurry."

He looked back at Brett again, and the man's face was pale under the glow of the fire. He looked DJ in the eyes and spoke, just as Lisa dropped into the snow next to him. "I'm not sure why I haven't fallen over yet, but I can't feel my legs. I've been trying to stand, but they just won't work."

"Is there any numbing sensation?" DJ asked his friend.

Brett nodded. "From the waist down.

With this new information, DJ moved the agent's shirt up and out of the way so he could see the exit wound in the center of his back. Blood ran out in a steady stream, but mixed with it, was clear fluid.

Spinal fluid, maybe? Crap.

DJ shouted at the top of his lungs to Cash who had already vanished into the cabin. "HURRY!"

Abbi plopped down next to Lisa and removed her belt as instructed, starting the process of binding her leg wound. Lisa, for her part, was letting her. But she pressed in close to Brett, lifted his head to look her in the eyes, and telling him he better hang on, or she was going to inflict a lot more damage on him.

Mighty Pebble had ignored DJ about having a seat in the snow. He made his way around the fire, removed his own belt, and before DJ understood what he was about to do, the guard yanked the blade free from his leg.

"You idiot!" DJ exclaimed. He watched with anger as MP then wrapped his belt around his own leg and cut off the flow of blood.

Cash came charging through the open door of the cabin, then, and tossed the roll of duct-tape to DJ before he even got close. DJ caught it in one hand, and started wrapping it round Brett's middle. There was little DJ could do beyond this. What was really needed was a fast trip to a hospital.

Brett spoke up again. "The Russian," he said simply.

DJ had forgotten all about the mobster, and he jerked his head around to find him. He spotted him still motionless in the snow, as more of the white stuff descended from the sky to cover him in a white blanket. DJ jumped up, and the wound in his side bit at him. It was a grazing wound, but it reminded him he was not exactly at full health himself.

He traveled the short distance to Sergei, and realized why the Russian had not tried to call for help, or even crawl away. The man was dead, staring sightlessly into the night above him. The round DJ heard fired from Shark Bait, but somehow did not connect with him, must have been for the fallen Russian at his feet. It was a last act of vengeance before the assassin made his escape.

Brett called out to him from behind. "You need to go after him. Before it's too late."

"Brett," he shook his head. "I need to get you out of here. All of us need a hospital."

"But if he gets away, he'll only come back again. It's what he does. He finds people and takes their life."

"Brett, I can't do that. No, the rest of you help me load him up in the Russian's SUV. We need to get out of here."

"DJ," Brett reasoned, "Don't risk our lives again. Cash and the others can get me loaded. You have to go after him. They probably have vehicles waiting for them near the road. And there is only one way across that ravine. He's got a bad leg, remember? If you hurry, you might catch him before the bridge. We'll meet you at the road in a minute. We have to end this. We can't risk him coming back and killing the people we love."

DJ knew he was right. If Shark Bait managed to make it out of here, he would use his experiences to vanish from the earth. Then, when he was healed up, when he had time to fully plan, the man would be back when they least expected it. And he would not settle for killing DJ. He would want to focus on hurting the people they loved. He would kill Lisa and Abbi first. He would wound Brett and DJ psychologically and make them suffer before finally snuffing all of them out.

Abbi stood and raced back into the cabin, returning almost as quickly with both of their jackets which had been hanging by the front door. She tossed his over to him, then moved over to the body of Geek. Removing DJ's weapon free from the dead man' belt, she tossed that to him as well. She thrust her arms into her jacket, then bent to pick up the fallen rifle from Sniffles. "What are you waiting on?" she asked as she flipped on the tactical light mounted to the front of the rifle. "Let's go."

There would be no arguing or reasoning with her, he knew. If he didn't lead the way now, she would turn and head off without him. There would be no denying her.

He pulled his own coat on and took off at a jog, following the deep grooves from the tires of the Russian's SUV. Calling over his shoulder, he issued a last order to the wounded group behind him. "Cash, get them loaded, but move Brett slow and careful. If we aren't waiting for you at the entrance, you get to the hospital without us."

And then they ran.

DJ was sure the man went into the woods behind his cabin first. How far he would travel before he turned back in the direction of the road, DJ was unsure. But he would have to. The long drive was the fastest way out of here. If you didn't use his bridge to cross the ravine, you would need to travel quite a way before the terrain would allow you back across. Of course, the man could not bother with the road, and instead head deep into the woods. But this would be the most foolish course of action. The assassin would end up lost in unknown terrain in the middle of a snowstorm.

The road. He had to be headed to the road.

Moving through the woods behind his cabin before eventually connecting back with his winding drive would eat up valuable time for the killer. Time, DJ was hoping, could be made up by Abbi and he taking the most direct route.

DJ ran in one wheel-track, and Abbi in the other. He reminded her the killer could be alongside them in the woods. And, he was still armed. If DJ's count was right, the assassin fired nine rounds in the exchange at the cabin. His weapon had been a full-sized Glock in 9mm. That was a seventeen-round magazine plus one in the chamber, if that is how the guy functioned. DJ reasoned it was. So, eight to nine rounds left.

DJ, on the other hand, rarely loaded a round in the chamber along with a full magazine. He wasn't really sure why. It was just not a practice he followed. Of course, he wasn't a trained combat soldier. He learned the use of weapons from being involved with 3-Gun competitive shooting. The one extra round to protect one's life was not ever factored into the equation.

That was a habit he would need to change. One extra round could make all the difference.

So, seventeen rounds for DJ, and approximately nine for Shark Bait. Oh, and Abbi carried a thirty-round magazine in her rifle. He couldn't forget about her. They had the numbers on their side. But all Shark Bait would have to do was hole up alongside the road, wait for someone to follow, and he could ambush them with no problems. He would just need to hide in the dark and look for Abbi's bouncing light as they ran along.

It was cause for concern.

DJ considered turning off Abbi's light, but the cloud cover overhead was too dense. There was no moonlight or other illuminating sources. Without the flashlight, you could barely see your hand in front of your face. It made him wonder how the assassin was faring in the darkness

And then he saw the first sign of their enemy.

Up ahead, a clear set of tracks came from the woods on their left, a single person carving their way through the snow and onto the long gravel drive. Shark Bait had merged with one of the tire tracks himself, and was moving along somewhere ahead of them. From the gate of the killer's footprints, DJ didn't think he was in a full out run. But it did look like a slow shambling jog.

He brought them to a halt. "Kill the light," DJ instructed. Abbi did as he said, and their world was plunged into snowy darkness. He closed his eyes and listened carefully. He thought he heard a car door slam from way back behind them. His friends would be along soon.

But then he heard it, the sounds of crunching snow somewhere up ahead. They were catching him, DJ realized. He opened his eyes and looked in the direction of the road. He wasn't sure, but he thought he saw a dim, shifting glow far ahead. Was it Shark Bait with his own light?

DJ reached over and disconnected the tactical light from the end of Abbi's rifle. "Let me have this," he said softly. "As quietly as you can, as fast as you can, let's go." DJ knew as they got closer, if Shark Bait saw the light, it would be the first thing the man shot at. The last thing DJ wanted was for Abbi to be the first target.

They took off again. This time moving even faster, lengthening out their gait as much as possible in the thickening white fluff. The tires had pushed down the snow in the tracks, but the largest flakes of the storm were now coming down. Peppering their face and eyes. There was already a good four inches of fresh powder on top of the packed tire tracks.

As they ran, he could tell they were making progress and closing the gap. What was once a flicker of light up ahead from a possible flashlight, turned into a confirmed moving glow.

They followed along quickly, their breath coming in easy and measured falls. They were used to running. They liked to run together, though Abbi was clearly DJ's better. Quite often when they got back from a run, she would take off and cover a few more miles. She was like a deer, he mused. She was just built for running, and embraced the opportunity for a good long one.

They crossed the bridge and could see the bouncing flashlight of Shark Bait clearly. The man ahead of them seemed oblivious of pursuit. If he would have stopped suddenly, he would have heard them coming. If he would have turned his head, he might have seen their own flashlight pulling in closer. But he was focused on escape. He burrowed straight ahead through the storm to the vehicle waiting for him somewhere up ahead.

At the thought of Shark Bait seeing his flashlight, DJ cupped it tightly in his palm, allowing only a thin sliver of light to escape from between his fingers. He permitted only the smallest amount to show them the path to follow.

He could make out the killer then for the first time for something more than a bobbing light. He could see the outline of the man as he turned left onto the road ahead. They were at the opening now, DJ realized. He could see the man moving left along the road through the trees. Were it not for those trees, DJ would have stopped and taken his shot. As soon as he cleared the trees and stepped onto the road, he would shoot the man. He had never shot someone running away from him. It certainly seemed cowardly. But DJ didn't care. The man needed to die. By any means necessary. In the back or not.

He heard a car then. At first, he thought it was the SUV from the cabin, carrying his friends to them. But it wasn't. Not yet. He wasn't sure what was keeping them. They should have caught up by now, he thought. But this vehicle was much larger, and it was coming from the road to his right.

Around the bend it showed itself. Its headlights stabbing through the snow and darkness. It was a plow truck scraping the road clear for the rich skiers who would travel it as soon as the storm broke. They would head out as early as possible, eager to take on the fresh powder.

Using the headlights of the snow plow, DJ hunted for the assassin. He saw him cross the road ahead of the big truck and into the trees.

DJ brought the both of them to a halt allowing the plow to pass. Waiting to see what had become of Shark Bait. Would he stay in the trees? Or was he merely in hiding until it passed, preferring to follow the freshly plowed road? It all depended on where the hidden vehicle was Shark Bait was heading to.

It rumbled and scraped its way past and DJ probed the darkness behind it, searching for the flashlight of the assassin. He cupped his own light tightly, killing it completely. For a good minute there was nothing, and DJ was about to charge forward anyway. But then he saw Shark bait's light flick back on, their prey emerging from the woods on the far side of the road. He must have paused there looking for pursuers.

Close call, DJ thought.

The man was shambling down the road again, and DJ took off after him. This time he ran as fast as he could. He needed to make it to the road, clear the trees, and take his shot before their enemy knew what happened. Fifteen steps to the road, and DJ would finally have his chance to end this ordeal.

He sprinted hard, dropping his flashlight in the snow for Abbi to pick up behind. All thoughts of Abbi were lost to him. He slid to a halt into the center of the road, turned to face his fleeing target, and paused to take a long slow breath to try and calm his racing heart.

Then he took his aim.

DJ had outfitted his Sig with something commonly called night sights. Each of the three sight posts on his weapon were filled with a radioactive material called Tritium. They glowed a dim green, and allowed you to line them up in even absolute darkness. No batteries were ever needed, and they functioned for a lifetime. He positioned the three dimly glowing green dots on the shambling figure ahead of him, a good eighty feet away. It was a long shot, to be sure, but not extreme. It was nothing for DJ to be able to hit a man-sized target in the center of the chest from this distance. Especially considering the target was moving away from him, and not side to side.

But then he was. Shark Bait took a hard right, and disappeared into the trees up ahead.

DJ never took the shot. His sights never lined up just right. He didn't want to give away his one chance at a surprise risking a lucky shot. His adversary could shoot as good or better than DJ. As long as Shark Bait didn't know DJ and Abbi were behind him, the odds were firmly on their side.

DJ took off again, leaving Abbi behind, and sprinting down the newly paved road. As he ran, he was conscious of his feet crunching across the snow. The sound would surely give him away if the assassin paused. The killer was making his own crunching noises as he moved. And now with him off the road and into the trees, he was making further noise bending branches out of the way and forging through the underbrush. But if he paused…

The vehicle Shark Bait was heading to must be somewhere just off the road, DJ thought to himself.

He took the same path, following in the footprints of the killer. His flashlight had been scooped up by Abbi, and she was only a few feet behind him now. She cupped the light in her palm as he had done to minimize the glow, but he could make out the footprints of their adversary easily.

He hit the tree-line and stopped.

Once more closing his eyes, he concentrated on the sounds around him. The first he noticed were louder ones coming from Abbi as she caught up to him and stopped as well. As the silence closed around them, he listened as the storm dumped snow from the heavens. It peppered them from above and coated their shoulders and head. He could actually hear the flakes as they struck the warmer skin of his upper neck and head close to his ears. Above and around him, a soft wind made tree limbs offer up a creaking noise in the upper reaches of their canopy. But in the distance, where there should be the sounds of Shark Bait fighting through the undergrowth, there was nothing.

Had the killer sensed their following? Was he waiting to ambush them in the darkness?

An engine started. Not too far away. They were about to lose him, DJ realized. He charged blindly into the trees, then. Limbs slapped at his frozen cheeks. He held one arm up and in front of his face in response, and pressed on towards the sound of the engine now idling in the darkness. He smacked straight into a tree trunk, the cold bark pressing into him, and he almost dropped his gun and went down. He could hear Abbi behind, but could not see her. She had killed the light, and had not turned it back on.

He pushed and fought the forest as it reached and grabbed at him, desperate to reach the running vehicle before it took off. He had to end this. They were all depending on him. *He* was depending on him. The man could not be afforded another opportunity to hunt them down again.

And just like that, he burst into a clearing and skidded to a halt. He could hear the vehicle just ahead of him. But he could see nothing. Where was it? He held a hand up and moved forward cautiously, his sig at his waist but pointing forward into the black.

Abbi body-slammed him from behind, and they both went down in a tangle of bodies. The end of Abbi's rifle caught him in his frozen ear, sending shooting pain. He was thankful she had absorbed his gun safety advice and kept her finger off the trigger. Otherwise she might have accidentally shot him from the collision.

"Light!" He whispered loudly, scrambling to his feet, and pointing his Sig in the direction of the invisible vehicle.

He heard her shuffling around. "Trying," she whispered back.

Then, the light he begged for, suddenly illuminated the world around him in blinding fashion. But it wasn't from Abbi's small flashlight. It was from the headlights of the large SUV as Shark Bait finally prepared to drive off.

It was pointed right at them.

They were standing on a road of some sort. Probably one of the many fire lanes the government created through the National Forest surrounding his cabin.

For a second he was blinded and confused, then the realization of his situation sunk home and he fired. His bullet tore into the headlight on the driver's side and it winked out. In response, Shark Bait planted his foot into the accelerator and the SUV launched at them through the thick snow. Abbi was still on one knee looking for her flashlight in the folds of her coat. DJ could not afford to take another shot into where he imagined the driver would be, past the blinding light of the one headlight. He scooped Abbi into his arms and shoved her hard off the road.

He tried to follow after and jump clear. But, the thick snow bogged him down. The front bumper struck him in his left knee, and the fender connected with his hip. The impact spun him around in the air in a full three-sixty, as the SUV raced by.

He landed on his face, but miraculously managed to still hold on to his gun. He tried to launch himself upwards, but his body was bruised and battered, and he did not move near as fast as he would like.

The SUV was pulling away.

He took careful aim and fired three measured rounds at the back of the vehicle, desperately trying to visualize where the driver would be. The gun bucked in his hand, but the big truck-like vehicle tore through the snow undeterred.

Fourteen rounds left.

He was running then, with everything he was worth. His last shot at ending this whole thing was escaping. This fire trail would intersect with the main road they were just on. Once the man made the turn onto it, he would be gone. There would be nothing they could do but wait for the next attack the assassin would surely, eventually, follow up with. Staying in the tire tracks, he put his head down and strove forward, willing himself to run faster.

Abbi shouted after him. But he ignored her. She pleaded with him to hang on a second, but he couldn't. DJ was a man of single minded purpose. His knee and his hip screamed at him in pain, but he shoved it aside. The SUV would turn onto the road just ahead. When it did, it would travel in a near straight path away from him. If DJ could make the road in time, he would have fourteen rounds to send at his enemy. Fourteen chances at justice.

The SUV reached the main road, and Shark Bait turned the wheel. But he hit the corner too fast. Either the vehicle did not have all-wheel drive, or the assassin had not engaged it. Either way, the thing went sideways and skidded across the slick surface. All the way across the road, the thing slid, until it traveled off the snow-covered blacktop and into the icy drifts on the other side.

DJ silently shouted in triumph as he continued to sprint. He was going to get his chance. His enemy would not escape him.

Again, Abbi shouted from behind him to wait. But he could not afford to pause for her. The SUV had its wheels spinning in the snow. Shark Bait was working the wheel back and forth, trying to free himself.

And, he was having success.

With jerking gradual progression, he was pulling forward and back onto the road.

DJ had a choice. He could skid to a halt, or he could continue to run. He had a profile shot through the passenger side window and door. If he stopped where he was, he could rattle off several rounds and hope a few of them connected. Or, he could continue to push his way to the main road, now only forty or fifty feet ahead of him. He would be much closer then, increasing his chances of success at hitting the man.

He opted for the later.

DJ was closing the gap between them rapidly, making up ground as he continued to pump his legs. His lungs were on fire from the frigid air sucking in with each deep breath. His left hip howled in pain, and the grazing gunshot wound that tore across lower left back only made it worse. His knee may have even suffered permanent damage from the bumper strike, as it felt like someone was repeatedly stabbing him with an icepick. But if he pushed through the pain just a bit more, he would only be ten or fifteen feet behind the SUV. He would be able to place well calculated rounds into the front seat area from behind. There would be no avoiding his precision.

Fourteen opportunities at closure, he told himself. The end was in sight. Press on to the finish line and the goal, he ordered his failing body.

The SUV pulled back onto the road, its rear wheels spinning on the icy surface as it pushed itself forward. DJ was right there as planned when it did. He was maybe only twelve feet behind the back bumper as it pulled away. Inwardly, DJ smiled. Payback was here. Justice was now being served. His enemy had killed hundreds of people over the course of his life. But no more. His reign of ruthless terror was over.

DJ aimed carefully at the tinted back glass of the SUV, softly illuminated by the glowing red tail light in the upper-middle of the frame. He did not try to make a calculated shot at where the man's head should be. He just visualized the killer's body behind the wheel, and squeezed.

Once. Twice.

And then he stopped.

The back glass shattered and fell away from the impacts of the bullets. He could see clearly into the rear of the vehicle now. What the crimson radiance of the tail light revealed, caused his heart to sink. There were large storage boxes stacked up in the rear compartment behind the back seat. They were not wimpy plastic storage containers. They were the hard kind soldiers would use to transport gear.

Storage containers for Geek's flying robots, he thought to himself.

He wasn't sure how many there were between him and Shark Bait, or what items were maybe still in them, but it would make it harder for his slow moving 9mm rounds to penetrate and make their way to the assassin.

In anger, DJ refocused and began to hammer away with his Sig. *One round*, he prayed. *I just need one round to make it through.*

Over and over again, he fired at the imaginary body of Shark Bait, silently urging his rounds to punch their way through and find the killer on the other side. To no avail, the slide locked back and he was empty. The infamous assassin shot away from him down the road, pulling away ever faster as he went.

He failed.

Abbi shouted at him again from his right. She was closer now, having caught up to him finally.

Again, he ignored her. Before, he was consumed by his need to catch the illusive Shark Bait. But now? Now he ignored her because he was consumed by his own remorse and guilt. Try as he might, the man was going to get away. He would return, of course. But the man would be fully recovered from his wounds, and strike at all of them when they would least expect it.

DJ had left his wounded friends behind. He had forsaken the desire to keep rendering first-aid to Brett Foster. The man was likely going to die now, if he wasn't dead already. Had DJ known he would fail in trying to kill Shark Bait, he would have stayed behind and tried to keep his friend alive long enough to make it to the hospital.

And where were the others, anyway? They should have caught up and passed them by now. Why had they not come barreling down the long drive and started their journey in to town?

"DJ!" Abbi was screaming at him now, furious at his ignoring her. "Look at me, you stubborn man!"

He did then. And what was a moment of self-pity and dejection, turned into one of hopeful promise.

Standing in the glow of her tactical light, was the love of his life, cradling a Russian made RPG. "Will this help?" she asked.

"Where in the world…" he began.

Cutting him off with exasperation, she answered his question. "If you wouldn't have run off like a crazy person, you would have seen the second truck parked behind the first. I opened the front door to look for the keys, but found this instead. I would have handed it to you a long time ago if you would have stopped."

DJ ignored the reproof and tucked his Sig into his belt behind him. He then snatched the big thing from her. "Stay to my side," he instructed. "Hold the light so I can see."

Anyone who served with a front-line combat group in a mid-east conflict or war, no matter the branch of service, was shown how to use and fire the Soviet era anti-tank weapon. Along with the AK-47, of course. They were common in that part of the world, littering the countryside almost as frequently as rocks. Since they were used by both friendly and enemy troops alike, it just made practical sense to teach everyone how to employ them if encountered on the battlefield. Even though DJ had been a corpsman, he was no exception to this policy. And, while he never actually fired an RPG, he knew precisely the process for making it happen. The Russians made it so a child could shoot the thing.

And they often did…

The first thing he did was check the end of the rocket already mounted into the launching tube. Screwed into the nose of the round, was a safety cap. Without the cap on, should you drop it while running around, it might blow up at your feet.

DJ unscrewed the cap under the flickering light of Abbi's flashlight and tossed it aside.

Next, he flipped on the power switch located on the side of the reticle and looked through the eye piece. Sure enough, the sites were illuminated and glowing.

Finally, he balanced the thing on his shoulder and aimed at his fleeing enemy. With his forefinger alongside the trigger, he used the thumb of the same hand to lock the hammer down into position behind the pistol-grip. Like a revolver from the Wild West, the weapon was fired using an old-fashioned hammer and firing pin method. And, it was now ready to be launched.

"Put your fingers in your ears," he barked. "This is going to be loud."

The SUV carrying the assassin away from him was now almost a hundred meters away, DJ figured. That was right in the sweet-spot of an RPG's accuracy. Shoot at a target beyond this range, and it rapidly increased the chances of the round flying off course. They didn't exactly have the greatest reputation of hitting their target because of this.

Secondly, they also failed to go off a lot of times. Soldiers in combat could share many stories of how many times the rockets refused to explode on contact. This was less true of newer versions. But how new was the rocket he was aiming?

It didn't matter, DJ knew. This was the only chance they had.

He pressed the trigger, and the rocket exploded forward with a simultaneous *pop* and *woosh*. DJ watched it streak forward like a gigantic bottle rocket. And with great satisfaction and relief, a fraction of a second after launch, the shaped-charge in the cone of the rocket exploded on impact. The SUV twisted and slid across the road, coming to rest against a snow bank created by the plow a few minutes before. The once expensive full-sized SUV meant for carrying people in style and prestige was now a burning pile of mangled metal on the side of the frozen road.

He tossed the launch tube away from him and started forward at a trot. "We need to make sure," he called to Abbi.

Together, they jogged forward, slowing as they approached the rear of the burning wreckage. DJ's faithful Sig Sauer now tucked into his belt behind him was empty. Any spare magazine he possessed prior to the attack was somewhere back at his cabin. And the rifle Abbi had once carried was missing. She had likely tossed it aside in favor of the RPG. If the man magically popped out of the driver's seat right now, they were in trouble.

But, DJ needed proof there was a dead guy behind the wheel. They had to advance anyway.

The former SUV was on fire, but it was not a raging inferno, and DJ moved up alongside the driver's side cautiously. His heart pounded in his chest from adrenaline, as he expected the door to swing open any minute.

But it didn't.

Slowly advancing to get a peek through the shattered driver side window, he could see the man slumped over the wheel. But, he was moving. He lifted a bloody hand into view, slowly. It wobbled around from muscles that had lost their ability to function properly. But, clutched in the still living hand of the assassin, was the man's Glock. DJ darted forward and snatched it from him with ease. He then yanked the door open and stepped back, aiming the killer's own gun at his face.

It was the face of defeat and blood. The look in the man's eye was one mixed with ragged submission, and vague consciousness. He was teetering on the verge of blacking out. The man's bloody head rolled around and pointed in his direction. "Slaughter," the man slurred, spraying blood out of his mouth. "You win. You're a worthy adversary. It was a good fight."

DJ could see the light fading from the man's eyes and knew he wouldn't live much longer. Abbi slid up behind him, looking on. "Is it over?" She asked.

"I think so," he answered. He lowered his weapon, and then tucked it behind his belt buckle. The dying man was no longer a threat. He probably should have just put the assassin out of his misery, but he didn't. Part of him said a quick end to the man would be merciful. The other part told him to let the man bleed out and die. Let it take as long as it would take.

He turned around to look Abbi in the eyes. There was relief there. There was closure there. She finally had the end she was looking for. He stepped close and put his arm around her, kissing her forehead. "He won't make it much more than a couple of minutes," DJ acknowledged. "Let's just let him die. We need to find out what happened to our friends."

As if on cue, DJ saw the fancy foreign-made SUV finally pull onto the road back behind them. It turned and headed their direction. At first it began to accelerate hard in their direction, obviously spurred on by the sight of a burning vehicle on the side of the road. But then, as the driver could see both of them standing near the shattered remains, whoever was driving backed off the gas. It coasted up next to them and stopped. The automatic window dropped, and they were looking at Cash behind the wheel, with Mighty Pebble in the passenger seat.

"Is it over?" Cash asked leaning their direction.

DJ nodded. "He's still breathing but he'll be dead in a second. What took you so long?"

"Got stuck trying to get out. Had to find a shovel and dig ourselves free. But Brett is bad. Find someplace to fit in here. We need to go now."

DJ nodded and made to do so.

Suddenly, he was being pushed aside by Abbi. She shoved him with all her strength, and he slipped on the slick surface, going down face first. Before he could roll over, he heard rapid gunfire and realized she had pulled the Glock free from his belt.

His heart skipped a beat before he could finally fix his eyes on her, desperately concerned for her safety. Shark Bait must have only been feigning death. She must have spotted him about to strike at them one last time.

And then his eyes finally found her above him. Standing upright in the snowy roadway, lit by the dancing reflection of flames from the burning SUV, was Abbi. She stood with both hands wrapped around the assassin's pistol just like he had shown her to do. And, she was firing a steady barrage of bullets into Shark Bait still behind the wheel.

Then she was empty and the sounds of gunfire subsided. The more than dead killer in the front seat relaxed in death, and his hand dropped into view from the open door. In it was held a smaller version of the Glock Abbi had just used. As he watched, the fingers loosened their grip and the gun fell into the road.

He had a backup gun, DJ realized. And he mentally slapped himself for not assuming the assassin would. This could only mean the whole time the man was on his knees sobbing back at the cabin, he was actually preparing to strike with deadly surprise.

Just like DJ had been.

Abbi looked down at DJ then, the reflection of the fire mirrored in her eyes. "Now," she said calmly. "Now it's over."

Chapter 25: Three Little Words

Tim Neville Checked his watch. 11:32 p.m. Nearly forty-eight hours had passed since being notified Brett Foster, his wife, and one of the missing guards from Denver, had all been checked into a hospital in Vermont. His own son had been the one to check them in and notify the proper chain of command of where they were.

And then, Agent Bradford Cashin vanished into thin air.

Tim had been a bundle of emotions and worry ever since. Part of him had been elated the assassin El Gran Blanco was confirmed killed. At least a life of the killer's extortion over him was finally over. The assassin, along with a hit-team associated with the Boston network of mercenaries, were all lying in a morgue. Not only that, but the Russian mobster Sergei Romanoff was also confirmed dead at the scene. That, in itself, mired Tim knee-deep in a giant bucket of crap. Romanoff was deeply involved with the Russian Government. The CIA informed him they long suspected the criminal kingpin was a pseudo-agent for Mother Russia. The communist country, having learned of the man's death, was demanding to allow members of its own FSB in to the country to participate in the investigation.

Tim sat in his plush office located in the J. Edgar Hoover Building, and reached a trembling hand for a glass of water on his desk. He considered for the millionth time all he was responsible for. For hours, he had flirted with grief and horror at not only getting his close friend almost killed, but unintentionally placing his own son into harm's way. His only solace was being informed they were both alive.

There was no word on any injuries for Bradford, as the agent turned into a ghost before the authorities showed up at the hospital. But the ER reported they had done no work on the man. Nor had he complained of injuries.

Brett, on the other hand, would have to grow comfortable with using a wheel-chair. The bullet he took on the account of Tim's treachery tore a pathway completely through the agent's spinal cord. He would be lucky if he didn't have to poop and pee into a bag for the rest of his life. Tim would know whether or not the surgeons could restore enough function to allow him to retain at least that much dignity within the next seventy-two hours. Right now, Brett was in an induced coma in order to try and minimize any additional trauma.

Tim was not sure whether his involvement in all of this was going to come to light, but the fact his own son had vanished did not point to a good conclusion for him. The only logical reason he could see for Bradford choosing to go off the grid was because he thought his own father might send someone to kill him.

If Tim went to jail over all of this, so be it. But to think he had lost the trust and love of his son? Well, that was almost unbearable.

And what of Slaughter and the girl? Where were they? Had they gone into hiding with Bradford? Had they split and traveled their separate ways? Tim was aware Slaughter had access to money and resources to live a life under another identity. But, had he offered to do the same for Bradford?

Tim shook his head. There were just too many unanswered questions. And the only choice afforded to him for now, was to sit back and wait for the dominos to fall. He couldn't help but wonder if the Department of Justice, located just across the street, would soon be launching an investigation focused on him.

His office door opened, and two men stepped into the room. The pit in the middle of his stomach which had been growing since the beginning of this ordeal suddenly opened and threatened to swallow him whole. The first man was his son, Agent Bradford Cashin. The other was the infamous David John Slaughter.

Slaughter was holding a silenced pistol in one hand. His son held nothing but contempt in his eyes.

The one holding the gun was the last to cross the threshold, and he closed the door quietly behind him. The man moved without the catlike grace of a predator Tim envisioned. Instead, he had the look of a nameless stranger one might pass on the street. There was no hint of uniqueness to him. He portrayed no indication he was anything other than the regular guy he appeared to be.

Other than the fact he was holding a silenced handgun, of course.

He was dressed the part of a nobody as well. He wore jeans, hiking boots, and a light jacket. And, draped across the man's shoulder was a well-used daypack. He stepped to one side of the room and slipped it off, dropping it into a nearby chair.

And then he aimed.

Tim's secretary and office staff had long since left for the day. He was the only one here. There were plenty of other people in the building, of course, but he was the only one in the director's offices. How they got past security and managed to walk right in here like they owned the place, Tim was certain he may never know. What he *was* certain of, were these men were here to exact justice from him in the most brutal way possible.

His son was here to kill him.

The gun held in Slaughter's grip jumped, and the muted clap of silenced gunfire bounced off the walls. The bullet he was sure had been intended to take his life, tore through the plush padding of his high-backed desk chair next to his right ear instead.

"Hi Dad." Bradford spoke with a flat and even voice. "You want to do me a favor and keep your hands on the top of the desk? My new friend here has a nasty reputation for shooting people in the head."

Bradford walked around to the side of his desk, and lifted the screen to his laptop computer.

"Bradford," Tim began.

"Shut up," his son cut him off. "I'm going to be the one doing all of talking here. When I am done, I'll ask you a question. I'll be looking for a three-word response. If I hear anything else, I will walk out of here and leave you alone with my friend. I honestly am not sure if I could watch him shoot you through the face. You are still my father, after all."

Tim said nothing. While he sat there in silence, he was sure his heart could be heard thundering in his chest. He was scared. Petrified.

Of his son…

The laptop screen lit up in response to Bradford pulling the lid open. Next, he turned and nodded to Slaughter.

Slaughter spoke into the room, then, to a person who could not be seen. Tim reasoned he must be wearing some sort of communication equipment he couldn't see. "Alright, Abbi. You're up."

The laptop screen changed a split second later. One moment it displayed the standard FBI screensaver of the organization's logo on a field of blue. The next, a multimedia player opened and began to play an audio file. Hearing it, made Tim sick to his stomach.

The file was a conversation between himself and El Gran Blanco. The assassin was giving him orders to betray his friend, his country, and the oath of his office. He was told to give up Slaughter's location so he could kill the man. He could hear himself plead with the assassin to spare Brett. The assassin said he could not make promises. Then he heard himself provide the information required for El Gran Blanco to attack them in Boston.

315

A new file began to play shortly after the conclusion of the first. In it, he provided intel for making the attack on the Denver Field Office.

To his horror, a third began to play immediately afterwards. In this one, he specifically told the assassin to make sure Brett Foster died. Because if he didn't, Brett would figure out Tim had given him up.

Hearing himself say the words was simply too much. Bile erupted from his mouth as he vomited right into his own lap.

He was humiliated. He was horrified at himself. He looked Slaughter in the eyes then, and begged him. "Kill me. Just do it now. Please."

His son spoke up then. "There's more where that came from. Turns out, every conversation you ever had with El Gran Blanco was recorded. Once we pulled his phone from his dead body, Abbi was able to hack the man's life. We have it all. The recordings, all of his bank accounts, his complete list of contacts. All of it.

"I'll never forgive you for what you've done. I can't say the same for Brett. He'll make his own decision. But he knows you betrayed him. He knew the moment that monster attacked us at the cabin. But, true to the way Brett likes to do things, he saw a way to spin it to his advantage. While he was lying in a pool of his own blood on the way to the hospital, not sure if he was even going to make it, he gave me an order. It's an order I intend to follow."

Bradford motioned to Slaughter, and the man responded. Reaching into his bag, he produced a thick folder of information and handed it over. Bradford, in turn, dropped it down onto a part of the desk without vomit on it.

"This," his son said pointing at the folder, "Is a chance for you to not spend the rest of your miserable life in prison. In all fairness, he came up with it before the attack on Denver. He was going to beg you to do it. He was going to call in every last chip he had with you for saving your life way back when you were still friends. He was pretty sure you would turn him down then. But now? Now we're not going to beg. I am here instead to deliver an ultimatum.

"It details an elaborate plan by you to set up an elite group within the FBI. One almost completely off the books, and completely self-contained. This group goes after criminal organizations, and does it outside the normal scope and procedure of the FBI. It was your brain child. Because of it, Big Chuck's organization was taken down.

"There is a complete paper-trail here showing how you recruited DJ and Abbi years ago, while they were still in training at Quantico. It reveals how you had their names removed from the rolls in order for them to be able to operate with complete anonymity. It explains how they have been undercover this entire time.

"According to everything here, you're a genius. And if you follow through with playing your part in this little ruse, no one will ever know what a complete traitor to your country you were.

"Now, if Brett does not manage to recover, I become the new leader of this group. We are going to continue to take down bad guys and criminal enterprises all over the world. You are going to find us some legitimate funding to make it all happen. And it better be a lot. As I understand it, Brett has become quite fond of flying around in his own jet. Abbi can help with that. She has some interesting ideas for creating as big a pile of cash as we need. But I'll let her get with you later on all of that.

"In addition, you are going to make sure we get first selection at any recruits coming out of training. Or, you will also allow us to take the unprecedented choice of recruiting outside the normal channels. For instance, I know a certain burly guard who worked at Denver. He watched all of his co-workers die, and he wants to get something out of all of this. He's already expressed an interest in the opportunity. If we add him to our group, you're going to need to give him an artificial bump in rank and pay to keep him from spilling the beans on all of this. But, I'm sure you can find a way to get it done.

"And now we have come to the conclusion of this little presentation. Here is the point where I ask my question, and wait for those three little words to come spilling from your lips. Or, like I promised at the beginning of all of this, not only will Abbi make sure every media outlet in the country gets a copy of those files, destroying your legacy forever, but I'll just step out of the room and let DJ do what DJ does best.

"Ready? Here it comes. Can I count on you to help us?"

Tim's head was spinning in circles almost as fast as his stomach was rolling over. He couldn't believe what he was hearing. He couldn't believe what Brett had dreamed up to make all of this go away. God bless Brett Foster, but he had not only invented an ingenious plan for exonerating Slaughter and his girlfriend, but he even provided a pathway for Tim to get away with everything he had done.

He should tell his son he couldn't do it. He should allow Bradford to step out of the room as promised and take the bullet in the face like he deserved. People died because of his choices. He should pay the ultimate price for his sins.

But if this is what Brett and Bradford wanted to happen, then he was sure participating in this charade would go a long way to somehow make up for all he had done. If it served to put people behind bars who deserved it as equally as he, then it also meant it would save countless lives in the long run.

Maybe, just maybe, by playing along, he could somehow redeem himself.

He met his son's penetrating, scorn-filled eyes, and gave him the three words he was looking for. "Yes, you can."

Chapter 26: New Beginnings

DJ stepped into the bright sunlight and came to an instant conclusion. Summers in East Texas could be brutal.

First of all, the humidity combined with high temperatures could take your breath away. One could step from freezing cold air conditioning, and be sweating buckets before you made it to your car. After a thunderstorm, it was even worse. You could see the humidity hanging in the air like smog. It would turn asphalt and pavement into sizzling sauna rocks.

Secondly, there was an insect the locals called "love-bugs." The tiny, black flying creatures were named this because they joined together with one another at their butts for mating purposes. Butt to butt, they would fly around in clouds. They were harmless in that they did not bite or sting. But, they would land in your food when grilling, and plaster the front of your car relentlessly while driving down the road. In Abbi lingo, they were just plain gross.

Thirdly, because of the moisture and heat, there would always be mosquitos. And the ones in this part of the country seemed to have a personal vendetta against DJ.

As he stepped off the private jet just outside of Jasper, Texas, those three things drove their way to the forefront of his thinking. Why? Because the heat sucker-punched him, a love-bug landed on his nose, and a mosquito flew past his face in a very threatening manner. It was only a matter of time before the little menace called in his swarming family for a sneak attack.

He brushed the love-bug off the end of his nose and looked around.

He was here in the middle of nowhere because it would be their new base of operations. This remote location in the Piney Woods section of Texas ticked all the necessary boxes for their secret hide-out.

First of all, they needed to find someplace far away from any other FBI facility, or other government influence. This aging airbase in East Texas not only answered that need, but placed them strategically in the middle of the country.

Abbi was the one to locate the old Air National Guard Facility. It had been closed a few years now, but was still in good enough shape to renovate and call home. Along with the runway and facilities for the plane, there were barracks for housing recruits, buildings for training and staging, and a major fiber optic hub for global communication ran right under the place on its way to Dallas. Abbi could tap in with all of her computers and do whatever Abbi did with stuff like that.

Even though Abbi and Cash had been practically living here for the last few months, it was the first time DJ set foot on the property. He had been spending all his time in Virginia.

Cash insisted he go through FBI training at Quantico. If he was going to be working in the FBI, and alongside agents who graduated the program, he needed to have the same basic knowledge and training they had. Otherwise he would be looked at as an outsider. Cash reasoned with DJ that he would have to occasionally interact with other FBI personnel outside of this facility. He would need to be able to engage with their procedures and protocols. Even though they would largely function outside the body of the organization.

Training was now over. Finally. While there was quite a lot to learn he found beneficial to his new job, he also felt the FBI was overburdened with unnecessary rules and regulations. The bureaucracy permeating the agency was mind blowing. Part of the reason they needed to function far away from any other departmental agency was for secrecy. But the other was to skip past all of the ridiculous red tape that could only serve to bog them down.

DJ had finally arrived here at his new home. But as he looked around, he was not exactly overwhelmed with awe. The entire time he was learning why he hated government procedure, also known as Quantico Training, Cash and Abbi had been setting up this new facility for taking down the bad guys. Over the many phone calls and video chats while he was in Virginia, Abbi had been referring to this place as their Bat Cave. She insisted he was going to love it. But other than the fact it had its own runway for the private jet sitting behind him, everything he saw said the word *love* was a bit overstated.

Instead of Bat Cave appearance, it looked exactly like what it was. An aging, small Texas Air National Guard Facility. The buildings he could see around the runway looked in desperate need of paint. He could only assume many of them were leaking. One unknown structure was actually in the process of falling down. His immediate reaction to all of this was Tim Neville had not lived up to their request of finding adequate funding.

The gruff voice of Mighty Pebble spoke up behind him as he stepped off the plane next. "Is it just me, or do I have a different memory of what the Bat Cave is? This looks like the very definition of *suck*. And dude, that building is falling down! You have *got* to be kidding me..."

Both men entered Quantico training together, and since then, he learned the ex-guard's name was Marion Peters. DJ remembered laughing out loud when the man told him. The guard actually took a swing at him, thinking DJ was laughing at what some considered to be a feminine name. DJ had to explain his whole process for nicknaming everyone he met until getting to know them.

Marion was actually quite pleased with the whole Mighty Pebble reference afterwards. So, DJ stuck to calling him MP throughout their training. After all, the initials matched up.

Even though they were completely different individuals, DJ developed a fast liking for the stocky ex-guard. He was brash and rough around the edges. And, he hated all the protocol probably more than DJ. If it were not for the fact his instructors were secretly ordered to pass him, he was sure MP would not have made it past week two. He had a tendency to let people know when he thought something was stupid.

He was also fearless and determined. Point the man in a direction, and he would knock down anything in his path in order to get to where he was going. What he lacked in social grace, he made up for in commitment to completing the mission. It was a trait DJ could appreciate. Just don't let him be the one to do all of the talking, and he would make a great addition to the team.

DJ replied to the burly new agent over his shoulder. "I'm sure they just aren't done with renovations yet. But where is our welcome party?"

DJ had not seen Abbi for more than twenty weeks, other than over video conference, and he was dying to see her. He wanted to wrap her up in his arms and kiss her until her face was numb. He was certain both she and Cash would be sitting on the runway waiting for them. But there was no one as far as the eye could see.

DJ would have run out and bought another ring, and proposed to her as soon as they left Director Neville's office that night. But, this new crazy plan of Brett's began to proceed at a rapid pace, pushed into high gear by a relentless Agent Cash hell-bent on making sure his father lived up to his end of the agreement. DJ never found the time to really do a proper job of asking her.

But he would get it done now.

As soon as he stepped away from graduation at the FBI training center first thing this morning, he and MP caught a ride straight to a jewelry store. He picked out a ring, and then he and his burly companion drove straight to a private airport for their trip west. As he stood on the tarmac wondering where the welcome committee was, the new ring seemed to burn a hole in his pocket. They were supposed to be looking forward to checking out their new facilities, and starting the process of taking down bad guys. But the only thing going through DJ's mind was slipping that small rock on Abbi's finger at the first available opportunity. Maybe tonight, even.

Where were they at?

He expressed his confusion to MP, and in turn, the new agent hollered back through the open door of the plane. "Hey! Didn't you radio ahead and tell them we were landing?"

A voice from beyond answered. "I was told to tell you they'll be here in a second."

As if on cue, DJ heard tires squeal against asphalt. He turned his head and found the source. A crew cab pickup was rounding their direction from between a couple of hangers. As DJ watched, the familiar head of Abbi poked out of the driver's side window. Her raven hair was whipping in the wind and she was waving her hand in joy.

DJ's heart was melting.

The truck raced up, braked hard, and Abbi came pouring out. She was smiling, and crying, and then pushing him backwards against Mighty Pebble and kissing DJ hard. He felt himself sag against MP with suddenly weak knees as blood flowed rapidly to other parts of his body.

He was embarrassed. He was thrilled. And he didn't want this moment to end.

"Really?" MP spoke behind him, trying to push them both away. "You're going to do it right here on this hell-hot runway?"

At that, Abbi pulled herself away. She stood there blushing and straightening her clothes and hair. She sported a white polo top that seemed to accent her body as her chest heaved with excitement over seeing him. And, she was wearing jeans that curved around her runner's legs and firm… DJ forced himself to avert his eyes. If it were even possible, it suddenly felt warmer standing out here on the tarmac under the Texas sun than it did just a minute before.

"Come on," Abbi instructed with a cheery lilt to her voice. "We have so much to show you."

DJ had been so consumed with seeing Abbi, he failed to notice Agent Cash. The man was standing there next to the truck, the passenger door still open, as stone-faced as always. He was wearing jeans and a short sleeved white polo matching Abbi's, and DJ finally noticed the blue embroidered logo in the upper righthand corner. Something with a plane on it.

As DJ finally acknowledged him with his eyes, Cash shoved a pair of dark sunglasses up on his head. "DJ," the man said simply.

"Cash," DJ smiled back.

From behind him, MP spoke up again. "Please tell me this Bat Cave is somewhere else. All I'm seeing right now is Bat Crap."

Abbi positively beamed at the both of them. "Nope. You're standing right in the middle of it. And that's what makes it so awesome. Now get your bags and come on!"

They didn't have much in the way of bags, as they weren't allowed to have much during their time at Quantico. DJ had the trusty daypack he appropriated during his assault on Big Chuck's riverside complex. But that was it. He figured on buying whatever he needed as soon as he got here. Yet, he was suddenly unsure if Jasper even had a department store. He wasn't sure how big the town really was. In fact, he realized, he didn't know much about Jasper at all. Maybe that was something he should look into. He would research the place tonight online. Maybe he and Abbi could go to dinner at a nice restaurant.

He and MP tossed their bags into the back and loaded up. Abbi was driving, so Cash climbed into the back seat. As DJ began to focus on other things beside the woman behind the wheel, he noticed the funny blue plane logo on magnetic sticker on the door as he got in. Curious now, he asked about it climbing into the front seat.

"It's our cover," Cash spoke from the back. "Our company is called PlaneTech, Inc. We focus on specialty mission software for aviation electronics. We have a government contract and everything. It explains why we need this facility, and why there is security at the gate. It will also be a plausible explanation for why military personnel will fly in and out of here from time to time."

"Military?" DJ asked.

"The scope of our job has grown a bit over the past few weeks," Cash answered. "When it comes to terrorists, the FBI sometimes works hand-in-hand with the CIA and special operations groups throughout the branches of the military. We pool our intelligence.

"Plus, the US has agreements with allied countries to allow the FBI to conduct investigations on foreign soil. We have offices all over the world. It's always been a way for the CIA and the joint special operations groups to gain a footprint in another country without arousing suspicion. Given the secret nature and purpose of this new program, it just made sense to lend a hand and provide special operators an alternate place to train and plan. Abbi, pull over here for a sec."

Abbi complied and pulled off under the shade of a pine tree next to a large hanger. "This," Cash continued, "used to be a hangar big enough to shelter a C5 Galaxy. But next week we have a group of Navy Seabees coming in to start construction on an elaborate kill-house. It'll be perfect for live-fire training for ourselves, plus a SEAL team can come in and plan out assaults for some overseas missions. Those Seabees will be stationed here permanently. They'll be able to construct a kill-house based on any blueprints we hand them in just a couple of days. Then, tear it down and build us something else a week later."

DJ nodded his approval of the construction of a kill-house. It was essential in armed combat training. Essentially, it was a building inside a building. The inside building consisted of walls only, designed to simulate a house or other structure. Instructors could look down into the room from above, evaluating how a team assaulted the structure and moved from room to room. Or, they could assess how an individual responded to various threats they could encounter. It was called a kill-house because it was built for live-fire training. Mess up your assault or not follow proper safety procedures, and you could accidentally get shot in the process.

DJ and MP spent time in one during training at Quantico. It was an area of training he naturally excelled at. In fact, DJ now had the unofficial record for every single one of their timed events. It was something he was proud of. Of course, he did have some prior experience.

"You see that hangar back there?" Cash was leaning forward now and pointing to another large metal building through the windshield. "That one will just store lumber, sheetrock, nails, and all the other supplies they need to whip up a copy of a building."

DJ was starting to see the size and scale this little clandestine group was fast growing into something much larger. And, he wasn't exactly excited about what he was hearing. Initially, this was supposed to be a small group designed to go after global organized crime. Now they were going to be working with Navy SEALs?

He expressed his agitation. "What happened to a small undercover group going against mobsters?"

"Well, our new FBI director needed to secure some funding. Enough funding to get us our own jet. The group with the biggest budget was the US Military. So, the director pitched his idea to some brass he knew at the Pentagon, they had been searching for options for training some of their elite teams off the radar from standard facilities, and the next thing you know, here we are."

"And we're supposed to be telling these SEAL guys what to do? I'm a former Corpsman that just happens to be able to shoot. These guys are going to eat me for lunch. Besides, I have no desire to go to war with the entire Mid-East. That part of my life is over."

Abbi jumped in then. "DJ, it won't be like that. Think of it more as sharing facilities and resources. Sometimes they will help us out, sometimes we help them, and sometimes we won't interact at all. I know you were thinking this would be a smaller operation. But the upside is, we now have the resources and funding to do whatever we need to do."

"But what about security and secrecy?" DJ asked. "As soon as a SEAL team leaves those front gates and heads in to town for a beer, civilians are going to start asking questions."

"First of all," Cash replied, "It will be other elite groups as well. Not just Navy SEALS. But the only way they will come into or out of this facility is in the back of a plane. The only ones allowed through the gates are us, and we'll be posing as workers for PlaneTech. This place will be like a smaller Area 51."

"What about the live-fire training you were talking about? Civilians are bound to hear that and want to know what's going on."

Abbi jumped in again. "That's the beauty of all of these hangars. Most of them are going to be converted to airconditioned, soundproof, and bulletproof facilities. No one outside the gates is going to hear a single thing. All live-fire walk-throughs for an upcoming mission will be done inside one of these buildings. It also means that you'll get access to practically any weapon you want, all the ammunition you can use, and as much of the kill-house time you desire. Guns, DJ. All the guns a guy could want, right here at your fingertips." Abbi was beaming with joy.

Cash and Abbi seemed to have thought everything through, and DJ certainly liked the idea of nearly unlimited resources. But it was all just a bit overwhelming. Again, he was a former Navy Corpsman that just happened to be able to shoot. He was feeling a little outside his comfort zone.

"You know," DJ said, "I would feel a bit better about all of this if Brett were here." Abbi turned her head to look over her shoulder, and pulled back out onto the maze of roads weaving through empty buildings. "He still won't change his mind?" DJ asked.

Cash shook his head. "He says agents aren't useful without legs. He says he's retiring to Florida."

DJ was instantly angry over those remarks. It was a direct slap in the face to every wounded veteran coming back from overseas. Your worth was not defined by your ability to walk. "Well, I don't accept that answer," DJ lashed out. "And I tell you what I'm going to do about it. I am going to spend a few days learning our new facilities here, and spending time getting to know a certain olive-skinned someone all over again. Then I'm going to take that new fancy jet we have, and I'm going to drag him back here. At gun point, if necessary."

Abbi patted his hand while still focused on driving. "I don't think that'll work, sweetheart."

"We'll see about that," he answered without masking the edge to his voice.

They pulled up in front of a rather nondescript two-story office building of sorts. It was surrounded by the tall pine trees indicative of this part of the country, and very little landscaping. From the architecture, it looked like vintage seventies. There was no signage, and it was about as spartan as one could imagine. It was the complete opposite to the shiny building back in Denver. DJ half expected to see plastic furniture and a receptionist with her hair in a bun when they walked through the door.

But, crossing the threshold was a shock. Everything was modern and current. The walls were some sort of warm textured material, the lighting all LED, and the furniture looked brand new. There was a receptionist, but she didn't have her hair in a bun. Instead, she wore Marine Corps camouflaged with a sidearm strapped low to her leg. "Agent Cashin. Abbi," she spoke crisply with a slight nod of her head.

DJ looked at Cash for more information, and the man smiled and gave it. "We have a number of security personnel on site. All Marines. They guard key facilities and watch the gate. They're on loan from the Pentagon. They all have security clearances and know why they're here, but they don't know where here actually is. They come in on a two-week rotation, and aren't permitted electronic devices. In fact, no one is. No one here has any outside contact with the rest of the world. There isn't even a television on the entire facility. So, don't mention what state we're in. It's part of what maintains our cover."

If DJ had not fully realized the size and scope of what he had agreed to, this one small thing made it stand out to him. They really were in a smaller Area 51. This facility was supposed to stay off the radar from not only other US based groups and entities, but all of the world's potential bad guys. From terrorists and foreign militaries, to criminal entities, everything had been done to try and keep this place secret. When even security for the base were flown in and not told what state they were working in, this was about as off the radar as they could get.

The young marine gave him and MP a slight smile, and handed them both a small envelope. "You must be Agents Slaughter and Peters. These are your key cards. Entrance to any vital area requires retinal scan, but these are for your private quarters. You're both located on basement sub-level three. Room numbers are on the front. Mess Hall is located across the street. The welcome packet in your rooms will detail hours for main meals, but the facility is open 24 hours. There is always someone on duty that can whip you up something if you come in late from an op."

DJ glanced at her rank. From the two chevrons with the crossed rifles underneath, he knew her to be a Corporal. He was curious about the Mess Hall, so he asked her. "Who maintains the Mess Hall, Corporal?"

"Sir?" She seemed confused by the question.

"Is it civilian run, or military operated?"

She smiled, now understanding. "Navy Culinary Specialist, sir. Straight from the Pentagon. You'll eat like an Admiral."

DJ smiled at Agent Cash. "Well, at least you got that part right."

Cash led them to a double door with a retinal scanner mounted next to it. He explained everyone entering must scan in. DJ was surprised to find it already loaded with his. Acquiring it must have been part of the initial physical he underwent at Quantico.

According to Abbi, there were sensors monitoring every sensitive area. If an extra person tried to cross the threshold without scanning, the artificial intelligence of the security system would sound an alarm. For example, if one person scanned, two people would not be allowed to enter without it going off.

While walking down the next hallway, she also explained how the building had its own source of electricity completely off the base's power grid, and how it had been isolated from electronic eavesdropping. Though he admittedly only understood about half of what she said.

She babbled on about things that fascinated her from a technological standpoint, with DJ only retaining bits and pieces. Everything was just far outside the size and scope of what he had been expecting. And, with Brett finally coming to the conclusion that retirement was a better choice than riding a desk seated in a wheelchair, he was starting feel like he didn't want to do this anymore.

It was then the statement from the ghost of his wife came creeping back to his memory. You can either embrace the change or watch as it rolls right over you, she had told him.

The truth was, as long as he was with Abbi, then it really didn't matter. Besides, not having to hide from both the law and potential bad guys was a bit relieving. This was a fresh chance at a new life with a real sense of purpose.

After snaking their way through the building, they finally arrived at another set of double doors and a new Marine manning a post at a desk next to it. There was a simple sign above the retinal scanner that read "TOC".

Speaking up for the first time since entering the building, Mighty Pebble pointed at the sign. "What does TOC stand for?"

"Tactical Operations Center," Abbi said. "Or, as I like to call it, our new Bat Cave."

Scanning through the doors found them in a large two- story room. It was constructed of steel, concrete, and glass. The lighting was dim, each area of importance illuminated by some sort of track-lighting or lamps. DJ could only describe it as mood lighting. There was a large open space in the middle occupied with several empty work stations and computers. He assumed the people intended to occupy them would be brought in at a later date.

Wrapping around the large square room were glass walled offices and conference spaces. Some of them he could see in, others had blinds drawn. It was two levels high with a balcony walkway making its way around the top. A stairway wrapping around a steel-caged elevator sat in one corner, providing access to the top floor.

Abbi pointed to the upper level. "Our offices are up there. But let me show you the director's office. It's pretty cool."

Cash cleared his throat and corrected her. "The FBI has only one director, Abbi. The agent who runs a facility is called The Special Agent in Charge, or SAC."

"Well the FBI is stupid, then," she told the man. "That title is simply too long, and I refuse to call someone a sack. It just sounds crass and rude."

Cash sighed and motioned them to the stairs.

DJ looked at the agent. "So, I guess we get to see your office first? And why is your office so cool? Wait, let me guess. You're the only one who gets a TV?" Cash laughed but didn't really answer, leading the way up.

As they made the landing, they passed by an open office that had an Air Force Colonel sitting behind a desk. He was the only other person DJ saw since entering the TOC, and he paused on seeing the man. The man had kind eyes and thinning white hair ringing the edges of an otherwise bald head. True to DJ's habits when meeting someone, he instantly assigned the man a nickname

Colonel Chrome Dome.

The officer stood and walked around to greet them. "Colonel Jack O'Kieffe. Welcome to your new offices. I've heard a lot about you two."

DJ shook the man's hand and wondered how much of it was true, and how much of it was the fabricated background Abbi had cooked up. "Call me DJ," he said. "The guy in back looking like a globe with feet, is Agent Marion. What do you do here? You're the only other person here, so you must do everything, right?"

Colonel Chrome Dome smiled. "Oh, those desks will all fill up soon enough. As I understand it, hiring of actual positions was on hold until you two guys got here."

DJ turned to look at Cash with surprise. The man shrugged and replied. "You didn't think you weren't going to get a say on who worked here, did you? You'll be right alongside me looking at applicant folders starting tomorrow." He patted DJ's shoulder with a grin.

Mighty Pebble laughed at the news. "Ha! Hiring people sounds boring. Boring is right in your wheel-house!"

DJ suddenly felt like pushing MP right over the balcony railing.

The Air Force Colonel continued. "My official title here is Military Asset Acquisitions and Liaison Officer. Or, as the sign will say on the door as soon as someone orders one, MAALO."

Abbi snickered at this. "*May Low*. The Government has some of the craziest titles I have ever seen. But he's our direct contact with the Pentagon. If we need something blown up with a drone, or we need a SEAL team to come and rescue us, he's the guy that makes it happen. Now if you will excuse us, *Mr. May Low*, we have a lot to show them."

Abbi led them a few doors down to a closed office and placed her hand on the knob. The blinds were drawn on the ample windows, and from the look on her face, she was quite pleased with whatever was concealed on the other side.

"I have to tell you," she said, her eyes glittering over what she was about to reveal. "This took a lot of doing. And, you're going to love it."

"Abbi," Agent Cash reprimanded. "Just open the door. Besides, I am sure he is not going to be as nearly fascinated with some button covered gadget as you are."

A stern look crossed her face. "Shut up, Cash!"

And then she opened the door with a flourish and stepped out of the way.

DJ's face broke into a huge smile. He wasn't sure what he was expecting, but Cash and Abbi both did a great job of hiding the truth from him. Sitting in the middle of the large office, facing the door as it opened, was one Special Agent Brett Allen Foster. Standing next to him was Lisa. Both were wearing the same jeans and white polo outfits as the others. Except, of course, for the fingerless mechanic's gloves Brett used for pushing himself around in the wheelchair he was riding.

His friend was smiling, but pointed a finger at him. With mock sincerity he said, "I know your panache for giving people nicknames. Legs or no legs, you start calling me Wheels, and I'll run you over with this thing."

"Sorry," DJ responded, rushing over to grab the man's hand. "It's only the first thing entering my head when I saw you. It's too late, Agent Wheels. You're stuck with it."

DJ couldn't help himself. He bent down and embraced his friend. He held it just long enough to not be weird, and stood back up.

Abbi had moved around and was hugging Lisa. The two shared glowing looks of joy and a sense of satisfaction. Brett must have made hiring Lisa a contingent on the deal they made with Director Neville. And DJ didn't blame him. There was no way he could do this not knowing Abbi would be by his side the whole time. She was every bit an important team member to him as the others. He imagined Brett felt the same way about Lisa.

Looking around the room, surrounded by his friends, DJ knew what he had to do. This was the place. This was the time. There could never be a better moment than right now. Nor could there be a better place than right here.

Stepping over in front of Abbi, he took a knee before her. Her face changed from one of happiness and joy, to one of frozen shock. He plunged his hand into his right-front pocket, pulling out the small velvet box with the ring he purchased only this morning. "Abbi Jackson," he said, finding his voice shaking and wavering with instant nervousness. "Will you marry me?"

Her hands went to her mouth in surprise, and she stared with wide open eyes as the small sparking diamond held before her. She didn't move.

She didn't breathe. And for a moment, DJ was beginning to have doubts about all of this. "Abbi...?" He said with questioning concern.

Her eyes lifted from the ring to take him in. And then her face changed as she had a thought that stitched her eyebrows together. "Wait right here," she instructed. Next, she was bolting from the room, rounding the corner of the doorway, and disappearing from view. "Don't move," She shouted from further away. "I have to get something from my office."

DJ, stunned and embarrassed, looked around the surrounding group of friends. "What...?" He looked from man to man. Brett shrugged and shook his head. They were all shocked. "How long am I supposed to wait here?" DJ asked them.

It was Mighty Pebble who offered up the answer. "Until she comes back, stupid."

Abbi was back then, sliding around the corner, and racing between Cash and MP. Coming to a halt, she snatched the ring box out of DJ's hand, and tossed it to Brett. Then, she handed over a small velvet bag. A burgundy velvet bag. The same burgundy velvet bag lost this past winter in Boston. He thought it gone forever, lost in the burning remnants of his row house in Beacon Hill.

"Again," Abbi said breathlessly. "Do it again."

"Where did you..." he started to ask. But he was quickly silenced by her.

"Shhh," she instructed, holding her finger to her lips. "Don't ask questions. I mean, other than the one you asked just a minute ago. Do it again. With the right ring this time."

DJ couldn't quite understand what was happening. This was not at all how he envisioned his proposal to take place. In dumbfounded response, he took yet another look around the room at his friends. They were all grinning at him. But, the answering look from Lisa finally got him moving again.

Lisa simply mouthed the words, *Do it again*, and sort of motioned him on with her hands.

DJ cleared his throat, looked up at Abbi once more, and repeated himself from a moment ago. "Abbi Jackson, will you marry me?"

"YES!" she squealed. And then they were kissing. In front of all of his friends, they were kissing. Unashamedly, and with unrestrained passion, they were kissing.

Things always change, he had once been told. Embrace the change or get rolled over by them. DJ could think of no better way of embracing the change than to marry this girl in a small quiet ceremony, surrounded by these people right here. He had new friends. He had a new career and purpose in life. He had Abbi.

He heard a pop then, and jerked his lips away from Abbi, reflexively looking for the gun that made it. But it wasn't a gun. Instead, Lisa was holding a freshly opened bottle of champagne. "This calls for a toast," she said.

DJ didn't drink, but this was an occasion he thought he might make an exception for. Lisa produced glasses that were waiting across the room, and began to pour. They had planned this moment, of course. DJ's proposal just made a good moment for toasting their new endeavors a great one.

Taking a glass from Lisa, he held it up and addressed the room. "To new beginnings," he proclaimed.

"To new beginnings," came a chorus of agreement.

To the readers who have made it this far: Thank You! From the bottom of my heart, Thank You! You have done me a huge favor by reading my book. But now I ask another. We writers depend on reviews and star ratings to help boost the chances of us being discovered. So, could you please perform this last act for me? It will take but just a second, and it will mean so much to me. Thanks in advance!

Also, I love to hear from fans. Please visit me on Facebook, my website, email me, or even just give me a call.

Facebook: https://www.facebook.com/JamesBeltzAuthor
Website: www.JamesBeltz.com
Email: James@JamesBeltz.com
Phone: 405-613-6279

Copyright

Slaughter: White Out

By: James Beltz

ISBN: 9781977004277

Published internationally by James Beltz

James@JamesBeltz.com

405-613-6279

Terms and Conditions:

All Persons Fictitious Disclaimer:

This book is a work of fiction. Any similarity between the characters and situation within its pages and places or persons, living or dead, is unintentional and coincidental.

Made in the
USA
Monee, IL